THE FARMER'S WIFE

Poppy Lovering is feeling somewhat frustrated with life as a farmer's wife in a remote corner of Cornwall in the 1950s. Spending her days baking bread or mucking out pigs under the watchful eye of her overbearing mother-in-law is hardly glamorous. Her husband Sam is a decent man, but taciturn and set in his ways, so when a handsome young reporter starts to pay her attention Poppy finds it hard to resist. A naïve and unworldly young woman, who has never ventured further than Penzance, Poppy doesn't realise an innocent flirtation can have devastating consequences...

THE FARMER'S WIFE

THE FARMER'S WIFE

by

Rachel Moore

Magna Large Print Books
Long Preston, North Yorkshire,
BD23 4ND, England.

British Library Cataloguing in Publication Data.

Moore, Rachel
    The farmer's wife.

    A catalogue record of this book is
    available from the British Library

    ISBN   0-7505-2459-6

First published in Great Britain in 2005
by Simon & Schuster

Copyright © Rachel Moore, 2005

Cover illustration © Johnny Ring

Published in Large Print 2005 by arrangement with
Simon & Schuster UK Ltd.

Magna Large Print is an imprint of Library Magna Books Ltd.

Printed and bound in Great Britain by
T.J. (International) Ltd., Cornwall, PL28 8RW

Chapter One

1950

Poppy Lovering had never considered herself anything out of the ordinary. An ordinary woman living an ordinary life – she was sure it was the way Sam thought of her. Sam was a rugged sort of chap, the kind that people called the salt of the earth, and although he wasn't the most talkative man in the world, he thought the sun shone out of her backside, if such a thing wasn't impossible.

She knew his feelings went deeper than he could find the words to say, but he never managed to say a lot until he'd had a few pints of ale. That was just about the *only* time he said anything, she thought, with a small pang.

No, she wasn't anything special, only to him as a good wife should be – well, and the rest of the village now. Poppy still couldn't quite believe that she was being treated like a local heroine. Of course, it wasn't every day you rescued a small boy from a mine shaft, though it had been sheer chance that she had been on the moors that day and heard the terrified shrieks of young Billy

Flint. He was only stuck a little way down the dank shaft and holding on by his fingertips and a prayer, but he was too paralyzed with fear to move, and Poppy had managed to haul him out.

It wasn't every day you had the whole village showering you with thanks and gifts, and the newspaper reporters coming to the farmhouse to interview you, and even the bigwigs of Penzance turning out to congratulate you.

'That was only to get their ugly mugs in the papers, mind,' Sam had said. 'Those buggers will do anything for a free bit of publicity.'

When he was in one of his talkative moods, Sam had an answer for everything, Poppy thought with a grin, remembering how he had hated every minute of it all, while she...

Well, she had to admit that her photos in the paper hadn't looked too bad, her normally wild, dark hair tamed into a tidy style, her blue eyes wide with shock at all the attention she was receiving (not that anybody could see they were blue in the newsprint), her mouth smiling.

As Sam said, she scrubbed up well. Certainly that chap with the camera had seemed to be taken with her, and had given her his card.

'Just in case you should need to get in

touch at any time,' he'd said, with a cheeky wink that brought a blush to her cheeks.

Poppy gave a sudden giggle. Imagine having a card with your name and address on it, and a telephone number too! What she would want with it, she couldn't think. It wasn't likely that she was going to do anything more significant in her life than being the wife of a farmer in a remote bit of Cornwall. Barras was hardly the most romantically named area to live, either, not like Polperro or Mevagissey, or one of the quaintly-named mysterious little moorland villages that lay half-hidden and swathed in mist in the early morning, and then appeared as if by a magician's hand once the sun came up.

By now the whole day of the interviews was becoming a blur in Poppy's memory, except for the way the camera chap – Jack – said that he'd love the chance to photograph her properly, because she had remarkable bone structure, and her glorious hair could have come straight out of a Renaissance painting, whatever that was. She remembered Sam laughing his head off when she'd told him.

'You want to watch yourself where that one's concerned, girl. All these newspaper chaps have got the gift of the gab, and 'tis easy for a silly young maid to get charmed by such daft talk.'

She had ignored the little gleam of jealousy in his eyes, more stung by being called a silly young maid. She was hardly a maid any more, not with Sam fumbling over her when he'd had a bit too much to drink. She'd pushed that particular memory away as she tossed her head and snapped right back.

'If the Yanks hadn't turned my head during the war, then I'm darned sure that a young chap with a trilby hat on the back of his head, just like Clark Gable at the flicks, won't make me go weak at the knees.'

'You weren't old enough for the Yanks to take a shine on you, and a good thing too. Not like some of them other fancy pieces we had to put up with during the war. You've got a sensible head on your shoulders, my girl, else why do you think I married you?' he'd added, chuckling, and giving her a playful slap on the backside.

Poppy thought it was hardly the most romantic of reasons for marrying anyone, and just managed to resist telling him not to call those nice land girls by horrible names, knowing it would only stir up an argument.

But she meant what she said about not going weak at the knees just because a good-looking chap had flattered her. She wasn't brainless, and she was cute enough to know it didn't mean a thing, and it was probably part of his job to get the best out of people.

She hadn't forgotten Jack what's-his-name, though, and she was right about one thing: he *could* almost double for that dashing Clark Gable in *Gone With The Wind*... And then the push of a damp snout in her hand made her yelp and get on with feeding the pigs.

Clark Gable and the flicks, indeed ... and how often did she get to Penzance to see the flicks? What with the farm and the demands that Sam made on her, and his mother snapping at her heels the whole time, always hinting that a wayward young girl like herself had never been the proper wife for her precious Sam.

Poppy swallowed the sudden lump in her throat. Maybe it hadn't turned out to be the kind of marriage made in heaven that Hollywood pretended it should be, but Sam was a good, solid kind of man who'd looked after her ever since she'd come to work on his farm five years ago near the end of the war, when she was just fourteen years old. If he didn't make her heart lurch in the way the cheap novels told her, and if he didn't make her blood zing with passion, she did love him, she thought loyally. She had a good home and she should count her blessings.

'Aren't you done there yet, Poppy?' she heard her mother-in-law's voice call from the farmhouse. 'Sam will be back from market soon, and there's bedrooms to clean and carrots to scrape for supper.'

Poppy's good mood faded as quickly as blinking. This definitely wasn't the way it was portrayed on the silver screen. Young girls who were not yet twenty were swept off their feet by dashing heroes, not expected to spend their mornings mucking out pigs and messing with pig-swill while slopping about in oversized wellies. Young girls who were not yet twenty wore dainty shoes and floaty, gossamer dresses, and were courted by handsome young men...

She shut the gate of the pig-pen quickly before going indoors, where the old farmhouse oozed with the various smells of beeswax, diligent cleaning and constant scrubbing and baking. It was homely and welcoming, except that a girl who was not yet twenty still had the occasional guilty dream that she might have done a lot better than being tied to a man fifteen years older than herself.

Her mother-in-law narrowed her eyes, just as though she could read every restless thought in Poppy's mind. 'Get yourself washed, girl, then start on those bedrooms, and don't let's see a speck of dust left behind.'

'I do know how to clean a room, Mrs Lovering!' she said resentfully.

She saw Sam's mother's lips tighten into

14

the straight line they so often did when dealing with her strong-willed daughter-in-law. No matter how she tried, Poppy couldn't bring herself to call this woman Mother, and didn't see any reason why she should, when she had a mother and father of her own. She knew Sam wished she could unbend towards Florrie Lovering a bit more, but she couldn't do it, and she wouldn't do it.

But she had to do as she was told in other ways. As well as the outdoor farming work, Monday was washday and Tuesday was ironing day; Wednesday was bedrooms day and Friday was baking day. Every blessed day had its regular task. And Saturday nights were when she and Sam made love, if that was what you called his enthusiastic pushing and grunting that sometimes left her feeling as bruised as she was satisfied.

She paused at the old stone sink, her hands still wet and cold, with the strong smell of carbolic soap in her nostrils. She knew instinctively that it shouldn't be like this. It was little more than drudgery, day and night.

She had arrived on the farm, innocent and gawky when the land girls were still here at the tail end of the war. The older girls had made a pet of her then, teasing her with their tales of evenings at the dances in Penzance, in the days when the glamorous GIs had been in the area, and it had all sounded fun and exciting, even though she guessed they exaggerated it all for her benefit. But those girls had long gone their separate ways now, and without their friendly chatter and laughter, everything had gone flat. It might be disloyal and wicked to admit it, but she had recognized for a long time now that she didn't love Sam the way a wife should love her husband, and that was a fact. He was kind to her, and she respected him, but she loved him more as she would a father. If she had someone special to care for, like a baby of her own, it might be different. So far, nothing had happened in that department, and she was probably a disappointment to Florrie Lovering in that way too.

'What on earth are you doing there, Poppy?' her mother-in-law's exasperated voice said right behind her. 'Those bedrooms aren't going to clean themselves. I swear I never saw such an idle girl as you in my life.'

For one blissful moment, Poppy felt the most enormous urge to fling the wet flannel right into the old bat's face. And a right carry-on there would be if she did, with Sam defending his mother and taking her side as always. He really should have married *her*, Poppy thought recklessly.

'I'm going. I can't be in two places at once, can I?'

If only...

Sam Lovering was a hard-working man who saw nothing wrong in leaving his womenfolk alone of an evening now and then while he drank his ale and jawed with the other farmers at the local pub in the village. It was what all good, honest hard-working men did. There was time enough for doing what came naturally with Poppy on a Saturday night when he had rolled home across the fields – providing he didn't have too many sweats on him, and didn't start imagining that the pale, moonlit cows in the fields were pink elephants. He never normally drank too much, but the other farmers in the district had always thought him a hell of a fine fellow for having married such a fine-looking girl as Poppy Penfold, and after seeing her photo in the paper they were always eager to know more and buy him a jug or two. And Sam was truly fond of her. If she buried her head in those silly *Picture Posts* and women's magazines a bit too often, it did no harm, no matter what his mother said.

The girl had to have some pleasure, as well as what he gave her. He'd never had a conscience about marrying her, despite the difference in their ages and the mutterings from some who told him he was cradle-snatching. He'd given her a good home away from the miserable hovel where her folks lived down in Zennor, almost on the edge of the sea where the waves crashed so magnificently against the cliffs whenever there was a storm.

Sam had only been to Zennor a few times before he married Poppy, and that was enough. Zennor was half a mile from the busy little town of St Ives, but a world away from such sophistication. Dominated by its church, legend had it that a local man had once enticed a mermaid from the sea with his fine singing, until she persuaded him to go with her and live forever beneath the waves. Such tales were still believed among the more receptive villagers.

Legends were easy to accept in remote areas like these, and the ancient standing stones and cromlechs on the moors all had their own tales for any gullible visitors who might venture so far west. But as a plain-speaking farmer, Sam didn't hold with all that nonsense.

Although by no means a centre of activity, he knew that when Poppy had first come to live on his farm, she had considered it a definite step up compared with Zennor. She had been wide-eyed with wonder then, not only at living and working on a farm, but also in the company of the girls the ministry men at the War Office had sent to help run the farm to replace the couple of farm-hands who had joined up. The girls his mother had condemned at once as flighty pieces...

At the time, Sam had thought he could manage perfectly well on his own, but the girls had settled in all right, and if Poppy had been dazzled by them in the last months of the war when she arrived straight from school, it had helped his cause when he'd finally got around to popping the question two years ago. And now she was nearly twenty, and it was time she stopped putting on airs just because she'd had her face in the paper.

Truth was, he'd felt more than uneasy about all that hoo-ha. Plain farming folk didn't get their faces splashed all over the papers, and although he was proud of Poppy for rescuing the kid, he wished the publicity had never happened. If Billy Flint's father hadn't been so keen to let everyone know about it, it probably never would have.

'You off home to the missus, Sam?' one of the other farmers called when he stood up to leave. 'God knows how she puts up with you when you've had a few.'

'We're all right, Poppy and me,' Sam said, 'and I'll fight anybody who says different!' He punched his arms about, windmill-like, playing up to his audience even though he was far from pie-eyed, and he left the pub to their echoing laughter.

But once outside, the cold night air hit him like a slap with a wet cod, and he swayed on his feet for a few moments while he got his bearings. He didn't like the feeling, especially in the middle of the week, and this was only Wednesday, but since some of the good ol' boys were still treating him and wanting to know more about Poppy's rescue, he'd be a fool to say no!

He wouldn't be sorry when all the fuss ended though, he admitted.

Away in Penzance, in the smart little house that she shared with her schoolteacher husband now that he had come up in the world, Shirley Bosinney had also read the newspaper account, as had everyone else in the vicinity. She remembered Poppy very well. She and the other land girls on Lovering's farm had taken a real liking to the young girl when she'd come to work among them. The three of them were older, and often teased Poppy about their goings-on at the dances in Penzance, especially with the Yanks when they were billeted there.

'I bet you wish you were old enough to come into town with us, don't you, Poppy?' they teased. 'Shirley might be engaged to her precious Bernard, but she's already got one of the Yanks under her thumb. At least I think that's where she's got him.'

Then they would burst into secretive laughter that effectively shut the younger girl out. They didn't tell her everything, of course, just enough to get her goggle-eyed and impatient at their teasing about things she didn't understand and would dearly like to know.

Shirley didn't tell the other girls everything, either. Some things were too private, too secret, too delicious – too awful – to share, except with really close friends, and these girls were never that. Shirley and her *real* friends had called them the imported ones. They would be going back to the cities once the war was over, and that time wasn't too far away when Poppy arrived on the scene, and then they would all revert to their former lives. And Shirley could start to plan for the day when she would be married to Bernard Bosinney and live happily ever after. That was the plan, and eventually everything had happened just as she wanted it.

But here in the newspaper now was Poppy's smiling face with the glowing reports on what she had done, and the amazing fact that sweet little Poppy who wouldn't say boo to a goose in the past, was now something of a celebrity. Shirley could imagine how it had turned her head. She had actually married Sam Lovering too. That was a turn-up, and none of them would have expected that. He was a decent fellow, and had always respected the girls, but he was still a bit of a mummy's boy; he must have thought the gods were smiling on

21

him when Poppy had said yes to his proposal.

With a touch of the Cornish intuition with which she always prided herself, in Shirley's opinion Poppy was an explosion waiting to happen – a bit like she herself had once been, which was something she would rather forget.

As always, Shirley's thoughts flitted about in her butterfly mind, but she had really liked the girl, and on an impulse she had sent a little card to Poppy at the Lovering farm, just to let her know that she was proud of what she had done. As a respectable schoolteacher's wife now, it was the least she could do.

Poppy was what people called a 'late baby', in that she was born when her parents had long given up hope of ever having a child. Her father was in his mid-seventies now, and her mother was only a few years younger. Neither was in the best of health, and Poppy made a point of visiting them every Thursday afternoon. That was one duty of which Sam's mother approved, anyway, and it took her away from the cloying atmosphere of the farmhouse for a few hours.

It was a long cycle-ride from Barras to the tiny coastal village of Zennor, but it also took her on a breathtakingly beautiful ride across the moors before they dipped down to the sea. As well as standing stones, those moors were dotted with the gaunt mine chimneys of yesteryear, and beneath the innocent-seeming stretches of scrubland, the dark, twisting tunnels of the mines still snaked through the earth.

Despite the warmth of the day, Poppy shivered, recalling that other day when the hoarse voice of young Billy Flint had seemed to reach out to her like an underground ghost, like one of the so-called trolls of the mines. At first, she had been tempted to throw down her bicycle and flee from whatever spectres lingered. There were plenty of such fanciful tales for those with a gullible imagination, and she wasn't about to put them to the test. But in the end, she knew she couldn't ignore his cries.

She pedalled more furiously now, knowing she had been foolish then, and she was being just as foolish now, for nothing could harm her on such glorious days as these. Besides, as one of the pompous Penzance bigwigs had told her, she was blessed now, for saving a life. Her own life was charmed ... and if anything had been guaranteed to make her preen, that was it.

When she reached the edge of the moors she looked down on the familiar vista of Zennor, the church standing square and solid, and picked out her family's thatched cottage, smoke curling from the chimney and the fire her parents always kept going, even on a summer's day.

A flash of unwanted memory came to her then, of gathering wood on the beach for the fire, and the village children running around her in a circle, chanting and taunting her for being a witch's daughter. She had hated those times; her mother wasn't a witch, just because she liked to keep herself to herself.

Poppy paused for breath, telling herself she was far too old to be taking notice of such superstitious nonsense, and then her throat caught raggedly as she heard a voice calling her name.

She whirled around, terrified that for a moment she had conjured up some unspeakable demon for daring to refute the old superstitions of the moors. Then her heart jolted as she saw a tall figure striding towards her, his face momentarily hidden in shadow as his large frame blotted out the sun. And then he came nearer and the illusion faded.

'Oh, it's you! I thought I was dreaming!' she stammered, unable to think of anything else to say.

'If you are, then so am I. I've just been talking about you, and here you are. It must be fate,' Jack Trevis said easily.

Poppy leaned on her bicycle, squinting her eyes against the sunlight, her hands clammy from the exertion, and something else. The sight of him, so handsome, so unexpected,

24

was enough to throw her into a tizzy, and she tried to remain cool and sophisticated – which she knew, to her chagrin, she never was.

'What are you doing here?' she went on inanely.

Jack smiled, wondering if she was even aware of how incredibly beautiful and desirable she was. He doubted that the dull stick of a husband ever told her so. He imagined their lovemaking to be a quick coupling and then the oaf would be snoring the night away.

'I came to see your parents,' he said, 'but they treated me with great suspicion and didn't seem inclined to talk, so I didn't get very far.'

Poppy looked blank. 'What on earth would you want to talk to them for?'

She couldn't imagine them being at all pleased. Her parents were as insular as it was possible to be. Her dad had hated seeing her face in the paper for all to gawp at, and her mum still held on to some weird and ancient superstition that to be photographed took away something of your soul.

Although she had never believed in the taunts of the village children all those years ago, Poppy admitted that she had some-times wondered if her mum had been a wise-woman in a former life. It was more than her life was worth to make any such comments to her, of course, since her parents probably wouldn't hold with such blasphemy. And they certainly wouldn't have welcomed some stranger with film-star looks accosting them in their own home.

'My editor thought our readers would be interested in a follow-up piece about your background,' Jack went on. 'We've had a number of letters praising what you did, rescuing that kid, Poppy, and it's fortuitous that you're here today, because I'd like to take a photo of you and your parents. I'm sure you can talk them round.'

She began to laugh at his persuasive voice, on safer ground now, even if she had no idea what fortuitous meant.

'You'll never get my mother to agree to that, even if I did, which I won't! She'd slam the door in your face if you even suggested such a thing.'

'Why is that, then?'

He was so nice, so interested, so friendly and unaggressive that, before she knew it, Poppy found herself telling him of her mother's beliefs. It wasn't such an unusual thing among country folk who rarely moved more than a mile or so away from the place where they had been born, to cling to the old country ways. Even halfway through the twentieth century, modern ideas hadn't yet caught up with people like her parents, and they didn't see any reason why they should.

She knew Jack was a reporter, but he seemed to be the kind of man that people naturally confided in. Besides which... Poppy felt that odd little jolt in her heart again. He was so different from Sam, and she didn't often have the chance to chat with someone nearer her own age. In Zennor, there had been few other girls as young as her, and she still missed the easy chatter of the land girls, knowing she had practically drifted into marriage with Sam Lovering without ever walking out with any other young man.

She stopped the disloyal thoughts at once, and told Jack quickly why her mother wouldn't allow her photograph to be taken, trusting him to respect her confidence. It was in her nature to be trusting, because being brought up in a tiny community where time had virtually stopped, there had never been any need to be otherwise. It was only other people who thought the family in the smoky cottage were stranger than most, and best left alone.

'Well, at least let me photograph you again, Poppy,' he went on. 'Out here on the moors, leaning against your bicycle with the wind ruffling your hair, you look absolutely stunning. I could get a view of the cottage and the sea behind you, and I'd send you a print of it to frame. I'm sure your husband would like to have it.'

She was instantly flattered by the image he created in her mind, and since he brought Sam into the conversation so naturally, she supposed it would be bad manners to refuse. He took half a dozen photos and gave her his card.

'You've already given me one of those,' Poppy said.

'Well, this is just in case you've lost it and want to get in touch any time. I meant what I said once before, Poppy. I'd really like to photograph you properly.'

'Wasn't this proper, then?'

He laughed. 'Of course it was. But you'll be amazed what can be done with proper lighting and filters in a photographic studio environment. I could make you look like a film star.'

She was out of her depth with all this technical information, even though he touched a chord when he mentioned making her look like a film star. But she couldn't ever see Sam agreeing to that, and without his say-so, she could never go to a photographic studio with a stranger, especially if she came out looking like a completely different person.

'I don't think so,' she said quickly. 'My husband likes me the way I am.'

'Pity,' Jack said. 'I think the world would love you.'

She didn't miss the way he emphasised the word love, when she had merely said that

Sam liked her. Of course Sam loved her too, and the unnecessary thought made her oddly uncomfortable with this man.

You didn't talk to a stranger about intimate and private things like love between married people. You didn't need to mention it to one another all the time either, she thought briefly, but that didn't mean it wasn't there.

She got on her bicycle, preparing to free-wheel down the hill to her parents' cottage, and to forget all this nonsense of looking like a film star, which she certainly did not.

'I've got to go now, but thank you for taking the photos.'

Before he could reply, she was gone, and once inside the cramped homely cottage where she had been born, calling out a cheerful hello, it was to listen immediately to her parents' grumbling about having their day interrupted by some flash chap who talked too fast for them to understand what he was going on about.

Poppy grinned as she moved the always simmering kettle on to the hottest part of the range for some tea. If there was ever anything destined to bring her back to earth, it was these two, in their ancient armchairs with their arms folded, mouths clamped tight with resentment and suspicion, like matching bookends on either side of the fireplace.

The half-comical thought flashed through Poppy's mind that one of these days she would probably turn up for a visit and find them still sitting there in the smoky atmosphere, dead as mutton, and mummified into those blessed armchairs.

Chapter Two

'What's all this?' Sam Lovering roared a week later, when he opened his newspaper and found his wife's face smiling up at him again. 'Have you been seeing that newspaper chap again?'

Poppy flinched. It was unlike Sam to get so riled up; his tone made her feel more like a naughty schoolgirl than a wife. But schoolgirls didn't have clandestine meetings with handsome chaps who looked like Clark Gable. And neither had she, she thought indignantly, snatching the paper out of Sam's hands.

Then she gasped. She hardly registered that the photograph was good, almost good enough to frame, as Jack had said, with her hair blowing in the breeze as she leaned against her bicycle, the old stone cottage and the blue sea and sky in the background. She didn't look like a film star, but she didn't look bad either. She quickly ignored such thoughts and registered instead that

Sam was very, very angry.

'*Well?*' he snapped. 'Where did he get all this claptrap about your mother being practically a witch and your father sounding like a country bumpkin? How do you think that makes me feel, for all the world to know I've married a halfwit?'

Poppy's eyes smarted. 'I don't know how it makes you feel, but I know how *I* feel to hear you say such horrible things!' she yelled back. 'And I never said anything like that to Jack–'

'Oh, *Jack* now, is it? I'd say any girl who's soft enough to get into conversation with a reporter would know how they twist things to make a good story. So what did you say to him, and just where did you say it, I'd like to know?'

She tried her best to stay calm, knowing she would only incense him more if she continued raging at him.

'It was last week when I went to see my parents, and we met by chance. I didn't know he was going to try to see them, and of course they wouldn't talk to him. When he asked me a few things about my background, it seemed harmless enough to tell him. I didn't know he was going to make us sound so – so *weird!*'

'Well, now you know just how harmless it was, don't you, girl? I'll be a laughing-stock in the village for ever marrying you.'

31

'Is that all you can think about? What about me? And what about my poor mum and dad being made to sound so dippy?' she almost sobbed. 'I wish I'd never met Jack Trevis, and I don't ever want to see him again. But if I've shamed you that much I'll probably never go outside the door again,' she added wildly.

Sam's face softened, seeing how distressed she was. He didn't find it easy to express what he called lovey-dovey feelings, but he didn't like to see her like this. He put his arm around her and squeezed her roughly. He smelled of earth and outdoors, but right then Poppy found it more comforting than offensive.

'Well, perhaps some good's come out of it if it's made you see sense, so don't talk so daft about never leaving the house. You're a good girl and a good worker, and you'll want to see your folk as usual on a Thursday, so go out and hold your head up high. Maybe you should go into Penzance occasionally and see other people too,' he said vaguely, as if realizing how rarely she did anything of the kind.

'What people?' she said sullenly. 'I don't know any people.'

Shirley Bosinney hadn't wanted a reply from Poppy, nor had she expected one. Sending her the card had been merely a gesture for old times' sake. She repeated as much to her best friend, when she caught the bus to Penhallow and walked to Tinners' Row, to the old stone cottage where Carrie Pollard lived.

Like Carrie, Shirley and her husband had been born and brought up in this village halfway between Penzance and St Ives, and she was still faintly surprised to find how strange it seemed to come back now, even though she had left here several years ago when Bernard got the new job in Penzance. She still missed the village in many ways, having had a far closer friendship with the women she had known all her life in Penhallow than she ever had with the transient land girls on Lovering's farm.

There were reasons for that, of course. They had all shared so much in those days when they all desperately prayed that their menfolk would come home safely from the war; things you only shared with very close and trusted friends.

'What's up?' Carrie said, when Shirley seemed lost in thought as she bounced Carrie's three-year-old Walter on her knee. 'You don't seem your usual madcap self. You and Bernard are all right, aren't you?' she continued delicately.

'There's nothing wrong in that department, thanks very much. It's all that business with the girl in the newspaper. Poppy

Lovering. You must have seen the stuff about her rescuing that boy, and now there's this new stuff about her parents and their creepy background. I can't imagine old Sam would be any too pleased about that, nor his mother,' she added with a grin.

'Of course, that was the farm where you worked during the war,' Carrie said. 'Me and Archie both read it, and it brought back some bad memories for him. When he was a kid some older boys kept him down a mine shaft for hours before they came and rescued him. Any mention of being in a dark pit, like he was in the POW camp, stirs it all up again.'

'He should have had some sympathy for the Flint kid, then,' Shirley snapped, reverting to the more pithy mood that Carrie recognized.

'I'm sure he did, but why are you so bothered about it?'

'I'm not, except that I felt obliged to send Poppy a card saying how well she had done – you know, all that kind of rot. I wish I hadn't sent it and I hope she doesn't write back, suggesting that we could meet in Penzance sometime.'

'What's wrong with that?'

Shirley held Walter more tightly until he squealed and asked to be put down, and ran to his mother for a cuddle. Shirley had finally discovered that she was not such a maternal kind after all. Not with other

34

people's kids, anyway.

'I don't know. I just don't want to meet her,' she said flatly. 'I suppose I got carried away with the unlikely thought of her being a heroine, and I sent the card on the spur of the moment in my usual stupid way – and we all know how that kind of thing can lead to trouble!'

Carrie frowned, seeing where her thoughts were leading. 'The thing is, Shirley, how well does she know you?' she asked carefully.

'Not as well as you do. But she's part of the past that I don't want to remember, and I wish I'd never sent her that damn card,' she said in frustration.

'I daresay Bernard thought it was a nice thing to do at the time.'

'Oh yes. The minute I said I had worked with her, he was all for it. You know how sweet he is with kids, well, being a schoolteacher and all that, and Poppy was just a kid in those days. But not any more. You can see that in the newspaper. She's turned into quite a looker now.'

'I still don't see why it should bother you.'

Shirley sighed uneasily, knowing she had to say what was on her mind.

'We all egged her on, the other land girls and me. Teasing her, I mean, making out what we got up to at the dances in Penzance, and going overboard with it. What if she believed it? What if she's got some idea of making me her bosom friend now? A kind of older sister to confide in? The newspaper made her out to be a bit of a dummy with no real friends, just her husband and her crazy-sounding parents. I just don't want her to latch on to me, Carrie, and that's flat.'

'Whatever you and the other girls said to her, I'm sure she'll have forgotten it by now.' Carrie ignored the fact that Shirley had always been a blabbermouth, and Lord knows what she might have said to a gullible girl on the farm, eager and ready to absorb everything from glamorous older girls. Shirley had always been a looker too, with her fluffy blond hair and baby blue eyes. But there were things that were far better left unsaid, and not even hinted at.

'I'd better go,' Shirley said, brushing Walter's cake crumbs from her skirt. 'Forget I ever said anything, Carrie. It's probably me being paranoid as usual.'

'Crikey, it's easy to see you've married a schoolteacher, kid!' Carrie said with a grin, taking the sting out of the words.

'Oh, I'm not just a pretty face,' Shirley said airily. She gave Walter a last hug and accepted his sloppy kiss before leaving Penhallow to catch the bus home. At the same time trying to forget worries that should have been buried deep – and were, most of the time.

The day the letter came to the farm for Poppy, Sam's mother handed it to her silently. There had been a number of letters since she'd hauled Billy Flint out of the mine shaft, but they had dried up recently. This one had the words 'Photographs' printed on the outside of the envelope, and Poppy sighed, knowing Mrs Lovering wouldn't be pleased about her receiving anything from the newspaper chap. Poppy had no doubt that it was from him, and took the letter to her bedroom to open it, ignoring the disapproving looks following her.

She had never had any photographs taken in her life before the mine incident, and now she discovered half a dozen of them inside the envelope, taken on that day on the moors when she had gone to visit her parents. She was pleased with the way she looked in them, all wind-blown and sparkly-eyed, a real child of the moors as her dad had once told her. She was pleased with the brief little note from Jack Trevis, because after reading it several times she knew there was nothing in it to which anyone could object.

Dear Mrs Lovering – Poppy,
These are for you to keep, and I'm sure your husband would like to have one or two of them framed.
Yours respectfully,
Jack Trevis.

In particular, Poppy was glad he'd used the words 'Yours respectfully', as well mentioning her husband so prominently in the note. She hoped Sam would see that it seemed to bring the association to an end. If there was a small sense of disappointment in this thought she wouldn't allow it to surface.

'I hope the chap doesn't expect us to ask him how to go about getting one of them framed, always supposing we were of a mind to do such a thing,' Sam said at last, when she had shown him the note and the photos that evening.

'I'm sure there'd be no need for that,' Poppy said quickly. 'There's probably a place in Penzance that would do it.'

'And they'd cost a pretty penny too,' his mother put in. 'When did God-fearing folk like us ever have our likenesses put in a frame and stuck up on a wall for all to see? It's plain vanity, that's what it is.'

'Well, you can't call our Poppy plain, Mother,' Sam said with a grin. 'You must admit she looks a real bobby-dazzler like them Yanks used to say, and if you don't want to see it framed, we could always keep it in our bedroom.'

Florrie Lovering snorted, but Poppy was so taken aback by Sam's apparent readiness to have one of her photos framed that she flung her arms around his neck and kissed him right there in front of her mother-in-law.

'Oh, I'd really like that, Sam,' she said breathily. 'It would be really special to me, so I'll find a shop in Penzance that would do the framing if you like.'

After all, he'd been the one to tell her to get out a bit more and to go into Penzance and see people. And going there with a purpose would be far better than wandering about aimlessly. For a moment she was tempted to say she could have one of the photos framed for her parents too, but she knew that they would never look at it if she did.

'You don't know anywhere in Penzance that does such things,' Florrie said, 'and you'll end up being overcharged. People always take advantage of young girls with their heads in the clouds.'

Poppy refrained from answering back as she had a sudden inspiration.

'I do know somebody. I'll ask Shirley who worked here in the war. She's a respectable schoolteacher's wife now, and she'll know where I can get the framing done.'

'A schoolteacher's wife now, is she?' Florrie said. 'Let's hope he's tamed her then, for a wilder young miss I never did see. I'm surprised she didn't end up like some of them others we all know about.'

'Leave it, Mother,' Sam put in. 'If Poppy

wants to visit Shirley and see about this photo framing, then that's the end of it.'

Poppy knew instinctively that what he really meant was that anything was better than having Jack Trevis involved any further. But she didn't care about his reasons as long as she got her way, and now that Sam was being quite understanding about her not being so tied to the farm all the time, that was good news too.

In fact, he seemed so taken with her that night, that they had what Sam called an extra bit of a cuddle in the middle of the week, and perhaps because of her own excitement, she relaxed a lot more than usual, and found an unexpected enjoyment in their lovemaking.

She knew Shirley's address, because it was on the top of the card Shirley had sent her. She started to write her a letter, asking if she could call, or perhaps they could arrange to meet in one of the tea rooms near the sea front. But then she'd have to wait for a reply and Poppy was too young and impatient for that. Besides, now that Sam was indulgent about having her photo framed, she wanted to see it finished.

So, on the following Monday afternoon, after a strenuous morning's washing and scrubbing Sam's longjohns and workshirts on the washboard, putting the sheets through the blue dip, then getting through the tortuous mangling and hanging them out on the line in a blustery breeze, she washed herself and changed into a pretty frock, rammed on her best hat and cotton gloves, and took the bus into Penzance with the envelope of precious photos.

Shirley was humming a ditty as she whisked a duster around the neat little house that she shared with Bernard. Across the bay, opposite the long and beautiful stretch of sands at Marazion, the gaunt, beautiful fairytale castle of St Michael's Mount reared up into the sky, and she never tired of looking at it. It was only occasionally that the wayward thought crept into her mind, that it was a good thing those sands couldn't talk ... and if they could they'd be talking about far more daring adventures than those of the young and headstrong Shirley Loe she had been then, she chided herself.

She looked around the pristine house with loving eyes, glad now that Bernard had persuaded her that this new job he had been offered was well worth the effort of moving away from Penhallow. They had been perfectly content in the prefab where they had lived right after their wedding, but this was so much more suitable for a school-teacher's wife, Shirley thought with a surge of pride.

When the doorbell rang that Monday afternoon she wasn't expecting visitors, but she never minded the chance to show off her housekeeping skills, which she knew none of her old friends would have expected her to have.

'Poppy!' she said, somewhat confused. 'What are you doing here?'

Realizing how ungracious she sounded, she opened the door wider, and invited the girl inside, automatically asking her if she would like a cup of tea. Anything to keep her hands occupied while she wondered what on earth she wanted. As she went into the kitchen, she told herself not to get in a state about it. It was only a casual visit from a friend.

'You've got a lovely house, Shirley,' Poppy said, sitting on the edge of a chair and glancing around the front room, where Shirley and Bernard's wedding photograph had prominent position on the mantelpiece. 'You married your soldier, then?' she said, as if she didn't already know.

Shirley flinched. 'I always said I would, didn't I?'

'Oh yes, of course. He looks nice.'

Not dark and exciting with Clark Gable looks. But nice.

Shirley came back to the room while they waited for the kettle to boil on her brand new gas stove. The more she looked at

42

Poppy, she couldn't help thinking she was almost like an echo of herself, except for the dark hair, and the more annoyed she became, with no apparent reason.

'So what can I do for you, Poppy?' she said, forcing a civil smile to her face. 'Have you come back to earth after being a bit of a celebrity? I'm sure Sam's mother will have helped you to get over that!'

Poppy laughed. 'She did that all right. She didn't like me having my photo in the paper in the first place, and now this other stuff has appeared – you have seen it, I suppose? All the rubbish about my mum and dad?'

Her lips trembled slightly, and Shirley spoke quickly, seeing that for all her sparkiness, the girl was vulnerable after all. Just as she had been.

'I doubt that anyone with any sense thought it was more than newspaper talk. You know how these people make a story out of nothing. Bernard reckons that most of them are a lot of rogues with an eye for the main chance.'

'Not all of them are like that,' Poppy said defensively.

'Well, the chap who made your folk out to be so ... uh ... so *countrified* – certainly was, wasn't he?'

The kettle boiled and Shirley went to make the tea. By the time she brought in a tray a few minutes later Poppy was sniffing

43

noisily, and blowing her nose hard.

'Good Lord, Poppy, what's wrong?' She had a sudden suspicion. 'You're not telling me this newspaper chap took advantage of you, are you?'

She suddenly felt so much older than this girl, so superior in what she was saying ... when in truth, she was anything but. Didn't she know exactly how it felt to be swept away by the heady feelings of romance and sweet-talking in the moonlight...?

'No, he didn't,' Poppy said crossly. 'He was perfectly respectable, and very nice, and now he's sent me these.'

She thrust her hand into her bag and pulled out the envelope of photographs. Although Shirley had seen one of them in the newspaper, she could see at once how charmed Poppy must have been by the provocative way she was smiling into the camera. This was how the newspaper chap would have seen her ... and why Sam would have resented his wife's face being splashed about like this for all to see. Sam had been a tolerant man, Shirley remembered, if a bit out of his depth with the lively land girls the War Office had foisted on him.

'They're really nice, Poppy,' she said finally, not knowing what was expected of her. She poured out the tea and offered Poppy a biscuit.

'I'm not hungry. Mrs Lovering insists on

feeding us up, as she calls it, so I'm always feeling bloated by the end of the day.'

'Good thing farmers don't have to rely on rations like the rest of us still do, then,' Shirley said dryly. 'You certainly don't look bloated, anyway. You were always as skinny as a rake.'

She eyed the girl warily. She wasn't skinny now, but she wasn't fat either. She had rounded out nicely over the years, and presumably Sam hadn't put her in the family way yet.

'So come on, Poppy. You haven't just come here for a social visit after all this time, what's troubling you? I sometimes help Bernard's pupils with their problems, so I'm sure I can help you, whatever it is.'

She groaned inwardly, knowing she was sounding like one of those so-called agony aunts in the problem pages of the women's magazines, offering help and advice to young girls in trouble. She was only twenty-six herself, for goodness' sake, Shirley thought, annoyed again at being unintentionally made to feel ancient.

Poppy took a deep breath. 'Jack – that's the chap who took the photos – Jack Trevis, well, he sent me these, saying he thought that Sam might like to have one of them framed to hang on the wall.'

'And what did Sam say to that?' Shirley said, aware of the way the girl lingered over the newspaper chap's name, even if she didn't notice it herself.

'Sam said he wouldn't mind having it framed as long as we kept it in our bedroom, as a kind of memento of me rescuing the Flint boy. Mrs Lovering disapproves, naturally, and my mum would think I'm practically going to the devil. She never did hold with photographs of folk.'

Shirley tried not laugh at her gloomy expression, seeing how serious this was to her. She remembered Poppy once telling them about her elderly parents with their doggedly Victorian attitudes, and she remembered Florrie Lovering all too well, having encountered the woman's disapproval herself more than once.

'And what do you think?'

'That's what I've come to see you about. Getting the photo framed, I mean,' she went on, seeing Shirley's blank expression. 'You being a woman of the world and all, and me being a country farmer's wife, I thought you'd be the one to tell me where I should go to find out about it.'

Shirley laughed out loud now. 'I don't know about me being a woman of the world, Poppy! But you certainly make me feel less matronly for saying so.'

'You couldn't be matronly if you tried. I always looked up to you when you worked on the farm, Shirley. Those other girls talked

46

posher than the likes of us, but you were everything I wanted to be. You were blonde and pretty, and you always had such exciting tales to tell about the Yanks you all met at the dances in Penzance. I was always green with envy, for ever wishing I was old enough to go with you and the other girls.'

'Is that right, you daft kid!' Shirley kept the smile fixed on her face, and not for a moment letting her eyes flicker with remembering.

'I'm not a daft kid. I might have been then, but not now,' Poppy said crossly. 'I know you all kept the best secrets from me and only teased me about what you got up to. I wasn't as daft as all that.'

Shirley's heart missed a beat. It was crazy to think that the younger woman knew, or guessed, or had any idea. There were only three other people in the world who knew her secret and, like her, they would never tell. But suddenly, without warning, the image of Hank flashed into her mind, dark and dynamic and so wonderfully handsome in his GI uniform, and wanting her so much. And the soft whispering sands of Mount's Bay would never tell either...

She jumped as Poppy's cup clattered into her saucer.

'So do you know where I can get the photo framed, Shirley?'

Poppy had inadvertently stirred up memories that Shirley wanted to forget. She amended that in her mind as they walked into the town that afternoon. She didn't exactly want to forget, she *chose* to forget because she knew she had to do so. She had a very comfortable life with Bernard, who was the love of her life, and there was no room for the intrusion of those other wild and crazy times. Her good friends, Carrie, Gwen and Velma, had impressed it on her so often and she had known they were right. It was the only thing to do.

'I'm sorry to be such a bother to you, Shirley,' she heard Poppy's uncertain voice say as they strode along, and she realized she had been silent for a good few minutes.

'Don't be a goose, Poppy. I was just trying to think which way we should go, and when we've done the business, we'll go to a tea room and have a couple of sticky buns, my treat. Mrs Lovering's not the only one who can feed you up!' she finished with a laugh, putting on her best acting performance, the one that Velma always called her Sarah Bernhardt voice. She hadn't had a clue who Velma was talking about at the time, but she was older and wiser now, and Bernard had put her right on that score.

'That's all right then. I thought I'd offended you, and I'm so enjoying being here instead of being stuck at the farm,'

Poppy said, relieved. 'Penzance is so busy and exciting compared with Barras, which is a real dump. Sam says I should come here more often and meet people, but I don't know any people except you.'

'You should have friends of your own age.'

She knew damn well she was saying it to put Poppy off the idea that Shirley was her only friend, and that this was the start of a friendship Shirley didn't want. As for having friends her own age, she was being a bit of a dog in the manger herself now, because Velma in particular had been a lot older than she was, older than any of the other close-knit friends of the war years. She would be over forty now, Shirley thought with a little shock.

It hadn't seemed to matter then, when they had so much in common, but Velma had been gone from their lives for five years now, moving upcountry to be a proper army wife with her soldier husband and baby son. Gwen, too, had eventually married again after her David's tragic drowning, and gone to live in Devon, so of the former quartet only herself and Carrie were left. And Shirley wanted to keep it that way, with no young farmer's wife being the spectre at the wedding feast, she thought in her usual dramatic way.

'Here we are,' she said quickly, trying to ignore the uneasy thoughts this girl was giving her. She'd been fond of her in the days when she'd arrived at the farm; a gawky village girl, just out of school, but those days were long gone, and they were two different people now. Once today was over, they could go their separate ways and resume their ordered lives.

They were outside a neat little shop in one of the alleyways leading off Market Jew Street, the busy main thoroughfare of Penzance. The modest shop sign that swung in the warm summer breeze announced it as 'Palmer's Picture Framing, no job too large or too small'. A bell above the door tinkled as they went inside, and a jovial man came to greet them.

The man recognized Poppy from the newspaper and once the order had been given, he promised to do a fine job on framing her photo for her husband.

'He wasn't the only one who recognized you,' Shirley remarked, after she and Poppy left the shop and found a corner table in a nearby tea room. 'Quite a few people nodded as we passed them, so how does it feel to be famous, Poppy?'

'Peculiar,' Poppy said flatly. 'I'm not famous, anyway, and if Jack Trevis had just written about me rescuing Billy Flint and not put my picture in the blessed paper, nobody would have known it was me, would they?'

'Don't you like it, then? Most film stars would give their eye teeth for a bit of recognition.'

'I'm no film star, nor likely to be. Sam didn't like it. His mother hated it, and my mum and dad think it's nothing short of devil worship to have your face on show for everybody to gawk over.'

'Well, as long as they don't stick pins in it, you're all right, aren't you?' Shirley said, laughing at Poppy's theatrical manner. She *was* like an echo of her younger self, she thought silently and unwillingly.

'They do that to effigies, not newspaper photos,' Poppy said. 'Don't you know anything, Mrs schoolteacher's wife?'

Shirley felt suddenly cold. There was no denying that Poppy's parents were odd people, and Poppy herself wasn't smart and up to the minute in the way she dressed and did her hair, but to talk about sticking pins in effigies in that calm and controlled manner as if it was something normal and not several centuries old that smacked of witchcraft, was something she didn't want to hear.

'Look, I'll have to go soon, Poppy. Bernard gets home early today, and we're going to the pictures tonight,' she invented.

'How lovely. Sam never takes me anywhere like that. Nor dancing. You used to go dancing a lot, didn't you?'

'We don't any more. Bernard still has trouble with his war wound.'

She elevated his old dragging walk to being far worse than it was now.

Poppy smiled. 'I bet you miss it, though. Dancing, I mean. All those lovely Yanks to dance with and then to go walking in the moonlight. I bet it was fun.'

'There was a war on, Poppy. It wasn't all fun, as you very well know. We might not have been bombarded with any air raids down in Barras or Penhallow, but even Penzance didn't miss out on the occasional hit and miss from a German bomber.'

She groaned, knowing she was making it sound as if they had won a prize, but Poppy still had that dreamy look on her face.

'All the same, lots of girls were glad the Yanks were here for a few months to make up for all that. It must have been wonderful to be a GI bride and go and live in America, even if some of them *had* to get married. I remember Sam's mother talking about shotgun weddings, and what a disgrace those girls were while their boyfriends and husbands were away fighting for their country, but they didn't all have boyfriends anyway, and I think it must have been so romantic!'

She was still rabbiting on as Shirley got up to go.

'You don't know what you're talking about,' Shirley said tightly. 'Those days are long gone, and a good thing too.'

But before she went home to prepare Bernard's evening meal, she slipped inside the coolness of the church and lit a candle, then after a moment she lit a second one, and said a private prayer. Poppy might not have known what she was talking about, but Shirley did.

Chapter Three

Jack Trevis had always had an eye for a pretty girl. It went with his profession, and the naively beautiful young farmer's wife who'd rescued the kid from the mine shaft was certainly that. Despite his casual suggestion of photographing her in a studio with proper equipment and lighting, he'd never really thought she would agree. If she did, the husband certainly wouldn't. He knew the type – solid and dependable as they come, and possessive over what was rightfully theirs – and he couldn't blame him for that where Poppy was concerned.

Jack didn't consider himself a wife-stealer, but he had a healthy young man's appetites. He also knew that he fell in love too easily – and fell just as easily out again – and he didn't deny that he'd been smitten from the moment he saw her. He hadn't expected to see her again, though, until his editor had suggested the follow-up feature with the girl's parents.

And seeing her so unexpectedly on her bicycle that day, so stunning and vital, with the wind blowing through her hair, it was more than he could resist to photograph her again, and then, when she had been so innocently open about her weird parents he had considered it his duty to write it all up for the paper as a piece of social interest. Besides, it didn't do him any harm professionally.

He really hoped she would get one of his photos framed, though. Once they had been read, newspapers were thrown away or twisted into firelighters, or used as lavatory paper in country places with only an outside privy and no running water, as was still the case in the most remote areas.

He didn't want Poppy's photo to end up like that. She deserved so much more, even if her lovely framed face was only for the husband to enjoy. He quickly smothered the stab of jealousy running through his veins at that moment, and concentrated instead on studying the latest photos emerging from the fixing bath in his dark room. She wasn't for him, and he had better remember that.

Jack didn't necessarily believe in fate, but being a Cornishman he wasn't going to tempt bad luck by denying that things happened for a purpose. The feature about Poppy's parents, and the brief background about the coastal village of Zennor he had included, prompted a small number of readers to write in about their own sometimes creepy and unexplained experiences with old legends.

Whether these were true or invented, the letters prompted more, and finally his editor called him into the office. 'We're on to a good thing here, Jack, and I've got a proposition for you. I'd like you to write a few sample columns about various parts of Cornwall, illustrating them with your own photos. You can bring in as many old legends and eccentric characters as you can find, and if it increases our circulation, which I think it will, I might consider making it regular. What do you say?'

Jack's interest was caught by the idea, but he was also cautious. 'It sounds good, the way you say it, but don't you think folk will start to think that the farther west you go, the more weird we are? Now that there's no more petrol rationing, people are starting to discover Cornwall and coming down here for their holidays. Not everybody agrees with that situation, mind, but we'll be in danger of turning them away if they think they're about to find witches and spooks around every corner.'

The editor's eyes gleamed. 'Then you'll have to make sure they don't see us like that, won't you? Don't get squeamish about this, Jack. You know how folk love a ghostly tale, and anything to make the hairs on the back of their necks stand up is good for business. Give them good pictures to accompany your articles, and they'll be flocking down here in droves to see our quaint places for themselves.'

'Is that what this is all about?'

It was well known that Graham Strang, the newspaper's editor, had his finger in many pies, not least the tentatively flourishing tourist trade now that roads were opening up to the far western corner of the country.

During the war years, when everyone had to tighten their belts and the only travel was that involved in fighting the enemy, people chose to remain cocooned in their own homes, and many still did. The exceptions were the poor evacuee kids, packed off to the country for their own safety, and often seeing farm animals and the vastness of the sea for the very first time in their lives. On the rare occasions that any of their families managed to visit them in their temporary homes, they gradually began to realize that the country wasn't such an alien place after all.

Some of those kids and their parents had come back again to visit their wartime hosts, and if tourism wasn't exactly booming yet, then, given time, the shrewder among the Cornish population thought that it surely would be. It was a situation that pleased a few local folk, but was far from acceptable to others.

Strang was still pursuing his case. 'You've got to look to the future, Jack, but if you don't want this assignment I'm damn sure I can find somebody else willing to take it on. I'm giving you first choice, because I know you'll make a bloody good job of it, so let me know your decision by the end of the week.'

He removed the cigarette he usually kept at the corner of his mouth, to the amazement of junior staff who wondered how he could snap at them and still keep it dangling there, and blew his famous smoke rings into the air. Knowing that this indicated that the meeting was over, Jack left the office to think things through.

But he knew, just as Graham Strang knew, that he would take on the job. The mercurial and visual part of his brain was already taking him to areas of the county that the general public knew little about; the picturesque fishing villages down on the Lizard; the wild remoteness of Land's End; Zennor with its myths and legends; even Barras with its unique position in an unexpectedly fertile hollow in the middle of the barren area of the moors; the quaint village of Penhallow, a half-way stop between Penzance and St Ives; Hayle on the northern coast where the placid sands could turn to quicksands in moments as the sea rushed in, and had even been known to swallow a horse.

In his mind, he was up to several months in copy already, and he hadn't even touched on the legends of the tinners and wreckers, nor travelled farther in his imagination than the south-western tip of the county. There was a wealth of material under his nose that was his for the taking, and Jack wasn't about to turn it down. He went straight back to Strang's office and asked when he wanted him to start.

Sam Lovering had never been slow to agreeing to rent out his fields for the annual village fête and the fair that arrived every August. There had always been an annual fair at Barras, and its origins went back into history, with quack doctors selling potions to cure everything; knife-throwing acts; and deeds of daring-do on horseback by the itinerant and colourful gypsies who came with it.

Some of those activities had been frowned on in more recent times, and during wartime the displays had been either toned down or completely curtailed. But now that folk were feeling a bit more affluent and ready to throw their pennies about at coconut shies to win a goldfish in a jam-jar, and to buy the village produce of jams and cakes and chutneys, Sam Lovering was more than ready to continue cashing in on it. He was even prepared to set aside a part of his land that was lying fallow for a car park for those who travelled from farther afield. His mother might not hold with such commercial dealings, but Sam was not such a stick-in-the-mud that he didn't know a good thing when he saw it. Besides, the weekly newspaper always sent a chap down to report proceedings, and it could only do him good to be seen as a genial farmer.

'You never know,' he joked to his women-folk one evening when they were about to eat supper, 'Poppy's part in rescuing young Billy Flint might also have something to do with folk wanting to visit the farm this year. You're still a bit of a heroine, girl, and country folk don't forget easily.'

'I'm not sure I want people coming here just to gawp at me,' she said with an uneasy laugh, at which Florrie Lovering slapped down the platter of rabbit pie on the table and spoke her piece.

'That's not what our Sam meant at all, you silly girl, and you want to get them fancy ideas right out of your mind.'

'Well, what did he say it for, then? I don't mean I'm like a film star or anything so daft, but if Sam thinks people might remember what happened and want to come and say hello, I'm not going to hide away, am I?'

Sam was openly grinning as his mother slashed a knife across the pastry pie-topping now, and the succulent flavours wafted out, teasing their nostrils.

He always enjoyed watching these two have a little spat. Deep down, he sensed that his mother was quite fond of Poppy, but it wasn't in her nature to throw compliments about, and any talk of film stars always got her dander up. She didn't hold with images on the silver screen being treated almost like gods and goddesses.

'Nobody asked you to hide away, Poppy,' she was still going on. 'You'll be expected to help get everything ready, same as always. Sam will organize the games for the children and you can help with that, as well as helping to set out the tables for the village women's produce. There'll be plenty to do and no time for any idle hands.'

'Yes, Ma'am,' Poppy said daringly, wishing that for once she had the nerve to stand up and click her heels, laying one finger under her nose like old Adolf Hitler's moustache and giving Florrie a German salute. And a right old hoo-ha there would be if she ever did such a thing.

She caught the wicked twinkle in Sam's eyes, and had the strongest feeling that he knew exactly what she was thinking. She

60

couldn't hold back a giggle, and at the sound Sam couldn't contain his laughter, so that Florrie stood back with her hands on her hips, glaring at the pair of them.

'I'm sure I don't know what I've said that's so funny,' she snapped. 'You're behaving like a couple of infants, and I'd have expected better of you, our Sam, never mind the flibberty child that you married. Stop that noise at once, the pair of you, and get on with your supper.'

If anything was guaranteed to make the laughter continue, that was it. But providing they avoided looking at one another, they somehow managed to hold it in until it finally exploded in the privacy of their bedroom. Then they clung to one another helplessly, until Sam accidentally let rip with a fart that reverberated around the room, and started them both off again. The sound of Florrie's complaining voice from downstairs and a bang on the banister with a broom handle had them falling on to the bed and howling with laughter.

'My God, you're a caution, Poppy,' he gasped.

'You're not so bad yourself,' she choked back, and then they both rolled about on the bed until she felt his hand steal towards her breast and caress it gently, sending a shooting pleasure through her already aroused senses.

'So why don't we pretend it's Saturday night?' he whispered.

The moorland village of Barras was in a good position to hold an annual event that attracted visitors from miles around. The hollow in which the village sat enabled it to miss many of the fierce winds that blew across the moors when storms rocked the coastlines and whipped up the sea into foaming torrents. But there were also mornings when the villagers awoke to find they could hardly see hands in front of faces for the mist that descended in silent, cobwebby fronds at first, and then enveloped the whole area in a ghostly shroud.

Some found it scary, while others were enchanted by the whole panorama, especially in seeing the emergence of the sun through the clouds burning off the final trails of mist as if by a giant's hand.

But in August such magical moments were still a long way ahead in the mild winter months, and the sun always shone on Barras on fair days. Shining on the righteous, as most of the locals remarked, fat with satisfaction at the coffers that would be swelling for them all, not least the local publican, who knew that ale would be flowing like water for the few days that the annual festivities took place on Sam Lovering's land.

The long-awaited day was still several

weeks away, but with its usual expected contingent of colourful characters and sideshows, it had always merited a bit of a splash in the local paper. Jack Trevis knew of it, even though he had only been living in Penzance for a few months, his previous post having been in Truro.

Now, with everyone talking about the Barras event, and folk preparing to dress up and come from pretty well the whole of the surrounding area for a day out, he seized the opportunity to cover it, assuring Graham Strang that he could probably chase up a few entertaining stories for his forthcoming features on Cornish life.

'It's all yours, Jack,' the editor said slyly, having always known the young buck wouldn't be able to resist such a challenge. And wondering, in passing, if seeing the farmer's young wife again had anything to do with his enthusiasm.

Poppy loved fair days. Even Florrie Lovering's comments that there was work to be done in the house and the fields before any of them could enjoy themselves, wasn't going to put her off the anticipation of these few days of excitement and the crush of people all intent on having a good time.

It was her birthday month too, and Sam's gift of any one of his prize sow's latest litter as a pet might not be enough to put a sparkle in many girl's eyes, but she knew what a precious gift it was from him. Pigs brought money into the farm when they went to market, and farm animals weren't intended for pets. She threw her arms around his neck and kissed him excitedly, already thinking of a name for her little pet, and of where she was going to keep him.

'Perhaps I'd better give you a gift more often if this is the treatment I get,' he said, laughing at her spontaneous gesture, and feeling surprised to realize what a glow it gave him to know he had pleased her so much.

Without thinking what he was saying, he went on: 'Perhaps when the fair's over and we're left in peace again, we could take the car to a beach one evening and have a picnic. We could build a bonfire and toast some bread and cook some sausages for a treat, just the two of us.'

He didn't know why he'd said it, but Poppy's eyes widened, never having heard him say such a romantic thing before. The creaking car was mainly for farm purposes, and not for gallivanting around the country-side. But she hugged his arm and almost sang that it sounded like a marvellous idea. Being twenty was a truly wonderful age to be, she thought joyfully, and Sam looked so much younger when he wasn't fretting over farming business and his mother's nagging. At times like these, she knew just why she had married him.

And on Friday she was going to Penzance to collect her framed photo, which was to be her gift to him, as a sort of *un*-birthday present.

Shirley hadn't really wanted to pursue the acquaintance with Poppy. It wasn't that she didn't like her, because she did. It was simply the association with those other days that was a small barrier between them as far as Shirley was concerned, even if Poppy was unaware of it. It should have cemented a friendship, but somehow, for Shirley it never could. But she didn't have the heart to say no when Poppy turned up and begged her to come to the framing shop with her again to collect her photograph.

'I'm almost afraid to look at it,' Poppy said, her bubbling enthusiasm over such a small thing making Shirley feel positively ancient. 'I'm sure it'll be awful!'

'It won't look any different from before it went into a frame, you ninny!'

'I suppose it won't. Oh, I'm so daft, aren't I?' she'd said delightedly.

'Just a bit,' Shirley said dryly, trying not to laugh out loud.

'Shirley, me and Sam would really like it if you'd come to the farm sometime during fair days. You and your hubby, of course. Come and have tea with us for old times' sake,' Poppy said recklessly, even though she hadn't mentioned any such thing to Sam, nor his mother.

Shirley groaned inwardly. The last thing she wanted was to get involved with any of these people 'for old times' sake'. She replied quickly. 'Well, of course we were thinking of coming to the fair, Poppy, but with one of my old friends and her husband and son, so we wouldn't impose on you for tea. But it's kind of you to ask, and it would be nice to see the old farm again – and Sam too, of course.'

She didn't know where the words came from, but although they were a bit stiff, they were as impulsive as any of her thoughts had ever been. In any case, she was sure Carrie wouldn't object to a day out, but if she did, there would be far too many people milling about at Lovering's farm to miss one or two who were meant to be there.

'Oh well, that will have to do then,' Poppy said, half relieved that her invitation hadn't been accepted. She was sure Sam would have been all right about it, but his mother would have had the usual frown on her face that a slip of a girl had taken to issuing invitations, especially to former flibberty-gibbety land girls they hadn't wanted there in the first place. Florrie Lovering still ruled the roost in that household, Poppy thought, and probably always would. But it would have been nice to preen herself as Sam's wife instead of the gauche schoolkid on the farm that she had been when Shirley first met her.

Her framed photo took away any small sense of disappointment. The frame had been done by a craftsman, and it brought back an instant memory of that day on the edge of the moors when bumping into Jack Trevis had set her heart jumping all over the place in her chest. The day she'd do better to forget.

By the time she returned to the farm, she had reminded herself that the photo was for Sam's eyes and no-one else's. His pleasure at seeing it was reward enough, and that evening it had pride of place on the dressing-table in their bedroom.

'It's a good likeness, and now I can always see you smiling, even when you're not here,' he said, in one of the softer remarks he came out with occasionally.

If he said them more often, Poppy thought fleetingly, she probably wouldn't treasure them so much, so perhaps it was a good thing that he didn't. She'd never really thought of it like that before, but she was still feeling mellow about his gift of the piglet which she had now named Henrietta, ignoring Florrie's acid remark that it was a crackpot name for a male piglet and enough to give it a complex.

'When am I not here?' she said to Sam now, with a small pout that was unconsciously provocative. 'This is where I belong, isn't it?'

'Just as long as you remember that, wench,' Sam said, a certain gleam in his eyes that she recognized.

Sometimes she was slightly repelled by it, because he was often so tired by the end of the day that even though he washed himself regularly, there was still the whiff of the farmyard about him. But tonight it had the opposite effect as he pulled her down beside him in the bed they shared, his rough hands in her hair, his mouth seeking hers before it inevitably strayed elsewhere.

All her senses were stirred, and she shivered in his arms, but not with any feeling of repugnance as she opened up to him, body and soul. This was how marriage was meant to be, she thought, with a huge sense of well-being.

'I'm not sure about this,' Carrie Pollard said doubtfully in response to Shirley's request. 'I'd quite like to go to the fair for a day out, and I'm sure Walter would enjoy it, but I doubt that Archie would think it such a good idea. He's not much for crowds as you know, and he and Bernard never got on all that well, did they?'

'Oh, for goodness' sake, Carrie, I'm sure you can persuade him. You always said you could get round Archie any time you wanted,' Shirley said impatiently, not totally sure her friend had ever said any such thing.

By now she had got used to the idea of the fair and managed to persuade Bernard that it would be fun. The tightness of his skin where he had suffered such awful burns when his plane had come down in France could still give him problems if he had to stand around for too long, but she had assured him that he could always sit in the car to take a rest at any time.

She knew very well he'd do no such thing, and if it made him sound more like an old man than a healthy chap in his mid-twenties, she ignored the thought. The war had made old men out of many who were younger than him, and corpses out of a good many more. She shuddered, wishing the thought hadn't entered her head.

'It's all very well you saying that,' Carrie went on, 'but I didn't think you'd be too keen, either. Going back isn't always a good idea.'

'I only worked there, Carrie.'

What she didn't say, but what they both knew she meant, was that Shirley hadn't actually met her GI at the farm. He was part

69

of another life, a heady, frivolous, dancing life in the days when local girls were encouraged to be nice to 'our overseas allies', so far from home and missing their families. The fact that some girls were far nicer than they should have been was something it was better to forget. But some of them could never forget.

'Anyway, it was a long time ago,' Carrie was saying. 'You know what they say about laying ghosts, so perhaps that's what you've got in mind, but I'm sure you have no need. Go and enjoy the fair – and if it means that much to you to have a bit of moral support, I'll see what Archie says about coming as well.'

Shirley hugged her. 'I'll feel so much better if you do, Carrie, and if it means I won't have to sit through afternoon tea with Florrie Lovering looking down her nose at me the whole time, I'll feel a darned sight better about that too.'

Carrie was still smiling about Shirley's obvious ruse to get out of a farmhouse tea at Lovering's farm by asking her friends to accompany her and Bernard, when Archie came home. But she decided to wait until after supper, when Walter was safely tucked up in bed, before she broached the subject with him.

Predictably, he objected at once. Archie

had spent two years in a German POW camp during the war and wasn't keen on any social gatherings. Carrie didn't know how he could possibly connect the two, although the fact of being kept in close confinement with a group of unwashed men for months on end was probably enough to explain it. But a day in the open air should be enough to attract anybody.

She spoke more firmly. 'Well, I definitely want to go, and you know how Walter would love to see the animals as well as the fair.'

'I suppose it's a chance to see how Lovering's pigs are fattening up,' Archie replied. 'A nice tasty bit of pork always goes down well for Sunday dinner.'

'Don't you dare tell Walter any such thing,' Carrie exclaimed.

'I suppose you'd rather he believed meat grew on trees, would you?'

Carrie sighed, knowing that any affront to his livelihood as a butcher, especially compared with Bernard Bosinney's more prestigious one as a schoolteacher, always rankled with Archie. One was just as important as the other, as everybody knew. And then she saw that he was smiling.

'Oh, all right, we'll go if it means so much to you. It'll do the little squirt good to have a day out, anyway, and I daresay I can put up with Bosinney for a couple of hours.'

'I don't know what you've got against him

71

– and before you say he's a fairy, or whatever other silly name you've got for him, you know very well that he's not.'

'Do I? He's taking a long time to prove it. I'd have thought Shirley would have been in the pudding club long before now. From the way she always flirted with anything in trousers, I'm surprised she hasn't managed to get her bloke to deliver the goods. Makes you think, doesn't it?'

'No, it does not make me think,' Carrie snapped. 'And don't you go making any such remarks when we see them, mind. I'm sure they'll start a family in their own good time.'

The unwelcome thought flashed through her mind that if circumstances had been different – horribly and disastrously different – the baby-that-never-was would have been older than Walter now. He would have been starting school and been branded for ever, and Shirley would have had to bear the shameful stigma of being an unmarried mother.

Carrie gave an involuntary shiver, thinking how precarious those times had been, and how very lucky Shirley had been after all. Whatever guardian angel had been looking after her had certainly done its benevolent work on the day when she knew the worst wasn't going to happen after all.

'When you've finished staring into space,

your husband could do with a cup of cocoa,' Archie reminded her.

She marched out to the kitchen with the supper plates at once, knowing how he never liked it when she seemed to vanish into her own little world where he couldn't follow. Thank goodness he couldn't, she thought feelingly, and not just on account of Shirley's secret that her best friends had vowed never to tell, but because you had to have some private places in your life, and thoughts were often the only privacy a person had.

As she put the milk on the stove for the cocoa, she felt a moment's sadness. The lovely girlhood plan in Carrie's mind had been for all four good friends to start their families together. They would all live near to one another in Penhallow, and push their babies out in their prams together. But nothing ever happened the way you wanted it to – except for her marriage to Archie, of course. That had definitely followed the path she had always wanted.

She felt uplifted at the thought, and pushed everything else out of her mind. You couldn't live other peoples' lives, nor interfere in what fate had in store for any of them, and a good thing too.

Chapter Four

Poppy was always sorry when the short hay-making season was over. It had been in full swing during July, when the fields hummed to the drone of tractors and mowing machines, the whinnying of horses, and men's voices. Unlike most farmers, Sam was reluctant to keep dogs on the farm since their last one was hounded for sheep worrying and caused such a disturbance among the local community. Sam had decided there and then that dogs were more trouble than they were worth. If his mother had had other ideas, she had finally given up airing them.

In haymaking season the air was filled with the scent of the sweet-smelling new-cut grass on the hay wagons, ready to be dried and stacked for the winter animal feeds, and there was a pervading sense of well-being that this perfect blue and golden Cornish summer would go on for ever.

Sam's farm consisted of a small herd of cows; the pigs that he reared for market; and a flock of chickens that supplied eggs for the village shops and local people. He jogged along nicely, with no wish to expand any further, in the same way his father had done before him. He only employed one general labourer, Len Painter, now that the fields no longer had to be used for the old wartime 'digging for victory', but as was usual in the rural community, the small group of neighbouring farmers always lent a hand for haymaking, and he reciprocated when required.

Poppy loved those times. The cheery good humour between the men was better than a breath of fresh air, and even her mother-in-law was reasonably affable. Between them the two women prepared jugs of cider and hunks of bread and cheese and jars of pickled onions, which Poppy would take out to the fields where the men were working.

Of all seasons of the farming year, it was the one that Poppy loved the best. But she had to admit that things were different – and even better – when the land girls were here, and she had had an insight into a different way of life from the one she had always known. There was always the July haymaking at Lovering's Farm, because nothing ever changed in the farming year, and in those days a good few larks and saucy banter went on between the local farmers and the female visitors.

At other times, while they were doing the back-breaking and unaccustomed jobs of raking and hoeing, planting potatoes or turnips in the ploughed fields as ordered by the ministry, or gathering whatever produce was in season, Poppy was the one who would take steaming mugs of tea out to the fields for the girls, with some of Florrie's seed cake for their elevenses. No cider was allowed for the girls.

This year, Poppy stumbled a little as she walked carefully over the hard-baked earth with the tray of cider for the men, and she made herself pause for breath for a moment as her head spun alarmingly, and her heart beat faster at imagining Florrie's wrath if she had dropped the lot.

She could hear the men's cat-calls from the far field, together with the drone of the tractor and mowing machine. Then, still dizzy from the stumble, and thankful that she hadn't spilled a drop of cider, she had one of those eerie, day-dreaming, almost delicious moments, when past and present seemed to mingle.

In her head she could still hear the land girls shouting and laughing to one another above the roar of Sam's tractor in another field. It was surprising how clearly the sound always carried over the still summer air, and Poppy was quite sure they never guessed how much of their conversations she had overheard and unconsciously tucked away in her memory. She never told them, and why would they bother about it, anyway? She was only a kid compared with them.

'So who's the target for tonight then, Mary?' came Shirley Loe's teasing voice, floating distinctly into Poppy's receptive ears, bragging with the latest RAF slang of her dashing boyfriend, Bernard Bosinney.

Mary was a Londoner, and not in the least impressed by country girls who thought they knew what was what. She teased her right back with some ripe words.

'I ain't made up my bleedin' mind yet, gel, but as long as I keep my 'and on my ha'penny, same as you should, I'll be taking my chances with them lovely GIs at the dance in Penzance on Saturday night.'

Poppy grinned, knowing Florrie Lovering would get her hackles up right away if she could hear Mary's language.

Her friend Lil, chimed in. 'Leave the gel alone, Mary. We all know she's only got eyes for her lovely air force feller, though since he ain't around just now, fightin' for King and country and all that, well, you know what they always say about the cat being away!'

'Bernard's not a cat,' Shirley said indignantly.

'No, and neither's that Yank you've got your eye on, is he?' Mary hooted. 'More of a tiger, I'd say. We saw you last week – and the week before that! What was it Lil called him – Hank the Yank, weren't it? Yanking in more ways than one if he gets his bleedin' way, I'll bet, eh Lil?'

'Don't be so coarse,' Shirley said, unable to resist giggling wildly at the daring way these girls spoke. 'Hank's a real gentleman, and I only dance with him, anyway. He's never even hinted at anything else and I'm sure he wouldn't!'

The other girls screamed as if she'd said the funniest thing in the world.

'Pull the other one, curly Shirley! Blokes are all after the same thing, so just you mind you don't get tempted to give it to him, right?'

Shirley's voice became shriller and crosser. 'You're both such know-alls, aren't you? You think we've all got hayseeds sticking out of our mouths. Anyway, how do you know I haven't ... uh ... given it to him already? If I had, I wouldn't be daft enough to tell you two!'

Poppy had groaned with frustration as the drone of Sam Lovering's tractor became louder as it moved across the field in her direction, and she hadn't heard any more of the conversation. She knew darned well they wouldn't tell her anything remotely saucy, saying she was too young to know about such things. But the words had stuck in her mind for days afterwards, alternately charming her and arousing her intense curiosity about what went on at these dances where all the GIs went on Saturday nights. At the same time, her fertile imagination wondered just how far – if anywhere at all – Shirley Loe had got with her Yank, and what her Bernard, away fighting for his country, would have to say about it if he knew.

It was a long time ago now, and both she and Shirley were two different people. Shirley had married Bernard, and in due course Poppy had married Sam Lovering, which would have been another cause for hooting laughter from the other land girls if they'd only known about it.

She hadn't had to marry him – certainly not in the way Mary and Lil would have meant it! She just hadn't known any other young men, and Sam had always been kind to her, and so she had said yes to his proposal of marriage.

It wasn't quite like the uneasy days of wartime, when you took happiness wherever you could find it, because you never knew what was going to happen from one day to the next. Even Poppy, naive as she was then, had known that, and had frequently mourned the fact that she had never been old enough to go to Penzance and dance with the Yanks like the other girls had done.

She had only really ever been able to guess what went on in overheard conversations and throwaway remarks from those other girls. Just enough to make her wild with impatience at never knowing more, and fuelling it with her own vivid imagination.

It was odd, though, and something that she couldn't rightly explain, how taking the cider out to the men on that summer hay-making day a month ago had stirred it all up in her mind again.

'You're making a fool of that animal, girl,' Florrie said severely as Poppy coaxed the bottle teat into the piglet's soft, eager mouth. 'Pigs are meant for fattening and slaughter-ing and eating, not being kept as pets.'

Poppy flinched, resisting the urge to put her hands over Henrietta's pink ears, just as if the piglet could understand every word the woman said.

'Well, Sam gave him to me as a pet, and that's what he is. And before you tell me I'm giving him a problem by calling him Henrietta, I know he's a boy, but he doesn't know it's a girl's name, does he? In any case, I like the name. It was my grandmother's name, if you want to know.'

Florrie continued banging pots and pans about, muttering under her breath about it being far too fancy a name for the family of a simpleton like Poppy.

'You can get him outside once you've fin-ished pandering to him, anyway. I'll not have him getting used to being in the house, and he needs to be in a proper pen, like the rest of the pigs.'

'Sam's making me a special little pen for

him today,' Poppy said defensively, 'he'll be outside then, but he's only a baby and he needs looking after.'

'Pity you don't get on and have a real one then, instead of wasting time on an animal. I don't know what you and our Sam are about, I'm sure. Every man needs a son to carry on the family name and you should have done your duty by him long before now.'

Poppy wouldn't listen to any more of this. They both wanted the same thing, if Florrie did but know it, but it still wasn't happening, and there wasn't much you could do about it, she thought resentfully. It wasn't as if they didn't do what those land girls had called 'the business'. In fact, just lately Sam had become quite keen on forgetting it was only a ritual for Saturday nights, and had surprised her on more than one occasion. She gave a giggle, because she quite liked to be surprised, and it was usually better than on the nights when he'd been drinking ale at the pub.

His mother might prefer to call her contrary, but Poppy had always kicked against things that were too predictable, which was why she had been delighted when Sam had mentioned building a fire at the beach one evening and cooking sausages for the two of them. It sounded so romantic – until she realized it was a couple of weeks ago, and he hadn't mentioned it since.

She took a deep breath. If Sam hadn't mentioned it, there was no reason why she shouldn't do so. She went out to the barn with Henrietta in her arms, where he was hammering on the new pen that was especially for the piglet.

'Won't be long now,' he said.

'It looks lovely, and Henrietta will love it, Sam.'

'He told you that, did he?' he said with a grin.

Poppy kissed the top of the animal's pink head. 'Oh yes, we understand one another very well.'

'You'd best be careful then, or my mother will think you're in league with the devil, talking to animals.'

'You talk to them!'

'Oh ah, but I don't expect 'em to answer back.'

He stood back, admiring his handiwork, and Poppy laid the piglet reverently inside. Henrietta had more of a squeak than a grunt as yet, but after a few moments he curled up on the straw bedding.

'He likes it! Oh, thank you for that, Sam – and now I want to ask you for something else.'

'What – more favours?' he said cautiously.

'It's about that bonfire we're going to build on the beach. Your mother will be out at her

church meeting, so can we do it tonight? We
don't have to tell her, because I know she'll
think we're crazy. I daresay she'd think we
were going to dance around the bonfire and
do all kinds of weird rituals.'

Sam gave a belly-laugh at her gloomy face.
'You don't have a very good opinion of my
mother, do you, girl?'

'Yes, I do! I know she's a good woman, but
I don't think she has a very good opinion of
me, that's all. She thinks I'm young and
scatty.'

Sam laughed again, and gave her waist a
quick squeeze. 'Well, you'll do for me, and
that's all that matters. So tonight it is.'

Poppy was hardly able to believe her luck.
She might like the unpredictable, but it was
rare that Sam did anything on the spur of
the moment. Farmers were ruled by the
seasons and their farming year. She gave
him a quick kiss on the cheek and went back
indoors, singing.

Florrie gave her a sharp look. 'Well, you've
certainly cheered up, miss. You can go and
collect the eggs if you've finished playing
with your pet.'

'Yes, Ma'am,' Poppy said smartly, glad to
get out of doors again, and determined that
nothing was going to dampen the thrill of
going to the beach with Sam later, and
having their own special evening.

Once Florrie had gone off to her church meeting, they took the sausages out of the cold store in the dairy and put them in a basket with hunks of bread, a couple of toasting forks and jugs of cider and lemonade, firmly stoppered. Then they drove over the bumpy farm tracks until the moors dipped down to the sea and one of the little coves beneath the cliffs.

They left the car on the headland and clambered down the sandy path to where the sea was mellow and golden from the low rays of the sun. The waves rippled across the shallow sands, but the tide was already at its height, so they would be quite safe in building their bonfire without any risk of being cut off. There was always plenty of wood and other flotsam on the shore, washed in by the tide and by the remnants of old and new shipwrecks that littered the coastline.

They had the cove to themselves, and it didn't take long to build a fire, and to watch the flames shooting skyward, blazing in the gentle breeze from the sea.

Poppy was so enchanted by it all that she laughed out loud. 'You know, I really do think there used to be folk who danced around bonfires in olden times, probably making good luck spells, or even ill-wishes.'

'It's a good thing you didn't let Mother hear you say that, then. You know she don't hold with such things. She don't have any doubts about you, mind, but she's always been a bit doubtful about your old mum and dad.'

Poppy pulled a face. 'Just because they keep themselves to themselves, that doesn't make them weird, does it? Or me?'

'I wouldn't have married you if I thought that. So stop talking, and let's get these sausages cooking.'

She did as she was told, holding her toasting fork gingerly as the heat threatened to burn her fingers. The fat from the sausages made the flames spit and spark and made her squeal with laughter and excitement, and in the end she gave up and left Sam to the cooking while she slapped the cooked meat on to the hunks of bread. They spent the next half hour alternately eating the food and washing it all down with cider or lemonade, and Poppy felt completely happy. The sun was reddening the sea to a glassy sheet of flame by now, though it wasn't yet dusk.

'Can't I try a drop of cider?' she said daringly, finding the sweet-smelling drink on Sam's breath more enticing than she had expected. 'There's no one to see, or to tell!'

'You'll get light-headed if you do,' Sam said with a grin.

'I don't mind that. In any case, I'm light-headed already. Please Sam, let me try. It's only apple-juice, isn't it?'

85

He laughed. 'Well, it's a bit stronger than that, but I can't see that it'll do any harm, as long as you don't make a habit of it. I don't want Mother thinking I'm leading you astray.'

At that moment, Poppy didn't care what his mother might think, or anyone else, for that matter. It was such a glorious evening and she and Sam were so in tune with one another. He handed her the jug of cider and pulled out the stopper for her to put it to her lips.

The liquid trickled down her throat, cool and tangier than she had imagined. She spluttered for a moment and then took a longer draught, with a new sense of exhilaration flowing through her.

'I think that's enough,' she said, choking a little as the sea and sky began to swirl in her vision, not unpleasantly, but just enough to make her feel expansive.

'I told you,' Sam said sagely. 'It's not a drink for young uns, not that you're a babby any more, mind. And you look different tonight,' he added.

'Do I? How do I look different?'

'Well, your hair's all wild and blowing about, for a start. You look sort of glowing, and your eyes are sparkling. That could be the cider, of course. And your mouth's all shiny from the sausages.'

Poppy felt her heart begin to beat faster.

The compliments – if that was what they were – were so unexpected, but it wasn't so much what he was saying as the way that he said it. As if he had never seen her before, which was daft when he had known her for so many years. He had never put such things into words though, as if he was seeing her like this for the very first time.

Perhaps he was. Perhaps she had never felt so alive, as if this was truly an enchanted place, and he was affected by it too. And she was sure that wasn't just on account of the cider, because she had really tasted very little of it. Just enough to make her relaxed and excited at the same time. She swallowed dryly.

'Sam,' she whispered.

The unaccustomed words brimmed on her tongue to ask him to make love to her, right here and right now – but a wife didn't ask her husband such things. If she did, she was sure he would be shocked. But couldn't he see what she wanted, what she was sure they both wanted, here in this secluded place with only the sea and the waving grasses on the moors above to whisper their secret?

'You're right. It's time we went,' she heard him say. 'We don't want to be climbing back up those cliffs in the dark and lose our footing, and you'll be feeling a mite unsteady now. We'd better pack everything up.'

'There's not much left to pack,' Poppy

said, sick with disappointment at his change of mood, and the way he hadn't seemed to be in tune with her after all.

She watched while he stamped out the remains of the fire, and tried not to think that he was stamping on her foolish dreams. For when would Farmer Sam Lovering ever do anything as spontaneous as making love beneath the first glimmering stars of twilight? She should be thankful he was here with her at all.

'Come on, my 'andsome witch,' he said, holding out his hand to her. 'We've done enough gallivanting for one night.'

She took his hand and let him lead her up the cliff path to the waiting car. She wasn't a witch and she knew he had only meant it as a clumsy term of endearment, but it sent a small shiver through her all the same. Her mum would have got that strange, narrowed look in her eyes and said it was an omen, that all good things had to be balanced by bad, and she wished to goodness that one of her mum's solemn old sayings hadn't come into her head right then.

Poppy woke up in the night with her nerves jumping. Something had startled her, and for the moment she couldn't think what it was. And then the sounds flooded into her brain, raucous, agonizing, screeching sounds, and she realized that Sam had already leapt out of bed and was struggling to pull his trousers over his pyjamas, swearing beneath his breath as he snapped on his flashlight.

'What is it?' she said as she became instantly and fearfully aware of the horrendous noise outside.

'Bloody fox if I know anything,' he bellowed. 'Sounds like it's got into the hen-house. I'm going for my gun.'

'Oh, Sam, no!'

He wasn't listening. She should be used to animals being slaughtered by now. It was part of being a farmer's wife. You reared the animals and then you had to let them go. Foxes were vermin and a menace once they got into a farmyard, but Poppy believed that all animals and wildlife were precious, and she couldn't bear to think of Sam shooting the fox's head off.

She jumped out of bed and pulled her dressing-gown around her, sliding her feet into her slippers before racing down to join him. Florrie was there before her, shouting after Sam as they both went outside. She'd have no pity on the fox either, especially if it had slaughtered half the chickens. Poppy's heart beat so sickeningly that she thought she might faint, both from the cold night air, and the dizzy aftermath of the cider she had drunk earlier. It hadn't been very much, but being unused to it, it had had an effect. They had got back to the farm before

Florrie returned from her meeting, but although she had said nothing, she had looked suspiciously at Poppy's flushed face and sniffed the air meaningfully.

Now, knowing what she called Poppy's ridiculous animal-worship, she snapped at the girl to stay indoors, since she would be useless in the chaos outside, and at the same time slating Sam that none of this would have happened if he'd got another dog or two to keep the foxes away.

'But I want to help,' Poppy shrieked, ignoring her tirade. 'I should be at Sam's side at times like this.' And *she* was the wife, not Florrie.

'Do as Mother says, Poppy,' Sam bellowed back from the yard. 'You won't want to see this.'

Did they both think she was so lily-livered that she couldn't cope? A farmer's wife had to deal with life and death. It was all part of the farming cycle. Even as a child she had seen her mum wring a chicken's neck more than once, and gagged at the smell and the sight of blood, but if it meant the difference between eating or starving, she knew these things had to be done, and at such times you had to forget your own squeamishness.

She pushed past Sam's mother and rushed outside to the hen-house, and then stopped short in horror at the scene of carnage that met her eyes. She was breathing so hard that she was in danger of swooning properly now. There was blood and feathers everywhere, and, even worse, there were heartbreaking shreds of poultry where the bodies had been torn apart in what seemed like a frenzy. Sobs rose in her throat at the slaughter.

The explosion of Sam's shotgun threatened to burst her eardrums, and for a few moments she was completely disorientated.

'I've got the bastard,' Sam roared. 'He won't do any more damage, though from the looks of things here I reckon there was more than one of the buggers.'

Still bellowing, he turned to his mother, as much to hide his own distress as in anger. 'For God's sake, get the maid back in the house. I've work to do here.'

Poppy stood transfixed at the way he was behaving. Foxes were the bane of a farmer's life, but she knew instinctively that there was something more, something he wasn't telling her. As Florrie grabbed her arm and tried to get her back to the farmhouse, she had a sixth sense about it. She twisted away from her mother-in-law and ran to the barn, to where Sam was clumsily lifting a small, very bloody pink body out of what looked like a smashed wooden crate.

'Henrietta!' Poppy screamed.

Before he could stop her, she had snatched the crushed piglet out of his arms

91

and held it tight to her chest, ignoring the blood running down her dressing-gown. She was weeping as if she had lost her best friend. That was exactly what he had been, she sobbed wildly, her best friend, the one thing that had loved her unconditionally, and for such a little time.

'Come on now, girl, there's no call for all this keening,' Sam said uncomfortably. 'Give the animal to me and I'll deal with it.'

'*No!* You'll just throw him in a pit with the remains of the chickens, and it'll be as if he never existed. Henrietta was my friend.'

Florrie's sharp voice sounded right behind her.

'You see, Sam? It's just like I said. There's no place for sentiment on a farm and the girl needs to be told. Take the thing away, before we spend all night arguing over it.'

'You're not taking him from me,' Poppy said wildly, backing away. 'He's going to have a proper burial, and I'll say some words over him.'

'Now, Poppy, stop this,' Sam began, beginning to sound alarmed.

'It's all the fault of that crazy mother of hers,' Florrie snapped. 'I always said you should never have tied yourself to the daughter of a madwoman, and now you know why. Giving a pig a proper burial, indeed. Next thing you know, she'll be asking the vicar to come and bless it.'

Without knowing where she was going, Poppy tore away from them and raced towards the moors with Henrietta still held tightly in her arms. His blood was still warm, seeping through to her nightdress and her skin. Still sobbing, but determined to do what she felt was right, she was also aware of an unwelcome sense of foreboding, wondering if she was truly going mad, and if what Florrie said about her mother was really true.

She wouldn't believe it. Her mum and dad were just simple country folk, that was all. They had no doings with witchcraft or any of that nonsense. This was the middle of the twentieth century, and such things belonged in a pagan past.

She suddenly tripped over a stump in her inadequate slippers, and went sprawling headlong in the coarse moorland grass. Whatever was left of Henrietta was now a bloody mess beneath her weight, and she wept anew as she realized it.

She had no idea how long she lay there, bereft and half stunned, before Sam found her, still cradling the soft, tiny broken body in her arms.

'It's time to come home, Poppy,' he said quietly.

She jerked up her head, her eyes clouded with tears, the words bursting out.

'I know you think I'm being a fool,' she

choked. 'I know your mother hasn't got time for me, and she probably thinks it's blasphemous to think about burying Henrietta properly, but he was my pet, and I loved him.'

'I know, and that's why we're going to do things just the way you want to, and never mind what other folk think. Come on now, girl, there's a touch of mist in the air. You'll be getting chilled in your nightclothes, and I've no wish to lose my wife as well as my livestock.'

His voice was rough now, embarrassed at saying such things. But she recognized the heart in him, and stood up slowly, leaning on him for support, still with the limp body in her arms. She looked at the piglet, a pulpy mess and smashed almost out of recognition now, but still with a soul, she thought passionately – if animals had souls.

'I'm ready now, Sam,' she said.

But she still couldn't rid her head of the dire words her mum used to drum into her. Every good thing the Lord gives you must be balanced by something bad. That was her simple message. Or, if you believed the scriptures, then the good Lord giveth, and the good Lord taketh away. But He didn't have to take Henrietta.

Chapter Five

Word soon got round that Sam Lovering had lost all his chickens to the rogue fox. The next day a neighbour turned up with a replacement hen, and then another and another until in less than a week they were almost back to full strength again. Poppy was touched by their kindness, and it was all that Sam and Len Painter could do to repair the broken hen-house in time to house the new arrivals.

'It's no more than our Sam did when his dogs savaged some neighbours' sheep a couple of years back. I thought you'd be sure to remember when he had the dogs put down, and pretty cut up he was at the time. But he saw the neighbours right for weeks with eggs, and a bit of his savings that he could ill afford as well,' Florrie told Poppy.

By now, after badgering him for days, Florrie had got her way, and there was a new dog installed outside, a snarling mongrel that would soon see off any predators, she said with satisfaction. Despite her love of animals, Poppy simply couldn't take to the nasty, yapping thing. She disliked the dog with a passion, and wouldn't go near it if she could help it.

'I do remember those dogs and how the city land girls hated them, but I didn't know about Sam helping out the neighbours at the time. It wasn't my business, was it? It was good of Sam though,' Poppy replied to Florrie's comments, and then added with a gulp: 'But nothing will replace Henrietta.'

'You want to forget that animal,' Florrie said. 'It does no good to brood on things, and Sam did as you wanted and buried him, more fool him for being so soft, so that should be the end of it.'

'Sam's not a fool. He knew how bad I was feeling.'

'We all knew that,' Florrie said dryly. 'But in the end, it was only a beast, Poppy, and a farmer's wife has got to remember that. It's not like losing a relative. That's the time for crying.'

Poppy was aware of a sudden odd note in her mother-in-law's voice. She hadn't known Sam's father, but his parents must have felt love at some time or a child wouldn't have been born. She supposed Florrie must have grieved when her husband died too, impossible though it was for Poppy to imagine the straight-lipped woman weeping and wailing.

'Did you cry when Sam's father died?' she asked, before she stopped to think, and immediately caught her breath, knowing how impertinent she sounded.

Florrie paused, her hands deep in washing-up water at the scullery sink. 'Everybody cries when a person dies. Just because we don't wear our hearts on our sleeves don't mean we don't feel pain. Some of us have the gumption to keep it locked up inside where it belongs. Grieving's best done in private, and you don't need to put on a show for other folk's benefit. Now, if you're going to get over to Zennor today, you'd best get on with it.'

Poppy was shocked at her vehemence, it was as if she hated herself for giving away the slightest inkling of her feelings and so had skilfully changed the subject. But those few words told Poppy more about her mother-in-law than she had known in all the years she had worked on the farm.

'I'm sorry for stirring things up, Mrs Lovering,' she said humbly. 'I know Henrietta wasn't a person, but he was as helpless as a baby, so you'll know how I'm feeling about him now then, won't you? Especially dying in that awful way.'

She turned and left the scullery before she burst into tears at the memory, and, more importantly, before she had to listen to Florrie reverting to her usual snapping again. It was really strange, though, how you never really got to know people at all, Poppy found herself thinking. There was always something of themselves that they chose to keep hidden, and probably a good thing too in some cases – except for someone like herself, who didn't have anything to hide.

Without warning, the memory of Jack Trevis leapt into her mind. She flinched, not having thought about him since the day she collected her framed photo from Penzance, and she didn't want to think about him now, she thought crossly.

Not now, when she and Sam were getting on so well, and he had been so understanding about giving Henrietta a decent burial in the corner of the yard where she grew her cooking herbs. She had particularly wanted him buried there, because Florrie left that bit of gardening to her, so she could whisper a few words of comfort to the piglet whenever she visited his little plot.

No, she and Sam were all right, and good-looking chaps with a look of Clark Gable about them belonged in a different world from theirs. She simply wasn't going to think about him any more, nor the way her heart could still skip a beat whenever he did come into her mind. It was her day to visit her parents, and after she had rammed her straw hat on her head she went to the dairy to fetch the eggs and few slices of ham that she always took for them.

Living on a farm had its benefits, she thought, as she struck out across the moors, vainly trying to put behind her all the misery of the past week or so.

'Hey Missus,' she heard a voice calling a few minutes later, and she turned around to see Billy Flint running across the turf towards her, his thatch of yellow hair as unkempt as ever, his ready smile making up for his grubbiness.

'Hello Billy,' she said, relieved to put a stop to her meandering thoughts. 'I hope you're behaving yourself lately and not falling down any more mine-shafts.'

He pulled a face. 'I ain't doing that no more! Me dad still says I was a bloody raving lunatic for wandering off and not looking where I was going, even though I'm always up here on the moors. It scares me when he says stuff like that, though, 'cos they lock up bloody raving lunatics, don't they, Missus?'

Poppy tried to keep a straight face at Gus Flint's choice of words and the innocent way Billy invariably repeated them.

'Oh, I'm sure nobody's going to lock you up, Billy. You were just unlucky, that's all.'

'Well, me mum still thinks you're a bloody female hero, and me dad keeps the paper in a drawer to remind me of what a bloody raving lunatic I was instead of using it in the lavvy.'

'Does your mum say that too?' Poppy said, choking, but thankful that her newspaper

99

photo wasn't going to end up in the Flints' privy and its inevitable use.

'She says what me dad says,' he told her solemnly. 'Where are you going?' he added, falling into step beside her, whether she wanted company or not. She didn't really mind, because he was a nice enough kid, despite his ripe language, and he had his father to thank for that. He was all of six years old, and having his company kept her mind off other things.

'I'm going to see my mum and dad in Zennor,' she said.

Billy stopped walking, and stood with his legs apart and his arms folded, a miniature of his aggressive father.

'I ain't going there. Me dad says there's a lot of bloody loonies living there and they cast spells on you.'

'That's a lot of silly talk,' Poppy said, laughing, and uncaring if she was calling Billy's dad silly or not. 'I was born in Zennor and I'm not a loony, am I?'

'I s'pose not, but that paper chap thinks they're all up to summat. He said so in the paper and me dad read it out to me mum and me.'

Poppy counted to ten and back again. She hadn't missed the latest piece Jack Trevis had written in the newspaper – some juicy article about strange goings-on in Zennor and the surrounding countryside, no matter that it happened centuries ago. It was enough to make decent folk quake in their shoes, but as Sam had snorted when he read it, it was to sell more newspapers, that was all, and anybody with an ounce of sense would tear it into squares and put it in their outside privies where it belonged. Just as the Flints should have done, she thought, seething. She wouldn't have minded *that*, since her photo wasn't in it.

'You don't have to believe everything you read in the newspaper, Billy,' she told him sternly.

'Why not? Ain't it all true, then? It was true about you getting me out of the bloody mine-shaft, weren't it?'

'Yes, that was true,' Poppy said, feeling as if she was getting into deep water now. 'I'm sure a lot of it is true, but all that stuff about putting spells on people, well, that's just fairy stories.'

'I'll tell me dad that then, but I still ain't going nowhere near bloody Zennor. I like the moors best, anyway,' he said, and raced back the way he had come.

Poppy chewed her lip, not sure how Gus Flint was going to take her interfering in his son's education. She hoped the family would come to the fair as usual at the end of the month, and still buy their eggs from them, and that there wouldn't be any trouble. Gus was well-known for his hasty

101

temper, and although she had been very much in favour when she'd rescued Billy, she knew he'd have no truck with her undermining what he had told his son.

Undermining, she thought, with a faint smile. That was a rum word to use, considering where she'd rescued him from. And then she put him right out of her mind as the village of Zennor came into view, and the wood-smoke from her mum and dad's chimney sent up a cheery welcome as usual.

Jack Trevis was pleased with the first of his local articles and the way it had been received by his editor, and also from the letters that had come after it had been published. Folk were keen to tell their own stories and for him to print them, which gave him plenty of material to build into a publishable piece.

He half regretted that the first one had been about Zennor, and that he had felt obliged to mention in passing that Poppy Lovering, the mine-shaft heroine, came from there. Graham Strang had been keen for him to report more about the fertile background of old Zennor legends and to mention the link with Poppy, and Jack admitted that he wasn't averse to bringing her name into his consciousness again. He managed to resist using her photo, but he hardly needed to do so to remember the way she looked, with that strange mixture of innocence and wantonness that he was quite sure she didn't even realize she possessed. He knew he was guilty of falling for a pretty face again, but he scoffed at thinking this was why he couldn't quite forget her. Or that she had put a spell on him...

He brought his thoughts up short, refusing to allow the spooky goings-on of remote hamlets and past times to colour his thinking. He had become so immersed in them for his work recently, delving into archives and old books until he felt too steeped in ancient folklore for comfort. He was glad now that it had been decided that the feature was only going to be an occasional one. It was far healthier to deal with the everyday problems and interests of local folk than to have his head befuddled with the myths and legends of a sometimes murky past. And far better to tease readers with always wanting more, than to bombard them with a regular dose of nostalgia, the journalist in him added.

But he had every intention of covering the fair and fête at Lovering's Farm. It gave him a genuine reason for being there, and he didn't deny how much he looked forward to seeing Poppy again. The husband was genial enough, and he could easily ignore the harridan of a mother-in-law. It was Poppy who lit up that whole household, like a star in the darkness.

As the flowery words came into his head, he gave an impatient sigh and returned to the more prosaic reporting of a local cricket match. The hacks on the local paper weren't called Jack-of-all-trades for nothing, and even apart from his name, he knew he more than aptly fitted the description.

Billy Flint's father came striding over the fields to Lovering's Farm that evening, hammering on the door of the farmhouse with his son in tow.

'What's that wife of yours been telling our Billy?' he snapped the minute Sam opened the door. 'You should be man enough to keep her under control, Lovering, and to make sure she keeps her bloody daft opinions to herself.'

Sam riled at once. He might be an easygoing man but he wasn't going to be browbeaten on his own doorstep by this madman. Behind him, Florrie began tut-tutting loudly at the man's language.

'Since I don't know what you're talking about, perhaps you'd better explain yourself before you start insulting my wife, and let's have less of the swear words,' Sam snapped back, arms folded tightly across his chest in just the way Billy's had been earlier, Poppy thought instantly.

'I'll say what I bloody well like,' the man

shouted. 'She's been saying I tell lies to my own son, and I'll not have it from the daughter of a couple of – well, I don't rightly know what to call them.'

'Leave them out of it, and you weren't so particular when Poppy dragged your boy out of the mine shaft, were you? Or have you forgotten that?'

'I ain't forgotten, but there's no call for her to fret him like she did, saying stuff in the paper's all made up, so now he's started asking me if I believe it all. What if other folk start listening to her daft talk? She'll be sorry if they start wondering if she ever bloody rescued him at all, and how will that make your precious wife look?'

'You're not making any sense, man,' Sam said angrily. 'I don't know what Poppy said, but I'm damn sure she didn't mean to alarm young Billy.'

Poppy had held her tongue for long enough. She pushed her husband aside and glared at the visitors, ignoring the way Billy was snivelling now, and clearly wishing he'd said nothing at all about their meeting on the moors.

'Don't I have a say in this?' she said shrilly.

'You've said enough, madam,' Gus Flint said rudely. 'And in future, keep your bloody opinions to yourself.'

He turned and marched away, grabbing the unfortunate Billy by one ear and making the boy yelp with pain and fury.

Sam slammed the door behind them, his fists clenched, and then saw that Poppy was upset and trembling. 'Whatever it was you said to the kid, there's no sense in upsetting yourself about it now,' he said roughly. 'The man's an oaf and everybody knows it.'

This wasn't enough for his mother. 'She must have said something to make him take on so,' she said accusingly. 'Aren't you going to ask her about it?'

They both looked at Poppy, and for a weird moment she felt as if she was on trial. Putting her in the ducking-pond would come next, she thought wildly, the way they did with all witches. And then she'd have no chance. Right or wrong, she'd be doomed. Furious at herself for thinking such a thing, she sent the stupid thoughts away, and her head cleared, knowing she had done nothing wrong.

'I met Billy Flint when I was on the way to see my parents, and he said he wasn't going anywhere near Zennor because the newspaper chap said people there put spells on you, and I told him that was all fairy stories, and anyway you couldn't believe everything you read in the papers. That's what *you* always say, isn't it, Sam?' she said, gasping for breath.

'Well, maybe I do, but a child that age believes everything he's told. You should know that.'

'How should I know? I've never had a child, have I?'

Her eyes brimmed with tears as she hurled the words at him, because it wasn't for want of trying. He knew that. He had been more tender than usual in bed lately, and if anything could produce the child she longed for, she thought it would surely have been that.

Her thoughts raced on again, knowing she had lavished all her love on Henrietta, treating him as the baby she never had, until he had been cruelly murdered, which was the way she thought of it. She could never feel the same towards the wretched mongrel dog, and didn't want to try. He wasn't to be considered a pet, anyway. He wasn't even given a proper name. He was just Dog.

'Mother, go and make us all a strong cup of tea,' Sam ordered, breaking into her thoughts. 'Me and Poppy have got some talking to do.'

She had never expected Florrie to soften towards her, but she supposed there was a certain amount of thawing in the farmhouse after the Flints' visit. It may have had something to with the straight talking between herself and Sam, and the even straighter talking he had then had with Florrie. She wasn't eavesdropping in the avid way she once enjoyed eavesdropping on the land girls' saucy conversations, but she could hardly avoid listening to Sam and his mother, because their sharp voices carried up the stairs long after she had left them and gone to bed, wearied by the whole affair.

'You've got to understand the girl, Mother,' he said angrily. 'If her words run away with themselves it's because she's no more than a kid herself. She'd have enjoyed the company of the Flint boy, and meant no harm in what she said.'

'That's as may be, but you should never have married her,' Florrie snapped. 'I said at the time she was far too young for you, and look where it's got you, bringing trouble into the house. Her head was turned by all this newspaper business, and now she's rattled our neighbours.'

'It'll be a long time coming before I care what Gus Flint thinks about my family, and it's time you remembered that Poppy's part of this family too. She's my wife, and she deserves to be respected for that. It wouldn't hurt you to try thinking of her as a daughter, instead of an interloper.'

Poppy drew in her breath at the way Sam was carrying on. He rarely raised his voice to his mother, and there he was, becoming quite eloquent for once, and championing her. Then her heart jumped as her attention was caught again.

'A *daughter*,' Florrie's voice quivered. 'How do you know what it means to have a daughter? The pair of you are lacking in that department yet. I went through the pain of it all years ago, and I don't want reminding of it, thank you, and nor do I plan to make this flibbertigibbet a substitute.'

Poppy felt her mouth drop open. It was the first time she'd heard of any daughter, but if she had her way it certainly wasn't going to be the last.

'Well, I'm sorry, Mother, but it was all a long time ago, and you can't dwell on it for ever. Anyway, that's not the point. All I ask is that you give Poppy a little more leeway, for all our sakes.'

Poppy hadn't heard any more, but she had lain awake in the darkness until Sam came stumping up the stairs, saying nothing as he got undressed without putting on a light, and then sliding in beside her. But it wasn't in her nature to keep quiet for ever.

'You'll have to tell me now,' she whispered.

'Tell you what?' he said, startled by her voice into giving a smothered oath beneath his breath.

She turned towards him in their big old bed. She couldn't see him clearly, but there was enough moonlight shining through the curtains to see the shape of his profile, and that his jaw was tight.

'I couldn't help hearing you and your mother arguing, and I'm glad you stuck up for me, Sam. It's what a husband ought to do, isn't it?'

'Well then, you got what you wanted, so now let's sleep on it.'

'But who was the daughter she was talking about? Did you have a sister, Sam?'

This time the oath was louder. He turned towards her, and she could feel his breath on her cheek as he began breathing more heavily.

'It's none of your business.'

'Yes it is. You said yourself that I'm part of this family now, so I have a right to know, haven't I? What happened to your sister, Sam?'

She didn't often persist in challenging him, but she wasn't a cabbage, and if there was something hidden in this family ... her heart began to beat more quickly, wondering if there was some intrigue she was about to discover. Some sinister dark secret in the past, involving Florrie Lovering. Not that she could ever imagine the woman having a *lover*, but she'd been young once, and she wouldn't always have been the dragon she was now.

Sam gave a short laugh. 'I'm sorry to disappoint you if you're cooking up some sort of scandal in your head, because it was nothing like that. I didn't even know my sister and probably never would have known about her if my gran hadn't told me what happened. The baby died of the whooping cough when she was a few weeks old, long before I was born.'

'Oh, that's terrible!' Poppy said, appalled.

'I daresay it was. My gran said Mother never really got over it, which was why she was relieved when I was born a boy. She'd never even wanted another child, but my father wanted a son to carry on the name. Gran said that if I'd been born a girl she'd threatened to strangle me at birth.'

'She would never have done such a wicked thing!' Not even Florrie Lovering. And whose family was touched now? Poppy couldn't help thinking.

'Of course not, but apparently Mother was quite deranged after the baby died, and she could never have borne to see another girl in the family. Are you satisfied now?' he finished savagely, as if the story had been wrung out of him.

Poppy reached out her arms to hold him, and feeling the rigidity of his muscles, she knew how much it had cost him to reveal this bit of family history. He was essentially a private man – and he got that from his mother too.

'I'm sorry for asking, Sam, but it was best that I know, or I might have said the wrong thing to your mother without realizing.' She finished lamely, for when would such a conversation ever have arisen between them? But unwittingly, the evening's upset and this latest revelation seemed to have aroused Sam, and he pulled her into him.

'Then maybe we should do a bit more towards filling the house with babbies of our own, and I'm damn sure I've no preference for boy or girl.'

If Poppy didn't bother to examine too closely the slight thaw in the female relationship at Lovering's Farm, she knew in her heart it had something to do with both sides. Florrie was undoubtedly unbending a little towards her daughter-in-law after Sam's sharp reprimands, and Poppy had a new understanding of how a once contented wife and mother could turn into the sour woman Florrie so often was.

So many comments that Florrie had made became more significant now. In particular she never harped on about Sam and Poppy having a baby, but if it was ever mentioned at all it was always a *son* that would carry on the family name. Never a daughter. Never a little girl like the one Florrie had lost.

Poppy didn't forget how distraught she herself had been over losing Henrietta, and he was only a piglet, she thought, trying to put it into perspective. It wasn't a child. Losing a child after carrying it inside you for nine months must be the very worst thing that could happen to a woman, so she was prepared to go more than halfway to being pleasant to her mother-in-law.

In any case, the annual fair at the end of August was only two weeks away now, and there would be plenty of work to keep them all busy then, and no time for reminiscing over something that happened forty years ago.

But although she never told Sam or his mother what she intended to do, the next time she went to Zennor to see her folks, she sneaked a look in Barras's small village churchyard and found the grave of Sam's father and the even more weathered one of his grandparents.

Beneath the name of Sam's father, Will Lovering, the faint words 'also Evie' had been simply scratched on the stone. It was as if the grieving parents had felt compelled to acknowledge her existence, but couldn't bear to do more. There was nothing else but her name to mark the spot where the baby daughter had been buried, which only added to the huge feeling of sadness Poppy felt for them. She had gone on her way, sobered, and given her own parents a special hug before she left their old cottage that day.

But she knew without being told that Florrie would be furious to think her

113

daughter-in-law knew of the chink in her armour, and vowed never to tell her of the conversation she had overheard between her and Sam that night.

As the days drew nearer to the end of the month, such things were put to the back of her mind in the growing excitement in the village and surrounding farms. The noisy village children gathered as if led by the Pied Piper as the painted wagons trundled down to Barras and set up in Lovering's field. As usual all seemed to be in total chaos, until almost miraculously, rides were erected, and amusement stalls made their appearance for the event which would continue for several days.

This was the commercial venture, but Sam always took on the organizing of childrens' games himself, and the first day of opening was when local folk dressed up in their best, not only for all the fun of the fair, but to visit the more homely stalls the village women had set up for their fête and to buy their produce.

As well as the rent for his fields, Sam expected to do as well or better than anyone else. His mother excelled too, with her famous sponge cakes made even more splendid now that wartime sugar rationing was at an end, and filled with her special butter icing. Poppy had never professed to be much of a cake-maker, and wouldn't dare to intrude on Florrie's province. The kitchen was Florrie's kingdom.

She was looking forward to seeing Shirley Bosinney again, and intended to look out for her on the opening day. It would be the first time Shirley had been back to the farm since the land girls had been disbanded. It didn't escape Poppy that she was no longer the gauche schoolgirl Shirley had first met here. She was the farmer's wife. She had a place here, and this was her home.

'Come on, girl, don't stand there stargazing,' she heard Florrie's impatient voice say. 'I haven't been baking all day for these cakes to sit in the dairy. Help me get them outside and set them out nicely on my table.'

Poppy picked up one of the trays holding half a dozen sponge cakes and hid a smile. No matter what the occasion, there would always be something she had neglected to do as far as her mother-in-law was concerned. But today it didn't matter. Today she was going to see her friend again, and hopefully have a good look at the airman-turned-schoolteacher she had married. But Poppy couldn't deny that Shirley wasn't the only one she was hoping to see.

Chapter Six

Although the fields for the August festivities were leased by Sam Lovering, the fête was organized and run by Barras village committee, who arranged the prizes for the best vegetables and flower arranging displays. The fair went on for a few days, but the fête was a one-day event.

Nobody ever dared to challenge Florrie Lovering's sponge-making expertise, and throughout the food-rationing war years she had become ever more adept at producing something from virtually nothing. Nor did she deign to enter hers in any cake-making competition. By silent agreement the other village ladies bowed to the inevitable, and the only other cakes for competition or sale were scones and fairy cakes. This little bit of snobbery on Florrie's part had always been a source of fun to the land girls, though they had never dared to show their amusement to her face.

Poppy was remembering that now as she helped to prepare the tables for the village ladies, as animated as any of them. Although she was looking forward to seeing Shirley Bosinney again, she didn't expect her to arrive too early in the day. Shirley and her husband would do the elegant thing and arrive later. She had always liked to make an entrance, Poppy thought with a grin – and an exit too, considering how long she used to take fluffing up her blonde hair and reddening her lips and cheeks with scraps of Tangee lipstick before she and the other girls left the farm on a Saturday night to go dancing in Penzance. The familiar twist of envy, even after all this time, curled around Poppy's heart.

But there was too much to do to waste time thinking of what was long past. By mid-afternoon the sun was hot enough for Florrie's home-made lemonade to have done good business, and for them both to be thankful that the sponges had all been sold before the butter icing became mush. It was a glorious day now, sweltering enough to make uncovered skins start to prickle.

The village stalls had been well patronized, and as usual half the funds would be going towards the church and local amenities. Among the stalls was one selling home-made soft toys; a Tombola bin with small prizes donated by the local farmers' wives; several second-hand books and comic stalls; a small refreshment tent where the older ladies were glad to sit on benches on the hard-baked grass for a breather; and a 'Pin the Tail on the Donkey' game that Len Painter had made, and which he produced, newly painted, every year.

Music blared out from the fun-fair – a useful consideration that Sam always said saved them the bother of trying to provide a band. There was so much noise and laughter going on, nobody would have paid much attention to it, anyway.

Poppy wasn't even looking for anybody in particular when she saw Jack Trevis. She could hardly miss him, since he stood head and shoulders above everyone else. He was throwing his head back and laughing at something one of the village women had said, as if it was something clever and wonderful. It occurred to Poppy at that moment that he had the knack of doing that, giving all his attention to whoever he was with, as if they were the most important person in the world. Perhaps it was part of his trade, or perhaps it was just him.

Poppy licked her dry lips, aware that her heart was beating much faster than usual, and that her palms were damp. She knew he would eventually come and speak to her. They were old acquaintances by now. Not friends, exactly, but they had formed a kind of intimacy in their discussions – and through the photographs.

She wished that word *intimacy* hadn't entered her mind. It wasn't what she meant. She just meant that she knew him slightly.

As if aware of her gaze on him, Jack turned his head slowly and looked directly at her. He was all of ten feet away and there were a dozen people jostling and chattering in between them but for those few seconds when she saw a smiling recognition in his eyes, they were the only two people who existed.

She flashed him a small smile before attending to the customer at her mother-in-law's table, now full of jams and chutneys, and tried to ignore how inept she was suddenly feeling. It didn't matter about the way he had photographed her and made such flattering comments about her, or that he had made her feel such a heroine by the way he had written about Billy Flint's rescue in the paper.

She didn't feel much like a heroine today, all hot and bothered. The dismal thought churned around her head that he couldn't fail to see her now for exactly what she was, a country farmer's wife doing the homely and rural things that country farmers' wives did, and there was nothing remotely glamorous in that.

'Everything seems to be a great success, and you're to be congratulated, Mrs Lovering,' she heard his voice moments later. 'I wonder if you would be kind enough to give me a quote for my paper?'

Poppy started at the formal use of her

name, and then she realized he wasn't talking to her at all, but to Florrie, who was just as flustered from the heat, and not at all keen on being accosted like this, which was the way she would see it. That much was obvious enough to Poppy from the shortness of her reply.

'I don't know why you'd think I've got anything interesting to say, young man. The fair's here as usual and the fête's always a success, because we women make it so. If you want to know anything more, I suggest you ask my daughter-in-law and let me get on.'

Poppy smothered a groan at her highhandedness. For heaven's sake, they weren't holding a royal garden party, and the women here were hardly dressed in the height of fashion in their homespun cotton frocks and flat shoes, and hair that had been tortuously curled and waved for the occasion. Just like herself.

She instantly felt angry and ashamed at demeaning, for the merest fraction of time, who she was and the way she lived. Her chin lifted as Jack turned to her and waited for her to respond, notebook in hand, his camera slung around his neck, and the smile she remembered all too well lurking at the corners of his mouth.

'I can't tell you anything more than Mrs Lovering,' she snapped. 'I'm sure you'll do far better to ask the folk who've come here for a day out than asking me.'

'I'd much prefer to talk to you,' he said. 'I've been biding my time so that it wouldn't look too obvious, but I couldn't wait any longer. And by the way, Poppy, you look stunning today. Not that a complexion like yours needs any help from cosmetics.'

His voice had gone considerably lower so that she wondered if she had really heard those words. Was this another of his tricks, so that any female he spoke to was obliged to lean closer to him? She was angry with herself for being so suspicious, but she couldn't seem to help it. Besides, it was a good way to keep him at arms' length, mentally, if not physically. But if her face went any hotter, she'd be on fire, Poppy thought wildly. He shouldn't be talking to her like this, in that deep, personal way that excluded everybody else.

She could see Sam making his way towards her, and she felt a rush of relief, as if she were being rescued from something as inevitable as sunrise.

'I've got to go,' she said swiftly. 'Me and Sam are organizing the children's three-legged race in a minute.'

There you are, Mr smarty-pants Trevis. That'll show you that me and Sam are a married couple, a team. We do things together, and we don't want you interfering in our lives.

'I want to see you again,' Jack said, as she made to move towards Sam. 'You know that, don't you? You can't avoid me for ever.'

'You're seeing me now.'

'Not like this. Properly, I mean. On our own with no husband or village folk around. I want to spend time with you. Think about it, Poppy.'

He emphasized his last words as if to put the images into her mind of what it would be like, just the two of them, somewhere where there was no husband or village folk around. Images that Poppy didn't want and wouldn't allow.

'Come on, Poppy, the kids are waiting, and I need you here,' Sam called out with a smile in his voice.

His words had more meaning for her than he knew. Of course he needed her. Her place was by his side, as always. And he was truly in his element now, Poppy thought, as she hurried across the field to join him, trying to calm her jumping nerves. For this one day in the year he became a different person, younger and more alive. She knew Sam loved this part of the fête, and he truly became a Pied Piper then, with all the local kids clamouring around him. There was nothing staid and stolid about him now, and it was a crying shame that he didn't have kids of his own. He would make a wonderful father. He could teach them so much about animals and the old country ways, and from his natural and easy manner with other people's kids, she knew he would be endlessly patient with them.

She hugged his arm for a moment, wishing it would happen, and for more than one reason. More than anything, she longed for them to be a close-knit little family unit with no dashing outsiders to turn her head and make her dream about something that could only be ephemeral – and excitingly dangerous.

And then she put all such thoughts out of her head as they were surrounded by the shrieking kids who wanted to be first to have their legs tied together for the race, and the small prize of home-made toffees at the end of it.

'Is this little one too small to be entered in a race?' Poppy heard a familiar voice say a short while later. She whirled around to see Shirley Bosinney holding the hand of a small boy of about three, and her mouth fell open.

'You never told me about this!' she stammered. Then she realized at once that it couldn't be Shirley's child. She was sure she would have known before now, and there had been no evidence of a child's presence in the house in Penzance.

Shirley laughed. 'No, you goose. He's a

little sweetie, but I can't claim him. This is Walter, my friend's son. You haven't met Carrie, have you?'

Poppy felt a ridiculous stab of jealousy at the good-looking woman standing beside her friend. 'Can't say I have, but I heard your name enough times in the past. Don't you live in Penhallow, where Shirley used to live?'

'That's right. We've known one another for ever,' Carrie said with an affectionate smile at Shirley. 'So, is Walter big enough to join in the race?'

Poppy tried not to sound sharp at the possessive way these two were behaving towards one another. 'We don't have a three-legged race for the little ones. It's too dangerous, but they'll have a normal race of their own in a few minutes' time if you want to wait or come back. Sam always takes care that they don't get pushed over or forgotten by the bigger ones.'

'God yes, Sam was always a softie when it comes to small things, whether it was animals or kids, wasn't he?' Shirley asked with a grin.

'He still is. So where's your husband? Didn't he come with you?'

She didn't know why she felt so awkward and resentful, unless it was because Shirley and this other woman shared a past of which she knew next to nothing. Although, when she was working here, Shirley had

124

often mentioned her three best friends who had all grown up in Penhallow with her. All through the war they had met once a week come rain or shine, no matter what war jobs they did.

They were all older than Poppy, and she immediately felt her lack of years beside these two. Her annoyance at feeling that way, when this was her husband's farm, and her home, made her even sharper.

'Don't worry,' Shirley was saying, 'you'll meet Bernard in a while. He's gone to look at the horses with Archie, Carrie's husband, but I insisted that he had to come and meet our famous Poppy.'

'Good Lord, I'm hardly famous,' she muttered, her self confidence diminishing by the second.

'Yes you are,' Carrie said. 'Shirley was really proud of you, Poppy, for rescuing the boy from the mine shaft. It was a brave thing to do.'

'It didn't feel brave. Anybody would have done the same thing.'

'Not everybody gets thanked by the mayor and has their photo in the paper, do they?' Shirley said. 'Stop being so modest, Poppy. It's not like you at all!'

Well, thank you, thought Poppy. However unintentional it was, if anything was designed to make her feel dismissed as the nosey, over-eager schoolgirl she once was, that was it!

In the small awkward silence that followed, she was called to where the boys were lining up for the start of the three-legged race. Sam always began the race and she would stand at the winning end, cheering them on, and presenting the winner with his prize.

'I've got to go,' she gasped. 'The race for the small children will be in about ten minutes, so you can bring Walter back in time for it.'

She almost fled away from the little group, hardly noticing the two men who came to join them.

'So that's Poppy, is it?' Archie Pollard said. 'She's a fine looking piece of goods, wouldn't you say, Bernard?'

'Oh, she's pretty enough,' he agreed, and Shirley squeezed his arm, laughing into his eyes.

'Bernard knows better than to go overboard with remarks about other women, don't you, darling?'

'It's not worth it,' Bernard said with mock solemnity. 'Keep the womenfolk happy and contented, Archie old boy, and you won't go far wrong.'

The two women glanced at one another, trying not to squirm at this patronizing remark. Bernard taught art and music, and had read a lot of books, and Archie had never had much patience with what he called 'a girlie profession'. But their wives both knew that Bernard was as tough as any man, and had proved his resilience when he was so badly wounded in France during the war, while Archie had what Bernard privately scoffed as the easy packet, locked up for two years as a POW. The two men would never truly be friends, but they met when they had to on account of Shirley and Carrie's friendship, and by mutual consent, the women avoided the subject of wartime whenever the four of them were together. Whatever happened during the war was in the past, and best kept that way.

Poppy had managed to take a quick look at Shirley's schoolteacher husband before she joined Sam. She knew he would be fair-haired and good-looking from the way Shirley had gone on and on about her Bernard when she worked on the farm. Poppy recalled how the others had teased her about having to choose between her old flame and her new fancy for Hank the Yank, but she had never really thought the teasing meant anything; Shirley had always been so set on marrying Bernard as soon as she was twenty-one. And when he had been wounded in France, she could have gone on the stage with all her dramatics about it.

Poppy gave up thinking about any of it as the kids in the three-legged race came hurtling towards her, legs tied together and arms around each other for balance, as tightly entwined as Siamese twins, their mums and dads screaming them on towards the finishing line. The winning pair fell into her arms, and she laughingly hauled them to their feet and looked right into Billy Flint's excited eyes.

'Me and Ron told 'em we'd bloody win, Missus!' he yelled. 'We've been practising all bloody week, wiv our legs tied up in knots!'

'Good for you, Billy,' Poppy said hastily, as several matrons turned away in annoyance at such language. 'Now let's untie your legs before you get your prizes.'

A woman hovered at her side, and she looked up to see Billy's mother.

'I'm sorry about that, Mrs Lovering. I warned him to watch his language, but when he gets excited he can't seem to help himself.'

'I don't think anybody heard,' Poppy lied. 'But I'm glad to see you today, Mrs Flint. I wasn't sure you'd come.'

'Oh well, you know how my Gus gets above himself sometimes. He didn't want us to come, but our Billy created such a fuss he gave in to keep the peace. We've never missed the fair and fête in ten years, so I didn't see why we should do it now just because Gus got a bee in his bonnet. He don't always get his own way.'

She dragged off the still screeching Billy and his friend, and Poppy saw them go

128

thankfully as Sam came to join her.

'Everything all right?' he said.

'Everything's fine. Mrs Flint's not so soft when it comes to dealing with her husband after all, Sam. I'm glad Billy won. It was fair and square, but at least it'll show his father there's no favouritism here. And do you think we could have the race for the little ones in a minute? Shirley's friend has got a three-year-old who wants to have a go.'

She had to be impartial, and she could never be vindictive towards a child, but she didn't really mind too much when the cherubic Walter didn't win his race and went off crying to his mother. It was the usual thing among this age-group, and only the winning child was all smiles. Some of the little ones had decidedly damp patches in their trousers from all the excitement and disappointment too. Being a mother wasn't all fun and games, she decided.

It all added to the fun of the fête though, Poppy told Sam much later, when the races were all done, the women's stalls had been dismantled with the coffers swelled satisfactorily, and the fairground people had closed down their rides until tomorrow. And now everything was quiet in the farmhouse and she and Sam were each enjoying a cup of cocoa before bedtime.

Florrie had taken her drink upstairs to bed, saying that her legs were too tired to keep them anything but horizontal for one more minute, and Poppy was glad of these blissful minutes when they could be alone and relax.

'You enjoyed today, didn't you?' Sam asked her.

'Of course I did,' she said, her eyes glowing. 'It's the best time of the year! Everybody had a marvellous time, and when I took the children round the farm to see the animals they enjoyed it as much as anything else.'

No matter how much she tried, it was impossible for her to avoid thinking how much the children would have enjoyed seeing and petting Henrietta too, and she had to swallow the lump in her throat as she thought of his little warm pink body.

'Sometimes I wonder if all this is enough for you, Poppy.'

She looked at Sam, startled. There was no possible way he could have overheard what Jack Trevis had said to her, and she was sure nobody else had heard it either. So he couldn't have meant anything like that, but he must have meant something by it. She remembered Florrie's words. *She was too young for you.*

'What do you mean? Am I such a bad wife?'

Without warning, tears started to her eyes, and she blinked them back angrily. It had been a very long day and they were all tired, but she had never expected this, and nor could she think that she had done anything wrong. But his words upset her all the same.

He came to sit beside her on the old sofa and took both her hands in his. They were such strong, capable hands, yet she knew they wouldn't hurt a fly, and she knew how tender they could be too. When they untangled an animal caught up on a fence, or fed a newborn piglet, or held his wife in his arms. Lately he had been drinking less too, she reflected. He was becoming a proper family man, without a complete family.

'Of course you're not a bad wife, Poppy. I don't say it often because you know it's not my way, but you know how much I think of you.'

'I don't know if you don't tell me.'

'Well, I've said it once, so don't expect poetry,' he said with a hint of a smile in his voice.

'So what did you mean by wondering if all this is enough for me? I've been here since I was fourteen years old, so what's changed?'

He didn't say anything for a minute, just stared into the fireplace, empty of flames at this time of year, and adorned with his mother's tapestry firescreen.

'You have, my dear.' He turned to look at her stricken face. 'Don't look like that, Poppy. Everybody changes, and you can't expect to stay the same as you were at fourteen. Have some sense.'

Her face flamed. 'I do have some sense. Of course I'm not the same as I was when I was fourteen. I can't imagine you'd have asked me to marry you if I'd still been such a child. So in what way have I changed? And why are you saying this now? What have I done to upset you?'

As her voice rose Sam leaned forward and put his arm around her, giving her tense shoulders a squeeze.

'So many questions! And keep your voice down, or Mother will be shouting down to ask what's going on.'

'I don't really care what your mother thinks,' Poppy said, pulling away from him. 'I'm your wife, not *her*.'

'Well, of course you are.' Sam was uneasy now, and she guessed he was wishing he'd never started this.

But he had, and she wasn't going to let it go until she heard what had made him say such things. She suddenly felt calmer. She hadn't had much schooling, but she had a quick brain. She was better with words than Sam, and always had been.

'So you think I've changed. I've certainly grown from a child to a woman, and I've got you to thank for that, haven't I? I don't know how it could be any other way, but I've always tried to be a good wife to you, even though I can't make sponges the way your mother can, and you know I'm not all that keen on feeding the pigs!' She didn't mean to be provocative, and was merely stating facts.

'It's got nothing to do with bloody sponge cakes and pigs,' Sam said roughly, startling her.

She could see the blotchy colour in his neck and knew he was having a struggle in saying exactly what was on his mind. She felt a tug of sympathy towards him for his inability to put into words something that was clearly so important to him. She put her hand on his arm.

'Look, why don't you just say it? Whatever it is, I'll try to put it right. I can't say any fairer than that, can I?'

He gave a heavy sigh and he wasn't looking at her now. 'All right. It was seeing you with those two women. And the Flint woman. And chatting with the other women here for the day. And the kids. And even that bloody newspaper chap.'

Her heart jolted. 'Sam, please stop swearing. I still don't understand. Didn't you want me to talk to people? I couldn't stand there like a village idiot all day, could I? And you know how much I was looking forward to seeing Shirley again. You even managed to say a few words to her yourself, didn't you?'

'That's just it. You should be seeing more of other folk like that, not stuck on the farm all day long with just Mother and me for company. I'd forgotten how young you are, and it was seeing you with them that made me see how you could be thinking I'm holding you back,' he finished clumsily.

Poppy stared at him. It was quite an admission from a proud man who was apparently examining his conscience, and for such a silly reason. Just because he'd seen her talking with friends, and the village women, and Jack Trevis. For a moment, despite his reminding her of how much younger than himself she was, she felt oddly protective of his feelings.

'I think you're being daft, but in a nice way,' she said softly.

'It's not daft to be thinking of my wife, and what I'm thinking is that you shouldn't be tied to the farm quite so much. You're young and it shouldn't be all work for you. You should be having fun sometimes, like you were having today.' He was sounding almost angry now, as if only just realizing it.

She didn't quite know how to handle him in this strange new mood, guiltily knowing very well that there were times when she *was* restless, and not quite as content as she might have been. But that wasn't his fault. It was something inside herself. It was being twenty.

'I've never said I was unhappy here, have I?' she said helplessly.

'Of course not,' Sam said, as if such a thing had never occurred to him. 'But I was thinking that perhaps we could go out together sometimes as well.'

She grinned mischievously. 'You're not suggesting taking me to the pub on Saturday nights, are you?'

He snorted. 'I'm damn well not! Women don't go in pubs, not respectable women, anyway. No, I thought we'd have a drive to St Ives one Sunday afternoon, or anywhere else you like.'

Poppy's mouth fell open. Taking time away from the farm wasn't something Sam cared to do very often, but she wasn't going to object.

'I think it's a lovely idea, Sam!'

'We'll arrange it when Len's here to do the afternoon milking then. You should go and yarn with those friends of yours some afternoons too. You looked real pretty when you were talking to them. You face was all livened up.'

She didn't bother saying they weren't both her friends, just one of them. But if he thought she needed female companionship, that was fine by her. And she had to admit that when he was talking to her like this, so concerned and thoughtful, his rugged face was all livened up too. He may not be strictly

135

handsome in a film-starry way, but he wasn't ugly either, and he could be as caring as the next man when he chose to be. In his own way.

Right now he was looking at her as if he wanted to care for her in a very physical way, and she wasn't arguing with that either. Not that she would think of doing such a thing. A wife didn't. It had been such a wonderful day, she thought, her heart singing, and now that they had got this little problem sorted out, it wasn't over yet.

Chapter Seven

Shirley wished that she was either going to be sick or she wasn't. This constant retching was making her throat sore, and she was pretty sure that it wasn't due to something she ate. Having missed two monthlies now, she knew only too well what it meant. She was leaning over the washbasin in the bathroom for the third time that Friday afternoon when the doorbell rang.

'Leave it a minute. Don't rush. Whoever it is, they'll wait. Be dignified,' Bernard always said with a resigned smile when she leapt up to answer it, knowing he was wasting his breath.

She was too eager, too impatient, wanting everything this minute the way she always had. It might be the postman with a letter from a faraway friend. Or a special visitor. Who knew? And Bernard wasn't here to chastize her today. But for once, she didn't rush to the front door to answer it. Her stomach felt too topsy-turvy, her breath short, her nerves on fire by the time she reached it.

'Oh – Poppy, it's you!' she said. 'You should have let me know you were coming. I haven't even tidied up properly today.'

Poppy glanced around the little house that was so immaculate, and smiled. Shirley was still playing at keeping house, and dust didn't stand a chance where she was concerned. She presumed Bernard liked it that way, being a schoolteacher and everything. By contrast, the big old untidy farmhouse at Lovering's Farm, with its well-worn sofa and chairs, and furniture that was never quite free of clutter, was always warm and homely. Somehow this house on the outskirts of Penzance never quite was. It was beautifully clean, but it wasn't yet a home.

'You know what the farmhouse is like, Shirley, so you should know such things never bother me!' Poppy said cheerfully, and then realized she was talking to thin air as Shirley rushed away from her and up the stairs to the bathroom.

A few minutes later she came down, smiling shakily. 'Sorry about that. I'm not feeling myself today.'

'Crikey, you do look a bit green. Is there anything I can do? Do you want me to fetch you something from the chemist to settle your stomach?'

'It'll take more than something from the chemist.'

Poppy stared at her. 'What's wrong then? It's not something serious is it, Shirley? You looked lovely at the fête the other week with your friend.'

She desperately wanted Shirley to be her friend. Well, she supposed she was, but not in the same way that the dark-haired Carrie was, whom Shirley had known all her life. It was silly to be jealous of a friendship that went back years, but somehow Poppy couldn't help it. She'd come here wanting some advice, but now it seemed that Shirley had problems of her own.

When Shirley didn't answer she turned towards the door, feeling ridiculously let down. Sam had urged her to get out and meet people, and here she was, having caught the bus into Penzance on this lovely late September day, and feeling a great sense of freedom to be calling on a friend and being offered a cup of tea and a cosy chat, even if it was a spontaneous visit – but it didn't look as if she was even going to be asked.

'I'd better go. I'm sorry I just turned up like this, Shirley.'

'Oh, for goodness' sake, sit down and let me catch my breath. I'll be all right in a minute. I can't stand the taste of tea at the moment, nor the smell of it, come to that, so you'll have to be satisfied with lemon barley. I'm sorry I was so off with you, but it comes and goes.'

'What does?' Poppy said, sitting down gingerly on the edge of a chair.

'This ghastly feeling. It's only supposed to happen in the morning, but I should have remembered how Velma said it happened to her at any time of the day, and often when she was least expecting it.'

It took Poppy a moment to remember that Velma was the name of another of Shirley's old Penhallow friends, otherwise she might have thought her mind was rambling. She was too caught up in that possibility to let the rest of Shirley's words sink in. When they did, her eyes widened as her glance flickered down over Shirley's shape, as slim as ever in her blue frock. 'You don't mean you're expecting, do you?'

Shirley gave a strangled laugh as the bile threatened to rise in her throat again. 'Well, don't sound so surprised, you ninny. It's all legal and above board, and I have been married for years, so it's about time, isn't it?'

Without warning, tears sprang to Shirley's

eyes, and Poppy stood there like an idiot, not knowing what to do. Despite the fact that Shirley looked so fragile and fairy-like, Sam had always said she was as strong as old boots. However, she looked anything but that at this moment.

'Don't bother about me,' Shirley said with a sniff, fumbling in a pocket for a handkerchief and giving a hefty blow into it. 'All this emotional stuff is one of the hazards of being pregnant, especially in the beginning.'

'Well, I wouldn't know about that, but I suppose you and Bernard have done plenty of reading about it, so you'd know what to expect,' Poppy said.

Shirley gave a weak smile. It wasn't only reading that had given her the certain knowledge that there was a baby coming.

'Anyway, I'll go and get us that lemon barley and then you can tell me what's on your mind,' she said, with an effort to sound normal, and not to let her thoughts drift, even for the tiniest amount of time, to the baby-that-never-was. The one that Bernard never knew about, and never would, and was a secret that remained locked in Shirley's heart for ever.

'Oh Shirley, you're so lucky,' Poppy said in a little rush as her friend went through to the kitchen. 'I want a baby more than anything, but nothing's happened yet. I thought there might be something wrong with me, but if it's taken you and Bernard all this time, I don't expect there is, do you?'

Sometimes it happens the very first time you make love, said the voice inside Shirley's head. *At the very worst possible time, and with the wrong person, even though the lovemaking may be dazzlingly wonderful.*

'Of course there's nothing wrong with you,' Shirley said, wishing the thoughts away and bringing the jug and glasses to the table. 'Some people just take longer than others, that's all. My friend Velma had been married more than ten years before she had her first baby, and she's had another one since then. Apparently, the more you worry about it, the less likely it is to happen,' she said vaguely, though she had never been clever enough to work out just why that should be. She wasn't clever at all. Her darling Bernard was the brainbox, and so patient with her sometimes, but this girl didn't have to know about that.

'Was that the reason for this visit today, then?' she went on brightly. 'To talk about babies?'

Poppy flinched. Now that she was here, she wasn't sure if she could bring it out in the open at all, or even if she should. Once something was said, it was no longer a secret, even if it was a secret she didn't want. But Shirley was interested now, and she was looking better too, with the colour coming back to her cheeks.

She looked more like the laughing girl who used to work on the farm and went into Penzance on Saturday nights to dance with the Yanks, and always insisted airily that she was only doing her bit to help our glorious Allies forget their homesickness, and it didn't mean a thing compared with her love for her dashing airman, Bernard Bosinney. And Poppy thought desperately that if she didn't say quickly what she had come for, she never would.

'You know a bit about men, don't you, Shirley? All those Saturday nights during the war when you and the other girls went dancing, there must have been times when you were a bit tempted. Not that I ever thought you did anything you shouldn't, mind! I wouldn't think that for a minute. I'm just saying you probably knew how it felt,' she ended lamely.

She was suddenly aware that Shirley's face had gone a brilliant red, and she scrambled to her feet, acutely embarrassed.

'Oh crikey, I've offended you now, haven't I? I didn't mean anything, honestly. But sometimes I couldn't help overhearing what you and the others were saying out in the fields. You had no idea how your voices carried, and, well, you weren't always talking about war work, were you?' she finished defensively, wishing she'd never mentioned it at all, since it had nothing to do with her worries about the attentions of Jack Trevis. But Shirley didn't see it that way.

All she saw was that this sparky girl, who was once such a nondescript little thing who had brought out their tea to the fields while they were working, had listened in on their private, grown-up conversations and put two and two together. She may even have written it all down in the diary she had been forever keeping. Shirley felt a tremor run through her at the thought.

'What is this, Poppy? If you're trying to blackmail me, you've come to the wrong place,' she snapped.

'*Blackmail?*' Poppy echoed, as if she had never heard of the word. 'I don't know what you mean. I'm sure you never did anything wrong, and I never meant that. I wouldn't believe it of you, Shirley, you know that.'

She was floundering now, becoming aware of all sorts of possibilities running around her head that she truly had never thought about before. But she had never expected this reaction, as if Shirley really did have something to hide that she was ashamed of.

She shook her head. Shirley was incredibly pretty, and Poppy had always envied her delicate features, but she was also a clean-living girl, and the others had often teased her about the need to rush off to church whenever she felt the need to confess about the slightest thing. There could never have been anything monumental in Shirley's past to make her believe somebody could think of blackmailing her.

'I'm really sorry, Shirley,' she went on. 'I've obviously offended you, and I didn't mean to. It's just that I'm so confused, and you're the only one I could talk to about it. I don't have anyone else.'

Shirley pulled herself together with a huge effort. The girl knew nothing of those tumultuous days, and after all this time she had just proved to be far more vulnerable than she had thought. It must simply be due to the emotional and physical changes in her body with the coming baby, she told herself determinedly.

'Well, I didn't mean to snap at you, so why don't you just tell me what's wrong, and if I can help, I will. It's not something to do with that photo you had framed, is it? I don't imagine Mrs Lovering was any too pleased to see it.'

'It's sort of to do with that. Well, not the photo. It's him. I think of him more than I should, and I know I was flattered when he said I was beautiful, which I'm not, and that he'd like to photograph me properly in a studio. That was all nonsense, of course, and I'd never agree to it, even if Sam would, which he wouldn't.'

'Slow down,' Shirley said, laughing as her

breathing returned to normal. 'There's no harm in thinking about somebody else, Poppy, providing that's all it is. Just because you're married, it doesn't mean you can't appreciate any other good-looking chap in the world, does it? That's not being unfaithful.'

And oh God, when did she turn into such a saint!

'What if he said he wanted to see me again, on our own, without my husband around?'

'Is that what he said?'

'Yes.'

She hung her head, as if she was the one at fault here, Shirley thought indignantly, when that bastard Jack Trevis was worldly enough to know just what effect he could have on a naive girl like Poppy. She might be married, but she was still one of the world's innocents as far as men were concerned, and right now she looked about twelve years old with her long hair falling over her face and hiding the expression in her eyes.

But oh yes, Shirley knew exactly how it felt to be so tempted...

'As long as you said no, there's no harm done, is there? You did say no, I suppose?' she asked casually.

'I didn't know what to say! But it's more than a month since the fête and I haven't seen him since then, and now I'm thinking he just saw me as somebody to flirt with. And it hurts, even though I would never do anything about it!'

A clever bastard too, Shirley thought, to tease the girl and then leave her alone to chew it all over. She didn't often use such words, but when they fitted the occasion and the man, she felt no compunction in thinking them.

'And I assume you haven't said anything to Sam about all this?'

'Good Lord no. He's normally easy-going, but he's nobody's fool and you know what his temper's like when he's roused.'

'You don't fancy the two of them fighting over you then?' Shirley said with a grin.

'I was thinking more of Sam fighting with me! Not that he would, mind,' she added hastily. 'I've never seen Sam hit anything, and I'm being silly, aren't I?'

'Just a bit,' Shirley said. Her stomach was starting to roll again, and she didn't know how much longer she could sit here being civilized. 'Look, Poppy, this is something you've got to work out for yourself. I think in your heart you know what's right, but come and chat to me again any time, all right?'

She stood up, hoping the girl would take the hint, and Poppy followed suit.

'Thanks, Shirley. It helps just to have somebody to talk to. I obviously can't talk to

Sam's mother about it, and mine would have forty fits if she thought some other chap was taking a fancy to me, sure that I was going to the devil.'

'Don't tell her then,' Shirley said, subtly moving her guest towards the door so that she could bolt upstairs again the minute she was alone.

It had been a lovely day when Poppy arrived in Penzance, one of those late September days when everything was calm, and the warm, lazy days of autumn lingered. Now, as she hurried back to the bus stop to wait for the afternoon bus back to Barras, the clouds gathered and darkened, a brisk wind whipped in from the sea, and without warning, the rain came hurtling down, dampening and chilling in seconds. There was no shelter at the bus-stop, and she was only wearing a frock and cardigan. The wool already smelled unpleasantly damp and clung to her arms. Within five minutes she was soaked, her long hair hanging in rat's-tails. She glared as a small car drew up alongside her, splashing her feet and ankles with water from the gutter, and then the driver leaned across to open the passenger door.

'You'll be drowned long before the bus arrives. Get in and I'll give you a lift.'

Her heart leapt at the sound of Jack Trevis's voice. He had been in her thoughts so much that afternoon, and for days past, that for a moment she thought he must be a mirage. His smile quickly told her that he wasn't.

'It's all right,' she began, embarrassed to be seen in such a state.

'It's far from all right. Do you want to catch pneumonia? Come on, I'm sure your husband won't object to me being a friend in need.'

Poppy felt her face go red. Just as if he was seeing her as the naive little farmer's wife that she was, afraid to get into a stranger's car. But he wasn't a stranger and, fuming, she told herself she had no need to be scared of him. Yet she still resisted.

'I'm sure you're not going anywhere near my direction.'

'I'm not going anywhere at all unless you get inside the car and shut the door and stop this damn rain coming in and ruining my car seats.'

She gave in, and slid inside gratefully. Though sliding wasn't the right word for it, because nothing about her was sliding anywhere. She stuck to the leather seat, which made her stockinged legs feel even colder. The water trickled down her back from her sodden hair, and she gave a small shiver.

'First of all I'm taking you back to my digs to dry you out,' Jack said as the car moved away from the kerb.

'Oh, I don't think that's a good idea. I just need to get home, and Sam will be worried if I'm late,' she said in panic.

'Calm down. I'm not going to eat you, Poppy, and I'll still get you home before the bus would have done. A few minutes in front of my gas fire and a warm towel to dry your hair, and you'll be as right as ninepence. There's nothing wrong in a friend offering you that, and I'm sure your husband would be far too busy on the farm to notice if you were a few minutes late.'

He sounded amused, making her feel even more idiotic, and she realized that they were rattling along in the car now. It wasn't new and it wasn't smart, but at least it took Jack from place to place, and she tried to relax and be grateful for the ride. He must really think her a child, to get in such a state about it. She was still uneasy about going to his digs, though. He was a bachelor, after all, and he'd made no secret that he wanted to see her alone. She pushed down the new burst of panic. Ten minutes and no more, she told herself.

'You said you were in digs. Don't you have a house of your own then?' she said, when she could think of nothing else to say.

'It's not worth it. My family came from Cornwall before they moved north years ago, but I don't plan to stay here for ever, so I'm just renting some rooms.'

She wasn't sure if surprise or disappointment or relief was uppermost in her mind. 'I can't imagine living anywhere else. Where would you go?'

'London, probably.'

'Whatever for?' She was too curious to be scared now. She turned to look at his handsome profile as he concentrated on driving.

He laughed. 'The world doesn't end in Cornwall, Poppy, only the last bit of England, and some of you diehards don't even think it's part of England, do you?'

'Are you making fun of us now?'

'I wouldn't dare. I like it well enough down here, but I wouldn't want to stay permanently, and it's a bit stifling to somebody with ambition.'

'And you've got ambition, have you?' She felt easier, talking about his work ambitions, rather than any ambitions he might have for her.

'Why not? I've a fancy to work for one of the nationals someday, which is why I'm taking care to create a good portfolio before I move on.'

If she had felt ignorant before, she felt even more so now, when she didn't have the faintest idea what he was talking about. But instead of making her feel inferior, it just made her angry.

'I'm sure you'll succeed in whatever you want to do,' she said crisply.

'I'm sure I will,' he replied, and there was something in his voice that made her shiver again, but he went on quickly. 'Here we are. Now, once you've dried off a bit, I'll run you back to the farm.'

She saw that they had stopped outside a small house in a narrow street. She didn't know Penzance very well, and had no idea where she was, but the house looked respectable enough. The curtains on the ground floor were different from the ones above, and when they went inside Jack led her to the upper floor.

'Welcome,' he said with a smile. 'I'll turn on the gas fire and find you a towel and you'll be dry in a jiffy. We'll have a cup of tea in the meantime.'

'Oh, there's no need for all that!'

'Of course there is. You're my guest. Sit down and for goodness' sake stop looking as if I'm about to ravish you. I promise I never do that on a first date.'

She knew he was teasing, and she managed to smile back weakly as she peeled off her wet cardigan. She wasn't comfortable being here, and she didn't intend to stay any longer than she had to. But it would be churlish to rush out like a scalded cat now that she was here, and she had no option but to accept his hospitality. And in this domesticated environment, there was nothing of the ravisher about him.

Her heart beat faster as the word came into her head. It wasn't one that was normally there. It spoke of excitement and wickedness and wanton behaviour, and things that were alien to her.

He came back to the room and handed her a towel and she could hear him busying himself in the tiny kitchen. It sounded so normal. She told herself to relax, and began rubbing her wet hair in front of the fire. He brought in two cups of tea and she sipped hers thankfully, glad of its warmth. Seconds later she felt the towel being taken from her hands, and his voice was right behind her head.

'It'll dry much faster if you let me do that for you, Poppy.'

She wanted to resist. It was far too intimate for him to be drying her hair, but her tongue seemed to be stuck to the top of her mouth and she was unable to utter a word. Besides, it was extremely pleasant to have someone else do what she had only ever done herself. Sam had never offered to dry her hair.

As his name came into her mind she jerked away from Jack. 'I shouldn't be doing this,' she said agitatedly.

He laughed softly. 'You're such a sweetheart, but there's nothing wrong in wanting to be your friend, is there?'

'As long as that's all you want,' she whispered, and immediately wished she hadn't said it. It sounded so pathetically childish, and she was a grown woman with a mind of her own. Besides, it may have put ideas in his head that weren't already there, and that hadn't been her intention at all.

'Let me show you something,' he said, and at the sudden fright in her eyes he laughed again. 'My God, you're so suspicious, aren't you? I told you I never ravish anyone on a first date.'

The first time he said it, it had sounded rather sophisticated. Now, Poppy couldn't help thinking it was more like a line from a bad Hollywood movie.

'Good, because I can't stay much longer. I really need to get home.'

'Come with me then.'

She stood up. Her frock was drying out quickly, but she was conscious that her cardigan was never going to dry in a few minutes, and that she'd have to put up with its clamminess later. She followed him into another small room with a dark curtain covering the window, reminiscent of wartime black-out, and then gasped in the dim red light.

'Don't be alarmed. I thought you'd be interested in seeing my dark room where I develop all my photos.'

Her curiosity was caught. She had never been anywhere like this before, and it intrigued her to see the many photos pegged up around the room, like so much washing. They were mostly of Cadgwith, the fishing village on the Lizard peninsula, where there was a long history of smuggling, and which was going to be the next subject for his newspaper series. There were also a few photos of Poppy, those she had already seen, and others that were enlarged to startling effect.

For a bizarre moment she felt that she knew exactly what her mum meant by saying there was something of yourself taken away when you were photographed. He had something of her. Her image. Her soul. She shook off the feeling angrily.

'Why have you done this?' she snapped.

'It's part of my business. My creative business, Poppy. I can experiment with them, changing light and shade and texture to get the best effect. It's what I do.'

It sounded so plausible, so glib, and it made her shiver again. It was as if he had control of her, and that was nonsense. All the same, he had said he wanted to see her again, without her husband around, and he had managed to do just that.

'I've got to go. Sam will be expecting me.'

'Don't worry, I'll get you home at the same time the bus would arrive in the village. Next time you must stay longer.'

'There isn't going to be any next time.'

She turned to the door of the dark room and fumbled with the handle. Her heart was beating so fast she thought she would die if she didn't get out of the stifling little room with its cloying mixture of chemical smells.

'Hang on a minute. This door sticks a bit,' Jack said, his hand reaching out to cover hers. She could feel his breath on the back of her neck, and the next minute his arms had closed around her and he was twisting her around so that she was enclosed inside them.

She had no chance to break away. She was pinned against the door and all she could see was his dark silhouette blotting out the dim red light bulb. She was Scarlett O'Hara to his Rhett Butler. She was every Hollywood heroine she had ever dreamed about, with the eerie feeling that she was spinning towards something inevitable, and then his mouth was covering hers in a demanding kiss, and she was clinging to him as her legs seemed to turn to water.

'I've wanted to do that since the beginning of time,' he whispered against her lips. 'That's how long I feel I've known you, Poppy Lovering.'

The words were as flowery and overdone as only a journalist could have said them, but he made a fatal error in using her full name. Her married name.

She put her hands against his chest and

twisted her mouth away from his.

'Let me go, Jack. Please. I want to go *now*.'

He released her at once, and opened the door with ease. Poppy almost stumbled out into the other room, blinking in the burst of sunlight coming through the window now that the rain had stopped as quickly as it had begun. She was at once exhilarated and ashamed. What had just happened should never have been allowed, and then Jack caught hold of her hand and brought it to his lips in a sweet, old-fashioned gesture.

'Poppy, sweetheart, it's not the end of the world. It was only a kiss. I won't tell if you don't,' he finished teasingly.

Her face flamed and she snatched her hand away. 'Of course I won't tell,' she snapped. 'And you're right. It was only a kiss, so don't read anything more into it. Do you think I've never been kissed before?'

Even as she said it, the truth flashed through her head. It wasn't only a kiss. It was far more than that, but right now she was too confused to analyze it. The fact was that only two men in her life had ever kissed her before. One was her father, which didn't count, and the other was Sam, and she suspected that his experience of girls had been almost as limited as hers was of men. She had never even been courted properly. She had simply been living and working at the farm and drifted into marriage. She had never had a date, as Jack called it. She flinched to think how insular she really was, and she was furious with him for making her feel that way.

She was already shrugging back into her damp cardigan and praying she wouldn't look too bedraggled by the time she got home.

'Please don't take me right to the farm. Drop me at the bus-stop in the village and I'll walk the rest of the way,' she said stiffly. In a silly way, just telling him what to do made her feel better. He didn't own her, and never would.

It would have been too much to hope for that they could drive back to Barras in silence, as Poppy dearly wanted. After the rain, the moors steamed in a peculiarly beautiful and ethereal way that normally enchanted her, the old mine chimneys seeming to rise out of the mist, but she was too agitated to bother about the mystic beauty of the panorama around her now.

Jack kept up a constant flow of small talk, and she answered in monosyllables, wondering if the guilt she felt was somehow stamped on her forehead for all to see. She knew how foolish she was being. Other girls had affairs and thought nothing of it, but she wasn't one of them and never wanted to be. It was a huge relief when he stopped the car near the bus stop at the end of the

157

village. She opened the door quickly, before he could reach across and do it for her.

'I'll watch out for you same time next week, if you're visiting your friend again. If it's a bit earlier, so much the better,' he said with an easy smile.

She slammed the car door shut and marched along the grass verge, not looking back as he swung the car around and headed back to Penzance. Her cheeks were burning with indignation. The damn nerve of him, thinking she would ever want to repeat today. Or that she would even remember that kiss.

Chapter Eight

If that kiss had meant anything, and if she had been a poet, she would probably have described it as an ... an awakening she thought, unable to forget it as she hurried along the dirt road towards the farm. One kiss, that was all it was, but one that created feelings inside her that she never knew she had.

She didn't want them intruding into her life. All she wanted was for things to be the same as before, with no thoughts of anything but the humdrum days of her life.

There was safety in that. There may not be great excitement but there was safety, even if it was a sad way for a twenty-year-old to be thinking.

All the same, the sight of the weathered farmhouse, hearing the noises of the animals and the endless cycle of farming work she knew so well, had a calming effect on her, and she was thankful that her jangling nerves were settling down. And if Jack Trevis thought she had any intention of seeing him again he could go and jump in a lake, she thought, with a burst of fury that he was arrogant enough to think he could disrupt a decent girl's life.

'Good Lord, girl, did you miss the bus?' Florrie asked her the moment she got inside the farmhouse. 'Sam came and met me in the village when the rain started, and we saw the bus come in, so we waited for you. Mrs Reddick was on it as she usually is on a Friday, and she said she hadn't seen you. Don't tell me you walked all the way from Penzance in that state,' she added sceptically.

If Poppy's heart was jumping before, it doubled its rate now. It was something she simply hadn't considered, that one of Florrie's church meeting friends might be on the bus as well. She couldn't think of a sensible enough reply, and she wasn't used to lying, so she said the first obvious thing

159

that came into her head.

'I was so busy talking with Shirley that I forgot the time, and when I got to the bus-stop the bus had gone. I did start to walk, and then that newspaper chap came along and offered me a lift in his car for part of the way. I was practically soaked by then, so I thought it was the sensible thing to do.'

Florrie set great store by sensible methods of doing anything, but she gave a great sniff at mention of Jack Trevis.

'It would be far more sensible to have nothing at all to do with the likes of him. Still, I can see that you got wet through, so you'd better go and change your clothes before you do any more damage. We don't want you coughing and sneezing all night.'

Poppy fled upstairs, glad to get away from her mother-in-law's suspicious eyes, and with the uneasy thought that the damage had already been done. But not the kind Florrie had been thinking about.

On Sunday afternoon, Shirley and Bernard were going to Penhallow to break the news of the coming baby to both families, knowing they would be ecstatic. Shirley's younger sisters had been longing to be aunties, although Bernard's adolescent brothers didn't feel quite the same way about babies. None of that mattered. What mattered was that the two people most closely concerned were thrilled that they were going to be parents. Bernard wanted a son, but Shirley didn't mind if it was a boy or a girl as long as it was healthy.

Nagging at the back of her mind was the knowledge that the other one had never stood a chance, and nor did she know whether it might have been wearing pink or blue. But Bernard knew nothing of that frantic time, and her big worry when she had seen the doctor and had her current condition confirmed, was that he would be able to tell. But she had replied calmly when he asked smilingly if this was her first baby, and said how much she was looking forward to it. That much, at least, was true. And only her conscience knew the rest.

But once the families had been told and they had all celebrated with cups of tea, since the middle of the afternoon wasn't the right time for a drop of sherry, there was only one person Shirley wanted to see. She and Bernard walked through the familiar village towards Tinners' Lane where Carrie and Archie Pollard lived, greeting old friends and acquaintances, and never giving a glance towards the now well-established colony of prefabs that Shirley had once so coveted. They had lived there for a year before Bernard got the chance of the new job in Penzance, but they had since settled happily into their new life.

161

Carrie and Archie were glad to see visitors, having just had words over one of Walter's tantrums. Shirley's secret smile told Bernard that this was what they could expect in the future, but nothing could dim her happiness. And being Shirley, she couldn't contain herself a minute longer before it all came bursting out.

'We've got something wonderful to tell you. We're going to have a baby next March,' she said, but she didn't need to get any further as Carrie gave a whoop of delight and hugged her.

'Didn't I say as much, Archie? I guessed there was something up at the fête. You had that look about you, Shirley.'

'You must be clairvoyant then, because I hadn't even been to see the doctor then. But I'm sure you'll tell me everything I need to know about bringing up babies.'

Carrie detected a tiny guarded look in her friend's eyes, and called out to Walter to come indoors from the garden. He tore inside at the sound of visitors, and threw himself at Shirley, excited to see her.

'This is what you can expect,' Carrie grinned. 'But if we're going to talk about babies, why don't you two chaps take Walter to the park for a while? I'm sure you don't want to hear all the gory stuff.'

'That's enough for me,' Archie said, getting up at once, even though Bernard

Bosinney wouldn't have been his first choice of companion. 'You might as well get used to pushing a sprog on the swings, Bernard. So let's leave these two to get on with it.'

Walter was even more excited at going out with the men, and once Carrie had made him go to the lav and be buttoned into his coat before he was going anywhere, she and Shirley were finally alone.

'So let's have it. You really are happy about the baby, aren't you, Shirley?'

'Of course I am. Can't you tell? It's just … well, a lot of things, really. It's odd how things come together when you least expect them to. When you never thought there was any possibility of them being connected at all. I always thought that was odd, and it happens far more often than people think, doesn't it?'

'Well, as I don't have the foggiest idea what you're taking about, perhaps you'd better start from the beginning,' Carrie said mildly, thinking that if Shirley had a dozen babies, nothing was going to change her scatterbrained ways.

Shirley looked at her crossly, aware that there was a small churning in her stomach again after the ride in Bernard's car. Carrie was always so sensible, and that was what she needed, of course, someone who would put all her worries into perspective, but without any smugness. She sighed, knowing

Carrie was never smug, and it was nothing more than her own perverse thoughts making her feel so ungracious when there was no need.

'What did you think of Poppy Lovering?' she asked suddenly, and Carrie burst out laughing.

'I see that being pregnant hasn't made you able to string your thoughts together any better. Where does Poppy come into all this?'

'I really want to know. What did you think of her?'

Carrie could see that this was important to her friend, though she still didn't have any idea why. But Shirley frequently went all around the bush before she got to what was really on her mind, so she was prepared to indulge her. It was just nice to have some female company on a Sunday afternoon, at a time when Archie was often tetchy after being with Walter all day long.

'She's a very pretty girl, but I already knew that from the newspaper photo when she rescued the Flint boy from the mine shaft.'

As always, she couldn't avoid a shudder, remembering Archie's own childhood tales of being thrown down a mine shaft by some vicious older boys, and then being sent to what he called The Pit during his POW days. Those terrible days had resulted in nightmares that even now occasionally reoccurred.

164

'He had his eye on her, you know. The newspaper chap, I mean – Jack somebody,' Shirley stated.

'Well, having seen Sam Lovering now, I wouldn't think he'd stand for that. I thought he was a big bear of a man, but so gentle and good with the children. Walter doesn't take to strangers very quickly, but he liked Sam.'

'Poppy's worried,' Shirley said flatly, as if she hadn't heard a word Carrie said. 'Jack told her he wanted to see her again, and she came to me for advice, because I'm a friend and she thinks I'm a woman of the world, but in a very proper way of course. That's a laugh, isn't it, Carrie? Coming to me for advice on whether or not she should have an affair behind her husband's back!'

She shivered, wishing she hadn't put it into words. Strictly speaking, it wasn't as if she had ever had an affair behind her husband's back, Shirley amended. She hadn't been married at the time the GIs swarmed into Penzance with their chocolates and nylons and glamour, but she had been as good as engaged. She knew she was only splitting hairs in her mind, though, and it was just as much a betrayal.

'Shirley, you're being stupid!' she heard Carrie's voice snap. 'For heaven's sake, if the girl wants advice, who better to give it to her, when you know all about the consequences.

And I don't mean that in a spiteful way, just that you'll know how to tell her delicately that it's not worth the heartache.'

'And you think she'll listen, do you? Any more than I did?'

For one glorious, insane moment, Shirley felt herself transported back to those magical times when she had floated around the dance floor in Hank Delaney's arms, when there were no thoughts of anything but these precious moments that were all any of them had, because nobody dared to think about what tomorrow might bring.

No thoughts, no foreknowledge that somewhere in France, Bernard Bosinney was about to be shot down and badly wounded. No thoughts that one magical night could end with her being more terrified than she had ever been in her life, until the relief of knowing that it wasn't going to end in disaster after all. No realization, either, that she would feel the bereavement of the miscarriage so deeply. There was nothing in her imagination to tell her that one day she would read the names of those brave GIs who would never come back for their reunion a year after the war ended ... and for Hank's name to be among them.

'Take a few deep breaths, Shirley. You've got your baby to think about now.'

Wasn't that exactly what she was doing?

After a few moments she managed to

speak, giving her friend a watery smile. 'I know you're right, Carrie, as always. And of course I shall tell Poppy what she should do. In her heart I'm sure she knows it already, but Jack Trevis is certainly a charmer. I can see how she would fall for him.'

'Newspapermen always have a good line in patter. That's part of their job,' Carrie said dryly. 'They can charm the birds from the trees if they want to, and pretty as she is, Poppy hardly seems the last word in sophistication.'

'Hardly! That's probably what attracted Jack to her in the first place.'

'And she reminds you of yourself.'

Shirley laughed. 'How did you guess? Perhaps that's why I'm starting to feel protective of her and, as usual, you've talked me into what I have to do.'

Carrie widened her eyes innocently. 'Me? I haven't said anything!'

The young woman in the car that trundled slowly through the village of Penhallow that Sunday afternoon, twisted her head around to look at the threesome strolling across the village Green towards the swings.

'Somebody you know?' Sam asked her.

'Not really,' Poppy replied. 'I thought I saw Shirley's husband with another chap and a small boy. I think they were the people she was with at the fête.'

'Of course, she used to live here, didn't she?' He glanced at her. 'You've got quite friendly with Shirley now, haven't you, girl? I'm glad. She was always a bit dippy, but it's good for you to have a friend.'

Poppy laughed. 'A bit dippy? I was always in awe of her and the other girls. They seemed so glamorous to me.'

'That's because you were only a kid. You're just as good a looker as any of them now.'

'Am I?' Poppy felt her face flush. Sam wasn't given to making compliments, even if it wasn't a flowery one. Coming from him, it meant just as much.

'You know you are, so don't go expecting any more old flannel from me. I leave all that to blokes who are slick with words, like that newspaper chap and Shirley's schoolteacher husband. That's their job.'

'I know,' Poppy said, keeping her gaze on the road ahead and not letting her heart flip for a single moment at Sam's words.

She wondered if Shirley was in Penhallow today too, and thought that she probably was, if Bernard was here. She guessed that she'd be gossiping with that other friend of hers, Carrie Pollard, while the chaps took Walter out of their way. It sounded such a civilized way to spend a Sunday afternoon.

But so was this, she thought immediately. They were on their way to St Ives, as Sam had promised. It was a sunny day, even if it was a bit blustery, and the sea would be its usual spectacular self. And she wasn't going to think about anything else. Especially not Jack Trevis.

'What do you want to do when we get there?' Sam said, breaking into her thoughts. 'There's a few beach shops, but I daresay they'll be shut on Sunday. There might be a trip around Carbis Bay on a boat if you fancy getting wet.'

'I don't think so,' Poppy said quickly, her stomach heaving at the thought. 'I'd rather just walk around the bay and look at the sea and enjoy the fresh air, and we might be able to buy an ice cream.'

Sam laughed. 'Well, at least you're a girl of simple pleasures. You don't cost me a fortune, like some might. You've probably forgotten how those land girls dressed up to the nines for their Saturday night dances. Mother used to make such a fuss about their perfume stinking the place out too.'

'I certainly haven't forgotten. I always thought they looked wonderful, and all I wished for was to be old enough to go with them. I don't think your mother remembers what it was like to be young. She always looked down her nose at them, and at me too.'

She hadn't meant to burst out with the words, nor to criticize Florrie. She wasn't sure she cared to be described as a girl of simple pleasures, either. Simpleton, more like.

'Well, don't let's get heated about it,' Sam said calmly. 'We're out to enjoy ourselves today. And Mother does care for you, Poppy, in her own way. It was never easy for her, having those city girls pushed on us by the ministry, talking so fast and looking so flashy, but you were a nice, wholesome girl.'

'I suppose that's another compliment then. We'll have to do this more often if you're going to talk to me so much, Sam.'

'I do talk to you,' he said in genuine surprise.

'But not like this.'

'Well, I'm not talking any more right now. If I don't keep my eyes on the road I'll have us in the hedge, so you'd better let me concentrate.'

Poppy smiled, feeling her spirits lift as they drove through the narrow lanes with the thick, high hedges on either side of them. Ahead of them now was the road leading down to the quaint, picturesque town of St Ives, with its hotch potch of little winding streets and cottages. There was a thriving fishing industry here, and the scent of fish was on the air as seabirds wheeled and screeched overhead.

St Ives was becoming known as an artists' paradise. Professionals and amateurs came here to paint, since the light was supposed to be particularly good for their skills. There were potters and a few sculptors in the area too, making good use of the local Cornish china clay for their work, and it was considered quite a bohemian place now, with many of them wearing colourful garb.

St Ives was a busy little place, and they weren't the only people coming here for a pleasant afternoon. Despite it being Sunday, there were a couple of small curio shops open near the harbour, selling ornaments and jewellery made out of polished Cornish serpentine stone. Several artists had set up their easels in advantageous positions in front of the cluster of fishing boats, and small crowds had gathered around to watch them work. To Poppy, it seemed a fascinating world away from the endless and everyday work on the farm.

'It must be lovely to be able to paint,' she said to Sam, as they paused for a few moments, watching them at work.

'Waste of time,' he said predictably. 'It's only idlers with nothing else to do that sit and paint all day. Lot of weirdos if you ask me.'

She was glad they had moved on so that the artist in question couldn't hear him. But it was so like Sam to pooh-pooh something artistic and therefore faintly suspect that he didn't fully understand, that she burst out laughing.

'Oh, Sam, you are funny. There's nothing weird about doing something you enjoy. And I bet they make a bit of money from it too.'

'What, from daubing paint on a bit of canvas? Pull the other one.'

'I mean it! What about famous artists?'

She knew she was going nowhere with this argument, because she couldn't remember the names of any, even if she had ever heard of them in the first place.

Sam guffawed. 'The only painters likely to scratch a living around Barras are house painters, girl. Which reminds me, the dairy could do with a lick of paint.'

She felt like stamping her feet if it wasn't so darned melodramatic. 'Oh, sometimes I think you've got no soul.'

He was tickled by the way she was getting so tetchy over something that didn't matter a damn as far as he could see. 'You're a daft maid sometimes, aren't you?' he said indulgently.

Unreasonably, Poppy's temper flared at once. 'I'm not a maid. You saw to that, didn't you?'

'Good God, what's got into you now?' Sam responded in like form. 'I thought we were having a nice day out when I could just as usefully have spent an hour or so having a Sunday afternoon snooze before milking. Maybe you're spending too much time with

172

Shirley whatsername after all if she's filling your head with fancy ideas about painters.'

'She's not. And it was you who told me I should go out a bit more, and you know very well what her name is too.'

She knew she was sounding like a petulant schoolkid now, but she couldn't seem to help it. This lovely day was spoiled as far as she was concerned, and for no other reason than that they were arguing over artists, for God's sake.

She wouldn't mind betting that Jack Trevis wouldn't waste a day out by arguing over daft stuff like that. In fact, if the subject of artists came up, she was pretty sure he'd know all about them and be able to tell her all sorts of stuff.

'So do you want an ice cream or not?' she heard Sam say heavily, and she knew this was his way of apologizing, even though he probably couldn't see that he had any reason to do so. He had always preferred to keep the peace, she knew that, and she was the one with the temperamental outbursts. She should count herself lucky, and in future she would try to remember it.

'Yes please,' she replied more humbly, 'and I'm sorry I got all huffy just now, Sam.'

'Ah well, you're a female, and a young un at that, so it's to be expected.'

With that remark, all her good intentions flew right out of the window.

'Were you in Penhallow last weekend?' she asked Shirley the following Friday. 'Me and Sam went for a drive to St Ives, and I thought I saw your Bernard with that other chap and his little boy.'

'You did. They were taking Walter to the swings while Carrie and I got our heads together. You know – baby talk,' she said vaguely.

'Oh, yes, of course,' Poppy said, even though she didn't know, and all she could think of was this was something else that excluded her from being a real friend of Shirley's.

'Are we going to spend the afternoon in silence, or are you going to stop scowling and say something?' Shirley said.

'About what?'

'Well, you tell me. It must have taken something to stir Sam out of his Sunday afternoon ritual, so does that mean you're all lovey-dovey, and that you've got over the other little problem?'

Shirley knew she was being a hypocrite. You didn't get over a crush, if that's what it was, that easily. You didn't even see it as a crush, you saw it as the love of your life, the doomed, can-never-have love of your life. You saw yourself as the tragic heroine. You dreamed about a beautiful, forbidden, and unfulfilled love. You imagined it, and longed for it, and slept with it, until you could think of nothing else. Once you allowed it in, it took over your life – if you let it.

'I didn't think you'd be so unfeeling,' Poppy complained. 'I came to you for advice, and it was far more than a little problem to me.'

'Oh, love, I'm sorry! I didn't mean to imply that it meant nothing to you, truly I didn't. But now you've admitted that it *was* a problem, I hope you've seen sense. Nothing can come of it, you know. Nothing ever does.'

'You're talking from experience, are you?' Poppy said sullenly, meaning nothing at all, but finding the need to hit back, tit-for-tat. She didn't miss Shirley's small intake of breath.

'Of course not,' the older woman said crossly. 'But I know enough to warn you. Sam's a good man, Poppy, and he doesn't deserve to be messed about, especially with a chap with a roving eye like Jack Trevis. You made a promise when you married Sam. Forsaking all others, remember?'

'Of course I remember. What do you take me for?' And at least *she* hadn't forsaken her marriage vows, Shirley thought again. She hadn't taken them when she had fallen so madly for Hank. She knew it made no difference, but she brushed it aside in her mind, more concerned with the stark misery on Poppy's face now. This time her gasp was more audible, because she knew what heartache was ahead of Poppy if she didn't stop this right now.

'Don't tell me you've really fallen for the chap, have you? You hardly know him, Poppy. You'd be mad to risk everything you have for a few moments' excitement, because that's all it would be. His sort isn't the marrying kind.'

'You don't know that, and in any case I don't want to marry him.'

Shirley decided it was time to be brutal. 'So what do you want? A bit of slap and tickle on the sands? A quick fumble in the back of his car? Or do you want to give in to him completely and risk an unwanted baby? How would you explain that to Sam – and his sour-faced mother too. My God! Maybe you don't remember how many GI brides were married in haste for the same reason, and went off to their new life with no idea what was waiting for them. I doubt that it was all honey and roses.'

'Jack's not a GI.'

'I know he's not, but he's got the same kind of glamour about him, with those film star looks. Please think what you're doing, Poppy – and don't do it.'

Poppy hadn't expected such a lecture. She felt as drained as Shirley looked now. She knew she shouldn't have come here with her problems. It wasn't fair on Shirley in her condition. Poppy didn't know much about babies, but she knew about pigs dropping their litters and cows calving, and that it was an anxious time for everyone until the young ones were safely delivered. Florrie once said that animals giving birth hovered somewhere between life and death. If that was true, then Poppy guessed it must be the same for women, and just as scary.

'I'm really sorry if I've tired you out, Shirley. When did you say the baby was expected?' she asked uncomfortably, not sure if she even knew.

'Good Lord, not until the middle of next March, and I'm not tired at all, but I'm fed up with this wretched sickness that comes and goes. I really hope it will stop soon. It's so antisocial.'

She gave a rueful laugh, and then said something to make Poppy's heart jump. 'Look, I'll walk with you to the bus stop when you go, though. I'm supposed to take plenty of exercise, and I can call at the fishmonger's on the way back to get something for Bernard's tea. We always have fish on Fridays.'

And since there didn't seem any logical way of getting out of having her company, Poppy had to agree. Besides, in one way it would be a very good thing. There would be no chance of watching out for a familiar car chugging along towards the bus stop and the driver offering her a lift. She had had no intention of accepting, but in case she had been tempted, there was no way she could do anything about it if Shirley was with her. It was fate, she told herself. Fate was taking a hand, and saving her from herself. The hell of it was, she wasn't sure she wanted to be saved from herself – or from Jack Trevis, even now.

But Shirley didn't want to linger at the bus stop with her and Poppy wasn't sure whether to be glad or sorry. She knew she was being spineless, wanting someone else to make the decisions for her that she knew she had to make herself. Wanting to ward off the inevitable. She shivered, because nothing was inevitable, providing she had the gumption to walk away from temptation.

She was so deep in thought that the car drew up alongside her before she had time to register it. Jack leaned towards her from the driving seat, his smile wide.

'Sorry I don't have time to stop and talk today, Poppy, but if you're going to Zennor to see your folks next Thursday, I'll look out for you. I'm going that way to take some photos of Chysauster for a feature I'm doing.'

He waved his hand and the car shot away, scattering dust and leaving Poppy fuming. The damn nerve of him, thinking she would just turn up whenever and wherever he crooked his little finger. She wouldn't go anywhere near the ancient ruins of Chysauster, even if it was on a direct route across the moors from Barras to Zennor. She'd take a very roundabout route in order to miss him, and she wouldn't care how long it took. It wasn't even that she didn't altogether trust him. She wasn't sure that she could trust herself any more.

And then the bus came into sight, and she stepped inside thankfully, turning her attention instead to Florrie's friend, the gossipy Mrs Reddick. Anything was better than acknowledging how rapidly her heart was beating at the thought that she just *might* be tempted to meet Jack in Chysauster next week.

Chapter Nine

Poppy Lovering, born Poppy Penfold, had never been what her mother called a churchified person. This had a lot to do with the fact that neither of her parents had ever had any truck with what they called 'them religious nuts'. You didn't have to go to church to be a good person, according to Poppy's mother. Providing you kept yourself clean, and your thoughts likewise, then that was good enough.

When she was a child this suited Poppy very well, because it meant she didn't have to go to Sunday School like the other kids in the village, chanting hymns and reading the bible, and she became generally known as a wild child, if not quite a heathen. She didn't make friends easily, which also suited most of the other village parents, since in their opinion, there was also the darker side of things to consider.

If you didn't go to church to worship God, then there must be something of the devil inside you, and they didn't want their own children corrupted by the daughter of non-believers.

It had been a source of conflict between Poppy and Florrie Lovering from the moment she came to work at Lovering's Farm. Florrie was a church-goer and Poppy was not. Poppy had been sent here to help out on the farm, and she didn't see why that should include something her parents hadn't made her do.

Right from the start Sam had been tickled at the way the mere stripling of a girl stood up to his mother in that respect, but he was firm enough to tell Florrie to let the girl bide, and Florrie had eventually given in to the pair of them.

Now, for the first time in her life, Poppy

found herself wishing she had something that would force her to do what she knew in her heart was right. She almost wished she was like Shirley, remembering how the city girls had mocked Shirley for her belief in confessing her sins, even when she wasn't a Catholic and didn't have anything to confess. They had scoffed, saying it was no more than a ritual, intended to put the fear of God into sinners, but it had seemed to calm Shirley down on more than one occasion.

It was something to believe in. To remind her what was right and what was wrong, and to warn you of the ghastly consequences of being burned in hellfire if you didn't abide by it. Poppy needed that now.

'I might come to church with you on Sunday,' she announced to Florrie as she was helping to muck out the pigs.

'Why? What have you done?' her mother-in-law said suspiciously.

Poppy stuck her hands on her hips. 'Well, I like that! I thought you'd be pleased. You've been on at me for long enough.'

Florrie gave a snort. 'In my opinion, when somebody who's never shown the slightest interest in reading the Good Book suddenly wants to go to church, there's a reason for it. So what is it?'

Poppy felt her cheeks flush. Florrie was too damn knowing, and she should have expected the inquisition. 'Why couldn't the reason be that I wanted to please you instead of always being such an irritation to you?'

Florrie was silent for a few minutes – although it seemed to go on for ever as the smell of the pig swill wafted into Poppy's nose. 'I suppose I'll have to accept that, even if I don't believe such a cock and bull tale for a minute. And I'd much prefer your reason for going to church to be because you felt a vocation for it.'

'I'm not thinking of becoming a nun!' Poppy hooted.

'No, and that would be a blasphemy if I ever heard one!' Florrie snapped, and then Poppy heard the squish of her boots on the damp earth as she marched away, leaving Poppy to finish the task by herself.

She couldn't resist a nervous giggle, wondering if her slight mocking had indeed been blasphemous. Then she jumped as she heard a slow hand-clapping. She turned her head to find Sam leaning on the fence post.

'Did you hear all that, then? I thought you'd be telling me off as well.'

He gave a laugh. 'Not likely. I was thanking my stars that my wife isn't planning to be a nun.'

She pulled a face. 'It was just something to say, that's all.'

'You're not really going to church with

Mother on Sunday, are you?'

'I'm not sure now. It seemed a good idea when I said it, but I don't think she really wants me there. I'm too much of a black sheep. I might think about it if you came too, though.'

Sam shrugged. 'No thanks. I've no wish to listen to Vicar spouting on all evening. The buggers all sermonize about tending your flocks, and that's what we're doing, sheep or no sheep. I reckon as how a farmer's got a genuine excuse for not going to church. He's too busy with his beasts.'

To Poppy it sounded more like a good way of copping out. But she giggled again at the way Sam described vicars in general, and wouldn't mind betting that he wouldn't do so in front of his mother.

'Well, I might go and I might not,' she said. 'I don't have to make up my mind until the day, do I?'

And when the day came, she decided not to go. Florrie merely sniffed and said it was no more than she expected, and just a flash in the pan. So Poppy saw her off thankfully, and settled down for the evening with one of her magazines, knowing that would probably be wrong on a Sunday in Florrie's eyes too, while Sam sprawled out in his armchair and snoozed after his day's labours.

It didn't make her feel any more settled,

though, to read about the doings of glamorous film stars whose lives were a million miles away from hers. She envied the clothes they wore and the diamond rings on their fingers, and knew she could never hope to have anything of the same. She didn't realize she had given such a heavy sigh until she caught Sam looking at her through half-closed eyes.

'I thought you were asleep,' she said accusingly, wondering if her envy had been showing on her face.

'What's got you so interested?' he replied.

'Nothing.' She closed the magazine quickly. 'Your mother always says I'm idling my life away with such rubbish, and she's probably right.'

'Let's have a look then.' He held out his hand and she was obliged to give him the magazine. He flipped through the pages, saying nothing for a minute and then he tossed it back to her.

'I wouldn't like to see you dolled up like some of them painted women, and there's no need. But you can have a new frock any time you like if that's what you're craving, Poppy. I'll give you some money to buy something in Penzance next time you go. Now let me get a bit more shut-eye.'

He folded his arms and closed his eyes firmly before she could thank him. She had always been good with her needle and made most of her clothes, because that was what thrifty women did. During the war it had been a necessity, but that was a long time ago, and then the New Look came in, and shops were selling all kinds of nice clothes now. Her spirits lifted at the thought of buying something new.

With it came the treacherous thought that it would be nice to look less like a traditional farmer's wife and more like the woman Jack Trevis evidently thought she could be. And that might be a very bad thing, she told herself sternly.

In any case she couldn't really go to Penzance until Friday. On Thursday she would be visiting her folks, and if he had his way, she would be seeing Jack Trevis at Chysauster. There would be no new frock by then, and if she did go that way, he would have to take her the way she was. But of course she wasn't going to meet him and that was that.

'I knew you'd come,' he said softly.

Poppy propped up her bicycle against one of the stone walls of the ancient village, careful that the basket at the front didn't tip over and smash the eggs for her parents. Her heart was thudding madly. In an idle moment, she had asked Florrie what she knew about Chysauster village, and had been told that a century ago Methodist preachers

185

sometimes used the ruins of the old settlement as an open air pulpit. To Poppy's fertile mind, the knowledge that it had been used for religious purposes made this clandestine meeting even worse.

'I'm not staying. I just came to tell you that. I'm going to see my parents as usual, and this is on the way.' Her voice was jerky.

'You could have taken another way,' Jack pointed out.

'But then I couldn't have told you to stop this.'

He unfolded himself lazily from the wall of what had once been a house, covered now with the encroaching moorland vegetation, and a home only for rabbits and other wildlife, and came towards her. She took an involuntary step backwards, and he gave a short laugh.

'What am I supposed to stop? I haven't done anything yet.'

She almost stumbled over a root and his arms shot out to steady her. The next moment she felt his mouth on hers and it was impossible for her to break away, even if she had wanted it to stop – and she didn't want it to. This was an adventure, the like of which she hadn't known before. It was not quite like one of the daring Hollywood movies that she read about in the maga-zines, where sheiks in the desert captured beautiful maidens and made them their slaves. Oh no, it was hardly the same, nor as wickedly wanton, but for a country girl the dizzy excitement was the same. It made the blood sing in her veins.

'You're wasted on that clod of a husband,' she heard him murmur against her lips. 'Does he even know what a treasure he's got?'

Poppy wrenched away from him, rubbing her mouth furiously. 'Don't speak about Sam like that. He's a good man, and this is all wrong, and I don't want to be here.'

He pulled her to him again. 'For God's sake, Poppy, stop acting like a silly little virgin, which I know damn well you're not. What harm does it do to anyone to have a bit of fun? What the husband doesn't know, can't hurt him.'

She was becoming frightened by the intense look in his eyes now. Up here on the moors, they were completely alone. She had no idea where he had left his car, because unless someone regularly risked these old tracks on a bicycle and knew the pitfalls, the only way to reach the ancient village was on foot over rough ground. She wasn't sure he'd be satisfied with just a few kisses either, and she knew how foolish she had been to come here with the noble intention of telling him to stop pursuing her.

'Please don't hurt me,' she whispered.

'That's the last thing I want,' he said,

suddenly tender, and smoothing her dark hair back from her damp forehead. 'But let's find somewhere comfortable. There's plenty of grassy patches inside the ruins of the old houses, and if it's a bit stony I'll put my coat down for you, like good old Walter Raleigh.'

She had a vague knowledge of whom he was talking from her school history lessons, but she was sure old Walter's chivalry hadn't meant putting down his coat for a lady on top of the moors.

Her hand was gripped tightly in Jack's, and she didn't seem to have the will to pull it away. Or perhaps she didn't really want to. She was as soft and limp as Lovering's milk swirling around in the churn to make butter. She felt as if she didn't know herself any more. She shouldn't even be here at all, but she was. She shouldn't be allowing Jack Trevis to lay down his coat on the grassy ground, smiling that Clark Gable smile at her, and inviting her to sit down beside him, but she was.

She shouldn't be feeling her heart thud so fast with the heady and strangely detached sensation that this must be how it felt when a handsome hero and a beautiful girl took part in a Hollywood movie.

It wasn't real. It was just acting. All make-believe. She could think herself into the mind of one of those Hollywood starlets where she was in the middle of a romantic scene. It was just for the moment, and afterwards they would go back to being whatever they were before. She was intoxicated with the feelings.

'You're so very beautiful, Poppy. And I've wanted to do this from the moment I first saw you.'

Shouldn't that be from the beginning of time? Her thoughts were getting jumbled up now, as fast as her heartbeats. But he was getting the lines wrong. That wasn't the way he said it in his dark room.

'Have you?' she said huskily, imagining that this was how the movie starlet would respond.

But he wasn't doing anything yet. He wasn't kissing her, or touching her. He was just looking at her. His gaze was enveloping her, as if he could see right through the flowery frock she was wearing, right through the petticoat and stockings, and sensible knickers.

She drew in her breath raggedly. Sam never looked at her like this. Sam never made her feel this odd tingling in the pit of her stomach that went down and down and was suddenly electric. She had read about girls in love whose bones had turned to water, and always scoffed at the flowery words, but now she knew exactly what it meant. Sam never made her feel like that, either. She kept dragging Sam's name to the

189

peak of her senses, to remind her of who she was and where she belonged.

'You've wanted it too.' Jack was still speaking in that soft, persuasive way that made her shudder again. 'I've seen it in your eyes and in every curve of that delicious little body. You can't deny it, sweetheart. It's what you were made for.'

Poppy realized that one of his hands was brushing lightly over her breasts, in a way that was more arousing than if he pressed hard, while his other hand was gently inching up her skirt. His was such a smooth and easy seduction that she was almost unaware of it, but she found herself hardly able to breathe as a flood of desire swept through her. They were alone in this wild and rugged place. The lonely whispering of the bracken all around them and the intense blue of the sky above, made it a perfect setting for love, just as so many others, those sweet, forgotten ghosts of the past, must have made love here centuries ago.

When his body lay heavily on hers, she knew there was no way back, and she felt a small gasp in her throat that was delight mixed with despair. In one instant she knew she was betraying Sam and her marriage vows, and in the next she gave herself up to the sensations sweeping through her. She was Scarlett O'Hara to his Rhett Butler.

But if she had expected a slow sensuous

seduction, she was disappointed. It was over almost before she registered that it had happened. Jack threw himself away from her, his breath rasping now, while she lay there in bewilderment, tears starring her vision as she clamped her legs together as if to deny what had just happened.

She closed her eyes tightly, praying for forgiveness to a God she didn't altogether believe in except when it suited her, and wishing desperately that she could undo these last wicked moments.

It hadn't even been wonderful, an honest little voice said inside her ... as if that made it any better that she had been unfaithful. It had been a quick, frantic rutting, as urgent as one of Sam's beasts with a mare. It was degrading and shaming, and the deep sobs she was too proud to show, began to choke her throat.

'Are you all right?' she heard Jack say, and she realized he had been off in the bushes for reasons of his own. There was no hint of any tenderness after the lovemaking as all the romantic movies would lead you to expect, she thought bitterly, knowing that anger was the only way to make her strong, when she felt as weak as a newborn lamb.

'I suppose so,' she mumbled.

'You don't need to worry. I was careful.'

She stared at him, not sophisticated enough to think what he meant.

191

'Careful about what?'

He gave an uneasy laugh. 'Come on, you're not that dumb, are you? But if you need me to spell it out, I promise there's no risk of you getting pregnant. That's what I was careful about.'

Poppy scrambled to her feet, her face ablaze with shame. On top of everything else it was awful that she hadn't even given a thought to such a terrible thing happening. She hadn't *thought* at all.

She saw Jack pick up his coat from the grass, and calmly begin to brush it down. It was increasingly obvious that none of this had meant a thing to him, and she had been foolish to think that it would. He had merely seen her as a naive little farmer's wife, eager for a bit of excitement, and that was exactly what she was.

'So what do you know about this place? I told you I'm going to write about it for my paper, and I daresay you've been here before. Maybe you even did a bit of courting here,' he went on with a grin, unbelievably insensitive to her feelings.

'All I know is that I want to get away from here as fast as I can, and I never want to see you again,' she said, her breath a tight pain in her chest.

He laughed uneasily again. 'Come on now, Poppy, it wasn't that bad. Good God, you came here willingly enough. I said I'd never hurt you, and I didn't, did I?'

'Maybe not in the way you mean,' she said, her voice shrill now. 'But you wouldn't understand that, would you? Your sort never does.'

'My sort? What sort is that then?'

'The sort that takes what they can get and never mind the consequences!'

His smile faded and he put a hand on her arm, gripping it tightly. 'I told you, there won't be any consequences. Are you deaf or just stupid?'

She brushed him off as if he was something slimy. 'I'm neither, except for coming here with you. I've already told you I don't want anything else to do with you, so don't ever come near me or my family again.'

She turned away, stumbling over the stony ground on shaky legs to retrieve her bicycle, gripping the handlebars as if they were a lifeline.

'There's a name for girls like you, Poppy Lovering,' Jack called after her. 'Maybe you don't know it—'

She bent low over the handlebars and pedalled off, the bicycle wheels wobbling beneath her, and deliberately closing her ears to what he was saying. She couldn't hear the ugly words properly, and she didn't want to. She wasn't the one at fault; he had done all the running, and she had just been a silly little fool, dazzled by his sweet-talking. The sobs tore at her throat now, knowing that this day, which had begun so normally, had changed her for ever.

In her mother-in-law's code of sins, she had had carnal knowledge of a man who wasn't her husband, and that was considered one of the worst sins of all. She tried to get the sound of Florrie's condemning words out of her head as she continued over the moors towards Zennor until the Chysauster settlement was far behind her, but eventually she had to stop for a breather, and to try to let her skittering heartbeats slow down.

She tried to force herself to think more logically. She knew she had done a terrible wrong to Sam, whom she loved – perhaps more than she had ever realized. In a weird way she could appreciate his bluff kindness all the more now that she had had this brief experience of a rotter like Jack Trevis. But she hardly thought that he was going to go around bragging about it. He had his precious position at the newspaper to think about, and she knew by now that he was an ambitious man. She was also sure that he'd forget any more ideas about photographing her, and she expected him to destroy all those photos of her in his dark room. He'd done what he intended, Poppy thought bitterly, and she'd be no more use to him.

So if he wasn't going to tell, and *she* certainly wasn't, the most sensible thing would be to put it all behind her and try to forget it ever happened. In fact, it wasn't merely a case of trying. It was vital that she did so. She couldn't bear for Sam to look at her as if she was no more than scum. She needed his respect as well as his love. So what had happened today had to be a secret that must never be told.

And if God was as benevolent as He was meant to be, then surely He would forgive her this one little lapse.

Intentions were one thing, but by the time she reached her family's cottage on the outskirts of Zennor, she was still finding it hard to think rationally, and her nerves were in tatters. Nobody could tell what had happened, she kept repeating to herself. She wasn't stamped with a great red sign on her forehead saying she had been an unfaithful wife. Nobody could tell.

But she couldn't face the innocent, bland faces of her parents yet. At the last moment she turned away from the cottage, propping up her bicycle against the hedge where they wouldn't see it. With her arms folded tightly around her body, as if to belatedly ward off the thing that had happened to her, she continued on foot towards Zennor Head, a wildly beautiful place where the sea crashed incessantly against gaunt cliffs, and the evening sunsets were spectacular. Poppy had spent many solitary hours there as a child, stunned by the awesomeness of nature, and weaving all kinds of fanciful stories about the sea and its creatures. There were seals in the waters around the Giant's Rock, not too far from here, and she had often imagined them having human faculties and living human lives beneath the waves.

Only later, when she was older, did she look back and see just what an insular and lonely child she had been. She could see it even more sharply now, wishing desperately that she could return to those times again when the only thing to worry about was how long she had remained with her dreams on the cliff top, and whether she would get back to the cottage in time for tea before her dad came looking for her.

She caught her breath in a huge, gulping sigh of remorse, knowing how simple her life had been then, and what a complicated thing she had made of it now. And the truth hammered into her brain that what was done could never be undone.

The sound of voices made her jump. She turned to see some walkers striding along the top of the cliffs nearby, and she hastily got to her feet and skimmed over the moorland turf towards her parents' cottage. She was in no mood for idle conversation with strangers or requests for directions. They might even ask the whereabouts of Chysauster ancient village, she thought frantically. She would be struck completely dumb if they did, and they would see her as the village idiot.

Her parents were sitting in their armchairs exactly where they sat every week. Poppy found herself wondering what she would do if the day ever came, which it surely must, when she would come here and find one of them missing. She gave a small choking cough at the smoky atmosphere inside the cottage, and spoke in as cheerful a voice as she could manage.

'You really ought to open these windows a bit more, Mum. It can't do your chests any good to be breathing in this wood-smoke all the time.'

'Oh, stop your grousing, girl. It suits your father and me,' her mother replied. 'We've lived here too long to change our ways now, not for you, nor anybody else.'

'Has somebody else said something, then?' Poppy said sharply, finding it an odd thing for her mother to say.

Her father grunted. 'The blasted doctor came the other day, wanting to know how we were faring, and calling it a social call in case we need anything. I told 'im good and strong that we don't need folk poking around here telling us how to run our lives. We've done it for all these years without interference, and we ain't going to start asking for charity now.'

'Quite right,' Agnes Penfold retorted. 'We'll see out our days the way we want to, not as some newfangled doctor thinks fit.'

Poppy hid a faint smile, feeling a mite more normal at their grumbling. The doctor was sixty if he was a day. He'd been around for as long as she could remember and had brought her into the world, so he was hardly newfangled.

'I'm sure he's only thinking of your health, Mum, and I don't want to hear any talk of you seeing out your days, either. There's plenty of life in you both yet.'

But a small shiver ran through her as she said it, because they hardly looked in their prime – if they ever had been. They looked old and crumpled, and complacent in their habits. As for taking any exercise, she doubted that they even remembered what it was like to be young and to go running and skipping over the moors. They must have been young once, doing the kind of things that young people did – and since she didn't want to think about too much of that, she spoke quickly.

'I've brought your usual eggs and ham, and when I've put the kettle on, I'll make you some boiled eggs for your tea if you like.'

'Whatever you think, girl,' her mother said without any great enthusiasm.

For one awful moment, Poppy wondered what it must be like to be so lacking in life, like these two. They were simply sitting here, passing the hours of daylight until it was time to go to bed and sleep and for the ritual to begin all over again the next day. They didn't do anything. It was no more than waiting to die.

She hadn't really thought of it before, but she thought of it now, and it filled her with a kind of panic that two people with whom she had once shared a busy family life could let themselves decline without doing anything about it. It wasn't as if they were infirm. They were just uninterested in life.

'Why don't I get Sam to come and fetch you for a day at the farm one Sunday?' she said impulsively when she brought in the usual tray of tea and biscuits while she waited for the eggs to boil.

Her mother's eyes widened. 'What would we want to do that for?'

'We ain't dressing in our tidy clothes to sit and talk to that Lovering woman, neither,' her father said at once.

Poppy was pretty sure he hadn't worn his tidy clothes since the day she and Sam had got married. They were probably full of moth holes by now.

'I just thought you'd like a day out,' she said lamely, watching as her dad poured his tea into the saucer and slurped it noisily.

'Well, we wouldn't,' her mother said. 'We don't like company, neither, so don't you go bringing her over here.'

'I wasn't even thinking about it.'

She could just imagine Florrie's sniff as her gaze took in every speck of dust, and the untidy muddles and piles of old newspapers that never got thrown away unless Poppy did it. The furniture was old and worn, like its owners, but imagining Florrie's disapproval, Poppy felt a fierce protectiveness towards them.

'I expect your eggs will be ready now,' she said, almost in a gasp as she fled to the kitchen. Her eyes blurred, wishing perversely that things never had to change, that things could stay as they were for ever, and knowing that, in their own peculiar way, these two had achieved just that.

Chapter Ten

Poppy sipped her bedtime cocoa, wishing her nerves would stop jumping about as if she had a dozen grasshoppers fighting in her chest. She was fast discovering that it wasn't so easy to forget what had happened that day after all.

'I don't think I shall go to Penzance tomorrow,' Poppy said as normally as she could. 'I don't want to wear out my welcome with Shirley, and I really don't need a new frock, Sam.'

Before he could say a word, his mother had spoken. 'That's the first sensible thing I've heard you say lately. You seemed to be having your head turned by all that newspaper nonsense, but perhaps you've come to your senses at last.'

'Perhaps I have,' Poppy muttered. The fact was, she couldn't bear to face Shirley, knowing that if she did it would all come pouring out, and once the words were said out loud, the shame of it would be doubled.

'Well, if that's how you feel, that's all right by me,' Sam said. 'But we're not so hard up that I can't afford to buy my wife some new clobber now and then.'

'I know, and thank you,' she said, grateful that he didn't persist with it. 'Perhaps I'll go next week and buy some material to make something instead.'

Florrie was more astute than her son when it came to a young girl's emotions. She looked at Poppy shrewdly, noting the flushed face and the slightly trembling hands that she couldn't quite keep still around her cocoa mug.

'Was there anything to do at Zennor today? The old folks are keeping well enough, I suppose?' she asked now.

Poppy seized on the lead Florrie unknowingly gave her. 'They seem so, but I worry about them sometimes. Their lives seem sort of stagnant. I thought they might like to come to the farm for a visit one day, but I might as well have asked them to go to the moon.'

'There's no moving folk that don't want to be moved,' Florrie said brusquely. 'You do your best for them by visiting once a week as a dutiful daughter should, and if that satisfies them, you should let them be.'

Poppy glanced at her as she gathered up the empty mugs and took them to the scullery, making an unnecessary noise about it.

'Is your mother feeling all right?' she whispered to Sam, aware that Florrie had paid her some sort of compliment.

He shrugged. 'Mother's always a bit offish in October. I daresay you wouldn't have noticed it, seeing as she can often be cantankerous, but it's always the same. It's best to say nothing and let her be, same as with your own folk.'

As far as Poppy was concerned he was talking in riddles, but later, as she lay sleepless beside him in bed, listening to his regular breathing and thinking he was asleep, he suddenly spoke up in the darkness.

'It's to do with that other business I told you about, Poppy. It was in October when it

202

happened. She don't keep on about it, but I know it's still there with her, even after all this time. It comes of being a church-going woman, I daresay. It would probably be easier on her mind if she didn't believe in all that afterlife stuff.'

At first, Poppy couldn't follow what he was talking about, but when he got to the afterlife stuff, she knew he was referring to the baby daughter Florrie had lost all those years ago. Evie, who had died of the whooping cough when she was barely a few weeks old, and wouldn't have had the strength to fight it, no matter how much coal tar was burned beside her cot to try to clear the congestion in her chest and relieve the terrible spasms.

'Was your sister born in October, then?' she asked timidly.

'Born and died.'

'It must have been a terrible time for your mum, and your father too.'

She couldn't help thinking back to how devastated she had felt over the way her sweet little piglet had been savaged by the fox, but she knew that nothing could compare to losing a child. She remembered the odd conversation she had had with Florrie when Henrietta died, and knew that the pain in that stoical woman's heart must be as strong as ever. It was her one weakness, even though she kept it so carefully hidden and under control.

'Ah well, it don't do to dwell on things for ever,' Sam said now. 'You've got to look forward, not back. And it's time we thought about the same, my girl. My father always said a man needs a son to carry on his name, and I'm no different.'

To Poppy's alarm, she felt his hand creeping towards her nightgown and pushing it up none too gently. At any other time, she wouldn't have objected, even if it wasn't Saturday night. A wife didn't refuse when her man wanted to make love, and lately she had begun to enjoy it a lot more. But tonight, after what had happened that afternoon, she just couldn't bear it.

She had got back to the farm later than usual from Zennor, and had only had time for a cursory wash before attending to her duties. She needed to scrub herself properly from that other encounter, and until she did, she would never feel clean again. Until then she couldn't bear for Sam to be where that bastard had been.

She gave a smothered gasp as the word entered her head, and his hand paused on her skin.

'Is summat up?' he said hoarsely.

'I'm sorry Sam. I've got the cramps, and I think my monthlies are starting,' she mumbled, knowing that this would put him off at once. He wasn't religious like his

204

mother, but he had been steeped enough in her bible teachings to believe that lying with a woman while she was in her flow, as Florrie called it, was evil.

He pulled down her nightdress at once and gave her stomach a gentle pat. 'Then you just go to sleep, my lamb, and we'll leave it a few days.'

He turned away from her and was snoring in seconds, while Poppy lay with tears on her cheeks and a sick feeling in her soul, knowing she had never used such a lie before to stave off her husband's love-making. It was a bad thing to do. But not as bad as that other thing.

Jack Trevis had evidently got all the inform-ation he wanted about Chysauster, because the piece about it came out in the paper a week later. There were photos too, and Poppy's face burned as she gazed at the spot where she had lain with him for those few tumultuous minutes. Florrie was scathing of it all.

'The man needs something better to do, if all he can think about is wandering about the countryside taking photos of local places and telling tales about the history of it that we all know perfectly well – or as much as we want to know.'

'I suppose there are some who'd be inter-ested. People who have always lived around here take it for granted that the place exists and probably never even go there,' Poppy murmured, knowing she had to say something.

'Why the hell would anybody want to?' Sam put in. 'It's a godforsaken place now, by all accounts, and only of interest to them from upcountry coming down here to look at we quaint folk,' he finished, heavy with sarcasm.

'Well, when you've done with reading 'em, Sam, the pages can end up in the lav where they belong,' Florrie said.

Sam wasn't listening. He was studying the photos more closely, a frown between his eyes, and without warning, Poppy's heart was thumping again.

'There's summat else here among the ruins. Summat or somebody. Perhaps it's one of they ghosts that folk reckon they see up on the moors at times,' he finished with a snigger.

'Can I see?' Poppy said.

She felt compelled to look, even if the thought terrified her. She couldn't bear to discover that somehow, whether innocently or intentionally, Jack Trevis had captured a corner of her skirt in one of his photos, or perhaps the wheel of her bicycle, or the basket containing the eggs and ham for her parents. He surely couldn't have been so stupid – or so *cruel* – as to let such a photo be published.

'Just there, look. Behind that wall covered in ivy or summat. If that's not a couple of fingers, like part of a small hand, my name's not Sam Lovering. Looks like there was somebody there when he was taking the photo.'

'That's not a hand! It's just a couple of bits of bracken or something,' Poppy said in relief. 'If it was a hand, you can bet Jack Trevis would have made something of it in his article. He'd have started a rumour that there were mining trolls roaming about the moors.'

Florrie snapped at her. 'You should know better than to take notice of those old nonsense tales, Poppy. Though it seems to me you know the working of the newspaper-man's mind a mite well.'

'I don't know it at all! I just think an ambitious man like him wouldn't have wasted a minute in making up stories if he thought he could get away with it.'

She knew she was saying too much, but she couldn't seem to stop herself. Any minute now, these two would start getting suspicious.

She went on shrilly. 'I also think he'd have used a magnifying glass on that photo, and if there was anything that shouldn't have been there, he'd have said so. It's like you said, anything for a story. Anyway, I'm bored with looking at it now.'

'There's no need to get in such a huff, my girl!'

'Leave her be, Mother,' Sam said in a low voice. 'It's her time of the month.'

Poppy went out of the farmhouse, her head held high and her cheeks burning again that he felt obliged to make such an explanation to his mother. It wasn't even true ... but Sam didn't know that, and she was guilty and oddly touched by his clumsy consideration.

She had a difficult week, alternately fighting off feelings of shame at being such a gullible fool as far as Jack Trevis was concerned; and knowing that she had to be strong and get on with living the life she knew.

Late one afternoon, while Sam was stoking a bonfire of farmyard rubbish in the yard, she bundled up all the old film magazines she had kept for so long, and defiantly threw them all into the flames, as if to burn all her foolish dreams.

She knew at once she shouldn't have been so reckless. Not because she didn't want any more reminders of the glossy life she could never hope to have, but because the action had caused a shower of black specks and dust to erupt into the breezy air. The smuts flew straight into her eyes and made them sting like fury. The more she rubbed them, the more painful they became, until angry tears were streaming down her face.

'That was a bloody daft thing to do,' Sam shouted above the roar of the tractor that Len Painter was just bringing into the yard. 'You'd best go inside and ask Mother to get the muck out of your eyes for you.'

'All right,' she choked, turning away from the heat of the bonfire that made her eyes smart all the more.

She went indoors, hardly able to see, and called out for Florrie to see if she could help. The woman tut-tutted at once at the state of her, and made her go to the scullery sink while she bathed Poppy's sore eyes with tepid water until most of the smuts were washed away.

'What on earth were you thinking of to be so close to the bonfire when Sam was burning rubbish? You young girls don't have the sense you were born with these days, and nor does he to let you stand there.'

'It wasn't Sam's fault. It was me,' Poppy said sullenly, feeling now as if she had been wrung out in a mangle as she sat back on a chair, exhausted and shaking.

'What do you mean, it was you?'

The next words came in a torrent. 'I was burning all my old magazines if you must know. I thought you'd be pleased to know about that, since I can't seem to do much else to please you, can I?'

She hated the fact that her eyes were still watery, and she didn't want Florrie to think she was going all soft and weepy because she was being told off – even if that was half the reason.

Florrie was silent for a moment. 'Well, if you've got rid of those heathen things with pictures of young women flaunting themselves half-dressed, perhaps you're growing up a bit after all, so I can't argue with that. Now we'd best have a cup of tea to calm down, and I daresay you'll be feeling a bit under the weather with the other as well.'

For a moment Poppy didn't register what she meant. Then she knew that even if she had fooled Sam for a special reason, she couldn't go on with the charade.

'It wasn't my ... my flow that was troubling me, Mrs Lovering. I must have had an attack of the bellyache for some other reason.'

And please don't ask what that might be...

Florrie's sympathy was diminishing. 'I suppose your mother gave you some of that evil brew she calls her blackberry cordial yesterday. I swear she could poison half the village with the herbs she puts into it.'

'That was probably it, then,' Poppy said, feeling too limp to start defending her mum and her cordial, even though she hadn't tasted a drop. She closed her eyes for a moment, thankful that the worst of the stinging in them had gone, although they still felt very tender and sore.

'You're not a bad girl, Poppy, and I know you think I'm hard on you sometimes,' she heard Florrie say next. 'You can be a bit silly, of course, the way young girls are, but a girl who cares for her family is doing God's work all the same. So drink your tea and stay indoors out of the wind for a while to protect your eyes and let your belly settle down.'

'I think I will,' Poppy said, thinking that miracles must be happening, if she was getting more praise, of a sort, from Sam's mother. It wouldn't last, but it was surprisingly nice when it happened. She sipped her tea gratefully, finding comfort in the warmth that slid through her.

And then she spoiled it all. After living at Lovering's Farm all these years, Poppy should have known when it was best to keep quiet. This was totally the wrong time to be impulsive, or to take advantage of the warm and cosy atmosphere that pervaded the farmhouse while she and Florrie drank their tea and ate a slice of Florrie's sponge cake. But she had never been known for keeping her mouth shut when something was bursting to be said. And said it she did.

'Mrs Lovering, I know it's none of my business, but I wanted you to know that Sam told me in confidence about the baby daughter you lost, and I was so sorry to hear about it, and I can't imagine how awful it must have been for you.'

As Florrie's back stiffened, Poppy knew it had been a bad mistake.

'He had no right to tell you. It's family business.'

'But I'm part of this family now. Sam told you that. I'm his wife, and I'm your daughter-in-law. That's nearly the same as being a daughter, isn't it?'

She could hear herself floundering now, saying it all wrong, and making things worse. She had never intended what she said to be insulting or intrusive, but Florrie clearly took it that way, livid with anger now.

'You're not my daughter, and never will be. I don't have a daughter.'

Poppy jumped to her feet, her own face scarlet. 'Yes, you do! She's in the churchyard with Sam's father. She's called Evie, and how do you think she would feel to know that you never even visit her grave, which I'm sure you don't from the looks of it. But you don't forget when someone dies. You told me that yourself, yet it's as if you've decided to forget that Evie ever existed.'

Next second she felt a resounding slap across her face, and she reeled backwards in shock.

'How dare you speak to me about things you don't understand,' Florrie shouted.

'You think the pathetic feelings you had for that wretched piglet came anywhere close to the desperate feelings a woman has after a baby's death? You don't have the slightest idea how it feels to know real grief that cuts into the heart of you. Now get out of my sight before I do you an injury, girl.'

Poppy fled up the stairs to her bedroom and slammed the door. Her face stung now as badly as her eyes had stung before, and she was still stunned by the fury in her mother-in-law's face. Fury ... and the most raw, agonizing pain she had ever seen in another person. And she had been the one to start it all up.

She lay curled up on her bed like a foetus for a very long time, trying to blot out all her thoughts and to remain perfectly still, until her limbs were stiff and aching. Sam found her there when the afternoon had long gone cold, and it was nearing early evening.

'So there you are. Mother said you still had the belly-ache, love. Are you coming downstairs, or do you want me to fetch you anything?'

It was more than she could take to hear the rough concern in his voice. In an instant she had burst into tears and blurted out all that had gone on between herself and his mother. He rocked her to him until the worst of it had died down, and then he gave her a none-too-gentle shake.

'Didn't I tell you to leave well alone? But you couldn't do that, could you? You had to go reminding her.'

'There was no need to remind her. She never forgets. In fact,' she said, shivering, as if the uneasy thought had just occurred to her, 'I think she sees a reminder of Evie every time she looks at me.'

Sam stared at her. 'I swear you're a mystery to me sometimes, Poppy. What in God's name could you and Evie ever have in common? If she'd lived, she'd be a woman of forty by now.'

'But she'd have been a daughter, probably still living here with her family if she wasn't married with children of her own. I know I'm nothing like that, but I'm still a reminder, a thorn in your mother's flesh, another female in the house, when she never wanted another one after Evie died. She told your gran that, didn't she?'

'I reckon she was a mite deranged at that time, so soon after childbirth,' Sam said, uncomfortable at speaking about such female matters. 'You should never have brought it up, Poppy. I thought you were both getting on better lately.'

'I thought so too. But I suppose I'll have to say I'm sorry, even though I don't think I've done anything wrong. I'm sure it's not healthy to brood on something that happened so long ago, either.'

She realized she was criticizing Florrie now, and waited for another reproach. But it never came. Instead, Sam got off the bed and stumped towards the door.

'I daresay you could be right, but she'll never change. Make your peace with her when the time's right, Poppy, but don't make a meal of it. Let it go, and carry on as before.'

Poppy thought at once that even though he didn't know anything about it, he could almost have been talking about that terrible afternoon at Chysauster.

Let it go, and carry on as before.

There was no reason why she shouldn't do so, providing that bastard had done as he said, and been careful. And when the stomach cramps began for their proper reason a few days later, she breathed a huge sigh of relief. Now, perhaps, she could let it go, as Sam so innocently said, and allow everything to be as it was before. She thought she was also managing to persuade herself that *she* hadn't done anything wrong. The wrong had been done to her. She wasn't to be punished for simply being ignorant of the plausible sweet-talking rogue. If punishment was due, it was to Jack Trevis, not to her.

It wasn't easy to keep convincing herself of those thoughts, but she knew she had to do so if she was to remain sane. It was a secret

215

only known to two people, and she was sure Jack Trevis wasn't going to go around boasting of his conquest, she thought bitterly. His sort wouldn't want to alert the next gullible girl of his slimy intentions.

She gave a huge shuddering sigh as she went out early one morning to gather mushrooms. Because for all her good intentions, she had really imagined herself falling in love with him. It was wrong, and she had known it, but at the time she had been so caught up in the romance of it all ... the silly, tinsel romance of it all ... and she had been persuaded by his easy flattery that he was falling in love with her too. How gullible she had been. And how very stupid to go to his rooms with him.

She imagined that by now he had taken down every one of her photographs, filling the room with those of some other girl, and it was an added humiliation to think he could be inviting her there, turning on his seductive charm to someone else. It was a galling thought, and she vowed that she would never be so stupid again.

There were others about on this early morning, when the mist was still in the air, and the dew was spread like a thin layer of icing sugar on the moors. It was pleasantly cool, and people called out a morning greeting as they, too, gathered mushrooms for breakfasts or stews. Farmers and villagers sent their children out on tasks like these, for there was no danger of them coming to harm, providing they kept well away from the old mine shafts, as Billy Flint had forgotten all those months ago.

She could see him now with several other boys, all dressed warmly and bundled up in scarves and caps in the early morning, shouting and yarning with one another like a gang of little old men.

He caught sight of Poppy across the fields and waved. She was still his heroine then, she thought with a grin as she waved back, even if his father didn't think so. She bent to attend to her work, knowing that Florrie wanted the mushrooms to add to a rabbit pie, when she realized Billy had skimmed across the fields towards her. She straightened her back, glad of a breather.

'You were about early this morning. How many have you picked?' she said by way of greeting.

'I saw you,' he stated, setting down his basket on the grass.

'I saw you too,' Poppy said, smiling. 'You're with the boys from the Johnson farm, aren't you?'

'I mean, I *saw* you,' he repeated.

She looked at him in puzzlement for a moment, and then her heart began to beat in the sickening way it always had as a child when she knew she had done something wrong, and was about to be found out.

'Where did you see me, Billy?' she said quietly, trying to stay calm.

'That spooky place up on the moors. Sometimes other folk go there as well, courting couples mostly, and I keep out of sight then, watching 'em until they go away and leave the place to me. It's my secret den, see? Me dad said I wasn't to go there, 'cos it's full of ghosts and things, but I ain't seen none yet. There's a lot of places to hide up there, and rabbits as well, and if I catch 'em, me dad always gives me a few coppers for 'em.'

He was talking in a disjointed way, but his eyes never moved away from Poppy's face, and she knew instantly that he was speaking about Chysauster. She licked her lips, realizing how dry they had become.

'You should always do as your dad says, Billy, and keep away from such places. You could get into trouble otherwise. Remember what happened with the mine shaft? If I hadn't come along, you could have stayed there for ever with no one to hear you.'

She tried to divert his attention, forcing him to remember how terrified he had been on that day, but he still gave her that unblinking stare.

'I saw you with that bloke,' he said next.

Poppy jumped visibly. 'I don't know what you're talking about, Billy.'

'Yes, you do. That bloke from the paper. You were lying down in that creepy place up on the moors with him.'

If the early morning had been cool before, it was more than the air that was chilling Poppy's bones now. She couldn't speak. She felt as if something was pressing down on her, moving her towards something that was bad and inevitable, all because of her foolishness and her vanity.

Without realizing it, her piercing stare on his face had become as impenetrable as his on hers. She suddenly saw his eyes flicker, and now he was the one to run his tongue around his lips, as he began to gabble.

'Me dad would kill me if he knew I was playing about up there, and he says the spooks will come and get me if I do. They ain't bothered me yet, but if you give me a few coppers to keep me mouth shut I won't say nothing about the other stuff,' he said, his shrill high voice revealing a last attempt at bravado.

Poppy came to life and grabbed his arm, pinching it tight. 'You know what they call people who do what you're doing, don't you?' she hissed.

He gave a howl, and out of the corner of her eye she saw a couple of the other small boys glancing their way. She slackened her grip on his arm a little, but she wasn't done with him yet. She wasn't even started with the little wretch.

'You're a sneak and a bully, Billy Flint, that's what you are,' she snapped, using words he would understand. 'But you're even worse than that, because asking people for money to keep a secret is a wicked thing to do. It's called blackmail. Do you know what that means?'

He shook his head dumbly, his eyes as wide as the mushrooms in the basket he'd kicked over now. Poppy felt really sorry for the kid, but she knew she had to do this to save herself from certain disaster. She lowered her voice to a hoarse whisper, knowing it would frighten him just as much as shouting at him.

'If you blackmail somebody by asking them for money to keep a secret, the police will come after you and you risk being thrown into jail. If that happened, you could stay there and rot for ever, and it would be far, far worse than falling down a mine shaft. Nobody would care what happened to you, because you had committed such a terrible crime. Your family would disown you. You'd never see your father again, nor your mother,' she added, thinking he might not care about not seeing Gus Flint as much as he would miss his mother.

She heard him snivelling now, and she knelt down to his level, ignoring the dampness seeping into her skirt. Shame was sweeping through her at what she was doing to him, but she felt that she had no option. She had to go on. She put her arms around him, encircling him inside them, her voice softening now.

'Billy, do you remember the very special thing about us that was said when I rescued you from the mine shaft?'

He shook his head.

'It's that you owed me your life, remember? A little bit of you will always belong to me now because I saved you from a horrible death. We have a special bond between us that makes us closer than ordinary friends, Billy, and friends don't do bad things to one another, do they?'

He looked at her, the colour slowly coming back to his pale face. 'You mean I should never tell what I saw, or ask you for money.'

'That's right. I always thought you were a fair boy, Billy, and that's fair, isn't it? You should never ask people for money, but because I'm your friend I'll give you some of my mushrooms, as you seem to have spilled most of yours.'

He looked down at the basket he'd dropped on the ground, realizing he had stepped on half of them and squashed them to a pulp. He knew his dad would leather him if he went home with nothing, so he wiped his sleeve across his nose and sniffed noisily.

'I never saw nothing, anyway. I just heard you and that bloke arguing over summat. I ran away then, in case he saw me.'

Poppy could have hit him. The little toe-rag, trying it on all this time, and scaring her half to death at what he might have seen and what he might say. Instead, she hugged him for a second, forcing a laugh.

'Well, now we're friends again, aren't we? Here, take these mushrooms and get back to your friends, and tell your mother to send you to the farm whenever she needs some eggs.'

She said it as a pacifier, handing over her mushrooms quickly, wanting to get away from him while her legs still felt able to hold her up. What a fright that had been, and how dangerously near she had come to having her sordid secret exposed.

As she left Billy and turned back towards the farm, she picked as many mushrooms as she could, to allay Florrie's annoyance. Her thoughts were in turmoil, realizing again how easy it was to let feelings overtake common sense. And of course, it must have been Billy Flint's small fingers in the photo after all, and even if Jack had recognized them as such, he probably wouldn't have cared, she thought bitterly.

It made her think soberly all the way home. Blackmail was an ugly word with an ugly meaning. Shirley Bosinney had once asked her if she had blackmail in mind. At the time Poppy remembered thinking what an odd remark it had been. Now, as the jitters began to leave her, she wondered if she should have dug a little bit deeper into Shirley's remark. Didn't people who thought they were being blackmailed usually have something to hide?

Poppy's thoughts skittered on, and the one that kept on returning was a line that had always charmed her in one of the old school books that the class at Zennor infants' school had had read to them.

It was curiouser and curiouser, as Alice would have said.

Chapter Eleven

Carrie Pollard enjoyed the occasional day in Penzance while her mother and aunt took care of Walter, to their mutual pleasure. Carrie knew the town of old, having once worked in the library there, and she usually made a point of looking up her old colleagues. She also frequently called on her friend Shirley Bosinney, especially now that Shirley was expecting.

On that particular Friday she was hesitating about visiting her too early, remembering the need to put her feet up for a short nap in the early afternoon when she was expecting Walter. She decided to while away a bit of time in a tea room and have a pot of tea, a scone and a dollop of Cornish cream.

When she had given her order, she became aware that someone in a corner table was glancing her way. For a moment Carrie couldn't think where she had seen the slim, young girl with the rich, dark hair before. Then the girl smiled slightly, and Carrie remembered.

'It's Poppy, isn't it? From Lovering's Farm?'

Poppy nodded. She had recognized the other girl at once, if only because she had been mildly and ridiculously jealous of her that day at the fair, when she had seen what close friends Carrie and Shirley were.

'Why don't you come and join me?' Carrie invited. 'Bring your tea to my table, unless you're waiting for someone?'

There was no reason to flinch at the words, Poppy thought. No reason at all to think there could be some hidden meaning in them, as if this very attractive young woman, some years older than herself, was hinting that Poppy might be here for a clandestine meeting with someone.

It would be a man, of course. A man like Jack Trevis, who went in for such meetings, and then, when it suited him, dropped his conquests as if they were hot potatoes.

Her tea cup rattled in its saucer, her hand trembling slightly as she took it over to Carrie's table. She wouldn't mind betting that this girl had never had a clandestine meeting in her life. She looked the sort who would never stray. The sort Poppy had always believed herself to be, until that chance encounter with Billy Flint, which was the start of a crazy chain of events that had turned her life upside down.

'Are you feeling all right, Poppy? You look paler than the last time I saw you. And by the way, I don't think I ever thanked your husband enough for the way he looked after Walter that day at your farm. He was so sweet with him.'

She spoke easily, drawing Poppy in, making conversation and ignoring the dark shadows beneath the girl's lovely eyes that made her look as if she hadn't been sleeping properly. She saw the tinge of colour in Poppy's cheeks then as she began to relax, and Carrie could see at once how that newspaper chap had got the best out of her for his photographs.

'I've never heard Sam called sweet before,' she said with a grin, 'but I suppose you're right. He has a way with small things, children as well as animals.'

'I could see that.' Carrie paused as her pot of tea and scone were brought to the table. 'You'll be wanting a small thing of your own soon, I daresay,' she said.

Poppy looked blank for a moment, and then blushed more furiously. 'Oh, you mean a baby. Well, these things happen in God's good time, don't they?' she said awkwardly, and then she fumed at sounding so dippy, when such comments were more often in Florrie's mouth than hers.

'I can see how Shirley would have liked you, Poppy. I'm afraid she got ragged rather a lot about such remarks in the old days when she scooted off to church to make confession about the daftest things.'

And the worst things too, Carrie added silently, wishing they had never got on to this tack at all, even though she had been the one to begin it. She ate her scone and drank her tea, glad that the little tea room was bustling with people now.

'Are you going to see Shirley today?' Poppy said. 'I sometimes go there on Fridays, but I've come here today to buy some material to make a frock.'

'I'm sure she'd love to see you, and we could go together if you like.'

Carrie didn't really know why she was encouraging this meeting to continue, except that the girl looked somehow lost. And Carrie couldn't help remembering how she and three close friends had supported one another so much during the war years – and afterwards – and she felt an odd sympathy for this girl who seemed to have no confidantes of her own, according to Shirley.

'Well, if you're sure,' Poppy said. 'I do have quite a while to wait for my bus back to Barras.'

It hadn't been her intention to see Shirley today. She was still afraid she might blurt out all that was still troubling her, but with Carrie Pollard there as well, it was hardly likely that any conversation would get so personal.

As it happened, the discussion was mostly about babies. Shirley was showing now, bemoaning the fact that already none of her clothes fitted properly, and that she felt as huge as a whale, even though to Poppy she looked blooming and exceptionally pretty.

'You wait a few more months,' Carrie told her with a laugh. 'Remember how big I was with Walter? I could hardly waddle through the door of the cottage by the time he was born. And Velma was like a beached whale too. I never saw anyone grow so large in the last couple of months.'

They were shutting Poppy out, however unintentionally. They were part of a secret club she didn't know, and couldn't enter. It wasn't their fault. Poppy presumed she would be eligible to join once she too had a baby. The thought brought on a wave of envy. She had often dreamed of having a baby of her own, but it had always been because she felt there wasn't enough love in her life, and she knew that a baby's love would be unconditional. Now, she realized how, imperceptibly, the feelings had changed. She wanted a baby because it would be a part of herself and Sam, the often dour, uncommunicative farmer who seemed to have changed recently as subtly as she herself had changed. She did love him, more than she had ever believed she did. And perhaps it had taken that episode with Jack Trevis to show her his true worth after all...

'Come back to us from wherever you've gone, Poppy,' Shirley was saying with a laugh. 'I've just asked if you and Carrie want to see the baby's room.'

'Sorry, yes, of course I do!' she gasped, flustered. 'I was miles away then, off with the fairies again, as my mother-in-law is always telling me.'

'And how is the dear old bat?' Shirley could always be irreverent when she chose. 'Is she as strict on you as ever?'

'Oh, well, I suppose she means well.'

'Cripes, you're being generous, aren't you?' Shirley was dryly mocking now. 'When we worked on the farm during the war it was as much as she could do to be civil to me and the other girls half the time. I'm sure she thought we were dead set on corrupting her precious son – no offence,

Poppy – especially the girls from the big city with their smart talk.'

'You have to remember how much she ruled the roost until you all descended on the farm,' Poppy said, hardly knowing why she was going out of her way to defend Florrie, when heaven knew she'd been slated by her enough times in the past.

But Poppy knew things about Florrie now that none of those girls had ever known, and just as her feelings for Sam had grown, so had a little more understanding of her mother-in-law. Sometimes the only way to keep your feelings in check was to build a shell around yourself, and that was what Florrie had done ever since her baby Evie had died. By the time they were in the middle of a war and her world had been invaded by bright young things, she probably didn't know any other way to behave.

'So, are we going to see this baby's room or not?' Carrie put in, seeing the other two apparently lost in thought and almost glaring at one another. 'I have to get back soon, Shirley.'

'So do I. I daren't miss the bus back to Barras, or Mrs Lovering will really be on my tail,' Poppy added quickly.

She shivered as she spoke, remembering the time she'd missed the bus and gone to Jack Trevis's rooms with him. Remembering that first kiss, so sweet and chaste in comparison with other kisses, yet sending such a surge of unexpected sensation shooting through her that she had really believed it was the beginning of falling in love.

'Well, if you're sure you can spare five minutes, I'll show you how Bernard's painted the baby's room and put up a frieze of cartoon animals all around the ceiling.'

Shirley sounded cross and mildly sarcastic now, and the other two both knew how quickly she could take offence. But once in the little room made ready for the baby's occupation so well in advance, they both admired the work that Bernard had done, and Shirley's face resumed its usual smile.

'I've even done a small pile of knitting already,' Shirley said proudly. 'I was never as good as the rest of you in Penhallow, but I'm getting better at it.'

'The difference is that you were knitting for soldiers' comforts then. They were people you were never likely to know, and now you're knitting for a special little someone of your own,' Carrie reminded her.

'I am, aren't I?' Shirley said happily, opening a drawer with a flourish and producing several matinee coats and sets of bootees, all in virginal white, and as tiny as though they were made for a doll.

'Can I knit you something, Shirley?' Poppy asked suddenly.

'Of course you can, love! All contributions

gratefully received and all that!'

'I'll get some patterns and wool before I catch the bus home, then. I hadn't thought of it before, but it'll give me something to do, and I'm sure Mrs Lovering will prefer it to me idling away my evenings, as she calls it.'

But by the time she left the house, leaving the two old friends together, she was having second thoughts about it. She'd rushed in with the offer, charmed by the thought, without really thinking it through. But how would Sam's mother feel, seeing her knitting little garments for a baby and watching them come to life right under her nose? Would it be turning the screw on the secret she had kept buried for so long, and which three people now shared? Presumably there might be older folk in the village who knew about it at the time, but it was all such a long time ago now, and a tragedy only really affected those most deeply involved in it.

No, she'd better wait awhile before she did any knitting for Shirley. She wasn't going to change her mind about a child of her own though, Poppy thought resolutely. Sam wanted a son, and she too wanted a baby. Even Florrie had hinted more than once that it was time she did her duty and produced a child – meaning a son, of course.

So if, and when, it happened, Poppy

would be knitting and sewing for her own baby, and Florrie would have to put up with it then. In any case, it would be her grand-child, so she might even soften enough to make some of the small garments herself. Although somehow Poppy couldn't imagine those broad, gnarled fingers, more used to dealing with farm work, knitting delicate clothes for a baby.

But you never knew. You never really knew people at all, at least, not the heart and soul of them. They always kept something hidden. Didn't Poppy herself know that all too well?

Shirley and Carrie were quiet for a few minutes after Poppy left, and then Shirley, impulsive as always, found herself saying what she had never intended to say. 'I think Poppy's a bit troubled. That reporter took more of a shine to her than she had expected. Well, let's face it, with only Sam Lovering as a yardstick, I suppose any good-looking chap who took an interest in her would be enough to dazzle her, wouldn't he?'

'Well, as long as he hasn't been chasing her, I'm sure she's a sensible enough girl to keep her feet on the ground.'

Shirley gave a small shrug, already wishing she could learn to keep her mouth shut. She didn't want to give away any confidences, and Carrie and her other close friends in Penhallow had been the most loyal friends anyone could ever wish for when she had found herself in trouble. But Poppy had involved her, and she knew exactly how it felt to be so carried away.

Suddenly all the best-forgotten feelings, those wonderful, forbidden, delicious feelings, came rushing back to her and she was no longer sitting in her own pristine living-room with Carrie. She was wrapped in her lover's arms, sweet-talking GI Hank whom she was so crazy about. She was breathing in the scented night air on the soft sands of Marazion, and listening to the swish of the waves rippling on the shore. They didn't crash and roar, the way they did in Hollywood movies, they simply soared back and forth from the beach in sensuous movements that echoed the movements of Hank's fabulous body filling hers...

The passion was so real, so ecstatically intense, that it could surely never end. But end it did, when the GIs suddenly disappeared from the area, and the girls who had loved them too well were left behind with only memories, and sometimes more than memories.

'Shirley, I'll have to go. It's been lovely to see you again, but there's a limit to how long my mother and Aunt Phyllis can stand Walter's antics, however much they love him.'

Shirley jumped at the sound of Carrie's practical voice. They had always called her that. Carrie, the practical one, while she, Shirley, had been the foolish, reckless one, who had nearly ruined her life by loving too well. She had always fancied herself as having a sixth sense, but when Carrie spoke again, it seemed that she was the one with it now.

'We should all learn to let the past go,' Carrie said softly. 'Whatever memories Poppy Lovering's situation stirs up, just think of how much you're looking forward to your baby.'

She didn't add *yours and Bernard's baby*, but she didn't need to. They both knew exactly what she meant, and in a moment they were hugging one another as Carrie prepared to leave.

'But you do understand, don't you, Carrie?' Her voice was husky now, ashamed to think that even for a moment, she had remembered so vividly the passion between herself and Hank, and how disloyal it had been to Bernard who had been suffering somewhere in France.

'Of course I do,' Carrie said, even though the understanding was entirely hypo-thetical, since never for a second could she ever have contemplated being unfaithful to Archie while he was a POW. But you didn't judge your friends. You loved them and supported them, and if this Poppy was in need of Shirley's support now, she knew Shirley would give it unstintingly.

Poppy had a few calls to make before she reached the bus stop, and she was almost afraid to stand there for too long, in case a certain motor car came along. It would be even worse if it stopped beside her. She couldn't help being jittery every time she thought about Jack now. She was no longer besotted by him, if that was the correct word to use, and it shamed her to think she had been so gullible as to be taken in by him. She wasn't the first to be used by a good-looking chap, nor the first to be used by *him*, she thought, but that didn't make it any better.

She almost wished she had his gift of the gab, as Sam would call it, and could send in a letter to the readers' page of the newspaper to warn other women.

And how stupid would that be! Even if she didn't give her name and signed it 'anonymous' there wouldn't be much doubt in people's minds who had given the information, especially as the newspaper demanded a real name and address, even if it wasn't for publication. They might even expose her in defence of their reporter. Imagine that! Poppy Lovering, farmer's wife, and sometime heroine, writing to a newspaper to denounce one of their star reporters as a lecher and a rogue.

Her thoughts rambled on, because it wouldn't be simply a case of getting a small piece of revenge. It would be a terrible humiliation for Sam. For all his faults, and Poppy admitted that he didn't have many, he was a good man and a good husband. His mother would disown her too. The idea came and went as swiftly as blinking.

Out of the corner of her eye she saw someone approaching the bus stop, and turned with guilty relief to greet one of Florrie Lovering's friends. Even if Jack Trevis was cruising around the town in his car now, he'd never stop to speak to her if she was in the company of this stout countrywoman.

'So what have you been up to in town today, Poppy?' the woman puffed.

'I've been visiting an old friend, Mrs Dyer, and buying some material to make a new frock,' she said at once, thankful that she'd finally got around to doing what she had come for.

'That's nice,' the woman said comfortably. 'I'm sure Florrie's pleased to know that Sam found himself a thrifty wife as well as a pretty one.'

But not so pleased if she knew that he'd got an unfaithful one.

Florrie's sewing-machine was a grinding old

Singer treadle that could be temperamental, but she didn't mind Poppy using it, providing she tidied everything away afterwards, and did a bit of dusting to get rid of the cotton fluff. In any case, Poppy intended to wait until Florrie went out to one of her evening meetings before she cut out the material for the new frock and started on the noisy machine.

'It's nice to be indoors on our own sometimes, isn't it, Sam?' she asked, glancing at him reading the newspaper as she spread out the pattern pieces on the table. 'Not that I mean anything by it,' she added hastily, in case he thought she was criticizing his mother. 'It's just, well, cosier somehow.'

He gave a chuckle. 'I know what you mean, girl. Two's company, three's a crowd, and Mother does go on a bit about things sometimes. But she means well.'

'Oh, I know she does.' Hadn't she said so herself?

Poppy wondered briefly if it would be a suitable inscription to put on Florrie's tombstone. *She meant well ...* and immediately had to stifle a fit of the giggles.

'What's got you so tickled now?' Sam said with a smile.

'Nothing. It's probably the cotton dust getting up my nose,' she said, choking at the thought of how indignant Florrie would be to think Poppy was even contemplating her tombstone. From the way she carried on, and her hardiness, she'd be good for many more years yet. And not for a second was Poppy going to let such a thought depress her. It was evident to anyone though, that this farm was still very much Florrie Lovering's domain, and every married woman deserved to be mistress in her own home. It wasn't a thought that troubled Poppy very often, but it was always more in her mind whenever she had visited Shirley Bosinney in her neat little house. Shirley was so lucky, she thought wistfully. All that, and a baby on the way.

She put the scissors down. A thought was filling her head, and her heart was starting to thump, but after all, this was her home too, and she and Sam didn't have that many evenings to themselves. A married couple in their own home had a right to do whatever they liked, and whenever they liked.

'Sam, why don't we go to bed early tonight?'

He didn't look up from his newspaper. 'Don't be daft, woman. It's only seven o'clock, and I haven't finished the paper yet. You can't leave this stuff all over the table for Mum to carry on about. Besides, what would the neighbours think?' he said, with a heavy attempt at a joke.

But Poppy wasn't joking. 'I just thought we could have an early night. I didn't say I

238

was tired, Sam.'

Short of saying she fancied him making mad, passionate love to her, she didn't know how much plainer she could be. And she wasn't going to say anything like that. He'd be shocked – and she'd be tongue-tied before she got the words out.

Her meaning suddenly registered. He put the newspaper down and his face relaxed into a smile. He really was quite good-looking when he smiled like that, in a rugged, outdoor sort of way, Poppy thought fleetingly.

'Well, if you're not tired, and I'm not tired, there's only one thing to do about it, isn't there, you saucy maid?'

And since she was sure it would be the usual kind of lovemaking that wouldn't take the entire evening, she thought prosaically, she could always come downstairs later and clear away the sewing stuff. Right now she was bemused by the fact that he was holding out his hand to her and chuckling beneath his breath as if he was really taken by the fact that she had taken the initiative for once. As if the thought that they would be doing it before proper bedtime was unexpectedly exciting him – and her too, Poppy realized as they went upstairs.

'No point in pulling the curtains, is there?' Sam was saying, already unbuttoning his trousers and hopping about on one leg as he tried to pull them over his boots. Poppy resisted a giggle and turned away to unfasten her blouse with trembling hands. What happened between them now was going to be very important to them both. She didn't know why, or how, she just knew it.

'There's no need to turn your back on me, girl,' she heard him say more gruffly, and then he was turning her towards him, pulling her into him as her blouse was discarded. She felt the naked flesh of his chest against her breasts, and a searing excitement flowed through her at the warmth of his touch.

She still wore her skirt and under-garments, but they both found themselves tugging at them urgently now. Moments later they were standing, locked in an embrace that was shiveringly sensual, until he pushed her gently on to the bed, his body enveloping hers.

'Oh Sam,' she breathed, her arms clasped around his neck. 'I do ... I do—'

'And so do I, girl, but we didn't come up here for talking, did we?'

It might have been like a dash of cold water in her face, but somehow it wasn't. Somehow there was humour in his voice, and a matching need for laughter in her soul. They didn't bother with what Sam called the waiting time, and nor was there any need, because she was so ready for him, so wanting him...

She felt him forge into her, and she gasped at the sheer joy of it. Lovemaking had almost always been done in the dark until now, so she had rarely seen his face as they made love, nor thrilled to the gleam of desire in his eyes. She held on to his powerful shoulders as he bent to kiss her mouth and her breasts, pulling her ever closer into himself until she heard his shuddering groan of fulfilment, and knew the same rush of pleasure within herself.

He lay heavily on her for a few moments, not yet leaving her, and she could feel the rapid beat of his heart against hers before it began to slow down.

'Well, if that bit o' loving don't produce a babby, I don't know what will,' he said, the practical words whispered hoarsely against her throat.

She felt a wild urge to giggle again, and she could only put down such a wondrous carefree feeling to losing all her inhibitions in a way she had never done before.

The thought flashed through her mind that she should probably be shocked at his remark, and by the way she had behaved like a wanton too, but she wasn't. Nor did she feel used or affronted. A baby was what they both wanted, and impulsively she wrapped her legs around him, still holding him tight.

Sam disentangled himself reluctantly.

'You'd best stop your clinging, sweetheart, or you'll have me stirring again and a man needs a little while to get himself together after that little lot,' he said, laughing.

She laughed back, glorying in such intimate, earthy moments, as well as hearing him call her sweetheart, which he so rarely did. These things could never have happened if Florrie was in the house, not even late at night, when there would be the risk of a creaking bed or a few groans that neither of them could suppress.

This had been the best idea on her part, she thought jubilantly, and she hoped, oh, God yes, she *really* hoped, that a baby would be the result of it.

'Come on, wench,' he said next, slapping her on the rump. 'We can't stay here all night, much as I've a mind to. Mother will be back in an hour, and she'll be wanting to see what progress you've made with your sewing.'

By the time Florrie returned from her meeting, Poppy had cleared away all the paper pattern pieces and was tacking together the material parts of the bodice of her frock. The warm material was in shades of muted green – 'nature's colour', as Sam called it.

'You haven't done very much to it,' Florrie complained. 'I'd have got the thing half-made by now. What on earth have you been doing all evening?' she went on suspiciously.

Poppy didn't dare look at Sam, but she didn't need to. She knew that his shoulders would be heaving, just as hers were. She put the sewing down and fled to the scullery, leaving Sam to say whatever he chose. She gasped that she'd make Florrie a nice cup of cocoa, knowing she'd be parched from so much talking with her women friends.

Only then, with the door pushed shut between them, did she let out a howl of laughter, and spent the next few minutes trying desperately to hide it with a hefty bout of coughing.

Chapter Twelve

Jack Trevis was feeling decidedly restless again. He recognized the signs. Right from the start he had wondered how long he would be satisfied with living down here in the sticks where nothing ever happened. Penzance might be a thriving town compared with the villages and hamlets in the more remote areas of Cornwall, but it didn't have the excitement and energy of London. He always knew London was where he intended to make his mark in the newspaper business. Next year would be a very good time too, with all this talk of the Festival of Britain. A chap could make his mark reporting details of the rich and famous who attended the various events, maybe even working his way up to being a court reporter.

As his breath caught on an involuntary cough, he scowled. For all his good looks, he had always been prone to an annoying minor chest complaint. It flared up occasionally, and it had stopped him joining up during the war. At that time, he'd pictured himself as a dashing war correspondent in uniform, finding fame and fortune as a result of his dazzling special reports from behind enemy lines. He imagined hearing his voice on the wireless and seeing himself on one of the Pathe News Reports in local cinemas.

Jack was nothing if not self-confident about his abilities. Some said arrogant. And more than once he'd clashed with his current editor who wanted to hog-tie him now to these damn features about local antiquities. They had been intriguing at first, but as the months wore on towards the end of the year, he was already bored with them. Very soon now, he'd be looking for pastures new. Even the delights of Poppy Lovering had quickly palled. She had been a challenge, but there were plenty of pretty girls in the world, and Jack had every intention of taking his fill of them.

Winter was generally mild in Cornwall. It was only on rare occasions, such as the terrible winter of 1947, when the ground had been as solid as rock, the sky filled with snow, and cattle and other livestock had found it difficult to graze. Then, local folk were startled out of their complacency from living in the mild tail-end of the country, and forced to shiver in their shoes like the rest of the country. In normal years, even Christmas was pleasant in the far southwest, and already the promise of an early spring could be seen as the first delicate snowdrops appeared in the hedgerows, and trees began to lose their gaunt looks as they welcomed a pale sun. Misty mornings, when trees and shrubs were spangled with dew, turned fields and moors into a kind of fairyland and could soon give way to bright days. Then, it was only the old codgers who were buttoned up to their necks, muffled into scarves and woolly hats, constantly grumbling that things weren't the same as they used to be, the way old codgers did.

Poppy had to admit that her parents were more than typical of all the old codgers she knew. They rarely left their thatched cottage except when her dad went to collect driftwood, of which there was never a shortage for their constantly burning fire. She always had to take a good few deep breaths before she went inside the cottage, letting the air out slowly and gradually getting used to the muggy atmosphere indoors. Sometimes she wondered how they could breathe in it at all. Sam had told her long ago that they must both have lungs made of iron, and a damn good constitution to survive the way they did.

Poppy thought wistfully that it would be nice if they would come to the farm for their Christmas dinner, just once, to make it a real family occasion. But she knew it was pointless to ask them. As always, her mother would slow-roast the small chicken that a neighbour always killed for them. Other than that, there would be no trimmings, no festivities. It would be just another day.

It was not so very different from what went on at the farm, really. Farming didn't stop, no matter what the weather or the season. Cows had to be milked, pigs and chickens had to be fed, eggs collected. At least Sam always brought a small tree indoors to decorate with fir cones and bits of tinsel left over from the previous year. And no matter what Florrie said about the evils of drink, they got out the bottle of port and drank a toast to the king after dinner while they listened to his halting words on the wireless during the afternoon. But too much frivolity at a time when folk should be celebrating Our Lord's birth would be frowned upon as heathen by Sam's mother.

'Are you visiting them at Zennor today?' Florrie asked Poppy a couple of weeks before Christmas.

Poppy nodded. 'I wondered if I could take them some extra bits and pieces, Mrs Lovering. A bit of butter, perhaps, and one of your special seed cakes from the larder. Would that be all right? They don't have much.'

To her surprise, Florrie's eyes softened. 'Of course you can. It's good to know you think so much about the poor old dabs, so go this morning if you like. You're a good daughter, Poppy.'

It was the second time Sam's mother had said something of the kind recently, and Poppy felt her face flush at the unexpected compliment. She wasn't asking for the treats to find favour with her mother-in-law, but it certainly made life easier for all of them when they were living in harmony. Letting her off her morning chores was something to be thankful for too.

Florrie's voice became brisk, not wanting to show any hint of emotion in the words, but they caught Poppy unawares, especially since she was still harbouring such guilt over Jack Trevis.

'I don't say this often, but you're a good wife to our Sam, too. I didn't expect it to turn out as well as it has, but I reckon he could have done a lot worse.'

'Me and Sam are all right, Mrs Lovering.'

'So you are, now all that other business is over and done with. I never did hold with a young, married woman having her head turned by such nonsense.'

Sometimes Poppy wondered if she was a mind-reader.

She spoke quickly. 'You know, I didn't ask for all the attention, and if it hadn't been for me, who knows how Billy Flint might have ended up!'

'Oh, well, as long as you remember where your loyalties lie now, I daresay there's no harm done.'

Poppy didn't like this turn in the conversation; it was creepy and uncanny. It was getting to the heart of her, stabbing her conscience again, even though she was perfectly sure Florrie had no idea of the real circumstances. If she had... Poppy shivered. If she had any inkling of what had happened that day on the moors at Chysauster village, she'd have demanded that Sam threw Poppy out as a slut and a hussy. And it would have broken Sam's heart. He might not be able to show his feelings the way other men did, but that didn't mean he didn't have them, and she knew that Sam's feelings for his wife were as deep as any man's.

Anyway, Florrie needn't have worried. Poppy never wanted to see Jack Trevis again as long as she lived – and she was quite sure he wouldn't want to see her, she thought bitterly. He was like one of the worst villains at the flicks, the type who could fill a girl's head with flattery, have his fill of her and then disappear, much like those Yanks had been during the war, with the girls who'd been left with babies in their bellies and the shame of it all.

Except that Jack Trevis hadn't disappeared, and Poppy fervently wished that he would, instead of having to read his words in the newspaper every week. Now that Sam knew who he was, he never missed reading bits out to her and Florrie, with both of them scoffing at some of the things he wrote.

She stirred herself as Florrie came back with one of her seed cakes wrapped in greaseproof and brown paper. 'Here you are then, girl. As well as the usual, you can take a couple of extra eggs for the old folks too. They need plenty of nourishment at their age.'

Poppy went upstairs to get ready, thinking she couldn't get away quickly enough. It wasn't just the unhealthy atmosphere inside her parents' cottage that stifled her. For some reason, she felt stifled by the farmhouse today, as if the whole world was somehow pressing down on her. It was a feeling she couldn't shake off, the kind of feeling you had when a thunderstorm was threatening, oppressive and uneasy, when the birds stopped singing and the animals were still. Waiting, just waiting.

It was stupid to think that way for no reason, Poppy told herself a while later. She called out goodbye to Sam, who was working in the barn with Len Painter, and Dog yapping at his heels as usual. Cycling through Barras, she tried to put the feelings of unease behind her as people said hello to her, commenting on what a fine morning it was for mid-December. Once through the village she struck out across the moors, her laden basket at the front of her bicycle.

The sky was bright enough in the village, but the mist still hung about on the moors in patches, and with her countrywoman's knowledge, Poppy guessed that by nightfall there would probably be a frost that lingered until morning. She had always loved frosty mornings when the ground crunched beneath her feet as she went about her daily duties. She had reached the high part of the moors when she realized how hard she had been pedalling and she paused to take a breather.

Below her now she could see the Zennor rooftops, some thatched, some slate-covered, the village dominated by the church. Spirals of smoke from every cottage chimney soared up to the sky, drawn upwards by the crisp, still morning air. The Penfold cottage was wreathed in smoke this morning, and Poppy guessed that her dad had been stoking up the fire as vigorously as ever, before he and her mum settled down in their armchairs again for a morning snooze.

Then Poppy felt her heart begin to pound. There was surely far too much smoke to be coming from a single chimney. She was still some distance away, but she could hardly distinguish the smoke from the sky. She fancied she could hear shouting, but it must be all in her head, for there was no sound up here on the moors at all today, not even the rustle of ferns. She got back on her bicycle, feeling an overpowering need to check that the old people were all right, to reassure herself that it was only her imagination that was driving her on.

She was about halfway down the slope towards the cottage when she saw people running towards it, shouting and waving their arms frantically. Poppy could taste the smoke now, acrid and sour and filling the air with the smell of death. And then, as if someone had set a bomb beneath it, the entire place exploded. Scalding orange flames leapt skywards as the inferno enveloped the cottage, raging through it in an instant and devouring everything in it.

Poppy heard herself screaming. Without thinking, she flung the bicycle away from her, the basket spilling and the eggs rolling and smashing down the hillside. She could hardly breathe for the terror in her heart. She was scrabbling over the stony ground, sobbing hysterically as she rushed down the slope. When she reached the burning cottage the fierce heat and the strong arms of the villagers at the scene forced her back as she would have rushed recklessly inside to find her parents.

'There's no use you trying to save 'em, girl, they'd have been gone long afore the flames got to 'em,' someone shouted harshly in her ear.

Others who had known the family all their lives were shrieking hoarsely. 'They'd have suffocated from the smoke. There was nothing a body could do to save 'em, the poor buggers.'

'They never threw stuff away, and Vicar always warned 'em that thatch was going to go up like a tinder-box one of these days.'

''Tis the devil's work all right.'

On and on they went, these so-wise-after-the-event know-it-alls, and Poppy found herself screaming back. 'Shut up, God damn you! They're my parents you're talking about. Why won't somebody put out the fire?'

Even as she spoke, she knew it was futile to try. There was no fire station here, no-one with real knowledge of what to do. The thatch on the roof was old and desert-dry.

Her dad had always refused to have it renewed, saying it was good enough to outlast him. He hadn't expected it to take him and her mum with it, though, Poppy thought, near-crazy with grief and shock.

Old neighbours were trying to drag her away. People were feeling the effects of the heat themselves. It was as searing and painful on their skins as a blast furnace. Poppy felt it too. But how much more did her parents feel it? Or had they even felt it at all? Had they still been dozing in those bloody awful old armchairs and just allowed the insidious smoke to take them before they burned?

Everyone was talking at once now. Trying to make decisions. Thinking what was to be done, while it was clear there was nothing to be done. No amount of water thrown on to this raging inferno was going to stop it, even though a few diehards were attempting it now with buckets brought up from the nearest cottages.

Poppy was being held tight in someone's arms. She was as limp as lettuce, letting the world sway around her while her whole self was filled with anguish. She had already felt the hot, shameful gush of pee running down her legs as her muscles had involuntarily relaxed and her innards seemed to melt with the shock of it all. She prayed that no-one noticed her humiliation, and in the same instance wondered why she should even care if they did. This whole community had always thought the Penfolds an odd family, outsiders. There was no reason for them to think differently about the last of them now that the old ones had gone up in flames.

The vicar had arrived among them, panting and red-faced as he reached the swiftly-burning cottage and prepared to do his saintly duty. Now that the first terrible shock was diminishing the tiniest fraction, Poppy couldn't help the blasphemous thoughts entering her head about all the Good Works that would be going on around her now. But what good could the vicar do? And where was God while two of his lambs had burned to death?

'This is a terrible day, my dear, and we will all pray for your dear parents.'

Poppy let out her breath and found herself screaming furiously at the vicar.

'Is that right? I suppose you're going to tell me next that this was God's will, are you? As if He even *cared* about two old people who never did any harm to anyone, except to scare a few young 'uns because of the way they looked.'

She was railing at a man of the cloth, and she didn't bloody well care. She didn't care about the horrified faces all around her, or the mutterings that it was the shock coming out and she didn't know what she was saying, when she knew damn well what she was saying. Just as she knew there'd soon be a few other choice remarks as well. The Penfolds had always been a queer lot, boiling their herbs and keeping themselves to themselves, and the daughter was probably no different. Instead of being belligerent, they expected her to be pliant and grateful, and she wasn't behaving in the docile way they wanted.

'We must get the poor girl to the village hall and get her some strong tea, and possibly a drop of medicinal brandy,' the vicar declared, as if he was well used to such outpourings from a deranged female. 'The husband must be told what's happened as soon as possible, and I suggest that some of you men get on over to Barras and fetch him.'

He spoke with a certain meaning in his voice, as if to alert those around him that although Zennor would see to the poor girl for as long as necessary, the sooner the husband took charge of his wife and took her home, the sooner they could all get back about their own business.

Several men took off at a sprint, no doubt not sorry to get away from the scene of the disaster. Poppy was as pliant as they could wish for now, weeping silently and being comforted by the villagers. Others were still flinging buckets of water on to the burning cottage, but it only served to send fiery sparks high into the sky, the dry thatch cracking like whips as if in some bizarre firework display.

'Come away, my dear.' One of the village women soothed Poppy. 'There's nothing you can do here. Let's go and get that strong tea so you can calm yourself a little. Once your hubby gets here, you'll both be wanting to speak to the vicar later.'

'What for?' Poppy said dully.

'Why the burying arrangements, of course,' the woman said uncomfortably.

Stumbling a little over the rough ground, and trying to keep her legs tightly together to try to ignore their wet discomfort, Poppy stared at her as if she was stupid. It wasn't the time for levity, and nor had she ever felt less like it, but the most inane thoughts were spinning through her mind now.

'What's left of them to bury? We won't need coffins, will we? We could stuff them both into a couple of match-boxes and they'd never know the difference!'

The woman looked totally scandalized at such words, and when Poppy began laughing hysterically, she squeezed the girl's shaking shoulders more firmly.

'Now then, my dear, we don't want to hear that sort of talk, do we? Your dear parents might have gone to their Maker in unfortunate circumstances, but they still deserve a proper send-off. It's the custom.'

'Oh well, we mustn't deprive folk of the custom, must we?'

But for the life of her, Poppy still couldn't imagine stuffing a load of smouldering ashes into two coffins and trying to pretend that her mum and dad were inside while the vicar said solemn words over them.

In the village hall, they made her drink tea that was too hot and too strong, and made even more bitter by the addition of what the vicar called medicinal brandy. She was surrounded by people. She felt dirty and sick. The hall boasted an outside lav, and to get a bit of peace from their fussing she said she had to go and visit it urgently. Once there, she took off her offending knickers, rubbed herself as dry as she could with the upper part of them, and then stuffed them behind a bush before going back inside the hall.

Since half of her was ready to burst into weeping at any second and the other half seemed set on making her see the funny side of the whole situation, she could only imagine what these sturdy village dames would think if the wind suddenly blew up her skirt and revealed that Poppy Lovering, née Penfold, had come to visit her folks without wearing any knickers.

'Your man's here, Poppy,' one of the

women said after what seemed like a very short time to Poppy, and yet in reality was more than an hour. Time was beyond her comprehension now, and she looked up in mute anguish as Sam rushed into the hall, blinking in the dimness after the daylight outside.

She was in a kind of limbo again. She wasn't here, with this tragedy unfolding all around her. Her mum and dad would still be sitting in their armchairs like matching bookends when she called in at the cottage with their Christmas goodies. They'd grumble as usual, saying she didn't have to bother about them, but looking pleased all the same that she was a good girl, a good daughter, a good wife.

She heard a sudden howl of grief, as deep as that of an animal in terrible pain, and realized that it was coming from herself. In seconds, Sam had crossed the room towards her and was rocking her in his arms. She clung to him as if she was drowning. It was truly how she felt, as if the very substance of her life had been taken away from her.

'My poor sweet girl,' he muttered against her cheek. 'What a bastard thing to have happened. But the poor sods could never have felt a thing, Poppy. You know how they were. They always had a morning doze, and they'd have been asleep in their chairs long before the flames got to them.'

'You mean dead, don't you?' she said chokingly. 'If they'd been asleep, they'd have woken up by now. They were *dead*, Sam. And they'll go on being dead – for ever and ever, amen.'

'I know that.' He spoke quietly, his mouth still against her cheek, not letting on how her attitude alarmed him. He wouldn't let her pull away from him, and she was very aware of the strength of him. She needed that strength, when she felt as weak as a puffball.

The vicar was hovering around them now, and many of the women helpers had discreetly disappeared. No doubt to spread the gossip, thought Poppy, as the strange mood she couldn't explain refused to leave her.

'Mr Lovering, if you and Poppy would like to come to the vicarage when you're ready, we can talk more privately about what's to be done,' he said delicately. 'But please take as long as you like here. My time is at your disposal.'

'Thank you,' Sam said.

Whether or not the vicar gathered up his flock all around him, Poppy wasn't sure, but it seemed that the next minute she and Sam were the only two people left in the hall. And she was weeping silently against his coat, breathing in the familiar old wool smell of the material, mixed with the scent of the animals he loved and the farm that was part of him. Her words came out in jerking, choking sobs.

'It was terrible, Sam. I saw it all. The smoke circling, then shutting out the cottage from my eyes. And then the noise. Like an explosion. Then the flames. So red, so orange, so bright. So *beautiful* in a terrifying way. And knowing what it was. What it meant. And I couldn't save them, Sam. Nobody could.'

'Hush, my darling. I know that, and so does everyone else. That old thatch was always a death trap, but it also made the end come quickly. You've got to remember that. You're not to dwell on it. They couldn't have suffered. It was nothing you did that caused it, so you've got nothing to reproach yourself for.'

She hid her face against him, closing her eyes tight. *Nothing to reproach herself for?* One of her mum's old sayings was that for every bad thing you did, there had to be a reckoning. And Poppy knew she had done the worst thing of all. Fornicating with a man who wasn't her husband. She wasn't a Bible-basher like Florrie Lovering, but you didn't need to be to know that it was the worst sin of all, bar murder. She had committed it, and who was to say whether or not she had paid the price for her sin with her parents' deaths?

She felt the touch of Sam's kiss on her tear-stained cheek.

'So if you're ready, love, let's go and see the vicar and get it over with. He'll want to know about the arrangements, and we'll see that the old folks get a dignified send-off, never fear.'

In his clumsy way, she knew he was assuring her that they wouldn't be seen off in two match-boxes, Poppy thought, near to hysteria as the image entered her head again. He would take everything from her shoulders like the good man he was. He was so much more than she deserved. He was everything she wanted and needed, and more.

'Sam, I do love you,' she whispered.

He squeezed her tight. 'I know. Now dry your eyes and let's do what we've got to do.'

They walked slowly down the length of the hall and out into the daylight. Poppy was faintly surprised to see that it was still late morning. Since arriving here she felt as though she had gone through a lifetime of emotions, and it wasn't over yet. There were people in the streets and lanes, mulling over all that had happened, some huddling together as if to gain strength from one another in the wake of a tragedy among them. Others were probably pondering on the fate of those two weird Penfolds, but all of them were standing back as the daughter and her husband passed, the men doffing their hats, the women falling silent.

'I feel a bit like royalty,' Poppy whispered. For the life of her she couldn't stop the inconsequential thoughts entering her head. If Sam thought she was being disrespectful, she couldn't help it. It was the only way she could stay sane.

'Make the most of it, then,' he whispered back, just as if he understood. 'By tomorrow you'll be a commoner again.'

She held on to his arm as they made their way to the vicarage, where they were subjected to more tea and finger biscuits from the vicar's wife. Poppy wondered at the scandalized reaction of these two saintly beings if they knew that she perched on one of their best upholstered chairs in her cotton frock and petticoat and no knickers, and she prayed desperately that the cushion she sat on wouldn't show a damp patch by the time she stood up.

'You're bearing up very well, my dear,' the vicar told her approvingly. 'So if you're ready, shall we get down to details?'

She let it all wash over her. This was men's business, and Sam was prepared to deal with it all. The funeral was arranged for a week's time, so they could get it all over and done with before Christmas, his extra-busy time of the year. Before that arrangements would be made for the verger and others to keep a watch on the still burning cottage overnight, though what harm could come to it now, Poppy couldn't think. There had been nothing there worth stealing in her parents' lifetime and there was certainly nothing there now.

But the rituals had to be seen to be done, and tomorrow Sam would make arrangements with the coffin-maker and the undertaker to do the necessary. There would be no wake or eats after the funeral, for the Loverings would want to return to the farm once it was all over. And a good thing too. Kind though the Zennor folk had been today, Poppy couldn't bear to sit among them for several hours after the burying, listening to their hypocritical words.

At last they could get away in the creaking car Sam had left near the village hall. Someone had collected her bicycle and bits and pieces, and Sam had slung it all in the boot and tied it down. Poppy refused to look towards the remains of the cottage. The memories of all of her young life had been there too, and she couldn't bear to see it the way it was now. Sam urged the car over the tracks and didn't speak until they were well on to the moors.

'You'll feel better now that we're away from there,' he said awkwardly. 'That pompous old fool at the vicarage was droning on about stuff that had to be said, but I know you didn't want to hear it. You looked more than a mite uncomfortable, shuffling about on your chair.'

'Did I?'

The ongoing temptation to sob was halted by an outrageous need to giggle, and the giggle won. 'Oh Sam, you don't know what I did! If the vicar and Mrs Vicar only knew – and those po-faced dames at the hall too! Oh, I can't tell you. I wish I could, but it's too awful!'

Sam stopped the car. There was no-one else about on the moors at this point, and the breeze was whispering through the ferns and bracken, inviting secrets as the pale December sun hovered in the sky.

'Well, you'll have to tell me now. You can't stop there. What could you possibly have done that was so awful?'

He was grinning uneasily, though clearly wondering if her brain was turned to be giggling so soon after the tragedy.

'The shock made me pee myself,' Poppy said shamefacedly. 'I could feel it running down my legs and I had to clamp them together to stop disgracing myself completely. Then I went to the lav outside the village hall and took my knickers off and dried myself as best I could. I couldn't put them on again so I stuffed them behind a bush. The vicar didn't know it, but I spent half an hour on one of his best chairs without any knickers!'

It all came out in a rush, and she immediately wondered if she had gone too far in saying all this to her husband, and if he would be totally ashamed of her. The next minute she felt the car shake and she realized he was roaring with laughter, hugging her to him as she laughed and wept hysterically in his arms. It was the most bizarre sound of all on this most horrible of days.

Chapter Thirteen

Graham Strang's dyspepsia was playing him up something cruel as he stormed through the newspaper office, shouting for Jack Trevis.

'The bugger's never here when I want him,' he yelled to anyone prepared to listen. 'Send him in to me as soon as he gets back from dinner.'

Trevis wasn't the only reporter capable of handling the news that had come filtering through that afternoon, but he was the Goddamned best one. Especially as he'd got involved with the daughter of the couple who'd fried. Jack would be the best one to get over to Zennor to get the whole story, then interview the girl while she was still in an emotional state. And the sooner the better. By next week it would be old news and only fit for wrapping around fish and chips.

'Boss wants you PDQ,' one of the young lads called out to Jack a while later, seeing him stroll in from his lengthy dinner hour.

Jack shrugged, not really caring whether or not he was in for a bollocking from his editor. If Strang sacked him on the spot, it would decide his future for him. He went into the office, prepared for a fight.

'What's up?'

By the time Poppy and Sam returned to the farm she had become silent, huddled in the side of the car, feeling shrunk and spent. All kinds of thoughts were whirling around her head now. It was weird to know there was no one in the world who was her real family now. She had Sam and his mother, but no one of her own. She had moved up a notch in the great scheme of things. Once the parents died the children were the next in line to die. It was the right order. Everyone knew that. It was only in times of war or serious illness that the order shifted.

She shuddered, wishing such ghoulish thoughts wouldn't enter her head. She was also trying desperately hard not to imagine those final moments when her parents' bodies had shrivelled and turned to dust, to be blown away on the wind and lost for ever, no matter how decent a funeral they would be given. And she wasn't sure just how dignified that was going to be, with gawkers from all around coming to stare.

'You're cold,' Sam stated. 'The sooner we get indoors and get a hot drink inside you, the better. Mother will have some rabbit stew warming for us too.'

Poppy's stomach threatened to erupt at the thought. 'I couldn't eat anything,' she said in a strangled voice.

'You must. You've got some upsetting days to get through.'

'Don't you think this day was *upsetting* then? Is that all you can call it?'

He glanced at her uneasily as her voice rose shrilly. 'Don't be daft, love. I know it was bloody terrible for you. But the ordeal's not over yet, and you've got to be strong.'

'It's over for them. I'm not the one who's daft if you can't see that.'

'Poppy, don't twist everything I say. I'm trying to help but you know I'm not the best chap in the world for saying things right.'

She bent her head. She knew that. She knew he loved her, and she loved him, but right now she felt so numb inside she wasn't sure she wanted anyone to help or that anyone could. She knew exactly how the animals felt when they went away to hide in

267

the dark and curled up with their grief. She thought she had known that feeling before, but it had never been as raw as it was now.

As they reached the farmyard she could hear Dog, tied up in the barn and whining and yapping excitedly as usual. For no reason at all the sound incensed her.

'Can't you shut that thing up?' she snapped.

'Come on, let's get indoors and I'll see to it,' Sam said roughly.

She had expected him to take offence, but in her heightened state it seemed she was to be treated with kid gloves – if a country girl like her could know what that was like, she thought scornfully.

She didn't know why such stupid things kept coming into her head. It was as if her brain was playing tricks with her. Perhaps she really was as mad as Zennor folk always suspected the insular Penfold family to be. That was probably it.

Sam helped her out of the car and she tottered on ahead while he calmed down Dog. Once inside the farmhouse she stood motionless, letting the sense of familiarity wash over her and hoping it would calm her down. This house was warm and alive, while in what was left of her old home, everything was dead and burned to ashes. Dust to dust, she thought with a shiver, just as the Bible said.

She could see Florrie through the open scullery door. Poppy must have made a small sound in her throat, because the next moment Florrie had turned and was moving swiftly towards her. Unbelievably, her arms were outstretched, and with a small cry, Poppy went into them.

'There, my lamb, you just cry it all out.' Florrie's voice was as gruff as Sam's. ''Tis a terrible bad business, and even more shocking that you had to see it all. Go and sit yourself down and I'll fetch you a drink and then we'll have some food. You'll feel a deal more able to cope with things when you've got something hot inside you.'

They separated just as quickly. The unnatural contact between them couldn't last and nor did Poppy want it too. But just for those few moments she had felt comforted, and she sank down on a chair, still snuffling like a child.

She truly didn't think she could eat anything. It didn't seem right to eat and enjoy food when her mum and dad would never eat anything again. But some sliver of common sense told her that was plain stupid. She couldn't drink anything. She was awash with drink, but she managed to pick at the nourishing stew, enough to satisfy the other two who were watching her like hawks.

'I'm not going to break into little pieces,' she said crossly, when she realized she was being inspected so closely. 'I know what's happened and that I've got to face it. I'm not made of straw.'

'That's my girl.' Sam's face showed relief, even though Poppy knew he couldn't even guess what it cost her to speak reasonably normally. 'Then tomorrow I'll get on over to Zennor and see to things.'

'We'll go together.'

He looked alarmed. 'I'm not sure that's a good idea, Poppy. The place won't be cleared yet, and it won't be very nice.'

She glared at him and spoke shakily. 'I know it won't be *very nice*, Sam. It's not very nice that my mum and dad have died, but it was my home and I've a right to see what's left of it – and to know what's happening,' she added, faltering.

'I still don't like it, but if you insist I can't do much about it. We have to see the doctor, as well as other people.'

'What do we need the doctor for?' She couldn't see the point. You only saw the doctor when you were ill, and her parents always resisted seeing him even then, preferring to mix up their own herbal potions for whatever ailed them.

'We have to get death certificates, Poppy,' Sam said delicately. 'The vicar won't agree to have them buried in the churchyard otherwise.'

'Well, nobody can actually prove they're

dead, can they? Or that they were even there.' She knew she was off in one of her contrary moods again, but she couldn't seem to stop it. 'Is the doctor going to sift through the ashes to find a few teeth or something? Dad didn't have any left to speak of, anyway.'

She swallowed hard, seeing how Florrie's face was getting more and more scandalized at her seemingly callous words. They weren't callous to Poppy. They just had to be got out in the open so that she could try to make some sense of what had happened.

'I'm sure those people know what to do, Poppy. Please don't keep fretting yourself about it.'

'Well, I can hardly forget it, can I?' she shouted, her face flaming now. 'In case you've forgotten, my mum and dad have burned to a crisp. They were decent folk and they never did any harm to anyone. All they ever wanted was to merge into the background, and now their names will be on everybody's lips, and people will be digging up all kinds of dirt about them, just because they liked to keep themselves private. What was so wrong about that?'

Her anger faded as quickly as it had come, and she was crying quietly now. She would probably go on crying for the rest of her life, she thought wildly.

She felt Sam's arms around her again, and his mother was urging him to get her to bed with a hot water bottle as if she was ill or infirm. She was no longer his wife, she was his child. She wanted to rage against them both, but all the fight was going out of her, and she leaned into him, thinking dully that she would do whatever they thought best. It was simpler that way.

She didn't know how long she had been asleep. She hadn't thought she would ever sleep again because of the nightmarish visions that kept assaulting her. Her parents weren't cosily dozing in their armchairs when the first sparks flew out of the fire-place; they were fully awake, fighting against the smoke that so quickly overcame them and made every breath an agony. But not so overcome that they weren't horrifically aware of the thatched roof turning into a blazing inferno and raining down on them.

Poppy had constantly buried her face in the pillows and tried to sleep, while being half-afraid to do so for fear that the night-mares would become even more real, and she would taste the smoke and feel the heat of the flames on her skin. She reached out for Sam, needing his comforting presence, but his side of the bed was cold. She knew he had been there beside her a little while ago, and then she became aware of Dog yapping wildly and voices shouting, and she was instantly awake, her brain crystal clear.

It was Sam's bellowing voice she could hear now.

'Get off my land, you bastard, before I set my shotgun on you. We don't want your sort here, poking and prying into folk's pain.'

'Look, Mr Lovering, I'm just trying to get the facts. It will stand your wife in good stead if people hear her side of the story.'

'This is no fairy story, you scumbag. The poor maid's out of her wits with grief, and she don't want you adding to it.'

Poppy jumped as she heard Florrie shouting too.

'Get out and leave us alone. You've done enough damage already, turning a simple girl's head the way you did. We're God-fearing folk, and she don't need to be flaunted again for all to see.'

That was enough for Poppy. She knew the voice of the intruder. It was Jack Trevis, come to get a scoop or whatever they called it, or to try to wheedle his way into her life again because of what had happened at Zennor that day. She leapt out of bed, her senses alive with fury. She wrapped her dressing-gown around her tightly and sped down the stairs to the open front door.

'You heard what my husband and mother-in-law said,' she screamed at him. 'Decent folk should be left to their grief, not hounded by scum like you.'

His foot was still over the doorstep, his

273

elbow leaning against the door as if he had no intention of moving. One blow from Sam with the butt of his shotgun and he'd be knocked senseless, Poppy thought dizzily. It was a miracle he hadn't done it already.

'Poppy, my dear girl.' Jack turned to her now, his voice oozing sympathy.

Once, she would have thought it sincere. Now, she knew he could switch on the charm at will. Anything for a story, as Sam had said.

She forestalled him quickly, her voice icy now. 'It's Mrs Lovering, actually, and I've got nothing to say to you. What happened today is painful and private, and I won't have my family's personal details splashed over the newspaper for all to see.'

'So may I quote you on that?' Jack said, silkily smooth.

Poppy stared at him. 'I haven't said anything for you to quote!'

'Well, actually, you have. You've said that the terrible disaster that happened to your parents in their cottage in Zennor is too painful and private to bear, and you're obviously far too upset to want our newspaper readers to learn about your family's personal details.'

'I didn't say all that!' Her heart was thudding again. Sam had said she was twisting his own considerate words to her, but how much more stealthily could this rat do it! It was part of his stock-in-trade.

'Then why don't you let me come in and take a proper statement from you – Mrs Lovering? You can dictate what you want people to know, and it will be taken down verbatim.'

She had no idea what the word meant. She just knew she wanted him out of here and out of her life, because the more she saw of him the more she saw the shame of her own betrayal to Sam.

'You don't have to do anything you don't want to, Poppy,' Sam said harshly. 'I'll not stand in your way if you feel up to it, but if you don't, then you only have to say the word and I'll kick the bugger out of here and set Dog on him.'

'That wouldn't be a very clever idea, Mr Lovering.'

Jack's voice was cool, but as he glanced her way Poppy felt her nerves jumping. This man had far more power than Sam realized. He could make statements in his newspaper account that could easily be twisted. He could make pointed hints that Poppy Lovering wasn't such a clean-living wife as she appeared. He could suggest that her parents had made a kind of suicide pact in their cottage where few visitors were allowed, and that the accident hadn't been an accident at all, nor the will of God, but a deliberate act on the part of two lunatic old people.

Poppy shuddered, knowing what the man

275

could do and that she couldn't let it happen. She may have been a simpleton once, but Sam was more innocent than she was in this respect. If Jack Trevis wanted a story then she would give it to him. She took a deep breath and gave a small nod.

'I think I should give him the details, Sam,' she said, speaking directly to her husband. 'It's far better that he hears the truth than makes up some lying tale.'

'I assure you I would never do that, Mrs Lovering,' Jack snapped.

'Well, we shall never know about that, providing you give us your word that you will faithfully record what I tell you.'

Her chin tilted as their eyes clashed, but she felt she had got the better of him when she saw a small flicker of shame in his gaze.

Sam spoke coldly. 'You'd best come inside then. The night's turned cold and my wife will be getting chilled, so make it quick.'

Minutes later they were sitting down. Poppy was glad to do so for her legs were trembling now. The last thing she had wanted, or expected, was to confront Jack Trevis across the table, with Sam and Florrie listening intently to every word.

But she had nothing to hide or to be ashamed about in telling how she had come upon the scene of her parents' cottage, smoking and smouldering. And then the horrific moment when the thatch seemed to

276

collapse and burst into flames in front of her eyes. Her voice grew husky as she related it simply, her plain words making the imagery all the more terrible for those who were listening. She wasn't aware of Sam's arm around her shoulders until she had finished, and then she sagged against him.

'You've got what you came for,' Sam snarled at Jack. 'Now get out.'

'I won't let you down, Poppy,' he replied, ignoring Sam. 'It will be a very sympathetic account, I promise.'

Sam hadn't finished yet. 'It had better be, or I swear I'll be over to that newspaper office and telling your editor how you came here harassing my wife in the middle of the night.'

Poppy was unable to look at Trevis any longer. She felt so weary she could drop, but she still kept her chin high until Sam showed him the door and then slammed it behind him. Florrie had already gone to the scullery, banging pots about and saying that since they were all up, they had best have another cup of cocoa or they'd never sleep. They could hear Dog barking for fully ten minutes until the man's car had gone away into the night. Only then did Poppy's tears come again.

'The bastard had no right to come sniffing around you late at night like this, stirring it all up again,' Sam began angrily, but she shook her head.

'I'm almost glad he did. I've got it all out of me now. I've said it all, and when folk read it in the paper perhaps it'll stop them asking me what happened.'

'Decent folk wouldn't do that, anyway.'

But they both knew that folk would always be curious. It was human nature, which was why Sam so often preferred the company of animals. And Poppy knew she'd been right to face up to Jack Trevis. She had had to look him in the eyes, challenging his attempt to persuade her into giving him a gory account of the burning cottage. And she'd seen that flicker of shame in his eyes for what he had done to her at Chysauster village. She had faced her demons, and she had poured out all her anguish over her parents' deaths in a dignified manner, and in a strange way the telling had begun a small healing.

The three of them drank their cocoa in near silence, hardly knowing what to say to one another now, and then Florrie cleared her throat and paid Poppy another rare compliment.

'Your folks would be proud of the way you handled yourself with that man, and what you said about them. You've got nothing to be ashamed of, my dear.'

'Thank you, Mrs Lovering,' Poppy whispered, lowering her head over the cocoa mug.

If she only knew ... but nobody knew, and nobody would ever know.

'It's time we finally put this day to rest,' Sam said. 'I've to be up early as usual in the morning, and once I've got Len sorted for the afternoon, me and Poppy will go over to Zennor, unless you've changed your mind, girl?'

'No. I need to see for myself and I'm not going to scream and shout any more. I won't let you down, Sam,' she said, hardly aware that she was repeating Jack Trevis's words.

'That's my girl.'

She was so exhausted that by the time she crept into bed again and was comforted by Sam's arms, she fell asleep almost at once and didn't wake until the first sound of cockcrow.

It was a day like no other. It was almost Christmas and never had it seemed less like it to Poppy. Only yesterday she had cycled to Zennor with such pleasure, taking extra farm produce for her parents. Today, she and Sam went there in a strange and sombre mood, but she was calmer now, even though it was obvious that the news had travelled like wildfire. Men still doffed their hats when they passed through Barras village, and women bent their heads.

Yesterday, in that queer, near-hysterical

mood she had been in, it had made her feel like royalty. Today it made her sad that it was the deaths of those two harmless, self-sufficient old people that had made it so.

'I suppose I've got something to be thankful for,' she said, breaking the silence between her and Sam.

'What's that?'

Poppy gave a twisted smile. 'I thought your mother might have suggested we went to Barras church and said some prayers. I half expected her to pull me down on one knee to say them in the farmhouse. Thank goodness I didn't have to go through such a farce.'

It wasn't that Poppy hadn't said a few herself in the long hours of the night, but the thought of sharing her feelings in a churchified ritual with anyone right now was more than she could bear.

'Mother's not all flint, you know,' Sam said shortly.

'I know that. I didn't mean to mock her, Sam. I just didn't want any sort of communal wailing, not yet. The time for that will be at the funeral.'

'You won't get that from Mother, either.'

Poppy looked at him, seeing that he was holding in his anger with an effort. She hadn't meant to upset him. She was merely trying to explain how she felt.

'Just as long as she doesn't expect me to

call her Mother from now on,' she said, attempting lightness.

'I doubt that very much. You're not her daughter, are you?'

Poppy stared straight ahead. Now, when they should be so close, when they had already been so close, they seemed to be putting up barriers between themselves and to be drifting farther and farther apart. She had always thought Florrie was put out because Poppy never referred to her as Mother, but that was before she knew about the baby daughter who had died, and the huge resentment that her mother-in-law felt towards another female in the house. No wonder she had hated having the skittish land girls here during the war.

They lapsed into silence again until the car lurched over the tracks towards Zennor. The remains of the Penfold cottage came into view, roofless now, like a king without a crown, its stark, crumbling walls blackened and still smoking.

'It'll be pulled down, Poppy. You won't have to see it in that state much longer,' Sam said harshly.

'I'll never see it again. I'll never come back here after the funeral.'

'Not even to put flowers in the church-yard?' The implication was plain. She had been scathing over Florrie's lack of flowers on her baby's grave.

'How do I know they'll even be there? It's just a ritual, Sam. I've made up my mind to that. Your mother had what was once a living, breathing child to bury. What do I have? We'll put up a wooden cross with their names on it, but they won't be there. They'll be scattered to the wind by now, which is probably the way they'd have wanted it. They never did hold with church doings.'

Her voice was brittle, but the more she thought about it, the more she knew this was the right thing to do. Zennor would be forever in her past, but the memories of her parents would remain in her heart. Nothing could change that.

'The vicar won't approve.'

'The vicar can go and stuff himself then,' Poppy snapped.

Sam began to laugh, breaking the tension between them. 'Thank God. I began to think you had gone all peculiar on me. That's much more like the Poppy I know and love, ranting and raving against things. It's more the way you were when you first came to the farm, when Mother had the daft idea that she was going to tame you. She never stood a chance, did she?'

'Not much,' Poppy said with a wry smile.

They were moving away from the area where the cottage stood now and entering the village. There were people to see, arrangements to be made, and Sam was going to take it all from her shoulders. She had no idea how she would have managed this alone, nor how different it might have been if one of her parents had eventually died a normal death. How would she have coped with the one who was left? Guiltily, she knew how difficult it would have been, and since everyone was insisting that they couldn't have suffered and would have been overcome by smoke long before the flames took hold, she made herself acknowledge that a small part of her was grateful that at least they had gone together.

In a couple of hours all the business had been concluded. The doctor had signed the death certificates and added his assurances to all the others. The site had been thoroughly inspected by then, and what was supposedly the remains of the Penfold couple had been taken away. The coffins had been ordered, the burial plot paid for, the time and date of the funeral arranged with the vicar. Sam saw to everything, including paying some labourers to pull down the remains of the cottage. He doubted that Poppy would keep to her word never to return to Zennor again, but if she did, he wanted no visible reminders of the tragedy that had occurred.

'Now let's go home,' he told her.

They knew the news would have spread

quickly, even before Jack Trevis's account and the unexpectedly ghoulish photos of the smouldering cottage. There was also a small photo of Poppy herself, which made her lips tremble, but he was true to his word and hadn't embellished her halting account.

Before then, farming neighbours and village folk had come to the farm with small tokens of flowers and produce, the way they always did. The Loverings always knew when folk were about by Dog's excited yapping, but although these visitors rarely knocked at the farmhouse door, each morning some small token would be left on the doorstep.

'People are really kind,' Poppy said, choked by it all.

The initial shock was over, and she was quickly recovering her senses. The final ordeal would be the funeral, but then it would be Christmas, and although it could hardly be celebrated in the same spirit as in other years, it was a time for heralding Christ's birth, and soon afterwards, the start of another new year. It was a time for looking forward, not back.

Shirley and Bernard arrived at the farm on the day the newspaper had the account of the tragedy. Shirley looked at Poppy warily for a moment, and then folded her in her arms after Bernard made a few murmured comments of sympathy and then went outside to jaw with Sam, leaving the women to their own way of dealing with things. Shirley began talking at once, covering her awkwardness.

'You poor love, what a time you must have had. If there's anything I can do, just let me know, but of course you'll say there's nothing you need, won't you? It's what everybody does, but I do mean it, Poppy. If you need company or a shoulder to cry on, come over to my house for an hour or two, any time you like. Oh, and I've brought you this to wear over your head on the day – well, you know – on the *day*. I don't suppose you've got a black hat, and in any case you're much too pretty to be smothered by one.'

She paused for breath, and Poppy found a hint of laughter rising in her throat. Shirley could always rabbit on, whatever the circumstances, despite being overly delicate about the day of the funeral, and after rummaging in her bag for a few minutes she was still muttering as she handed Poppy a black silk scarf.

'It would be just like me to have forgotten it, but if I had, I'd have sent Bernard right back home to fetch it. So how are you really, darling?'

'I'm all right. Well, I have to be, don't I? No amount of moping about the place is going to bring them back, is it?'

285

'That's the spirit. You're so brave, but I always knew you would be. Bernard said you'd survive too because you've got a lot of backbone.'

'Did he?' As far as Poppy knew, he didn't know the first thing about her – except what Shirley would have told him.

'Oh yes. Bernard's good at summing people up. He didn't take much time in knowing what that newspaper chap was like, either. We saw all the stuff in the paper, of course, and I'm sorry he had to come bothering you, Poppy. It couldn't have been easy for you to have him poking around, asking questions when you were feeling so rotten.'

'It was horrible, and if I never have to see him again, it will suit me fine.'

Shirley nodded, noting how the other girl's mouth trembled, and immediately wished she had never brought up Jack's name.

'Where's the old dragon today?' she said in a loud stage whisper, knowing this would bring a certain smile to Poppy's wan face.

'The old dragon's right here,' came Florrie's disapproving voice from the stairs. 'And how are you, Shirley? You're looking very well, and I see that marriage has done nothing to improve your cheek.'

'I'm sorry you had to hear that, Mrs Lovering,' Shirley replied defiantly. 'It was

286

nothing personal, of course, just a slip of the tongue.'

'Oh yes, I should have remembered your slips of the tongue from the old days. And I suppose you'd like a cup of tea now you're here,' Florrie said with a sniff turning to the scullery and completely missing the way Shirley made a cross-eyed face at her retreating back.

Poppy felt her spirits start to lift just by Shirley's presence. There was only so long that you could be steeped in gloom and misery. This was a welcome respite, even though she knew the bad feelings would return. You couldn't get over something so traumatic in a day or a week, but no matter what the season Shirley always seemed to bring a breath of springtime with her, but the way she made Poppy feel at that moment was better than that.

If she had been feeling poetic, she'd have said it was like seeing a small glimmer of light in the darkness. It was like Christmas, she thought again, which wasn't going to stop just because two old people had died a ghastly death. It wasn't going to stop the old year ending and the new one beginning, when everyone looked forward to better times and brighter days. Whatever else happened, she had to hold on to that thought.

Chapter Fourteen

The funeral was going to be a small family affair. They had invited no outsiders, but it was inevitable that Zennor folk would turn out, and a sprinkling of Barras neighbours and farm workers came too, all wanting to show their respect and sympathy for what had befallen the parents of Sam Lovering's wife. Shirley and Bernard Bosinney were the only other outsiders to attend.

Once the short service was over, Poppy clung tightly to Sam's hand, aware that his mother was walking behind them in the small procession from the church to the churchyard, as tight-lipped as Poppy herself was trying to be. Perhaps Florrie was remembering other times like these, Poppy thought fleetingly; the time she had buried Sam's father; and before that the time they had buried the tiny baby who had hardly a chance to live. Florrie knew the loneliness of bereavement.

Without thinking, she stretched out her free hand to draw Florrie closer alongside her and Sam, and the three of them moved as one unit towards the open plot that had been prepared for Poppy's parents.

'We bring nothing into this world and we take nothing out,' the vicar intoned, hovering over the open grave like a spectre himself.

Well, that was for sure, Poppy thought irreverently. Her mum and dad had had little when they were alive, and they had even less now. Not even a body between them to call their own. She kept her eyes down on the plain coffins that were being lowered into the grave, one beside the other, and it was impossible to prevent that other wickedly irreverent thought coming to the surface again.

They could have saved a lot of space in the churchyard if they'd only stuffed them into two match-boxes as she had said so flippantly. She caught her breath on a shuddering sigh, and Sam clutched her hand, assuming she was trying to stifle her sobs. But she wasn't.

She knew to her shame that she was perilously close to hysterical laughter. She would disgrace herself for ever if it erupted on such a solemn occasion, and then it would surely prove to the worthy citizens of Zennor that she truly was mad. She would also disgrace herself in front of Sam and that was far more important. It was enough to settle her crazy, irrational thoughts, and she squeezed his hand in return to let him know she was composing herself.

Out of the corner of her eye she could see a tall figure in the shadow of the trees beyond the main part of the churchyard, and in an instant whatever else she had been feeling was overcome by a red rage.

How *dare* he come here today of all days! How dare he come to stare and gloat and ask questions of local folk in order to make yet another piece of newspaper rubbish for his own ends.

Hardly knowing what she was doing, Poppy shook free of Sam and went storming across the dank earth towards Jack Trevis, who straightened up at once as he saw her furious approach.

'What do you think you're doing?' she shrieked. 'You have no business to be here today. Do you have no shame?'

'Poppy, control yourself,' he said tightly. 'People are staring, and wondering what the hell you're thinking about, leaving your husband at the graveside like that. Have *you* no shame?'

She couldn't believe what she was hearing. 'You dare to talk to me about shame, after the things you've done?'

'Be careful what you're saying, sweetheart,' he warned in a small smooth voice, 'unless you want everyone to know what a little slut Sam Lovering married.'

Poppy gasped with fury. The next second she had swung her arm with all her strength and struck him full in the face. As he staggered, it was Sam who was pulling her away, puce with embarrassment that his wife was making such a spectacle of herself, but she still had enough sanity to hope frantically that he hadn't overheard what Trevis had said.

'Poppy, for God's sake, what's got into you?' Sam shouted in her ear. 'The man was an insensitive oaf to come here at all today, but there was no call for violence.'

'You've no need to apologize for your wife, Mr Lovering,' Trevis replied, his own face dark with anger now. 'What she witnessed last week was enough to turn even the sanest person's mind.'

His emphasis was all too clear, and with a sick sense of foreboding Poppy knew that this was all going to be reported in the newspaper in the juiciest way. Poppy Lovering was far from being the sanest person in the universe, and Jack Trevis would put in as many little barbs of poison as he chose to make everyone think that way.

'Come away now, Poppy, darling. The vicar's waiting to finish the service.'

It was Shirley's anxious voice in her ears now, and she felt her head drop with shame as she saw the entire group of people gathered around the graveside looking her way. She leaned into Sam's chest for a moment.

'Sam, I'm so sorry,' she whispered. 'I just couldn't bear to see him there and something inside me just exploded.'

She was probably making things worse. Adding to the fantasy that she was completely mad. Things didn't explode inside a person. People should have control of their emotions, especially at a time like this, when so much was expected of a grieving daughter. The ritual had to be seen to be completed. It was the done thing to weep and mourn, and those who had come out of curiosity or to pay their respects could go away satisfied that Poppy Lovering, née Penfold, was a good girl, and not the screaming harridan she had turned into for those few humiliating moments.

Still raging inside, Poppy allowed Sam and Shirley to take her back to where the vicar stood waiting as if carved in stone. Obviously, nothing like this had ever happened at a burial before. This would be something for Zennor to talk about for years to come. She glanced at Florrie, knowing she would be washing her hands of her wayward daughter-in-law for ever now, and was startled to see a glint of something like sympathy in Florrie's eyes.

But at last it was all over, and people dispersed from the churchyard, muttering among themselves until the only ones left were the three chief mourners and Shirley and Bernard Bosinney.

Shirley hugged her tightly as they prepared to leave. 'Come and see me whenever you like after Christmas, Poppy. We'll have some cosy afternoons together, and you'll be able to put all the bad memories behind you. The worst is over now, darling.'

Poppy nodded, knowing there was a double meaning in her words. She had coped with her stupidity in falling for Jack Trevis, and she had somehow got through today despite her disgraceful behaviour. Neighbours had come to say goodbye to her and Sam, and hadn't seemed to be too outraged by what had happened after all. Perhaps they too had considered a reporter's presence here an intrusion. Nobody had heard the exact words that had passed between her and Jack, and at least she could be thankful about that.

'It was such a terrible thing to happen, and I felt so sorry for Poppy,' Shirley told her friend Carrie when she went back to Penhallow with her Christmas gifts for Walter. She and Bernard would be here again for Christmas dinner with her parents, and for afternoon tea with his, but this was her precious time with Carrie, when they could let their hair down and be themselves.

'And then for that man to turn up at the funeral too,' Carrie said.

Shirley snorted. 'He's got no decent feelings. He might look like a Greek God, but he's all shallow inside. You can't go by looks, can you?'

'Is she all right?' Carrie said delicately. 'About him, I mean? You said she made quite a scene in the churchyard.'

'I don't know. I haven't seen her since then, and I do feel sort of responsible for her in a way, although it was something I never expected to happen, nor wanted it to. I hope she'll come to Penzance once Christmas is over so we can chat.'

Shirley sounded almost cross as she said it. But it was true. There were only half a dozen years between her and Poppy, yet she felt so much older. Even so, the role of mother confessor didn't sit comfortably on her shoulders.

'Is that wise, Shirley?'

Shirley gave a deep sigh. 'Probably not. But like it or not, we do have something in common, don't we? Her brief infatuation with Jack Trevis, and mine with Hank.'

'But that was more than an infatuation, wasn't it?'

'I don't want to talk about it any more. It's in the past, and I've got this little one to think about now.' She touched her belly lightly and gave a crooked smile.

Carrie was glad to change the tone of this conversation. 'Oh, that reminds me, Shirley,

I've got a few things of Walter's I'd like you to have for the baby. I know you want everything new at first, but these are for when he's a bit older, providing it's a boy, of course!'

'Are you sure you don't want to keep them for Walter number two?'

'Walter number two doesn't seem in any hurry to put in an appearance, and I don't like to hang on to things for ever.'

'All right then, and thanks. I must get back soon, Carrie. Christmas is always a busy time at school for Bernard. We've got the carol service to go to tomorrow afternoon, and then the nativity play tomorrow evening. All the mums and dads go to it. Your Walter's sure to be one of the little angels once he starts school.'

'You really enjoy being a part of it all, don't you?'

'Of course I do,' Shirley said brightly.

It was only at certain times; the anniversary of Hank's death – as far as she knew it – and that of the baby-that-never-was; and Christmastime when everyone got nostalgic and reminisced about other times; times when she simply couldn't help her thoughts straying to those secret places of her heart.

Poppy wasn't sure how she was going to get through Christmas. Florrie always expected them to go to church on Christmas morning, and it was always a joyful service, unlike some of the ponderous ones the Barras vicar gave. This year there would be two services since Christmas Day fell on a Monday.

How could she be expected to sing carols and smile at folk and wish them the compliments of the season, and all those other cosy platitudes that came out on these occasions? How *could* she?

She flatly refused to go to church on Sunday. It was too soon. It was just too soon. Sam was fretting over Dora, one of his cows, soon to calve so late in the year, so he decided not to go at all, and Florrie could make what she wanted of it.

He'd obviously had second thoughts by that evening. 'I know neither of us felt like going to church today, and if you don't feel you can face the service tomorrow morning, Poppy, no one will think the worse of you,' Sam told her on the Sunday that was Christmas Eve, daring his mother to say otherwise. 'Dora seems more settled now though, so I'll be going tomorrow,' he added.

'I'll see. I don't know how I shall feel yet.' She couldn't help feeling a bit guilty about staying home the following morning now, knowing that Florrie would be fielding off all the questions people would be asking about her parents.

'You'll be feeling like hiding away from folk, just as you do today,' Florrie said briskly. 'It's quite natural. You won't want them looking at you or avoiding you, or trying to think of the right thing to say. It's how everybody feels at such times, but the sooner you go out and face folk, the better it will be.'

'I daresay you're right, but it's not so easy as it sounds.' Poppy was more than a touch resentful at Florrie for sounding such a know-all.

'Do you think I don't know that?' Florrie said shortly.

She wasn't taking over the role of a parent, and neither of them would welcome it. It was as if she knew exactly how Poppy was feeling, how mixed-up and unsure of anything any more, which of course she did know, having gone through bereavements of her own. But Poppy had never expected Sam's mother to express any of those feelings out loud when she normally kept such personal opinions to herself. And Poppy wasn't even sure if she wanted someone knowing exactly how she felt. In a totally selfish way, it was as if she felt protective of her own grief, and she had to be the one to deal with it in whatever way she could.

'So what's it going to be?' Sam said, clearing his throat and looking from one to the other of his womenfolk as if not too sure if they were arguing or agreeing. 'Do you want to stay home tomorrow, Poppy, or will you be joining Mother and me?'

She looked at him, seeing the troubled look in his eyes. He was suffering on her account too. He'd had to put up with her weeping and her guilt, and he'd been far more patient than she deserved. He was more than a bit worried over Dora too. She was now in the loose pen, away from the others, and probably feeling as lonely and lost as herself, Poppy thought incongruously.

She gave a deep swallow as the ludicrous comparison with Sam's best cow entered her mind. 'All right, I'll go to church tomorrow. I have to face them all sometime, don't I? But don't expect me to sing carols, because the words would stick in my throat.'

'That's good enough for me, and you won't be on your own, Poppy. You'll have Mother and me beside you, and if anybody starts being too kind, we'll soon ward them off.'

His clumsy words brought a smile to Poppy's face, because when did the thought of anybody too kind demand any kind of warding off! But she knew what he meant, and she had already had enough kind words to last a lifetime.

Eventually, she realized that going to church on Christmas morning was the best thing she could have done. The church was decorated with holly and berries, the service was bright and cheerful, giving praises to the Lord, and the local children sang the carols lustily, having already had plenty of practice on Sunday. If Poppy didn't join in with the singing she doubted that anyone noticed, and by the time the congregation spilled out into the morning sunshine with no more than sympathetic glances coming her way, she felt a fraction better.

Her grief was still raw and new, but it was a personal grief, and today the whole world was celebrating a very special birth, not mourning the deaths of two old people. She tried not to spoil the rest of it for Sam and his mother, even though their family celebrations were modest and more subdued than usual.

Sam never stayed so long at the pub on Saturday nights now. The first flush of excitement after Poppy had saved the Flint kid from the mine shaft had long since faded, and he was no longer treated to his pints of ale in return for embellishments on the story. Not that he minded. It had become too much of a ritual, and he had never been that much of a drinker. He still went to the pub on occasion though; it was what local farmers did. The only exception was when some family drama intervened, or one of their animals was sick.

A light flurry of snow had come and gone during recent days, but the week after

Christmas was cold and Dora was nearing her time. The separate loose pen away from the rest of the herd where Sam had moved her to, had clean straw on the floor, a trough for her feed and plenty of water, and a lantern hanging ready on a hook if he should be needed during the night.

'Animals are like humans,' Florrie said sagely one night when Sam had gone outside to check that Dora was comfortable. 'Birthing is as much a time between life and death for them as it is for us. They feel the same kind of pain, but they're usually cleverer than us. They manage it all by themselves without any of these new-fangled methods the doctors give a woman these days.'

Poppy glanced at her. 'I suppose you mean gas and air. I know Shirley intends to have it if it's offered, and I don't know that it's such a bad thing if it helps to prevent such a lot of pain.'

Florrie spoke shortly. 'A woman expects pain when she's giving birth, and if nature never intended her to have pain it would be as easy as shelling peas. Anything worth having is worth going through a bit of pain for. Our Lord knew that.'

Without warning Poppy's already fragile nerves seemed to snap. 'I suppose you'll be saying next that my parents had to go through their *bit of pain* in order to reach eternal life. Well, if you want to know what I think, I think God was being damn spiteful to two harmless old people!'

She didn't know where the words came from. She hadn't meant to say anything so blasphemous that was certain to shock and outrage her mother-in-law. Florrie looked so furious that for a moment Poppy thought she was going to strike her. But she wouldn't take it back. She *wouldn't*. And then she was shocked to see Florrie's shoulders slump.

'We all have our faith sorely tested at one time or another, Poppy. We all rant and rage against the things that grieve us the most, but in the end we always come back to Him, because He's all we've got. And He always forgives us, which is why I'm able to forgive you for saying such things.'

Dear *God*, the woman must be in line for sainthood, Poppy thought furiously. She didn't want to be forgiven. She didn't want to be pacified. She still wanted to feel anger at the horrific deaths her parents had suffered. But in an instant she knew why Florrie had said those things. How sorely had her own faith been tested when her baby Evie had died! She swallowed back the harsh retort that had been brimming on her lips with a great effort.

Then Sam came back indoors, bringing in a rush of cold air, and a feeling of relief to both women that this difficult conversation was brought to an end.

'How is Dora doing, Sam?' Poppy asked quickly.

'As well as can be expected,' he replied glibly. 'Well, that's what all the smart medical folk say, isn't it? She's a good beast, but truth to tell, I'm not too easy about her so I might decide to sit up with her when her labour starts.'

'Your father always said a cow's quite capable of delivering without any outside help, Sam,' his mother said.

'So she is, but a bit of human kindness never hurt man nor beast. I'll do what I think best when the time comes. Now I'm off to my bed for a few hours' sleep.'

Poppy stood up at once, more than ready to join him and glad that this awkward evening was at an end. When Florrie carried on with one of her Bible lectures, it always made her feel uncomfortable. It wasn't that she didn't believe in God – well, everybody did, she supposed; but you didn't have to have it rammed down your throat all the time.

'Are you really worried about Dora?' she asked Sam once they were in bed.

'I'm not sure what to think. If it didn't sound so daft I'd say it's not me that's worried that something's not quite right. It's Dora.'

'I don't think that's daft. Why shouldn't cows know when something's wrong? They

302

always lie down when they know it's going to rain, and they've got feelings too, haven't they? They feel pain just like we do. Your mother made sure to tell me that.'

She recognized the smile in his voice. 'Has she been giving you a lecture?'

'Just a bit. But I think we understood one another in the end.'

'I bet she didn't get the better of you, either.'

Poppy gave a short laugh, and realized what a rare sound it had been these last few weeks. 'Not completely, anyway.'

He held her close for a few minutes, before turning his back on her and saying they should try to get some sleep. She didn't mind. She did the same and snuggled up to him, back to back. It was a comfortable arrangement, as long as she could feel his warmth in the bed they shared.

Late on New Year's Eve she awoke with a start, wondering what had startled her. Sam's side of the bed was cold, and Dog was yapping frantically in the yard. But there was another sound too, the bellowing sound of an animal in pain. Dora.

Poppy leapt out of bed, sure that Sam would be in the loose pen with her. She had never witnessed a cow giving birth, and didn't particularly want to do so now. But she knew how precious this animal was to

Sam, as all his animals were, and she felt the need to be there with him. She couldn't do anything to help, but she could be by his side.

She dressed quickly and padded downstairs, surprised to find Florrie already in the scullery in her dressing-gown with the kettle singing, and a bucket of water heating up.

'There's no need for you to be here, Poppy. Sam's decided to sit with the beast, so I'm making him some cocoa.'

'I'll take it to him, Mrs Lovering. It's a cold night, and I'll have a cup too. You go back to bed.'

She challenged Florrie with her eyes. She was Sam's wife and it was her place to be a helpmeet to him. She remembered the vicar saying as much when they were married. At the time it had seemed such an old-fashioned word, but it was the right one to use now. She was his helpmeet.

A few minutes later she stumbled across the cold farmyard to the loose pen where she could see the light of the lantern through the cracks. She hovered outside for a moment, scared of what she might see, and then she went inside to where Sam was leaning beside the cow, stroking her back and murmuring gently.

'Not long now, old girl. 'Tis a bad time for you, Dora, but 'twill be all worth it when

304

you see your bab.'

Poppy felt her throat constrict and tears stab her eyes. The words were said with a peculiar rough tenderness, and not at all as those of a man who saw his beasts merely as milk producers and a way of earning a living for his family. This was a man who cared for the pain that an animal was going through.

'Is she all right?' she said huskily.

Sam glanced her way. 'She'll do. She knows what to do, love, but she's having a hard time of it and she might need some help.'

Poppy's heart thudded. She gave a shudder and put the two cups of cocoa down with a clatter on the stool beside Sam.

'What kind of help? Shouldn't you call the vet?' she stuttered. 'I could go if you like. It wouldn't take long.'

Anything to get away from here, she thought frantically, hearing Dora give another loud bellow.

'I doubt there'll be time for that,' Sam said keenly. 'The feet are already through and it looks to me as if the calf's stuck. I may have to draw it.'

Poppy shuddered more violently now. 'What do you mean?'

He reached behind her to where a looped rope was hanging on a nail beside the lantern. His voice became sharp. 'I'll need you to hold the lantern for me. She's already been in labour too long, and each time she gives a contraction now, I'll have to draw the calf a bit further out.'

Poppy's mouth was dry. She couldn't watch this. She couldn't. She couldn't stay here. And then Dora bellowed again, and she knew she must and she would. She watched numbly as Sam looped the rope tightly around the calf's feet that were visible now from the birth opening.

He constantly murmured to Dora, and just as he had said, each time there was a contraction he pulled gently on the rope to ease the calf further away from the cow. The whole operation of giving birth seemed a nightmarish and impossible task to Poppy, and she wondered how any female, human or animal, could ever go through with it.

'We're nearly there,' Sam said at last.

Dora gave a last violent convulsion, and in a rush, the calf slithered out on to the straw below, steaming and wet, a perfectly-formed miracle.

Sam reached forward at once for some hay to wipe the calf's nose and mouth, clearing the airways before it gave its first bleating sound. Almost at once, Dora shuffled around and began licking her calf to clean it. In doing so she kicked away the stool, and the two cups of cold cocoa disappeared into the straw. Nobody noticed or cared. Poppy was too much in awe of the miracle she had witnessed, and by now Sam was busily ensuring that the afterbirth had come away and that Dora was feeling no more distress.

They were vaguely aware of a sound in the distance that grew louder in their ears as the farmyard sounds died down. Church bells.

Sam gave a half-smile. 'Welcome to 1951, bab,' he said softly, stroking the calf's silky nose.

'You can't call it that,' Poppy said, her throat still tight with emotion. 'What kind is it, a boy or a girl?'

'It's a girl,' Sam said, grinning at her choice of words.

'She's lucky then, because she was born to the sound of church bells at the start of a new year. We should call her Belle. Can we, Sam?'

'Why not? You took part in her birth as much as anybody tonight,' Sam said, reaching out his hand to squeeze Poppy's.

About fifteen minutes later, they watched as Belle staggered to her feet on splaying, spindly legs, and as she nuzzled towards her mother it was the second most amazing sight Poppy had ever seen.

They stayed a while longer to keep a check on both animals, and to see that Belle was suckling properly, and then Sam spoke gruffly.

'You did well for standing by tonight, Poppy. Many a young girl would have thrown up or fainted if they'd had to witness what happened here.'

They hadn't been aware that Florrie had come out to the loose pen to see what was happening, and they both started when they heard her voice.

'And this one wouldn't have been the first, but I reckon she can be called a proper farmer's wife now. So move aside and let's have a look at the new beast.'

Poppy stood back as Florrie's voice resumed its usual forceful tones. But as Florrie inspected the newborn animal, nothing could take away the glow of that unexpected moment when her mother-in-law had called her a proper farmer's wife.

Chapter Fifteen

In a strange way the euphoria of Belle's birth seemed to give Poppy a temporary respite over the trauma of her parents' deaths. She knew it couldn't last, but while it did, she was glad of it. And in that brief time she felt as if she had finally grown up. She had had to cope with death in a most terrible way, and she had witnessed a birth. It wasn't quite a natural birth, since it had needed Sam's intervention and help, but it had been a revelation to Poppy all the same.

However, as swiftly as the boost to her feelings came, it just as swiftly disappeared. Once Dora and Belle were back in their winter quarters with the rest of the herd, the general routine of the farm continued. Sam was as busy as ever, and she had never felt at such a loss. There was nowhere to go on Thursday afternoons now, and Florrie seemed as tetchy towards her as usual, as if that special moment between them in the loose pen had never happened.

By February, spring still seemed a time away. The nights were still long and the mornings were still misty and dark and unwelcoming.

'If only I had something to do,' she moaned to Sam one night when Florrie had gone out to Barras church hall on one of her regular jaunts.

He was only half listening, more interested in the newspaper he was reading, and he replied absentmindedly.

'You could always go with Mother to one of her meetings.'

Poppy grunted. 'I'm not ready for that yet, thank you, Sam! They're all like ancient monuments, except for the mother and baby groups, and I'm not eligible for that either. Even your precious Dora could do better than me in that respect!'

He laughed, not yet registering how

restless she was becoming. 'Don't tell me you're jealous of a cow?'

'Maybe not,' she snapped. 'But I might just be jealous of Shirley Bosinney having that smart house in Penzance and a baby to look forward to and all.'

She hadn't meant to say it, but Sam looked up from the newspaper article he had found so intriguing, finally realizing how miserable she sounded but still not really listening to what she had said, except for mentioning Shirley.

'There's no reason why you can't go and see her, Poppy. You haven't seen her since the funeral, have you? I know it might be tricky for you both, but the longer you leave it, the more awkward it will be. Never mind what Mother says about the house-cleaning and other jobs about the farm, you go and make your visits and get some fresh air.'

'It's not the answer though, is it?' She was still resentful at what she felt were patronizing words. 'I still have to come back.'

This time he put his newspaper down and looked at her uneasily. 'What's this really all about, then? Are you so unhappy here with me? I know I'm not every maid's dream, but I thought we rubbed along pretty well.'

'We do! And for goodness' sake stop calling me a maid! I've told you before, I stopped being a maid on the day we were married.'

310

'You did that,' Sam said with a grin, and then he saw the shine of tears in her eyes and his face darkened. 'By Christ, Poppy, what do I have to do to please you? I'm bloody sure I don't know if you don't tell me what's wrong.'

'I can't tell you because I don't know – apart from the fact that I'm still missing my parents like hell, and thinking I should have done more to help them.'

It wasn't what was really troubling her, but she had to say something. The truth was, she didn't know *what* was wrong with her. She just had this persistent feeling of unease inside her, and the only person to take it out on was Sam.

He got up from his chair and put his arm around her. 'You were everything a daughter should be, and don't let anybody tell you different. Now, I'm going to make us some cocoa and then I'll show you this piece in the paper that might interest you. How does that sound?'

Sam didn't often make cocoa, since that was women's work, and Poppy thought she would burst if she drank many more cups of the bloody stuff. Besides, if the piece in the paper had anything to do with Jack Trevis, she didn't want to see it. But she knew Sam was doing his best to appease her.

'It sounds good, and I'll do as you say, Sam. I'll go and see Shirley next week.

She'll probably be glad of some company now she's getting near her time.'

But she found herself biting her lip as Sam went out to the scullery, because thinking of Shirley nearing her time reminded her all too clearly of the distress that Dora had been in while she was calving. And of herself witnessing it. Her imagination had always been vivid, but it wasn't her imagination that was sending her back now to that loose pen on New Year's Eve, it was the memory of Sam putting the rope around those fragile legs and easing the calf out of the cow's belly.

At the thought, Poppy felt the bile rise into her throat. She clapped a hand over her mouth and rushed out to the scullery, pushing Sam aside from the stone sink before she retched over it.

'Well now,' Sam said, when she had recovered a little and he was mopping her sweating brow with a towel and holding on to her trembling body. 'What do we have here?'

Shirley looked at her friend cautiously. Poppy still seemed in a precarious state of mind, and it would be all too easy to say the wrong thing. Shirley knew that feeling herself and she was too uncomfortable with her baby lying awkwardly to be able to deal with too much emotion from anybody else.

But this was Poppy, the sweet kid who had so wanted to be grown up like the rest of the land girls, whom they had teased mercilessly about the Saturday dances in Penzance and flirting with the Yanks.

'Are you sure? Have you seen a doctor? Or told Sam and the old dragon?'

She tried to coax a smile to Poppy's face, but the poor kid looked so damn unsure of herself right now that Shirley doubted if anything could do it short of a miracle. She should be looking happy. It was what she'd wanted, for God's sake.

'I haven't told anybody but you and Sam, and he's certain about it now that he's seen me throwing up a few times. He's seen enough cows and pigs giving birth to know when his wife's likely to be expecting.'

'Poppy, forgive me, but I have to ask this,' Shirley said hesitantly, trying to ignore the reference to cows and pigs. 'It is ... well, it is Sam's baby, isn't it?'

Poppy glared at her furiously. 'Of course it is. At least I know that for certain. If it hadn't been, I'd probably have killed myself.'

'All right, calm down. So aren't you pleased? And since when did you start comparing yourself with cows and pigs? Just because you're a farmer's wife doesn't mean you have to think of yourself as being fattened up ready for market.'

'That's just how I'll probably look. You've managed to look all neat and tidy all the time you were expecting. I'll probably end up looking like a prize porker.'

'My goodness, you are down in the dumps, aren't you?' Shirley said with a laugh. Then her face softened.

'Poppy, darling, you've had a rotten time lately, with your parents dying in that awful way, and all that Jack Trevis business, which I'm sure is well and truly behind you now,' she added hastily. 'But expecting a baby is a magical time, and if there's anything you want to know, I'll be happy to tell you. You'll have such a lovely time for it too, with the summer ahead of us. We'll be able to take our babies out together come next autumn.'

She did her best to encourage Poppy to look more cheerful, though sharing baby secrets with this girl was certainly not something Shirley had ever imagined. Once, she had dearly hoped that it would be herself and her three best friends in Penhallow who would be pushing their babies out in their prams together, but circumstances changed everything and it was not to be. As for certain other baby secrets ... that was something Shirley preferred not to think about.

'It sounds nice,' Poppy said with the ghost of a smile. 'And of course I'm pleased – and damn scared too, if you want to know.'

'Well, of course you're scared. Everyone's

scared of doing something they've never done before. But you'll be fine when the time comes, I promise you.'

'How do you know that? You've never had a baby before, have you? You've never gone through it, any more than I have.'

It was just a brickbat remark, no more, hitting out at anyone who didn't seem capable of understanding the fear in her heart. It was too soon after seeing what Dora had gone through for Poppy to want to hear that giving birth was normal and natural, and that thousands of women did it, and had always done it.

She suddenly became aware of the choking sound coming from Shirley's throat, and the agonized look in her eyes. 'You're not scared too, are you, Shirley? I always thought you could deal with anything. Even when you knew Bernard was badly wounded in France for all those months, you managed to keep smiling. I always thought how brave you were.'

'Well, I'm not smiling now, am I?' Shirley managed. 'And you must be stupid if you thought I was being brave when I was so worried about Bernard. Like most people I just went through the motions. It was important to have as normal a life as possible, no matter how much your heart was aching.'

'Like going to the dances in Penzance, and

flirting with the GIs, you mean?'

Poppy tried to cheer her up in the only way she knew how. She was the one who was supposed to be depressed, but for some reason she seemed to have completely deflated Shirley. And her friend's tone was less than friendly now.

'You were such a naive kid, weren't you, Poppy? You knew nothing in those days – and you don't know much more now!'

Poppy glared at her. This wasn't what she had come to hear. Everything seemed to be going wrong between them, and she didn't know how to put it right.

'If that's what you think of me I might as well go home. I don't know why you ever asked me to visit you if you're just going to insult me!'

'Oh, for God's sake sit down! I'm not insulting you. I'm sure there are plenty of girls who wished they'd been as young and innocent as you were. Then they wouldn't have been tempted to do things they would always regret. You must remember the days when the GI brides went off to America with their babies. Do you think they were all as happy as they pretended, going so far away to another country and meeting strangers who were going to resent them? Especially the girls who expected their boys to come safely home to them,' she added with a shiver.

'Well, crikey, I didn't expect you to go on like this about it. Anyway, nothing like that happened to you. Bernard came home safe and sound, and you've got nothing to reproach yourself for, have you?'

At that moment, it was so very tempting for Shirley to blurt out everything to this wide-eyed girl who was looking at her as if she was a saint, when Shirley knew she was anything but that. She kept her eyes lowered, trying not to let her hands twist the handkerchief in her lap. She still had her secret ... but she had reckoned without Poppy's acute perception.

'You *did* have a Yank, didn't you, Shirley! I always thought none of them could resist someone as pretty as you. I don't blame you either. What was he like?'

Poppy's mood changed, and she couldn't stop the excitement in her voice now. It explained so many things. All those whispered conversations between the other land girls, the way they constantly teased her about the exciting moonlight walks after the dances with the GIs. She'd always thought they exaggerated it all for her benefit, but perhaps there was some truth in it after all. Then there was the way Shirley had known exactly what she was going through in her infatuation with Jack Trevis. It was because Shirley had been in the very same situation.

'Oh, come on, Shirley!' Poppy persisted,

when Shirley said nothing. 'It always seemed so exciting and glamorous to me, and I envied you girls so much.'

Perhaps after all, it was time to shock this little madam, Shirley thought furiously. Time to take that eager, sparkling look from her face … and then she remembered with a stab of compassion what Poppy had gone through recently, and she knew she couldn't be hateful about it. It wasn't in her nature, anyway.

'All right, I did have somebody,' she said slowly. 'He was the most beautiful young man in the world, and I truly loved him. You might not think you can love two people at the same time, Poppy, but you can. I still loved Bernard with all my heart. He was my childhood sweetheart and I knew we were going to get married when the war ended. But Hank was just as you said – exciting and glamorous, and very hard to resist. And in the end, I didn't resist. It broke my heart when the Yanks left the area in preparation for D-Day. I never knew what had happened to him, nor heard from him again, and when a group of them came back to Penzance for a reunion after the war ended, it was only then that I learned from the newspaper reports that Hank was among those who had been killed.'

Poppy's eyes were wide, her mouth slightly open, and Shirley could see that what she had just heard was the stuff of Hollywood movies to the younger girl. And so it was, she thought, with a catch in her throat. But not all stories ended happily ever after, and having started she had to go on. She couldn't leave it unfinished.

'Even when I didn't know if I would ever hear from him again, I always counted myself lucky to have known Hank and had his love for such a little time. And then came the terrible realization that I was expecting his baby.'

Her voice had dropped almost to a hush. The words hadn't been said for so long that it seemed an intrusion to all the love she and Hank had shared to say them out loud now.

'Oh God, Shirley, I don't know what to say,' Poppy whispered.

'There's nothing to say, and nor do I want you *ever* to repeat what I've just told you. You must promise me, Poppy.'

'Truly, I never would. I swear on my heart. But what ... where–'

'I had a miscarriage, and, of course, it solved everything. Can you imagine how awful it would have been for Bernard and my family if it hadn't happened? The disgrace would have been too much to bear. But even after all this time I feel terrible to admit that losing a child was the best thing that could have happened. I went through torment, wanting to confess to Bernard, wanting to tell him everything, but I never did. My very good friends saw me through it, just as I hope I've seen you through your problems with you-know-who.'

Poppy nodded, scalding tears filling her eyes. Shirley was always so bright and pretty, so full of life, and yet she had carried this burden for so long. It just proved that you never really knew people.

'You're the best friend I could ever have,' she said huskily.

'So that's why we'll both look forward to our coming babies and cherish them from the day they're born, won't we? No more long faces, no recriminations. This is a new year and only good things are going to happen from now on. Agreed?'

'Well, yes.'

'Was there something else? I must confess I'm feeling a bit tired after all that soul-searching,' Shirley said, not just tired but truly exhausted now.

'It's nothing to do with babies. It's something Sam saw in the newspaper that he thought looked interesting. I don't know if I like the sound of it or not.'

'Well, I won't know either unless you tell me what it is.'

She shifted uncomfortably, wanting to be alone, wanting to lie down on her bed and rest. But she could see that Poppy was still troubled about something, and she managed to resist a sigh.

'It had to be Jack Trevis who wrote it, of course.' Poppy couldn't help the bitterness in her voice. 'That man seems to be every-where, and now he's got Sam all fired up in thinking about this new enterprise, as he calls it.'

'You don't mean he's been talking to Sam?'

Poppy shook her head. 'He wouldn't dare come near our place again. If he did he knows he'd get a mouthful from me, and from Sam and Florrie too, I daresay. But he didn't need to talk to Sam. He just wrote about it.'

'Well, what the devil did he write about, then?' Shirley reasoned that it couldn't have been anything personal, or Poppy would have been in far more of a fright than she was. 'I don't remember reading anything spectacular. Hold on a minute, I'll get the paper and you can show me what this is all about. You're probably making a fuss about nothing as usual.'

Or was that herself she was talking about? It was what her old friends had always said about *her*. She rummaged in the magazine rack by the fireplace until she found the latest newspaper and handed it over silently.

'There!' Poppy said, stabbing her finger at one of the inside pages.

Shirley's eyebrows rose. 'What, this article

about some chap near St Austell who's opened up a museum of old farming equipment? What's that got to do with Sam? Does he think he could buy something useful there that's going cheap? I didn't think he was that much of a skinflint.'

'*No*, you dope,' Poppy said impatiently. 'But he's got this idea that we could do the same thing. Plenty of people know Lovering's Farm through the annual fair and fête, and he thinks it could be a useful sideline. He says it would keep me occupied making labels for all the stuff we are going to display.'

'It sounds like a good idea, so what have you got against it?'

'It sounds to me as if he's thought of it just to give me something to do. I don't want scores of people around the farm once I have a baby to look after, and I especially don't want Jack Trevis to get wind of it all and come and inspect it.'

'What makes you think he would?' Shirley said, when Poppy paused for breath.

'Because Sam said that for all that we don't like the fellow – those were his words – he'd obviously give us some publicity and help to make the thing a going concern. I can see why Sam is intrigued by the idea, but having Jack Trevis involved in any way is the last thing I want, Shirley. You must see that!'

'I think you're getting this all out of proportion, darling. Sam's being very forward-looking, if you want my opinion. You would need some publicity, but I'm sure there are other ways of going about it than by contacting Jack Trevis. You're bright enough to put words on paper, so you could write it all out and send it in to the paper yourself when the time comes. But since this is still only an idea in Sam's head, you needn't think about it for a long time yet.'

'I don't want to think about it at all.'

Shirley stood up, too uncomfortable to sit in a chair for a minute longer. 'Well, you obviously are, so go home and think about it some more, because I've got to go and lie down. There's nothing wrong, but I do need a rest in the afternoons, Poppy. We'll talk about it again any time you like, but don't say no to Sam right away. It's something you can be involved in together – as well as the baby, of course.'

'Oh well, maybe you're right. Florrie didn't put up lots of objections either, which was a minor miracle. Sam suggested we went to see this other farming museum first, to get an idea of what he's done.'

'There you are then,' Shirley said, edging her way towards the door. 'Come and tell me all about it when you've seen the other place.'

She shut the door thankfully behind

Poppy, wondering how she was ever going to last out another six weeks with the baby kicking more strongly every day as if she had a miniature footballer inside her – or two.

As Poppy walked towards the bus stop, a dozen thoughts were spinning around in her head. Perhaps it wasn't such a crazy idea. Perhaps Sam was cleverer than she had supposed in seeing the potential of a farm museum. People from upcountry were starting to discover Cornwall in their cars now that petrol was more plentiful and most of the wartime rationing had finally ended. People from upcountry would be curious about these so-called quaint folk with their legends and country ways. She had to admit that Jack Trevis had already proved the interest in it all through his local articles.

She pushed his name out of her mind as her imagination took hold. Maybe they could even have a tea room area alongside the farming implements, and Florrie could bake her famous sponge cakes to tempt the visitors.

The *paying* visitors, she realized with a little flutter of excitement. Maybe in this new year of 1951 there could be more to being a farmer's wife than the drudgery of feeding the pigs and chickens, and washing and ironing and cleaning and making beds, and selling eggs to the likes of Billy Flint's family.

'I didn't think you took to the idea,' Sam said in surprise that evening. 'Especially with the fuss you made about Trevis doing the reporting.'

'That's foolish talk,' his mother chipped in. 'If it was the thought of that young newspaper chap that's bothering you, Poppy, you should put him right out of your mind. He's got nothing to do with us, or whatever Sam decides to do.'

'Do you really like the thought of it, then?' Poppy asked her. She had quite thought Florrie might be up in arms at having what she would call an invasion of foreigners tramping about the farm, and would need to be talked round.

'There's more ways than one of making a go of things, and if this other chap up at St Austell is doing all right by it, why shouldn't we do the same?'

'Well said, Mother.' Sam smiled at her, and then at Poppy. 'But whatever's changed your mind about it, love, it's good to see you're getting over the sadness of past weeks. You've got some colour in your cheeks and your eyes are sparkling again. You look quite blooming tonight.'

If she had looked blooming before, Poppy felt herself blushing now. Sam wasn't a great compliment-giver, so she always felt especially pleased when he did so. Florrie's fingers paused over the crochet chair-back she was working on.

'Perhaps she's got another reason for looking blooming.'

Poppy couldn't look at Sam now. Instead she spoke in a rush. 'Well, yes, I had an enjoyable afternoon with Shirley today. She always does me good, though she's not feeling so comfortable now, and I think she's starting to wonder if she's expecting two instead of one! As a matter of fact I mentioned the museum thing to her, and she thought it was a good idea.'

'Oh, well, if Madam thinks it's a good idea, then it must be!' Florrie said sarcastically. 'But that's not quite what I meant. Are you sure there isn't something else you want to tell me?'

Without realizing that she was doing so, Poppy found herself hugging her arms around herself. Until this very moment the baby, which was little more than a speck inside her, belonged only to her. And to Sam, she thought hastily, but it was their precious secret. And Shirley's too, she remembered, still feeling privileged that Shirley had entrusted her with her own never-to-be-betrayed secret.

She wasn't sure she was ready yet to tell Florrie that she would become a grandmother in the autumn. She didn't know what the reaction would be, and she couldn't bear it if she didn't see the look in her eyes that she wanted. Once, she had imagined the day when she would go flying over to Zennor to tell her own parents, bubbling over with excitement and happiness, but that day would never come now.

She swallowed, knowing that Florrie was still waiting for her to answer, and that Sam was waiting too, wanting the words to come from her. And then her mother-in-law put down her crochet work and went across to the sideboard drawer.

She took out something wrapped in tissue paper.

'I've been keeping this for you to give to Shirley when her baby arrives,' she said. 'If you like it, I can easily make another one.'

Poppy opened the wrapping tissue, and blinked at the sight of the tiny white crocheted matinee coat inside. She wasn't sure if Florrie meant that if Shirley was having twins, she would need to give her two matinee coats instead of one, or if she was hinting that she knew very well why Poppy looked so blooming.

While she was still thinking of what to say, Florrie put her hand over Poppy's, her voice a touch gentler than usual. 'My dear girl, do you think I can't see what's in your face for all to see? A woman has a certain look when she's expecting a child, and you've had it for these past couple of weeks now. So am I to be the last to be told?'

'Of course not, and we want you to be pleased, Mother,' Sam said anxiously.

'Why wouldn't I be pleased? A man needs a son to carry on his name, and 'twill give Poppy plenty to think about during the summer, preparing for him, especially with this new idea of yours too. So when is it due?'

'September – I think,' Poppy said, stuttering a little.

She admitted that she had been vaguely dreading this moment. No, *more* than vaguely dreading it. She had thought Florrie would go all tight-lipped on her, and instead she was starting to bring out crochet and knitting patterns from the sideboard drawer now. Sam was looking like the cock of the heap, and for the moment all the talk was of babies, and any thoughts of the farm museum were put firmly into the background.

But one thought was very firmly and shiveringly in Poppy's mind. There was no doubt that Florrie was ready to welcome a grandson.

A man needs a son to carry on his name was what she had said, and the look in her eyes said that that was what she expected Poppy to produce. But there were no guarantees, and how Florrie would react if the baby was a girl was something Poppy didn't want to consider. Nor did she want to think that the ghost of Evie was going to mar this wonderful time of her life.

Wrapped in Sam's arms that night, she ventured to say as much.

'Stop worrying your head about it, sweetheart. As long as the child is healthy, that's all that matters. We'll love it whether it's a boy or a girl, and I'm sure Mother will feel the same as soon as she sees it.'

She nestled against him, feeling his breath on her cheek and the warmth of his body surrounding her. But it didn't stop her unease at the reaction she might get from Florrie if she didn't get the grandson she wanted. Already, the poor wee mite had a responsibility on its tiny shoulders, and it wasn't even born yet. But *she* was going to love it, Poppy thought, fiercely protective, no matter what.

Chapter Sixteen

'I thought we'd go over to St Austell in a week or two,' Sam told her. 'There's no sense in putting it off, so we might as well see how this other chap operates, and we could probably stay the night at a boarding house to save hurrying back.'

Poppy looked at him in astonishment. He was serious then. The idea hadn't been all that exciting at first, but she had time to think about it now, and it could be interesting as well as bringing in a few pennies.

The thought of staying overnight at a boarding house was intriguing her more. She had never done such a thing before. Getting married and coming straight from Zennor to live at the farm was the farthest she had ever been away from home, and until that moment she hadn't realized how very insular she was. No wonder Jack Trevis had found it so easy to take advantage of her – and she instantly wished his name hadn't come into her mind.

She dismissed it at once, her nerves still tingling with anticipation at the thought of having a night away from the farm, and certainly not by any memories of *that man*. Her smile was bright.

'Oh, I like the sound of that, Sam! Perhaps we could take a look around the town while we're there too.'

'Here now, I can't be spending too many hours idling away from the farm, Poppy, and besides there's not that much to see. It's just a hilly town, with a lot of spoil heaps and milky-looking pools to do with the china clay works, and then the port at Charleston where they dispatch it all from.'

'Well, as I've never seen anything like it

before, it sounds exciting to me!'

Sam laughed, seeing how her eyes were glowing, and at that moment he felt a rush of exquisite pleasure in his loins. With it came a fierce, possessive warmth in knowing that this lovely girl belonged to him and was soon going to bear him the son that he wanted.

'Well, maybe we can spend a few extra hours there like proper visitors,' he agreed. 'I daresay Len and Mother can deal with things for that amount of time.'

'It'll be almost like a honeymoon, won't it, Sam?' Poppy said without thinking, and then blushed furiously at a remark that was plain daft for a girl who'd been married all this time and was carrying a child.

'That it will, girl,' Sam said, with rare understanding.

She found herself humming over her chores during the next days. She had never expected to feel cheerful again after her parents' deaths, but a person couldn't stay in a state of gloom and despair for ever.

Florrie always said that the good Lord had seen to it that the passage of time changed everything, softening even the worst of anxieties. Poppy wouldn't have put it quite so pompously. Nor was she sure it was always true, but she had to admit that she was feeling easier in herself as the days passed, especially now the morning sickness wasn't quite so bad.

That was thanks to Florrie again, advising her to sip a cup of hot water and munch a dry biscuit before she got out of bed every morning. Florrie was never going to replace her own mother, Poppy thought, but she was the next best thing, and she realized it was the first time such a thought had ever occurred to her.

Late one evening there was a knock on the farmhouse door, accompanied by Dog's raucous barking at the arrival of a strange motor car.

'Now, who can that be at this time of night?' Florrie grumbled.

'You'll never know unless somebody goes to answer it, Mother,' Sam said lazily. 'I'll go and see to it.'

'No, I'll go,' Poppy said, jumping up too quickly, and wishing she hadn't as the room spun briefly. Shirley kept telling her to take things slowly to make sure the contents of her stomach remained in the right place and she wished she didn't keep forgetting the advice.

She was still thinking of Shirley, a smile on her face, as she opened the door. The smile wavered as soon as she saw Bernard Bosinney standing there. He should be bringing good news, but instinctively she knew that he wasn't.

'What's happened?' Poppy said, her hand going at once to her own stomach. 'Is everything all right with Shirley and the baby, Bernard? Sorry, I'm forgetting my manners. Please come inside – and please tell me quickly if anything's wrong.'

It was unthinkable that anything *had* gone wrong. Shirley had been looking forward so much to this baby, but right now Bernard looked haggard and unshaven, so different from his usual dapper style. It wasn't a good omen. Poppy felt the nervousness in her stomach become a great knot of fear. Somehow she felt that there was a special, close bond between her baby and Shirley's because of shared emotions and secrets, and she couldn't bear it if anything awful had happened.

Bernard came inside the farmhouse and spoke quickly. 'I'm sorry if I alarmed you, Poppy. And good evening Sam, and Mrs Lovering,' he added, polite as ever. 'Shirley's fine and so is the baby, but it was all pretty traumatic at the time.'

'You mean she's had the baby already? But it wasn't due for another month!' Poppy almost squeaked.

'Come and sit down, man, you look as if you could do with a drink,' Sam put in. 'We've only got cider to wet the baby's head – unless you feel you could do with a tot of brandy?'

'I won't have anything, Sam, thanks all the same,' Bernard said, but clearly glad to sit down. 'Yes, Shirley's had the baby, and a fine boy he is too, considering.'

'Considering what?' Poppy was fearful now, seeing how exhausted and worried Bernard appeared. Shirley had always been so breezy about having this baby until the last time Poppy had seen her, she remembered, when she hadn't been able to sit still. If things had started to go badly when labour began, surely her conscience hadn't started pricking her again, making her blurt out everything about the baby that hadn't lived.

Bernard spoke more agitatedly as memory took over. 'Last night we thought she might be going into labour early, so I sent for the midwife to come and take a look at her. She confirmed it, and said everything was coming along nicely, and so it was, until Shirley's waters broke with such a flood it made her scream out with shock. That was when it all began to go wrong.'

'Here. Take this.' Nobody seemed to have noticed Florrie until that moment when she thrust the small glass of brandy into Bernard's hand. 'No argument, young man. Drink it down and tell us what's happened.'

He gulped the spirit back as if he hadn't even tasted it, and he probably hadn't, thought Poppy, her heart thumping sickly. Shirley was like her talisman. If things could

334

go wrong for Shirley, what did that mean for her? She shook her head, willing the superstitious nonsense away.

Bernard began talking again, his tone so different from his normal placid manner, betraying just how worried he had been. 'The midwife could see something was wrong, and by then Shirley was in a lot of distress and begging her to do something. Eventually I was sent to fetch the doctor, and he got an ambulance right away and took Shirley to hospital.'

'Oh, that was the last thing she wanted,' Poppy breathed, knowing how much Shirley wanted the baby to be born in her own home, and that she had visualized a birth that was smooth and easy and beautiful.

'It was the only thing to do. Apparently the force of the waters had dragged the baby's arm over his head and he'd got stuck in the birth canal. Sorry about all the medical details but that was how it was told to me. They had to put Shirley out so that they could turn the baby round and use forceps to deliver him. The poor girl had been drinking tea and eating toast so they had to put a tube down her throat to extract it all before she could have the anaesthetic.'

'But they're both all right now?' Florrie said in a firm voice, seeing how Poppy's face had gone chalk-white at the image his words evoked.

'Thank God, yes. They're both doing well, and Shirley's surprisingly perky now after all she's gone through, though I'm not sure I want to go through a day and night like that again. I've spent this evening over at Penhallow giving the news to our folks and to Carrie and Archie Pollard. She especially wanted me to let you know too, Poppy, as you've become such good friends.'

Poppy felt like weeping, even though the news was finally good. But in those few minutes she had begun to realize just how things could go wrong, and how precarious those hours of giving birth could be. And she was scared. Scared to death if anybody wanted to know.

She felt Sam's hand squeezing hers, and as their glances briefly held, she knew a moment of sheer empathy with her husband. It was as if he could see inside her soul at that moment, and if she had ever thought him insensitive, she took it back a hundredfold. He may not reveal his feelings in words too often, but they were there whenever she needed them.

'Can I visit Shirley?' she asked Bernard huskily.

'Well, not just yet. It's only close family for the first few days, while she recovers her strength, but after that I know she'll want to see you and show off our little Luke.'

'You finally decided on his name then? I

know Shirley was as superstitious as me about that,' Poppy said, tasting the name in her mind and liking the way it sounded. One-day-old Luke Bosinney was now a person in his own right. He could exercise his lungs and wave his little fists about and look at the new world around him with wondering eyes. She blinked away the silly tears at the thought.

'Luke's a good biblical name,' Florrie was saying. 'With a name like that he won't go far wrong in life. And before you go, Mr Bosinney, I'd like you to have this small garment I've made for him.'

She foraged in the drawer and handed the tissue-wrapped package to Bernard, while Poppy told him she would write to Shirley tomorrow, and urged him to let her know just how soon she could go and see her and the baby.

'She'll be in the hospital for two weeks, but I'll let you know the minute she can have other visitors,' he promised.

After he left, Sam decided that they should all have a tot of brandy to wet the baby's head too. Poppy didn't like the taste and wasn't sure that she should have it in her condition, but Sam told her it would help her sleep, and she could see the sense in that. Otherwise she knew she would be lying awake imagining everything Shirley had gone through, and her nerves would be in shreds by morning.

'I think we'll take that trip to St Austell the day after tomorrow, once I've got Len organized,' Sam said later, just before they turned out the light in their bedroom. 'It will give us something else to think about instead of having you bursting with impatience to see Shirley's new baby.'

She snuggled into his back, knowing that this was his way of conveying to her that she shouldn't let her vivid imagination send her crazy, wondering if what had happened to Shirley was going to happen to her. Or worse.

But as she drifted off to sleep, she guessed shrewdly that in Shirley's mind all the pain and trauma she had gone through to deliver Luke safely would be a kind of penance for that other time. She would be humbly thanking God for the punishment she always knew she deserved, and for giving her and Bernard their own sweet baby at last.

She reminded herself that first thing in the morning she intended to write to Shirley congratulating her on the birth of her son, and imploring Shirley to let her know as soon as she was fit enough for Poppy to come and see him.

Len Painter had no objection to doing extra hours on the farm while Sam and Poppy were away. So Poppy found herself packing a small suitcase with the few clothes they would need for a stay at a boarding house in St Austell, and the excitement was bubbling up inside her again. It *would* be like a sort of honeymoon to be away from the farm, and she was still marvelling that Sam had agreed.

They drove off in the car in their Sunday best, feeling strangely awkward with one another as they left Barras and then Penzance behind them, and ventured on to unknown roads as far as Poppy was concerned. They would drive through Helston, where the ancient furry dance was held every year, skirting Falmouth and going through Truro before they finally reached the moorland outskirts of St Austell where the established farm museum was situated.

She knew Sam had been to St Austell several times before, and it occurred to her that after all these years she knew little about any social life he might have had in his youth. Had he had other girlfriends before her? He would hardly have told her about them since she was such a kid when she had first come to the farm. Had he ever had a big romance, the way they were shown on the silver screen, and maybe been disappointed in love? When he was younger had he taken moonlight walks along the coast, or gone to the pictures with a girl beside him to slide his arm around in the back seat of the cinema?

'What's so interesting about my face?' he asked, glancing at her when she'd been staring at him intently for a few minutes. 'Have I got a smut on my nose or something?'

She felt herself go hot. 'I was just sort of wondering why you married me.'

He laughed. 'Good God, it's a bit late to be thinking about that, isn't it?'

'I didn't mean that, exactly. I mean, you must have known plenty of other girls before me. I was just a kid on the farm and the land girls were far more glamorous than me! Didn't you ever fancy one of them?'

He gave a snort. 'If you're fishing for compliments, I don't quite know how to answer that.'

'I'm not,' she said crossly.

'No, but if I say I wasn't interested in fast-talking glamour girls, you'll think I mean that you weren't glamorous.'

'Well, I might,' Poppy muttered, wishing she'd never started this. 'In any case, I'm not and I never was. Glamorous, I mean.'

Despite what that slimy oaf Trevis had told her, but she was wise to him now. His kind were only out for what they could get, no matter how many lies they told.

'There's no need for you think anything of the sort. You were always the prettiest of them all. You were far more natural and you didn't need to plaster your face with all that make-up and stuff, and you were the one I wanted, so you can get any daft ideas about glamour right out of your head.'

She laughed. 'That was quite a speech, Sam.'

'Make the most of it then, because I doubt that you'll hear it again.'

But he took his hand off the steering wheel for an instant and squeezed her knee to soften the brusque words. And she kept his rugged profile in her mind as she concentrated on the road ahead, aware that he'd been smiling as he said it. Her spirits lifted with every mile they took, because this was quite an adventure after all.

The farm museum was well outside St Austell, but in the distance and way above the town itself, Poppy could already see the strange white mountains on the vast stretches of empty moorland.

'Is that what you told me about, that's all to do with the china clay business?' she asked Sam. 'They look as if they should be on the moon, not here in Cornwall.'

'Maybe they should, but I doubt if the clay-workers would appreciate such a thought. They're just the worthless waste products left over once they've got the clay out of the earth.'

'They look far too pretty to be worthless,'

Poppy said, caught by the way the morning sun was glinting on the spoil heaps.

'That's just the minerals catching the light from the sun. You can't always go by looks, and some things that are attractive to the eye aren't worth a fig.'

She caught the slight change of tone in his voice. Did he mean that what he said applied to people as well? Maybe he was thinking of the land girls, whose glamour he always said was no more than skin-deep. Or maybe he was hinting obliquely that a certain newspaper reporter who thought he could charm the birds from the trees, was a worthless individual too. If so, she would fervently agree with that.

'We're here,' Sam said briefly.

Poppy blinked. Was it her imagination or had the day suddenly got colder, the distant spoil heaps losing their sunlit glitter and resembling nothing more than dull piles of dirty waste? Or was the coldness in Sam's voice, as if he was slowly beginning to wonder whether his wife had been as resistant to Jack Trevis's attractions as he believed? Although, after the way she had struck out at Jack like a harridan at her parents' funeral, Poppy could hardly think that he would be so suspicious.

Her heart jolted. Unless, of course, young Billy Flint had decided to slyly mention to someone that there had been a certain less than innocent meeting at Chysauster Village. She shuddered visibly, sick at heart at the thought of how she had allowed that rotter to take advantage of her, and even more humiliated and alarmed at wondering just how much that boy had witnessed after all.

'Well, are you coming inside, or are you going to sit in the car for the rest of the day, Poppy? You seem to be off in a dream-world. You're not unwell, are you? There's nought wrong inside, is there?'

She could see that he was anxious now, for her welfare and for that of the baby. And perhaps all her fears were merely in her imagination, and nothing more. She smiled as warmly as she could.

'There's nothing wrong at all, Sam,' she said shakily. 'I think perhaps I felt the baby move, that's all, though it's probably too soon. I think perhaps he's going to be a footballer.'

The words were out before she could stop to think that Sam probably wouldn't appreciate hearing such a thing. His son was destined to be a farmer through and through, the same as his father and grandfather before him. But it was true that she fancied she had felt a fluttering movement several times, and it was a glorious sensation that meant their baby was alive and well.

Sam leaned over before getting out of the

car and pressed his hand lightly on her belly. 'With you and me as his parents, there's no knowing what he'll be. He'll be strong-willed and robust, that's for sure, and as long as he's healthy that's a good enough legacy for any child.'

He cleared his throat, as if giving away so much of his feelings was enough for one day. 'Now let's get inside this museum and see what's what.'

Poppy stepped outside the car, breathing in the clear moorland air that had just a hint of the sea in it from the coast beyond St Austell. She loved this county with a fierceness akin to passion, she thought, and it would take an army to move her away from it. Or a war, she added silently, remembering Bernard Bosinney and all those others who had fought for their country, some of them dying for it.

She hugged Sam's arm as they crunched over the gravel path to where the placard announcing 'Callard's Farm Museum' stood firmly in front of the old outbuildings.

'I can't wait to see Shirley and her baby,' she murmured. 'She must be so thrilled that he's here at last, and I'm dying to see him and hear all about it.'

Sam grinned. 'Take my advice, girl, and close your ears to most of it. There's no use worrying yourself over what happened to Shirley. She was always the dramatic one.

She should have been on the stage.'

Poppy hadn't quite meant that, and nor was she sure that she wanted to hear *too* much detail of Shirley's experience, but as long as her friend had come through it smiling, it would all have been worthwhile when she saw her little son for the first time. Everyone said as much. You forgot the pain and only remembered the joy.

An hour or so later they had inspected all the old farm machinery and the knick-knacks that Frank Callard had collected for his museum. He had had leaflets printed to publicize the place, and, as well as taking one of them for reference, Poppy had made a careful note of everything.

Many of the displays were composed of objects that had been lying about on Lovering's Farm for years, Sam whispered to her, and he saw no reason why they couldn't do the same thing in Barras, as they were far enough away from Callard's not to be a threat to his business.

Eventually, the owner couldn't be unaware of the special interest these two were taking, and approached them with a smile on his weatherbeaten face.

'Good-morning, Sir and Ma'am. Is there anything of particular interest to you both? From the look of you' – he glanced down at Sam's polished brown boots and his capable country air – 'I'd say you might be a farming man yourself, and well knowledgeable about some of the things here.'

Sam nodded. 'And you'd be right. I'm Sam Lovering of Lovering's Farm in Barras, and this is my wife, Poppy.'

'So what's this then, so far from home? A trip down memory lane or summat?' Callard said with a grin.

Intuitively, Poppy realized that Sam was momentarily tongue-tied. He knew all about farming, rearing pigs and chickens and calving cows in trouble, but when it came to business dealings he was a novice. She plucked up courage and spoke before Sam could start waffling.

'Mr Callard, we've heard about this museum of yours and we wanted to take a look for ourselves as we're very interested in doing something similar. As you say, we live a good distance from here, so we would attract different visitors from yourself. We also wondered if you could give us any tips on how to begin, since it's no more than an idea at the moment.'

She added the last sentence quickly, seeing the frown begin to appear on the man's face. But then he nodded slowly, clearly accepting that they would be no competition.

'And you can see a way of adding a bit of income to the general farm work, I daresay.

Seems to me I've heard of you already. Lovering's Farm, you say? Ain't that down yonder, Penzance way, where the fair and fête is held every August?'

'The very same,' Sam said, bolder now that his name was recognized.

'Well then, since 'tis a quiet day for visitors today, you'd best come through to the house and take some tea with me and my missus and I'll tell you how we went about it. The young woman could do with a sit down and a cuppa, I'm sure,' he added, glancing at Poppy's gently-rounded belly.

Poppy grasped Sam's hand, hoping she hadn't done wrong in speaking out before he did, but his nod reassured her. And once inside the homely parlour she was glad now to let the men talk business in another room, while she and Mrs Callard discussed more female topics, such as Sam's vague idea of Poppy and Florrie dressing up in old-time costumes in their proposed museum, perhaps opening a small tea-room alongside and, more importantly, Poppy's coming baby.

'You'll forgive me for mentioning it, my dear,' Mrs Callard said in her soothing voice, 'but you've got such a bloom on you I'm sure it's going to be a very happy event. I'm psychic, you know, so I can see these things.'

'Really? My mother was reckoned to be a

bit psychic too. She always said I had the gift, but I haven't seen much evidence of it yet.'

'Oh, I suspect that you have, even if you don't recognize it fully. You'll have an instinct for good and bad, and such things always stand a body in good stead.'

Well, she hadn't had much of an instinct to sort Jack Trevis out, Poppy thought keenly. But since she was as much involved in this farm museum project as Sam, Trevis's name prompted her to ask this motherly woman another question.

'We saw the piece about your museum in the newspaper, but we don't really care to have a reporter coming to discuss it with us. My friend suggested I could write out the details and send it to the paper myself. What do you think?'

Mrs Callard stared at Poppy for a moment before snapping her fingers. 'Now I know why you looked familiar! I remember seeing your pretty face in the paper a while back. You were the young woman who rescued the boy from the mine shaft, weren't you?'

'That's right, but we don't want all that publicity raked up again.'

'Why not? It would put your new business on the map.'

'Oh, well, there are reasons, but I could send in the report myself, couldn't I?' Poppy went on, starting to shift uncomfortably as she remembered that if this woman was truly psychic she could probably see a lot more behind Poppy's words than she was willing to reveal.

The kettle sang out from the small scullery and the woman stood up. "Course you can, my dear, and you'll make a good job of it too, I'm sure. Now we'll have that cup of tea and talk some more about babies.'

Just as long as you don't tell me if I'm having a boy or a girl, thought Poppy.

Until it was born it was a secret known only to God and the infant itself, the way nature intended. She wanted no psychic predictions, no waving of a wedding-ring over her belly or other old-wives' tales to try to gauge the baby's gender. It was why she was knitting and sewing everything in white, both as a symbol of the infant's purity and to show that the final choice was in God's hands.

She blinked, wondering why she was suddenly turning so perishing noble. But she truly wouldn't want to know beforehand. Besides, Sam had his heart set on a boy, and so had Florrie, and even though Poppy would have longed to hold a baby girl in her arms, she knew how much of a disappointment she would be to both of them if it didn't turn out right.

She was glad when the men came back from their discussion and Mrs Callard busied herself in pouring out large mugs of tea and handing out home-made biscuits that were as heavy as lead, as Sam remarked afterwards. But it had been a good meeting, and he was more fired up with his idea now than ever before.

'We'll go and find ourselves a boarding house and settle in, and then we'll go and take a look at these clay mountains you're so curious about,' he said, as they walked back to the car, in good spirits now, and willing to indulge her.

'And the port tomorrow too. I'd like to take a look at the ships, Sam.'

'Not thinking of going anywhere, are you?' he grinned.

She tossed her head. 'Why would I want to go anywhere when I'm happy right where I am?'

He put his arm around her shoulders and gave her a hug right there in full view of Callard's Farm Museum, and she felt a renewed sense of love for him. It was undiminished as they found a comfortable boarding house and deposited their things into the room that was to be their home for the night, and then drove up above the town of St Austell and gazed at the strange white landscape all around them.

'I was right. It is like being on the moon,' Poppy said.

'Oh yes, and how would you know?' Sam grinned.

'I don't know, but I can guess. There seems to be so much power in these spoil heaps, yet you say they've had all the goodness taken out of them. I think the moon must be like that. When God created the universe, all the goodness was sent down to earth, and the moon has what's left.'

Sam let out a loud guffaw, but his voice was indulgent. 'I always thought I'd married a madwoman, and now I'm sure of it. My mother would be pleased to hear your godly words though. You're not going to turn into a saint as well, are you?'

'Not likely,' Poppy grinned back.

The wind caught at her hair and blew it in gossamer strands around her face. Her eyes were glowing bright from the sights all around her and the freedom and silence of the open moors compared with the restrictions and routine of the farm.

On the skyline were rows of clay-workers' cottages; far below them they could hear the drone of machinery and see the ant-like figures of the clay-workers themselves going about their tasks. The depths of the distant milky-green pool of clay water was motionless from here and they seemed to be in a world of their own, with nothing but the whisper of bracken and furze about them.

Without thinking, Poppy threw her arms in the air and yelled to anyone who could hear, even though there was no one within earshot. 'Thank you God, for giving Sam and me this day!'

She was suddenly caught in her husband's arms, and his voice was hoarse and rough against her cheek, his laughter at her uninhibited actions fading.

'By God, Poppy, if I ever wondered why I married you, it's because of moments like this when you seem like an enchanted child of nature. The perplexing question is why such a glorious creature as yourself ever married *me!*'

Her heart was beating fast against his chest, and she could feel the drumming of his in return as she answered him breathlessly and in an instant. 'It's because I love you, of course. Why else would a woman marry a man?'

'Or a man marry a woman,' he returned huskily.

He was kissing her face and her eyes and then his kiss was sweet and deep on her mouth as he found her lips, and she felt herself melting into him. This was the closest they had ever been, she thought faintly. There were no intruders into their intimacy, only the baby growing inside her that was a part of them.

'I want to make love to you here and now.' He spoke with sudden fierceness, his voice full of passion. 'Do you think we dare take advantage of a hollow on the moors, my wild witch?'

In an instant the spell was broken for Poppy. It was too reminiscent of another time, another place, when a seductive man with a silver tongue had persuaded her to lie with him and then pushed her aside as if she was of no more consequence than a troublesome fly.

'I would far rather take advantage of that double bed waiting for us at the boarding house where we can be sure of having all night to ourselves,' she whispered back, hoping that her trembling voice would convey her own restrained passion and not despair at knowing that that man could still come between them, no matter how much she tried to push him out of her mind.

'Well, that's an enticing thought and no mistake,' Sam said, reluctantly unlocking her from his embrace. 'And you're right, of course. We don't want to frighten the natives hereabouts. So let's go and see what sort of fare the landlady's preparing for our supper, and then we'll have an early night. How does that sound, Mrs Lovering?'

'Wonderful,' Poppy said.

Chapter Seventeen

A week later Bernard Bosinney called at the farm to say that Poppy could visit Shirley in the hospital the next evening between 6pm and 7pm. Sam said he would take her there, as he wanted to see several people in the Penzance area about his new project – besides which, his idea of an evening's entertainment wasn't making hospital visits. But he said it cheerfully enough to imply that if any such thing were to happen to Poppy (fingers crossed as she thought it), he'd be there like a shot. In any case, Poppy wouldn't have wanted him listening in when she visited Shirley. This was a time for women's talk.

She dutifully walked the antiseptic corridors of the hospital to the ward where she was directed, a bunch of flowers in her hands and her own knitted offering for baby Bosinney in her bag. She was unaccountably nervous. It was her first time in a hospital, and it seemed both alarming and forbidding, full of strange odours, and so very clinical. It made you wonder if anyone here had any heart or if everything was done to mechanical perfection.

Then she saw Shirley waving to her from the bed at the far end of the ward, looking bright and pretty and normal. She was chatting to a youngish-looking nurse who beckoned to Poppy after Shirley had obviously told her who she was.

'Thank goodness you've come to relieve me from this chatterbox,' the nurse said jovially, belying all the things Poppy had just been thinking. 'I'll give you five minutes together, and then I'll bring Master Bosinney into the ward for your inspection and admiration. She won't give me any peace until I do.'

Poppy sat down on the chair at the side of the bed, not knowing what to say for a minute. Did you kiss the patient? They weren't really kissing friends, and Shirley was hardly the usual kind of patient. She'd always insisted that having a baby was a natural, normal thing, and probably still would, despite all that she had gone through. At the thought, Poppy's eyes welled with tears.

'Oh, Shirley,' she began with a wobbly smile.

'Now don't start blubbing, or you'll start me off. I'm fine, except for a bit of soreness in what the vampire nurses call my tail, but I'm told that'll soon pass. You wait until you see my Luke. He's the most beautiful, adorable baby that ever lived, and I can still

355

hardly believe that he's mine. And Bernard's, of course,' she added with a beaming smile.

'Everything's all right then,' Poppy said cautiously.

She didn't know how it could be otherwise with Shirley looking so rapturous. And so disgustingly well after so short a time. But Shirley had always had the capacity to bounce back, no matter what the circumstances.

'Everything's as wonderful as it should be. And no matter how many babies I have, nothing will compare with the first moment I held Luke in my arms. You've got that to look forward to, Poppy, and you're going to love that special moment when he comes into the world and you say hello to him for the very first time. It's like magic.'

Her voice was almost awed, and Poppy knew instinctively that all the sad memories of that other time had been dispelled. Luke was the first baby Shirley had held and loved. Impulsively now, she leaned forward and kissed Shirley's cheek.

'I'm so very glad it all turned out well for you,' she whispered.

'So what's your news? Have you and Sam done anything about this farm museum idea?' Shirley said, as if determined to show some interest in something other than the baby, if only to be polite – however briefly.

'Oh yes. We've been to St Austell and seen this other place, and Sam's full of enthusiasm about it. He and Len are clearing out a couple of unused barns and seeing what junk we've got that could be of interest to upcountry visitors. Honestly, Shirley, that's mostly what it is, just old junk – apart from the corn dollies that I can make, but I suppose when folk have never seen old farm implements and stuff like that before, they'll be willing to pay to see it. Mr Callard seems to be making a go of it, so I don't see why we shouldn't.'

'That's good,' Shirley said vaguely, her mind already wandering, her gaze continually going to the door of the ward.

Minutes later, the nurse returned, pushing a wheeled cot towards them, and Shirley immediately sat up straighter, wincing only a little, and held out her arms.

The nurse picked up the baby, wrapped like a mummy in a white shawl, and handed him to Shirley.

'Here you are, Mother,' she said with that continuing jollity that would surely drive Shirley mad in time, thought Poppy. 'He's sleepy now, so don't go tickling him too much to try to make him perform tricks. The minute he starts crying, he goes back in his cot and back to the baby ward, remember.'

'You're a tyrant, do you know that?'

Shirley grumbled, but then immediately forgot her as she unwrapped the shawl from around the baby's face and Poppy got a good look at him for the first time.

She drew in her breath. He was so tiny. So perfect in every way, from his screwed-up button mouth to the long eyelashes on his cheek, and the fair wispy hair, so like Shirley's and Bernard's.

She couldn't speak for a moment, picturing herself holding something as small and as helpless as this, and then Luke gave a huge yawn in his sleep, his mouth suddenly wide and mobile in his face, and they both laughed out loud.

Right on cue, his eyes opened a fraction. They were as blue and fathomless as the sea, and then he closed them again, blissfully content in Shirley's arms.

'He's gorgeous, Shirley,' Poppy gulped. 'I've never seen a newborn baby before, and oh Lord, I didn't know it would affect me like this. It makes me want to cry, it does really.'

'It's your hormones,' Shirley said briskly. 'I've learned a lot about all the emotional stuff since I've been in here. Nurse Willis never lets up, but she's a good sort all the same. Here, you hold him a minute while I adjust these God-awful pads they put in my bosoms to stop the milk leaking out between feeds. I feel like a cow sometimes.

Who needs falsies when you're a new mum!'

She giggled as she handed Luke over matter-of-factly to Poppy, who held him gingerly. She could smell the soft, sweet baby smell of him, and as she touched his satiny cheek she knew a rush of emotion that made her want to gather him close to her and smother him with love. And if *she* felt like that, how much more intense must Shirley be feeling, knowing he was hers for ever.

'He won't break, Poppy,' Shirley told her. 'He's a fine, strong boy, even down to his little you-know-what. I made sure of that.' She giggled again, at once the old Shirley with dancing eyes and a mischievous streak.

'I hope mine will be just like him.'

'Good God, I hope not. Not with Sam's dark looks, and your lovely dark hair and film-star face. What's he going to say if you produce a little blondie?'

Poppy laughed. 'You know what I mean. As long as he's perfect, it doesn't matter about his looks. I shall love him, anyway – well, I already do,' she added, wondering if that was a totally daft thing to say.

'Of course you do, but that's enough mooning over Luke or I shall get jealous. You can give him back to me now. I only allow visitors to share him for a few minutes, except for Bernard.' Her brisk voice suddenly softened. 'Oh Poppy, we're so

359

lucky – both of us. All of us.'

As Poppy handed the baby over, their hands touched and their faces were momentarily close, their eyes meeting. And she knew without saying what Shirley meant. They had both done foolish things in their pasts, but they had both come through unscathed. Yes, they were the lucky ones.

'We'll have to arrange for some advertising in good time for the opening,' Sam said in mid-April, when it had been decided that for maximum impact the opening of Lovering's Farm Museum should coincide with the next annual fête and fair. In Penzance while Poppy was visiting Shirley, he had already contacted a sign-writer to make several signs for the doors of the barns announcing Lovering's Farm Museum. The few local farmers who had already brought stuff over to the farm that they were glad to get rid of had gone away with the promise that the notices beneath the objects would say who had donated them.

Right now Poppy didn't feel much like planning anything. The pleasure of seeing Shirley's new baby, and the excitement of going to St Austell and the thoughts of starting a new business concern had faded somewhat. She knew it was due to her condition, these *hormones* that Shirley had spoken about so airily, even if Sam seemed distinctly unaware of her moodiness. Despite Florrie's remedies the morning sickness hadn't abated much after all, and even though the midwife had told her it would ease off once she reached the halfway stage in her pregnancy, there wasn't any sign of it yet.

Not that she was quite halfway there yet, she thought almost crossly. In fact, the birth of her baby seemed an eternity away. Her restlessness wasn't helped by the fact that she was seeing Shirley on a fairly regular basis now, and saw how deliciously Luke was thriving. Each time she handed him back to his mother's arms, she thought wistfully how lovely it would be to be caring for her own. And nobody had ever told her just how bloody long these nine months could be!

'I told you I'd compose something for the newspaper, but it's far too early yet,' she snapped at Sam in response to his comment.

'All right, there's no need to bite my head off. It might be too early for that, but you could be writing out the labels for the stuff that we've got, since your writing's tidier than mine. I've scribbled out the names for you, and a bit of detail about what they're used for, and at least with your schooling you can sort out the spelling. You should have time enough to do that, now that

Mother's doing much of your farm duties.'

She glared at him. 'There's no need to be sarcastic, Sam. I can't help it if I'm not up to much in the mornings, and your mother did offer, remember?'

Oh God, this was supposed to be a happy time, wasn't it? A time when she should be serene and calm, awaiting her baby's birth. Instead of which she and Sam seemed to be forever scratching away at one another lately. She didn't know why, and she didn't know how to stop it.

'Mother's not a young woman, Poppy.'

She looked at him sharply, wondering if this was just a ploy to stir her conscience. 'She's not ill, is she? If she is, she's never said anything and if she thinks I'm not pulling my weight, why doesn't she say so? She never used to be slow in complaining about me!'

Sam sighed impatiently. 'She's not ill, but sometimes I wonder if you're making too much of this morning sickness. It wouldn't hurt you to hang out the washing or feed the chickens like you used to, instead of leaving everything to Mother and having a lie down whenever you feel like it.'

Poppy's eyes blazed. 'Well, if that's not just about the most damnable, bloody arrogant *male* thing I ever heard! Next time, *you* can have the baby, Mr high-and-mighty Lovering, and see how you cope with it. I've not heard of a man yet who'd willingly go through childbirth, nor care to look and feel like a useless lump for the nine months leading up to it!'

Without giving him time to reply, she flounced out of the parlour and into the yard, where Dog started yapping and leaping around her feet and legs the minute she appeared.

'And you can shut up too!' she yelled at him. 'What do you know about anything, you damn stupid animal?'

She marched away, seething at being so childish as to shout petulantly at a dog. It wasn't his fault that she felt so out of sorts with herself, with Sam; with his mother; with the world in general. She didn't know why she felt this way, but she wished the feeling would go away for good and all.

She reached the barns that had been partially cleared, except for the variety of old artefacts piled up inside. Prepared to be belligerent about anything and everything, she asked herself just who in their right minds would be interested in ancient dairy equipment and a range of different horseshoes; in a couple of country smocks someone had donated; in strange old tools that would have to have their purpose explained; an old farm wagon; baskets of various kinds; and all the other paraphernalia she had listed from the contents of Callard's Farm Museum.

Gradually, however, as she touched the old things her imagination made her think of what memories they must hold. And with a small renewal of the excitement she had felt in St Austell, Poppy guessed there would be very many folk from upcountry, and even from their own Cornish towns, who would have no idea what a horsegagging link was, or the difference between a pitch fork and a dung fork. The tools might be old and dusty, but some of the most ancient things were still in use among rural farming folk, and however commonplace they might be to them, they would all be new and strange, and arouse curiosity in those other people.

That was why she had to make a good job of labelling them, Poppy thought, using as much personal information as she could gather. The artefacts alone were cold and impersonal, but for the long-ago folk who had used them, they would have been an essential part of their livelihood, and had a history of their own.

A sound behind her made her start, and she turned around to see Sam standing there, his hands aggressively on his hips. He looked angrier than she had seen him in a long time.

'Have you done with your temper?' he said shortly. 'It's time you remembered you're a married woman, not a spoilt child, ready to run away the first time somebody crosses you.'

She snapped back. 'I wasn't running away. And if I was, it was only from you and your stuffy ways, old man!'

The minute she had said it, she knew it was a mistake. Sam's frown got darker as she seemed to emphasize the gulf of age between them.

'Well, I'm sorry if my ways don't please you, Madam. If you'd wanted constant attention you should have married a young whippersnapper like that Trevis bloke, or one of them film stars you used to gloat over in them trashy magazines.'

Poppy gasped at this tirade. It wasn't what she had expected or wanted. She didn't stop to think that Sam could have been hurt by her remarks. She was too concerned by his reference to Jack Trevis and her own guilt at how she had been seduced by him. She had thrown away the film star magazines long ago – and when did he ever offer to take her to the pictures, anyway? She could count the times on the fingers of one hand, and she was too stung with wounded pride to care what she was saying now.

'I daresay I could have married somebody like Jack Trevis if I'd wanted to, but I didn't bother waiting, did I? I married the first man who asked me, more fool me!'

'If that's what you think, then it's a pity you ever said yes and got landed with a countryman's babby. But if I'm so repulsive to you, you can be damn sure I won't be troubling you in that department again.'

He turned and stalked away, leaving Poppy trembling and shaken and wondering how it had all come to this, when minutes before she had been ready and eager to go back to the farmhouse and say she was sorry for her silly behaviour and that she had all kinds of ideas for the museum.

Then it dawned on her just what Sam had said. He wouldn't be troubling her in that department again. Did he mean he wouldn't want to sleep in the same bed with her ever again, or that there would be no more babies between them? And how would such a terrible situation and bad feeling affect the little one they had already created?

She was certain she felt the baby give a small lurch inside her then, and to her ever-receptive mind it was as if he knew exactly what was going on between his parents, and was reproaching her for it. She felt an enormous tightening in her throat, her limbs felt as if they were turning to water, and the next moment she sank down on the straw-littered floor, sobbing as if her heart would break for her foolishness.

How long she remained there she couldn't tell, only that she was stiff and cold when she finally got to her feet, swaying a little. She knew she must have been there ages, and that Sam hadn't come back to the barn to find her as she had half expected him to. But he wouldn't, of course. He had his pride too. He would never beg. And she had done an unforgivable thing by implying that he was too old for her and that she could have done so much better than to accept a proposal from the first man who asked her.

A shadow fell across the opening of the barn and she looked up anxiously, ready to make the most abject apology she could. She was acutely ashamed of the way she had behaved, and since her pride was in shreds now, what did anything else matter but to repair the damage between her and Sam?

'A fine state you're in, my girl. I swear I never heard such goings-on, and it'll do no good for the little 'un to have you ranting and bleating all the time like this,' said Florrie severely.

Poppy stared at her mutely, hating the fact that she might have heard most of it; disappointed that she wasn't Sam, come to take her in his arms and say they'd both said hasty things and that it didn't matter a damn in the great scheme of things; angry with herself for feeling so weak and so very, very young.

'I know,' she choked. Her arms hung limply by her sides, her shoulders drooped, and the next second she found herself being enclosed by stronger arms and her back was being patted and soothed as if she was five years old.

'There now, you shouldn't take on so,' her mother-in-law said roughly. 'A woman in your condition gets all kinds of daft ideas while her body goes through all the changes to prepare for the babby. A man knows nothing of the turmoil that goes on inside at such times, and 'tis up to the woman to make allowances.'

'Is that right?' Poppy mumbled against her shoulder, beginning to marvel at the knowledge that Florrie wasn't condemning her for being so cruel to Sam, but was actually showing her some understanding. She pulled slightly away from her.

'But you don't know the half of it. I was so awful to Sam, Mrs Lovering – Florrie – Mother-in-law,' she rushed on. 'I don't think he'll ever forgive me.'

''Course he will. You're his wife, aren't you? Do you think there's a married couple alive who don't have some sort of barney at times? It clears the air and it does no harm, providing they have the sense to make things right between them and don't let it fester.'

'Is that what you think I should do then?'

Florrie gave a grunt. 'Well, one of you has to make the first move, and 'tis certain sure that a man never had the sense to do it. We women have always been the wiser when it comes to putting things right. The good Lord only knows why they call us the weaker sex. Weaker in body, perhaps, but stronger in sense.'

Poppy managed to give a small smile at that, and was embarrassed to find herself still held tight in Florrie's arms.

'Thank you,' she whispered. 'I'll go and find Sam straight away. I couldn't bear for this to be hanging over us for ever. And you know, I do – I really do love him, Mrs – Mother-in-law.'

'Of course you do,' Florrie said, extricating herself now. 'And for heaven's sake, girl, if you find it so difficult to call me Mother, then start calling me Grandma. It's what I'm going to be to the boy, isn't it? And I'll have to get used to it.'

'Yes,' Poppy said, mentally crossing her fingers for more than one reason.

She made up her mind to find Sam as soon as they left the barn and went their separate ways. He would probably be out in the fields by now, mending fences. It seemed very apt. Mending fences was exactly what she had to do. She struck out, her heart thumping, knowing she had to humble herself.

She caught sight of him a long way ahead, near the outer lane of the farm. He was hammering nails into the fence that the cows had rubbed against and broken, and even from here, she could still sense the anger in him by the tautness of his body and the way he was furiously wielding the hammer. She stumbled a little, praying that she would find the right words to put things right between them.

And then her heart almost stopped as she saw another figure making his way towards Sam. She didn't know where he had come from, though he would probably have parked his car farther back along the wider part of the lane, but there was no mistaking Jack Trevis's tall, rangy shape and the arrogant set of his head.

Poppy's senses whirled. What did he want? Why was he here? Why now, when she had thought they were rid of him, and she had been so determined not to involve him in any publicity to do with their farm museum?

In any case, this wouldn't be a good time. Sam wouldn't be pleased to see Trevis at the best of times – and this was far from being the best of times, when she and Sam had just had that blistering row, and she had unwittingly compared the two men to Sam's disadvantage. She found herself quickening her pace, and then sprinting towards the two men.

Before she reached them, she could see how Sam's hand had tightened on the handle of his hammer, and her mouth dried.

'Sam,' she shouted, as if to divert his

attention from whatever Jack was saying to him, if only for a moment.

Her voice was caught on the wind, and either the two men didn't hear her, or chose to take no notice. She had a stitch in her side, and she held on to it tightly, mentally telling the baby that everything was all right, and that they would be resting soon. But not yet. Not until she found out what Jack Trevis was here for, and what kind of insinuations he might be making. She didn't trust him an inch.

She called out again, her voice a little weaker this time, but it was enough for Sam to turn and see her approaching in full flight.

'Leave us, Poppy,' he ordered.

'I want to know what he's doing here,' she gasped as she reached them.

'It's nothing of importance, nor anything that you need concern yourself with. I will deal with it.'

She looked fearfully at Jack whose face was darkening by the second, realizing he too was being dismissed as if he was no more than a pest.

'What do you *want?*' she asked him directly, ignoring Sam, even though this was doing the exact opposite of what she had come out to the fields to do. Ignoring his wishes wouldn't stand her in good stead for the future either.

'I came to offer my services for your farm museum,' he told her curtly, his gaze sweeping over her swelling figure and embarrassing her intensely as he instantly assessed her condition. But his words startled her.

'We don't want any of your help, and anyway, how do you know about that?' she snapped, while noting with relief that Sam had dropped the hammer although he had crossed his arms by now and was glaring at them both, incensed and affronted that his wife had taken the initiative.

'I'm well acquainted with Tom Woodword, the sign-writer, and I've seen the designs of the signs your husband asked him to make. I thought that as old friends,' he paused significantly on the word, 'you might appreciate a bit of advance publicity, so I've come to hear about your plans.'

She railed at him again. 'Our plans aren't to be made public yet. When the time comes I'm going to write something myself for the newspaper. It will be more personal that way and we don't need any outside interference.'

Jack had folded his own arms by now, and Poppy had the ludicrous thought that the men resembled two aggressive gladiators, each ready for the kill, with herself as the prize in the middle.

'You think you're capable of doing that, do you?' he said, oozing sarcasm.

'I may not have had your learning, but I can put words together and I'm not a dummy,' she almost shouted. At that moment they seemed to have forgotten Sam, until he grasped her arm and spoke harshly.

'All right, that's enough. My wife has spoken for us both, Trevis, and there's no need for a third party to intervene. Our plans are our own concern, and I think you've done enough harm here already.'

Poppy's heart stopped as his hand tightened on her arm until it hurt. Did he know? Could he possibly know that something had gone on between her and this oaf? She couldn't bear it if he did. He was too good, too upright a man to have to face his wife's infidelity. And too vulnerable if the whole truth ever came out, she thought with sudden deep perception.

'Please leave us alone, Mr Trevis,' she said, her voice trembling. 'I am not feeling well of late, and we need to get on with our lives without the kind of fuss that occurred after I rescued the Flint boy. I'm sure you know that we didn't welcome any of the attention we received.'

She brought Sam into it, as if the unwanted publicity at that time had affected him as well, as indeed it had, and in more ways than he would ever know. She jerked her arm away from him, and then she caught at his hand and held it tightly, lifting her head high. Showing a united front was the message she hoped to convey to Jack Trevis.

After a few moments she saw him give an insolent shrug, and when he replied his voice had more than a hint of cruelty in it. 'So be it if you're so short-sighted that you can't see what a good send-off I could give to your little tin-pot museum. In any case it was going to be my swan-song for old times' sake, and remembering the pleasant chats I had with your charming wife, Lovering. I'm leaving for London next month to take up a far more lucrative post than here in this back of beyond, so you won't be seeing me again.'

'Thank God for that,' Sam snapped. 'Now get off my land before I throw you off, you blood-sucking leech.'

Jack turned and walked away, but not before he had given a theatrical bow and blown an exaggerated kiss to Poppy, who stood there with her cheeks burning and her heart in her mouth, knowing the things he could have said, and wondering just how Sam would react to the things that he had.

She didn't have long to find out.

'Get back to the house, woman,' he said curtly.

'Sam, he didn't mean anything. He's so self-centred and full of himself he just can't bear it when he doesn't get what he wants.'

'Is that so? And just what did he want?'

She turned away, her eyes smarting with tears. 'You know what I mean, so don't twist my words. I came out to the fields to make amends for my bad behaviour earlier, and now he's turned up like a bad penny and somehow everything's worse than it was before. We mustn't let him come between us, Sam. He's not worth it, truly he isn't, and after all this upset I'm really not feeling well, and I think I *should* go back to the house and lie down for a while. Can't we leave all this until later when we've both calmed down – please?'

'Well, why don't you tell me just what we're leaving until later that's so all-fired important to discuss?'

She babbled nervously as he stared at her so uncompromisingly. 'About some of the things the other farmers have brought for our museum, so that I can label them correctly, and then what you think I should write for the newspaper, of course.'

'Oh yes. For the moment I was almost forgetting that all this was about our little tin-pot museum.'

Her cheeks burned anew. 'It will never be that. We'll make a go of it, Sam, I know we will.'

This time, she hoped he would see more than one meaning in her words, but she wouldn't make it any plainer, and with a smothered sob in her throat she began to run back the way she had come, to the haven of the farmhouse and their bedroom.

She lay face down on the bed, sobbing her heart out until the baby's presence made the position too uncomfortable, and then she lay staring at the ceiling, her eyes swollen and dull, wondering if Jack Trevis had finally done irreparable damage to their marriage.

Chapter Eighteen

She must have fallen asleep from sheer exhaustion because it was growing dark by the time she heard a tap on the bedroom door. Surely Sam wasn't being so formal? Surely he wouldn't bother, she thought bitterly, when this was his home. She mumbled a response, and then the door opened and Florrie came in, carrying a cup of tea with a biscuit in the saucer. Poppy sat up too quickly and, as she felt her head spin, she put out her hand to the side of the bed to steady herself.

'I've warned you about that dizziness, girl,' Florrie said casually, as if this was a normal day, instead of one that threatened to turn Poppy's world upside-down. 'Your balance will be out of sorts for a while, so you need to sit up slowly. Drink your tea and don't gulp it, and when you're feeling up to it, come downstairs and have some supper.'

As she put down the cup and saucer at the side of the bed and turned as if to leave the bedroom, Poppy reached out and caught at her arm.

'Please stay for a minute,' she pleaded. 'I feel so awful. It's been such an awful day, and I've said such awful things.'

She knew she was repeating herself, but she couldn't think of a better word to describe how she felt. She didn't have a literary way with words like some people, and what better word was there to try to explain the way her stomach was churning and that she felt as though she was going to bring up the contents at any minute?

Without warning, she knew she was going to do exactly that. She gasped, flapping her hands towards the pail that was always ready for her early morning eruptions, and then she retched violently, and Florrie was holding her head and smoothing back the tangle of her hair to keep it away from the bile.

'I'm sorry,' Poppy croaked at last, wiping the back of a trembling hand across her mouth. 'I just couldn't stop it.'

'For pity's sake, my dear, lie down again and stop apologizing. Do you think I don't know how a woman feels when she's carrying? 'Tis enough to be experiencing the ups and down of it all, without having to deal with the wranglings of short-sighted men.'

Poppy felt a swift shame. 'Has Sam told you what happened in the field?' she stuttered. 'I don't know what you must think of me, nor if he'll ever forgive me for the way I went on.'

'I've told him in no uncertain terms that he's the one who should be apologizing for upsetting you in your condition, but he probably won't, being a mere man. They think 'tis weak to say sorry, but it takes a strong 'un to do so, and all the more credit to them that do,' Florrie said with a decisive sniff.

Poppy wasn't sure whether or not she meant that Sam was intending to say sorry. He had no need to, she thought guiltily. He had every right to turn Jack Trevis off his land, and every right to expect to do so without his wife interfering on his behalf. It wasn't seemly. Thank goodness Florrie obviously didn't appreciate all the undercurrents that had gone on between herself and Jack Trevis, even if Sam suspected – and she prayed with all her might that he didn't.

But she registered that he hadn't come to say sorry, either. It had been left to his mother to do that, so although she didn't completely agree with what Florrie had

378

said, how much of a man did that make Sam after all?

'He didn't feel inclined to come upstairs himself, did he?'

'That's because he's gone out for a drink with his pals like I told him to. You both need time to cool down, and it's a long time since he's had a belly-full of ale. Once in a while don't hurt any man. It may muddle his brains for a while, but it'll clear his thinking in the long run.'

'That sounds like too much of a riddle for me,' Poppy said, as her stomach began to feel more settled.

'Maybe it does, but when you've been married as long as I was, you'll know that there's more than one way of getting a man to do what you want. When he comes rolling back across the fields later tonight, he'll feel so guilty at letting the drink get the better of him he'll be full of sweet words and wanting to make things right between you, you'll see.'

Poppy gaped. 'I didn't know you could be so devious, Mrs Lovering.'

'Well, now you do, Mrs Lovering. And since 'tis so cumbersome with two of us being Mrs Lovering, I thought you were going to start calling me Grandma in preparation.'

'Was I?' Poppy said awkwardly. 'Well, I'll try.'

She might have half-agreed to it, but she didn't think she was going to find it easy after all this time, though she had to admit that today she had seen a new side to her mother-in-law. She wasn't always the dragon she sometimes appeared to be, and she didn't always champion Sam over her daughter-in-law.

'I think I should have some supper,' Poppy said, as her stomach grumbled with emptiness. 'I'm starting to feel hungry.'

'I expect you are, so come down when you're ready, and have some of the onion soup I've saved for you. All this emotion makes a body hungry – and you're eating for two now, don't forget.'

If the thought of onion soup almost made Poppy retch again, she managed not to show Florrie that it was the last thing she felt like eating, and a bit of bread and cheese would be more welcome. But by the time she got downstairs and the succulent smell reached her nostrils, she was ravenous and made short work of the food put in front of her.

She was in bed and falling asleep again by the time she heard Sam stumbling up the stairs, and her heart began to beat uncomfortably. She wasn't at all sure whether to feign sleep or to open her eyes and make sure he knew she was waiting for whatever he had decided to say to her. But perhaps he hadn't decided on anything, she thought fearfully, hearing him swear colourfully in the darkness as he stubbed his toe on the bed a couple of times.

'Why don't you put a light on?' she whispered through lips as dry as salt.

'You're awake then,' he stated. 'Mother said she thought you'd have been asleep ages ago.'

'Your mother doesn't know everything,' Poppy said, and then bit her lip, because this wasn't the right time to be censuring Florrie, even if she hadn't meant it that way.

Sam sat down heavily on the bed, pulling off his boots and hurling them across the room, and then his socks followed suit. Poppy trembled for a moment, wondering if this was the time she had been dreading, when all her indiscretions – and worse – with Jack Trevis, would come tumbling out in the wake of his accusations.

Sam still didn't say anything as he wrenched off the rest of his clothes and slid into bed beside her without even putting on his pyjamas. Poppy's nerves were really stretched now, and she inched as far away from him as she could, smelling the familiar earthiness of his body and the drink on him, and wondering fearfully if she was going to get more than a tongue-lashing.

She lay rigidly in the darkness, and then at

381

last he spoke.

'Have I really been such a bastard to you, girl? So much less than you wanted?'

She twisted towards him at once. She didn't mind his body odour, because it was part of him and his livelihood, but she didn't like the smell of drink, nor the stale smell of smoke from the musty interior of the pub. At any other time she might have said something about that ... but nothing was more important as saying the right words at this moment.

'You've been a *good* husband, Sam, and I hope I've always been a good and faithful wife to you,' she said shakily, praying that God wouldn't strike her down dead for the untruth. But she needed to give him this reassurance, because for the first time since she had known him, she was sure she had detected a note of uncertainty in his voice.

He gave a smothered oath that made her catch the breath in her throat again. And the next minute he had turned to her and was raining kisses on her face and eyes, and she could feel the warmth of his naked body against her.

Should she pull off her nightgown and show him how much she wanted and needed him? she wondered. And was this the mute apology that he couldn't find the words for?

She heard him give a short, rueful laugh as

his hand caught hold of hers and thrust it downwards.

'You see what we've come to, my maid? The spirit's ready and willing, but tonight the flesh is too bloody weak to do anything about it!'

Please don't get upset, Poppy said inside. *Don't let it spoil these moments, because there's more to us than making physical love* ... but she knew better than to say it didn't matter, even if it didn't, knowing how fragile a man's ego could be at such times.

Instead, she leaned up and very softly kissed his mouth. 'I love you, Sam,' she said huskily instead.

'No more than I love you, sweetheart. And this little one too.'

Before she knew what he was about, he had dived beneath the bedclothes and his hand gently palmed her stomach before kissing it, oh so reverently. The tenderness of the moment, coming from this bear of a man, made the tears start to Poppy's eyes. She was hardly aware of how subtly his kisses moved downwards, but she suddenly drew in her breath with unexpected pleasure as his tongue found her moistness for a few blissful moments before he covered her with her nightgown again. He gave a small sigh.

'Ah well, it seems we shall have to wait for the old John Thomas to recover from his drinking bout before we can do the business properly again,' he said.

The sudden crudeness of the remark compared with his previous tenderness made Poppy giggle, and then she was being rocked in his arms and they were laughing fit to bust.

'Sam, stop it, or we'll have your mother wondering what's going on in here!' she managed to choke out eventually.

'Well, if she don't know by now what goes on between a man and his wife in their boudoir as the damn Froggies say, then I'm a monkey's uncle.'

Which only started her off again, and once they had finally managed to squash their laughter they slept locked in each other's arms.

'All's well between you, then,' Florrie stated with no more comment the next morning when Sam had left the house to go about his work.

'I think I can safely say that it is,' Poppy nodded, not knowing how else to reply, and hoping Florrie hadn't been aware of the early morning bedroom activity in the room next to hers. The old *John Thomas* may not have been up to much the night before, but he had enthusiastically awoken that morning.

Poppy felt herself blush, as much for

mentally using the term herself, as for the realization from the small smile on Florrie's face that she couldn't have made it plainer if she'd tried. But why wouldn't Florrie be pleased? Her grandson was the all-important factor now, and she wouldn't want any hint of trouble between her son and daughter-in-law.

Besides, if things ever did go wrong between them and Poppy became desperately unhappy here, where would she run to? There was no home at Zennor now. No mum and dad whose broad shoulders she could cry on. But she *was* happy, and the thought was quickly dismissed.

She knew she didn't think of her parents quite so often now. The realization didn't come with sadness, because when she did think of them it was with loving memories, and not the searing pain she had gone through at their horrific deaths.

Time did heal, she thought, the way others told you it did, even though it took a personal experience to fully accept it. Perhaps in time, the bad memory of Jack Trevis would disappear too, especially if he was no longer going to be around. They had had their showdown, as they said in the cowboy flicks, and London was a long way from here, and welcome to him. Her heart lifted as she cleared away the breakfast things and helped Florrie to wash up the plates.

'I intended to do some more of the labels for the museum today, but really I'd like to go and see Shirley. Would you mind?' she asked Florrie diffidently.

'Of course not. I think 'tis a good idea. You'll want to be seeing young master Luke as well, I daresay, and you don't want to be tied to the house every day. You need plenty of fresh air for you and the child, and there's time enough for doing those labels.'

Shirley wouldn't be expecting her, but she had said Poppy could call at any time. Their friendship was on a far more equal level now, with Luke already a little person in his own right. Poppy was also keen to know every aspect of baby care, even though she had to admit she sometimes looked at Luke's head, and wondered just how painful the process of giving birth would be. And that was something even Shirley didn't know, having been under the influence at the time, as Sam said.

Shirley opened the door with Luke in her arms.

'He's gone,' Poppy stated.

Shirley looked at her stupidly for a moment, none too pleased at being interrupted while she was changing Luke's nappy. She put her hand protectively over his bare bottom and told Poppy to come inside.

'Who's gone?' she said irritably.

For a few seconds it seemed inconceivable to Poppy that Shirley couldn't understand who she meant, nor see the significance of it instantly, when it was so all-important to herself. Without warning, she burst into tears.

'For heaven's sake, Poppy, what's wrong, and who's gone?' Shirley said, really alarmed now. 'Has something happened to Sam? He's not ... he's not–'

The gruesome warnings of farming accidents that had been drummed into the land girls during the war years swept through her mind. She recalled some of the things they had been told that had happened to other farmers and inexperienced farm-hands: falling off a tractor and getting maimed or worse by the huge wheels; slicing off a hand or an arm with a scythe; falling into some slurry and being choked to death in the filth; being crushed by an animal gone wild...

At the time they were sure such things couldn't *all* have happened in so relatively small a rural community, and that Sam had been merely trying to save them from any accidents through their own carelessness. And she prayed fervently that nothing terrible had happened to Sam knowing Poppy would be devastated, especially after the horror of what had happened to her own parents. And in her condition too.

Poppy almost snapped at her. 'It's not Sam. He hasn't gone anywhere. It's *him*. Jack Trevis. Well, he hasn't quite gone yet, but as good as. He's going to London next month and good riddance!'

'What on earth are you crying for then?' For once, Shirley felt out of patience with the younger girl. 'Isn't that the best news you've heard in a long time?'

'Well, of course it is. I just wanted to tell you, that's all. I thought you'd have been as pleased as I am instead of biting my head off.'

Shirley ignored the remark, thinking it was more the other way round. She laid Luke on the rug, knelt down beside him and carried on efficiently folding his towelling nappy, the curved safety pin fastened to her blouse like a badge of office. Normally, Poppy would have laughed at the baby's vigorous kicks and the sight of his so-vulnerable little tail, but right now she felt like having a huge attack of the sulks at Shirley's reaction, even though she knew that was no way for a pregnant married woman to behave.

As if to register his annoyance at the way he was getting less attention than usual and had been left nappyless for too long, Luke let out a stream of pee right into Shirley's face that had her spluttering and laughing at the same time. She mopped it up with the gauze nappy liner that was ready alongside.

'You see what you're in for, Poppy? They have no respect for the hand that feeds them!'

'I didn't think it was the hand that does that – and just be thankful he didn't spray you from the rear end,' Poppy muttered, and then her mouth twitched as well, and they were hugging one another helplessly while Luke kicked on regardless.

'I'm really sorry for the way I burst in on you, Shirley,' she said a short while later when Luke was clean and dry once more, and they were relaxing. 'It's just that I've had a bit of a chaotic time lately, and I had to come and tell somebody.'

'Oh God, he didn't come and make trouble for you before he went to London, did he? I did warn you that he was a rat, Poppy.'

She shook her head. The next minute she was pouring out all that had happened, about how she had wounded Sam with her thoughtless words, and how she knew damn well she had nearly betrayed herself over Jack Trevis. The thought of confessing had been so very near, and she knew that Shirley had once known that feeling so well.

'But you didn't make any stupid confession over something that should be well and truly forgotten, and as long as you and Sam managed to patch things up after all the arguments, I'm sure no harm was done,'

Shirley said. 'Sam's a good man, Poppy, for all that the rest of us always thought him a bit of a stick-in-the-mud, and I can't deny that we did that.'

'Oh yes, we patched things up. I know how lucky I am to have him – and he does have his moments, I promise you,' she added with a grin.

'Well, don't give him all the credit, darling. It takes two to make a marriage, and I'd say he didn't do so badly in marrying you. So now you've got that off your chest, how's the other business going?'

When Poppy looked at her blankly, still caught up in the memory of recent events, Shirley laughed. 'Poppy, even I'm more than happy to get off the subject of babies now and then, and in fact it's good to have something else to talk about. The blessed District Nurse pops in every few days and I'm up to my eyes in leaflets about breast-feeding and cradle-cap and childhood illnesses and immunization and suchlike. So tell me how Sam's project is getting on – and if his bright new ideas don't destroy any illusions of him being a stick-in-the-mud I don't know what does,' she added, to give Poppy a boost.

'It's going fine. At least, it will do once we've got some advance publicity organized. I'm going to write it out myself, but I don't know if I'll be brave enough to take it to the newspaper offices, or if I should post it when it's all ready.'

'If you want my advice you'll take it yourself. Put on your prettiest frock and dazzle the chief the way you dazzle every other chap who looks at you.'

Poppy laughed. 'Thanks for the compliment, even if I don't believe it, but I'm not sure that's the right way to go about things.'

'Why the hell not? You want Sam's museum to attract customers, don't you? What could be better than having his gorgeous wife doing a bit of self-promotion? The newspaper boss will be sure to recognize you from that rescue business, so cash in on it, Poppy, and don't be backward in coming forward.'

'Has Bernard been coaching you in giving speeches?' Poppy said.

Shirley tossed her head. 'He doesn't need to. I just think you and Sam should make the most of this, and I don't imagine he can string the proper words together, so it's up to you, girl. And presenting your advertising stuff face to face is far better than shoving it in the post-box.'

'Well, I'll think about it. So now that we've done with sorting me out, can I have a last cuddle with Luke before I catch the bus home?'

Florrie was out for the evening, and Sam looked at his wife quizzically when he'd scrubbed his face and hands and was ready for supper.

'You look different,' Sam said. 'Sort of sparkly and a bit feverish. What's up? You're not sickening for something, are you?'

She laughed. 'Oh, Sam, of course not! If I'm looking sparkly, it's because I'm starting to get excited about the farm museum – to say nothing of this other little production,' she said, touching her stomach.

He visibly relaxed. 'Well, I know you've been to see Shirley today, so if everything's all right, what's she been saying to put you in such a good mood?'

'I don't know why you think it's only Shirley who can put me in a good mood. You don't do too badly on that score yourself. But before you get a certain gleam in your eye, I want to show you something I've been working on. It's only a few rough ideas and if you don't like them I shan't be upset.'

She handed over the old, half-used school exercise book, and waited anxiously for his reaction.

'I didn't know you could draw,' he said at once.

She spoke self-consciously. 'I didn't know either, but if you think it's too silly and looks too childish, I can strike the sketches out and just have the words.'

'I don't think it's silly at all. It will catch

people's eyes far better than just a block of print, if you think the newspaper boss will agree to it.' He said the words so calmly that she knew it was his way of telling her they didn't hold any worries for him.

She didn't answer for a moment, just studied her own ideas that had come from nowhere after a number of attempts trying to see the information through other eyes. The block of print, as he called it, stated that the opening of Lovering's Farm Museum would coincide with the annual fête and fair at the end of August. Around the edges of the wording she had drawn little items of farm equipment, with a corn dolly in each corner.

It made a complete feature of the advertisement, rather than a brief mention that would probably end up wrapped around somebody's fish and chips in a week or so. Or worse, in somebody's outside lav.

'I didn't know I had such a clever wife,' Sam said at last.

She looked at him anxiously, not sure if he was mocking her or not. Then she saw that he was smiling.

'I think this is a brilliant idea, Poppy. I know the drawings aren't exactly perfect, and probably there will be somebody at the newspaper office who can tidy them up a bit. But the idea is a good one. I don't think we need to take it to them just yet, though.

If we give folk too much notice, they'll have forgotten all about it by the time August comes.'

'That's what I thought. We can easily leave it a month or two.'

The unspoken message between them was that Jack Trevis would be well and truly gone to London by then, so whoever else took an interest in Poppy's piece of advertising, and hopefully an interest in the museum itself, it wouldn't be him.

'You really are keen on the scheme, aren't you, Poppy?'

Her eyes widened. 'Of course I am. Why would you think otherwise? If I seem less than enthusiastic sometimes, it's only because I'm having a baby day, when he makes me feel a bit queasier than usual. I can't explain it any better than that, and I'm sure it will pass. Your mother says so, anyway – and I doubt that any grandson of hers would dare to question what she says.'

Sam laughed, hearing the teasing in her voice. 'Let's have an early night,' he said, and there was no doubting the meaning in his.

'Another one?' she said, her senses already afire.

Florrie was pleasingly complimentary about the rough sketches Poppy had done for the newspaper piece. She knew she was no artist, but as Sam said, it was the idea that counted, and someone more skilled than she was could pull it all into shape in due course.

She was determined not to present it until she was sure that Jack Trevis had left Cornwall, hopefully for good, and it was agreed that sometime in late June would be soon enough to take her idea to Penzance and see what the editor thought about it. Once it was made to look more professional and inserted in the paper for a few weeks prior to the event, those who normally came for the fête and fair would have their curiosity aroused, and others might be attracted to it too.

Over the next few weeks, it was obvious that Jack Trevis was making his departure well and truly known in his final articles for the paper. They were a compilation of all his previous ones, no doubt to remind 'we quaint Cornish folk' Sam said scornfully, how much they would miss his writings when he was gone.

Poppy was more concerned in how much he might have written about herself. It was unthinkable that he would ignore his big scoop of interviewing the girl who had rescued the young boy from the mine shaft. Sure enough, there was her face looking out at her from the paper again, making her heart turn over as she remembered how innocently and glowingly she had smiled up at the young reporter and taken his flattery as genuine, and so important in her life.

'You've changed a bit since then, girl,' Sam remarked, making her heart jump again, but for a very different reason.

'Have I?' she said cautiously, preferring to make no comment.

'Well, of course. You were always a good-looker in a girlish sort of way, but you've blossomed since then. You look more womanly now.'

He started to talk more clumsily, more awkwardly, and she knew he didn't have the words to say what he really meant. But she knew. Her face was more rounded – like the rest of her, she thought ruefully – and she may have lost the innocence she once had, but that wasn't altogether a bad thing, since she knew she also looked more fulfilled, more mature and more loved.

She was still young, but she felt as though she had finally grown up in these last tumultuous months, having had a brief clandestine affair and lived to regret it – and having been bereaved by losing her parents in a horrific accident. And through it all, she had always had Sam.

She hugged his arm. 'Well, if I've changed, I'm glad you haven't. You'll always be my Sam.'

She saw him go a bit hot under the collar

at her remark and then he muttered that if he didn't get on with the milking, the cows would be bellowing their disapproval all morning. But she knew he was pleased all the same.

On her own, she read the article again more objectively, and realized that there was nothing anyone could see in it to make them think it was anything other than a report about an incident that could so easily have resulted in tragedy, but which had had a happy ending. The following week she saw the photos Jack had taken of Chysauster ancient village, and avidly read the words he'd written. But it was merely a piece of geographical and historical interest, and by the time the day of his departure arrived, she felt able at last to breathe more freely.

It was unlikely that they would ever see him again, since his final farewell article had been full of anticipation about his new job in London, where he would be reporting on the events of the Festival of Britain in the coming months. Good luck to him, and good riddance, Poppy thought again. Besides, there was far more to do here on the farm now than to fret over something that was past. The seasons moved on, and the farming year never stopped for personal problems, and the Loverings had two exciting prospects ahead.

As always they would be preparing for the

August events, but this year there was far more to do to get the Farm Museum ready. For this first year at least, they had abandoned the idea of a tea room. Poppy would be nearing her time, and she was to sit in the entrance of the two barns, taking the entrance money and handing out leaflets, which still had to be designed, as well as a poster or two. This was going to be Poppy's task again, but then she would take them to a proper printer in Penzance.

'It still seems wrong to take money from folk just to look at old farming junk,' she observed later.

'Well, if that chap in St Austell does it, why shouldn't we?' Sam said. 'You can't let sentiment creep into business, Poppy. Whatever you do, don't get flustered about it all. There's plenty of time, and you need to take it easy now.'

It was probably good advice, except that she was starting to feel more energized than she had in a long while. The baby was settling down now, she no longer felt so sick in the mornings, and taking it easy was the last thing she wanted to do. In between writing and drawing, then scratching everything out and starting again, knitting for the baby and helping Florrie with the general household chores, it dawned on her that she had never been happier.

Chapter Nineteen

On a warm day in late June, Poppy took the bus into Penzance. She was armed with her sketches and writing, set out in the large unlined notebook she had eventually purchased for the purpose in the village. She was extremely nervous. She had never been to a newspaper office before, and the sight of the intimidating building almost made her forget the whole idea – and what a waste of effort that would be.

Before she went inside, she took a deep breath, told herself not to be an idiot, and tried to remember something she had once heard – probably from Shirley.

However aggressive they look, imagine them sitting there without any clothes on. That'll cut them down to size!

When she was shown into the office, which had the important words 'Graham Strang, Editor' on a plaque on the door, Poppy found it hard to think about anything except the way her heart was thudding. The man behind the desk stood up, quickly assessing her hot and flustered face, and offered her a chair and a cup of tea.

'Or would you prefer lemonade on such a

hot day, Mrs Lovering?' he asked.

'You know who I am, then,' Poppy said, immediately knowing she must sound dafter than ever. Of course he damn well knew.

'Well, apart from seeing your charming photograph again in the paper quite recently, I was given your name when you asked to see me,' Strang affirmed smoothly. 'So tell me if you prefer tea or lemonade, and then let me know what I can do for you.'

'Lemonade, please. And it's about this.'

She thrust her notebook on to his desk, acutely aware of how amateurish he was about to find her drawings. Sam and Florrie might think them clever enough, but Poppy knew they were only schoolgirl scribbles, and that she was probably about to be laughed out of the office. Who did she think she was, coming here to this busy, professional place, and displaying her crude drawings for the editor's inspection? She was a farmer's wife, not an artist, and for two pins she'd get up and flee.

The choice was taken away from her when Strang pressed a button on his desk and ordered his secretary to bring them two glasses of lemonade. And then he opened Poppy's notebook.

He didn't say anything as he turned the pages, reading all that she had written: her advertisement for the newspaper, framed with her drawings, and the proposal for the leaflets that would be handed out in the museum itself. She saw the corners of his mouth turn up a little, and she squirmed with embarrassment, wishing she was anywhere but here.

Finally Strang looked up. 'This is all very interesting, Mrs Lovering. And what exactly are you asking me to do?'

Poppy knew she was about to stammer nervously, and then her pride got the better of her. After all her work in trying to do the best she could for their project, couldn't the fool see why she was here, and that this wasn't merely a social visit? She owed it to Sam to make him see. Her shoulders straightened and her voice sharpened.

'I would have thought the plans for the farm museum were obvious. What I'm here for is to ask if one of your clever people will tidy up my drawings so that they don't look as if an infant had done them, and then put our advertisement in the paper for a few weeks before the end of August.'

She paused for breath and then went on before he could intervene. 'You don't have to take any notice of the leaflets we intend to hand out to people on the door. The outline for those just happens to be in my notebook and I can take them to a printer. But whatever you can do for us, we'll pay, of course.'

She tried to be as cool and efficient as

possible, considering how she disliked the way the man was leaning back in his chair now, hands behind his head, and watching her with calculating eyes.

As shrewd as a weasel, she thought ... and there was no way she could imagine a weasel without clothes ... she took a large gulp of lemonade and just managed to stop herself choking as it went down the wrong way.

'Are you all right, Mrs Lovering?' Strang said, bringing his chair legs back to the ground with a crash.

'Yes, thank you,' she replied, crimson with embarrassment now. 'And I'm sorry if I've been wasting your time.'

As she half-rose, he waved her down again. 'My dear young woman, don't be so indecisive. After the way you outlined your plans a moment ago, I suspect it's not your usual style. Am I right?'

She wasn't sure what he meant by that, unless he could see by the determined tilt to her chin and the flash in her eyes that she was quite prepared to gather up her work and walk out of here with her dignity intact.

And then he smiled, and became at once a sort of father-figure, if only for the briefest moment before the businessman took over.

'Mrs Lovering, you and your husband obviously think your museum has the makings of a going concern, or it wouldn't have gone this far. I never met a farmer yet who used part of his property on such a venture unless he thought it was worthwhile. Of course this newspaper will be pleased to give you some advertising. As you say, there will be a small charge, but we can discuss that with your husband. I presume he's too busy to come to the office himself, and I admire you for taking the trouble. One of my staff will tidy up the drawings, as you put it, although I think that in essence, the childlike quality of them shouldn't be altered too much. There's something very attractive about their naivety.'

This was all starting to go over Poppy's head now, but at least Graham Strang didn't think her stupid, and implied that her work was going to be appreciated. The relief made her almost tongue-tied, and she could only mutter a word of thanks.

'Can you recommend a printer who will print our leaflets, Mr Strang?' she thought to say at last.

'There's no need. I don't see why we couldn't do those as well, if only to keep the continuity of the drawings. We often do outside printing work. Would that be agreeable to you and your husband?'

He insisted on mentioning Sam's name at all times, she noticed. Well, of course he would, since it was normally a man's pre-rogative to be dealing with business matters. Poppy smiled for the first time since coming into the office. She hadn't used her so-called feminine wiles and done as Shirley had suggested and worn her prettiest frock. In any case, it was stretched too tight over her now, but she had worn a soft blue smock over her skirt, and brushed her hair until it shone. It was patently obvious to anyone that she was pregnant, but she still recognized the admiration in the editor's eyes as her face brightened.

'More than agreeable, I'm sure,' she said calmly.

'Then I'll send for Charlie Reynolds and we'll discuss the details while my secretary gives you a small tour of the offices if you wish. Then Charlie can drive you back to the farm with our proposals for your husband to approve.'

She was being temporarily dismissed, which was also a relief now, because having intrigued the editor she didn't want to see any signs of mockery in someone else's eyes. She hoped this Charlie wasn't going to be anything like Jack Trevis, but when he entered the office and she saw the bespectacled, earnest face of the middle-aged man, anyone less like him she couldn't imagine. You couldn't tell a roué by his appearance, any more than you could tell a bank manager or a teacher, but she was reasonably sure she would be safe enough with Charlie Reynolds.

Fifteen minutes later, after an awkward walk around the building with the secretary, whom she was sure would far rather be doing something else, and seemed more than impatient to have her working day broken into in this way, Poppy returned to the editor's office. The two men rose when she came in.

'Sit down again, Mrs Lovering,' Strang said. 'Charlie here is our chief draughtsman, and he'll make a very good job of your drawings, while keeping the original concept very much in mind as I mentioned. We've sorted out some figures for your husband's approval, so whenever you're ready Charlie will drive you back to Barras to discuss it all with Farmer Lovering.'

Again, he couldn't have put it plainer that although she might have made the first move in coming here, Sam Lovering was the head of the household, and he was the one to be doing business with. Poppy was merely the messenger, even if she had put the words and drawings in order. It hardly mattered. As far as Poppy was concerned, she and Sam were a team in this venture, and all that mattered was that it was going to happen, just as they had planned.

A short while later she was sitting beside Charlie Reynolds in his old jalopy on the way back to the farm. While her spirits were bubbling, she tried to concentrate on

Charlie's constant chatter about his daughter's wedding plans and his wife's back trouble, confirming the feeling that he was a family man and that she was perfectly safe with him.

The days moved more swiftly now. The farming year was at its height in the summer months with haymaking, and the plans for the museum were also pushing ahead. Charlie came to the farm again a week after his first visit, to get the Loverings' approval of what would be going in the newspaper, and the finer detail in their publicity leaflets. The drawings were definitely tidied up, thought Poppy, but just as Graham Strang had said, the essence of her original ones was still there.

By now it had been agreed that the museum would be fully open during the few days of the fair and fête, and then on Saturdays only until the end of October, by which time most of the summer visitors had left the county. Depending on its success in this first year, they would make further plans for opening times for the following spring.

'You've made a really nice job of it, Mr Reynolds,' Florrie told him, when they were sitting around the table with mugs of tea and slices of Florrie's sponge cake – a tribute which showed her approval of what was happening more than anything else, thought Poppy.

Charlie smiled. 'Most of the credit goes to this little lady, Ma'am. She's got a real eye for attracting the customers, both in words and pictures.'

Poppy smiled back, even though she squirmed at being referred to as 'this little lady' especially as she was starting to feel as big as a house now.

'You're right there, Reynolds,' Sam agreed. 'So once we've got the final costs sorted out, I'd say you could go ahead with the printing as soon as you like.'

Florrie stood up. 'That's our cue to leave the men to their business dealings, Poppy. I'm taking a walk down to the village, so if you want to come with me, we can clear these tea things later.'

Florrie didn't often leave anything until later, but Poppy could see that she was just as intrigued by their new venture as anyone else now.

'I'll get my hat,' she said at once. The sun was hot, and she didn't fancy a dose of sunburn. Like most countrywomen, Florrie walked everywhere and ignored the vagaries of the weather, come rain or shine, and Poppy was in no shape to ride her bicycle until after the baby was born.

She paused at the stairs, and turned to Charlie Reynolds.

'I expect you'll be gone before we get back, Mr Reynolds, so I just want to thank you again for not laughing at my drawings.'

'On the contrary, my dear. I think they will be a real selling point.'

He was being kind, but she knew her limitations. She was never going to rival a real artist, and nor did she want to. She had her own personal production ahead of her, and young master Lovering was going to take up most of her time in the future, no matter how successful the museum proved to be.

She felt in good spirits as she and Florrie set off for the village. It was a beautiful day and everything was going right at last. The traumas of the past were well and truly behind her now, and she and Sam were in good harmony.

'You're good for our Sam, Poppy,' Florrie said, striding out. 'You may not be exactly like two peas in a pod, but 'tis trust and understanding that sets folk on the right track to a good life together.'

Poppy almost missed a step, startled by such an unexpected compliment at first, and not too sure if Florrie meant anything by the last remark.

'Perhaps we're good for each other, and having this little one will prove it to one and all,' she said, not really knowing how to answer.

'Do you think there's any folk who need to have it proved?' Florrie said, looking directly at her now.

'None that I can think of. It's no one else's business, anyway. Me and Sam know we've got a good marriage, and that's all that matters.'

She didn't like the way this conversation was going. Was Florrie trying to probe? She remembered how cross Florrie had got when Jack Trevis sent her the photographs of herself, and wondered just how much she had suspected at that time. But the past was over, and raking it all up did nobody any good. Perhaps her mother-in-law was just making idle conversation – except that it was such an unlikely thing for her to do.

'I'm glad to hear it,' Florrie continued. 'Sam's an honest man, Poppy, and I wouldn't want to see him hurt.'

'Do you think I would ever hurt him?' Poppy said angrily.

'No, I don't think you would. So let's enjoy this sunny day and go to the bakery and buy some cream cakes as a treat for after supper.'

Poppy assumed this was her way of an apology and a concession. Florrie never bought shop cakes if she could help it, since her own were considered so much better. Sam had the sweetest tooth, so this would be mainly for him. As usual, Florrie had turned the smallest concession to her advantage. But she wasn't going to get it all her own way.

'Why don't we take a walk around the churchyard afterwards?' Poppy challenged her. Such a visit might not be everyone's idea of pleasure, but all those old headstones and flowers and inscriptions, together with the beautiful peace of the place, never failed to have a soothing effect on her.

'If we must,' Florrie said. 'Providing you come to church with me on Sunday. It's time you showed your face if you expect the vicar to christen my grandson.'

Poppy gave in, knowing Florrie always had to have the last word. But she was determined to put a small bunch of wild flowers on Evie's grave, no matter what Florrie thought. You couldn't give birth to a baby and then forget she ever existed. Poppy knew she couldn't anyway, and she felt a small shiver run through her at the uncomfortable thought.

By the time they returned to the farm there was a definite chill between them. Thankfully Sam couldn't see it, being far too taken with the thought of cream cakes after supper, and Poppy wondered miserably if she had gone too far in virtually forcing Florrie to face up to whatever remained of that tiny form in the ground.

But it was far too late to ponder on whether it had been a good idea or completely insensitive, considering that Poppy was carrying an increasingly lively baby inside her now. Anyway, there were other things to think about. In a week's time the advertisement would be in the newspaper, and they waited eagerly for its appearance.

A few days after it came out, there was a card in the post from Shirley, congratulating Poppy on her achievement.

'I knew you could do it, Poppy,' she wrote. 'It will be a roaring success, and we'll be there to see the opening. In the meantime, don't forget when you're feeling bored with yourself, I'm always here. I may bring Luke over to see you if Bernard will bring me on Saturday afternoon. I always enjoy showing him off – Luke, I mean, not Bernard. Well, him as well!'

Poppy was laughing by the time she had finished the note, and then read it out to Sam and his mother. Florrie gave her usual sniff, but it wasn't quite as derogatory as it used to be where Shirley was concerned. Shirley was a respectable married woman with a child now, and not the flighty piece Florrie had once considered her. Poppy wondered briefly how much different a person felt inside just because they had attained so-called 'respectability'. Not much, she suspected.

'I'd like to see that baby,' Florrie conceded. 'He'll be a bouncing boy by now, and Shirley will have her hands full.'

She made no secret of her preference for boys, Poppy told Sam later. 'How's she going to react if ours is a girl? There are no guarantees, Sam, and it's not a bit of use her going on saying I'm bound to have a boy because I'm carrying it all in the back. As far as I'm concerned, I'm very definitely carrying it all in the front, or else it's a sack of coal I've been lugging around all these months!'

He laughed. 'Don't let her get you down, love. She'll love it whatever we have, and so will we.'

'I know that, but what about you? Will it be too much of a disappointment to you if it is a girl, Sam? Tell me truthfully.'

He looked at her anxious face. 'Of course it won't. I find it natural to refer to the baby as him because I'd rather do that than call him an it – if that's making any sense to you,' he added as his words began to get muddled.

'It makes perfect sense,' Poppy said, her face clearing. 'So whether he turns out to be a ... a Gary or a Greta, we'll love him anyway, won't we?'

'Yes, providing you're not thinking of saddling him with either of those fancy film star names.'

'I wouldn't even think of it,' Poppy said airily. In any case, she had been too superstitious to even consider any names yet. They had both agreed that as soon as they saw him, they would know what to call him – or her. Providing Sam's mother didn't have too many other ideas, Poppy thought, crossing her fingers.

By the middle of August Lovering's Farm Museum was complete, with elaborately-painted signs above the adjoining barns, all the contents suitably labelled, and a pile of leaflets ready beside the main door to hand to paying customers, and anyone else who was interested. All they had to do now was wait for the day to arrive, and in the meantime make the usual preparations for the annual fête and fair, which left them little time to have the jitters about the fortunes of the museum. In amongst all this, Poppy's birthday had come and gone without fuss, just as she wanted.

Shirley and Bernard had brought Luke to see them several times since that first day, and Florrie was clearly taken with the boy, as she constantly referred to him, as if to impress on Poppy that she expected her to produce the same.

It all began to backfire in Poppy's mind. Where the feelings came from she didn't know, but not only had she begun to hope desperately for a girl, she was perfectly certain that a girl was exactly what she was carrying. She never said as much to Sam, but she knew that even if Florrie couldn't find it in her heart to love her, she and Sam would lavish all the love in the world on their baby girl.

'You could be wrong, of course,' Shirley said, her only confidante. 'But you've only got a few more weeks to wait, and then the big day will be here. Aren't you excited?'

'Excited and impatient – and scared to death.'

'That's normal. But once it starts you'll have no time for any of that. They don't call it labour for nothing, as somebody once told me.'

'It didn't all go as planned for you though, did it, Shirley?'

It was out in the open now, all the fear and the worry that was mostly kept inside Poppy's head where it belonged, but could sometimes burst out in a wave of panic, as it was doing right now.

'Good Lord, you don't want to think about that. You'll be fine, and even if you find it hard going, you'll forget all about it as soon as you see your baby. Just make sure the old midwife knows about bringing you the gas and air machine, that's all and take a good whiff of it before the contractions really start, then you'll be so woozy through the worst of it, you'll sail through it!'

'That's your best advice, is it? I'm not sure if you've made it better or worse.'

Shirley laughed. 'Oh, Poppy, everyone's different, but you're no shrinking violet. Look how you've coped with everything during this last year, and just think how lovely it will be once you've got your little whoever-it-is to look after. It's what you always wanted, isn't it? So cheer up.'

'I know you're right.' Her breath caught. 'It's just that I'd give anything if my mum and dad were going to see my baby, and the worst of it is, I know they never will.'

As always the population of Barras and the nearby locality swelled with visitors for the annual fête and fair at Lovering's Farm. Sam was in his element with the children as usual, but one of the attractions this year was undoubtedly the new Farm Museum, where Poppy sat inside the door, handing out leaflets and taking the small entrance fee.

She was also prepared to answer any questions, although she knew her detailed labels told city-dwellers and countryfolk alike the purpose of the many tools and artefacts the museum held. Those farmers who had donated things came to inspect them as well, and to ensure that their names were included on the labels, which Poppy had been careful to do.

'You and your man have made a fine job of it, Poppy,' one and another told her as they passed through. 'You should be very proud.'

'We are, but it's thanks to people like yourselves who have helped us.'

She remembered to compliment them, and also to waive any fee for those who had contributed.

Charlie Reynolds turned up with another reporter who took a few photographs of the interior and promised to give a good write-up of the museum as well as reporting the annual event as usual. Last year it had been Jack Trevis doing it, Poppy thought fleetingly, but like everything else in the farming calendar those days had moved on.

The museum did good business, but she had to admit that by the end of the first busy day she was weary, and when the three days finally came to an end, she was near-exhausted. Sitting all day in the extended barn, with short breaks when Florrie took over, she had had little exercise, and even though the door was left open to invite visitors inside, it had got stuffier and stuffier as the days wore on.

It was a relief to know that they were only opening on Saturdays until the end of October from now on, when either Poppy or Florrie would be in charge. And thank goodness they had abandoned Sam's one-time suggestion of them wearing olde-worlde costumes in the museum to make things look even more authentic, she thought feelingly. If Poppy had been obliged to do so, she was sure she would have roasted.

By the middle of Monday morning when Sam had left the house she told Florrie she had to get out in the lanes to breathe some good clean air.

'Do you want company?' Florrie asked. 'I could leave the washing for a spell if you feel uneasy at walking by yourself now your time's coming near.'

Poppy shook her head quickly, thinking that wonders would never cease if Florrie was prepared to alter her daily tasks on Poppy's account.

'Thank you for the offer, but I feel the need to be on my own for a while, and I know how you like to get on. I'll be quite all right, and I may pick some blackberries,' she added quickly, thinking this would sound better to a diligent housewife like Florrie, than to think of her wandering about aimlessly.

'You'd best take a basket then,' Florrie said, to Poppy's relief. The last thing she needed was to have her mother-in-law breathing down her neck in these last few weeks of her pregnancy. She needed to stay calm to prepare herself for the biggest adventure of her life so far, and she needed

to be at one with herself and her emotions –
and Florrie would never understand such
high-minded thoughts.

Poppy wasn't sure she understood them
herself. She only knew that out in the fresh
air, with the blue of infinity above; the
breeze whispering through the trees and
hedgerows; the pliant, soft earth beneath
her feet; the singing of birds and the droning murmur of summer bees, she felt in
tune with nature, and such times had always
been the most calming that she knew. But
she dutifully took the basket and picked
some blackberries, which were plentiful in
the hedgerows of the fields and lanes now. It
felt good to be doing something very
homely and ordinary, and to be alone with
her thoughts and her baby.

She had been picking for more than half
an hour, her basket filling with the succulent, juicy berries, when she caught sight of
something that made her heart jump. Two
eyes were staring at her between the tangled
branches of the brambles on the other side
of the hedge.

She wasn't sure if it was an animal or not.
The distance between the eyes made her
certain that it wasn't large enough to be a
cow, but it could have been a dog, or even a
fox, at which she shuddered, remembering
Henrietta.

'Go away,' she stuttered, not knowing

what else to say.

She picked up a stick and banged it against the hedge, and as she did so her basket fell out of her hand, spilling the blackberries. In trying to save them, she squashed some of the fruit against her smock, where the stain immediately resembled splashes of blood. To Poppy's receptive mind it looked so ominous that she burst into tears.

Next minute, she heard a shrill voice. 'I never meant nothing, Missus!'

Poppy stopped crying at once, and her nerves settled. 'Is that you, Billy Flint?' she snapped.

He scrambled reluctantly through a gap in the hedge, dishevelled and scared-looking. 'Bloody hell, are you going to tell on me? I was only looking, honest.'

'What's there to look at around here? There's only me picking blackberries, and you've seen plenty of folk doing that, haven't you?'

She realized that his eyes kept glancing nervously towards her belly, large enough now to house a whale, as she kept moaning to Sam. Self-consciously, she put a protective hand over it – or the portion of it that a hand would cover.

'There ain't really a baby in there, is there?' Billy whispered in awe. 'Me mum said there is when we came to the farm for eggs the other day, but I didn't bloody well believe her.'

Why not? Do you really think babies are found beneath gooseberry bushes?

She almost said the words out loud, and then she saw how young and curious he really was. She remembered the first time she had discovered where babies came from, and how disbelieving she had been too, and she forgot all about her stained smock and spoke solemnly to the boy.

'There really is a baby in there, Billy, and it's going to be born soon, which is why it makes me look so fat.'

And please don't ask me how it got there, or how it's going to get out.

'Does it hurt?' Billy said.

'No, it doesn't hurt. You can feel it move, if you like.'

He jumped back as if he'd been stung, but as she gently ran her hand over her bump he came nearer and cautiously put out his hand. She caught hold of it and held it against her until they felt the baby kick, and he jumped back again.

'Bloody hellfire, it's alive!' he yelled.

'Of course it is, and now you know it's real. But I don't let everyone feel it kick, so this is just between us mind. I know you like secrets, and when it's born you can come to the farm and say hello to it properly if you like.'

If she was reminding him of that other

secret she had threatened him to keep, she didn't need to say so. His eyes told her that this was far more awesome, and he nodded quickly.

'So how about helping me pick up the blackberries I dropped? If I don't go back with enough to make a pie, Mrs Lovering will give me a good telling off for getting my smock all dirty.'

Billy was obviously charmed by the thought that a grown-up would get a telling off from another grown-up. He did as he was told, and then helped her pick some more until the basket was full. Later, they walked back through the lanes together before going their separate ways.

Poppy was already wondering if it had been wise to let him feel the baby move. If he was going to blab to his parents, they would probably have his irate father ranting and raving at her again for destroying his son's innocence. Though, judging by his colourful language, she'd have thought that was gone long ago.

In any case, they wouldn't have long to wait to know if she had misjudged him. There wasn't very long until the baby was born, either. By the way things were going, and the way the lump felt as if it was about to drop down in her boots, it would be any day now, she thought cheerfully.

Chapter Twenty

She didn't feel so cheerful a couple of nights later when she awoke in the dark to find herself shouting. Sam leapt up in bed beside her, cursing loudly as he turned on the light. A farmer needed his sleep, as his mother was forever telling her.

'Bloody hell! What was that all about? Are you having a nightmare?'

She glared at him, blinking in the sudden light that hurt her eyes, and pressing her hand to her stomach.

'*No*. I don't *know*. All I know is that it was a very big pain.'

He looked at her sharply, a note of concern in his voice now. 'The baby's not starting, is it?'

'Well, how the heck do I know? I've never had one before.'

She didn't feel like being sociable in the middle of the night, any more than Sam did, but nor was it the time to be getting stroppy. It wasn't the time to be doing anything but sleeping.

'Anyway, it's going away now,' she muttered.

He snapped out the light again. 'Then lie

down and let's get back to sleep. It'll be morning before you know it, and I can't be doing with these upsets in the middle of the night.'

She fumed at the unjustness of it all. 'It would be different if it was one of your precious cows, I suppose. You'd be prepared to sit up all night with the blasted thing then, wouldn't you?'

He gave a heavy sigh, and spoke in the darkness. 'Poppy, you know damn well I'd sit up all night with you if I thought there was anything to worry about, but it was probably just a twinge or a bit of indigestion. Take some milk of magnesia if it's troubling you.'

It wasn't indigestion, and she knew it. An hour or so later she knew it wasn't the baby either. She leapt out of bed, hopping about as best she could with cramp tightening up her calf muscle.

The light went on again. 'What's up now?' Sam said, watching her ungainly progress about the bedroom.

'Cramp,' she gulped.

'Come back to bed and I'll rub it for you.'

'No, don't! You know that only makes it worse. I'll stamp about on the cold lino for a bit until it goes. Go back to sleep, Sam. I'm sorry,' she added, her eyes misting.

'Don't be daft. You can't help it.'

He was out of bed then, padding across towards her and holding her close as she tried to get rid of the biting cramp in her leg.

She had a sudden picture of what they must look like; Sam in his creased striped pyjamas, his hair stuck on end from sleep; and herself, in one of Florrie's voluminous nightgowns, since they were the only ones that would fit her now; holding on to one another as if they were drowning while she stamped up and down in her bare feet. She couldn't stop the giggle escaping her lips, and Sam released her slightly, staring down at her.

'Are you playing games with me, wench? If so, you could be in for a tanning – or I might have to have my wicked way with you instead!'

She giggled again as she saw the twinkle in his eyes. 'Oh, I'd much prefer to have your wicked way if I've got any choice. I'm not sure how, though!'

Sam laughed as the bulk of the baby was evident between them.

'You're right. Chance would be a fine thing now. But keep it in mind, and we'll be making up for lost time after the baby's born.'

'I reckon we will,' she said, conscious of his body and marvelling that she could still arouse the lust in him even when she was virtually nine months pregnant and literally twice the woman she used to be.

'So if your cramp's gone, can we get back to bed now?'

It had certainly eased, though it had left her with a dull ache in her leg as it usually did for a while. Nobody had warned her about the side-effects of being pregnant, Poppy thought, as she rolled into bed.

Sam was snoring in minutes, while she tried to settle down in the least uncomfortable position she could find without disturbing him too much, and willed sleep to come. Even more, she willed the baby to come early.

'Babies never come until they're ready,' Florrie told her, when Poppy had felt bound to explain all the rumpus during the night. 'But whether 'tis a fact of nature or not, it seems that they usually start during the night. It's as if they have some instinct to make their presence known when there are plenty of folk around to help their arrival.'

'More like Sod's Law,' Sam muttered, still bleary-eyed. 'They do it to deprive a chap of his decent night's sleep.'

Poppy glared at him. 'Well, I'm sorry if your baby has already disturbed your sleep. If you think that's the only time you're going to get woken up by him, you're in for a big shock.'

'That's telling him,' Florrie said. 'Men don't know the half of it.'

Poppy hid a smile to realize that Florrie was on her side, if sides were indeed being taken. Later, Florrie had more to say.

'I daresay what you felt last night was nothing more than a practice pain, and that's quite normal. Didn't the midwife tell you about it?'

'She may have done, but I probably wasn't paying much attention at the time.' Poppy couldn't recall Shirley saying anything about it, either, but then it dawned on her what Florrie had said. 'You mean I might get more of them? So how do I know when it's the real thing?'

Florrie grimaced. 'You'll know.'

All this talk did nothing to make Poppy feel any easier. She felt as though she'd be on a knife-edge from now on, wondering if every twinge was the real thing at last, or just another practice pain. Her leg still ached, but she offered to go out to feed the pigs, feeling the need for fresh air, and wrinkling up her nose at the irony of the thought. Farmyards were a mixture of smells, some very identifiable and others not.

Pigs were her favourite animals all the same, she reflected with a smile as they snuffled around her for their feed. And then she remembered Henrietta's fate and her smile faded. Farmyards could be vicious places too, as well as places of seasonal

426

rebirth. In fact, the whole cycle of birth and death was here – and if she didn't stop these morbid thoughts she'd do her baby no good at all. She had read somewhere that you had to think calm, positive thoughts when you were expecting, because your mood could be transmitted to the baby. She wasn't sure if it was poppycock or good sense, but she chose to believe it, anyway. She even sang to him sometimes when nobody was listening. They'd surely think her crazy if they heard her doing that.

When her task was done, she wandered towards the museum. Without the visitors, it was calm and quiet in there, and a place where she liked to be alone. She found herself wondering about the people who had once used all these old implements, about their lives and loves, and she felt a great sense of peace in realizing the continuity of carrying on what had gone before and not letting things die. Sam had done a good thing for the community in bringing the past to the present in this way, and she felt a renewed respect for him.

It was a lot more than that, of course. As Poppy allowed these soothing moments to wash over her, she felt her heart swell with love, more love than she had believed possible, for this quiet man who had cared for her all these years.

'You can be very proud of your daddy,

little one,' she told the baby. 'He'll show you all kinds of things that town boys will never know.'

She realized she was thinking and talking about the baby as if it was a boy now, partly to be the same as everyone else – and in order to mention to God or whoever might be listening, that whether it was a boy or a girl, all that really mattered was that the baby was healthy.

'Your daddy will show you how to milk a cow, and how to mend fences, and how to drive a tractor. You'll know that eggs don't just appear in shops like magic, and you'll know the wonderful taste of milk straight from the cow. You'll learn about the changing seasons, and how to tell when it's going to rain by studying the sky, and wonder at the way the animals sense it before we do. You'll know when to plant seeds, and which are good mushrooms and which are poisonous. Oh, and you'll love harvest-time and the smell of new-mown hay.'

She stopped abruptly as the door opened, sending in a stream of light. Sam was silhouetted against it, and for a moment Poppy felt her heart jump at the haloed figure he became.

'Good God, Poppy, it's you. What in hell's name are you doing in here? I heard a voice and thought we had an intruder.'

She saw that he had a shovel in his hand

and that he was restraining Dog with some difficulty. She knew he'd have been quite prepared to let him go if he thought someone was vandalizing their new museum. He wasn't that much of a saint, then.

'I was talking to the baby,' she said stupidly, still caught up in her own saintly thoughts of moments ago as he came inside and shut the door, before shooing Dog off elsewhere. They could still hear him yapping frantically as Sam came nearer.

'And did the baby have any answers for you?' he said, surprisingly tolerant.

She gave a shaky smile. 'Of course. Didn't you know babies can talk to their mothers, even when nobody else can hear them? He said how excited he is about being born, and how lucky he is to have such good parents waiting to say hello to him, and how impatient he's getting to meet them face to face.'

Sam laughed, moving forward and taking her in his arms. 'You're mad, do you know that? I always thought I'd married a crazy woman, and now I know it for sure.'

'Perhaps. But it's a good craziness, isn't it?'

'The best.'

It was one of those sweet, silly moments that didn't happen too often in a busy farming day. When they did, they were to be cherished. But the sound of working life outside the museum, and Len Painter's voice shouting at Dog to stop leaping up and down at the barn door, drew them reluctantly apart.

'Len will be coming to see what's going on in a minute,' Sam said. 'I have to go, but stay awhile if you want to do some more communing with the unborn.'

'I do. And don't call him that. It sounds disrespectful, and you'll be giving him a complex before he's even here,' Poppy said.

'Now I know you're mad!' But he was still laughing as he went outside.

'We don't worry about things like that, do we, darling?' Poppy said, smoothing her belly. 'If it keeps you happy, I'll go on talking to you until you open your eyes and let me know you can hear me properly.'

The baby gave a great lurch against her hand at that moment, and she knew in her soul, that no matter what anyone said, he was listening, and understanding. And most important of all, he knew he was loved.

By the time the date for the baby's birth had come and gone, Poppy was feeling less tolerant towards him. Well, not towards him, exactly, but towards everyone else, from Sam to the midwife to Shirley and any neighbours she happened to meet in the village, who kept repeating Florrie's words that he wouldn't come until he was good and ready.

'I know all that,' she said crossly to Sam. 'He might not be ready, but I am. I'm more than ready. I want to see him sleeping in the cot you made for him, and send you off to Penzance to collect the pram we've ordered. I want to see him wearing the nightdresses I've made for him. I want to take him out to show him off to people in the village, all wrapped up in one of your mother's matinee jackets and shawl. I want to see him and hold him, Sam.'

'Whoa! At this rate you'll have him off to school before he can crawl.'

'I want to see him crawl too. And walk. And talk.'

'Well, right now you're doing enough for both of you,' he said as she paused for breath.

She spoke ruefully. 'I was never the most patient person, was I? But I've had to wait nine months for the most important arrival of my life, and it's just not fair that he's keeping me waiting like this.'

She looked and sounded so petulant then that Sam laughed out loud.

'How did your parents ever put up with you, love?'

'I don't know. They were the most placid of people, and how they ever produced someone like me is a mystery.'

Her eyes clouded, because he had made

431

her think about them now, and when it happened without warning, it reminded her of how much she missed seeing them on either side of the fireplace in their old cottage, like matching bookends. And at a time like this, when they would be anticipating the birth of their first grandchild, she missed them even more.

Sam spoke briskly. 'I'm going to Penzance tomorrow afternoon to see about some feed-stuff. Do you want to come with me for the ride? It might jolt a certain person out of his laziness, and you could call on Shirley if you like.'

'No thank you,' Poppy said listlessly. 'Seeing Luke will only make me envious. I'd rather stay home and listen to the wireless with my feet up.'

The following day was Florrie's afternoon for doing the flowers at the church and Poppy had the house to herself. Not that she minded; sometimes she enjoyed being alone in the farmhouse. She liked to go through all the things they had in preparation for the baby, and to lie on the bed listening to whatever soothing music was on the wireless, dreaming of the day when she would have someone very small and helpless to cuddle. Right now her whole self seemed to be waiting ... waiting ... holding her breath for the magical day she wanted so much.

She slipped off her shoes before she got on to the bed, feeling very drowsy as she usually did in the afternoons. Somewhere in the distance she could hear the drone of the tractor, and was reassured by Sam's words that even if he and Florrie were not around, Len Painter was somewhere at hand if her pains started and she needed help. Not that she could imagine wanting Len's rustic presence in this most female of occupations.

The old song on the wireless that Sam had rigged up in the bedroom for these occasions was playing softly in the background. It was something about a woman doing something wonderful. Poppy only half-listened, soothed by the melody and by the breeze from the open window, all her muscles relaxed. She could almost imagine she was soaring high above the clouds, with nothing but sky above her and the patchwork green earth far below. Or maybe she was floating in a warm, enveloping ocean...

Her eyes suddenly opened, and her body went rigid. The warm, enveloping ocean was right beneath her, except that it wasn't an ocean, it was *her*. For a horrified moment she wondered if she had become so dreamy and relaxed that she had simply wet herself. Her next frantic thought was to dread what Florrie would have to say at having to wash bedcovers and blankets.

She struggled to get off the bed to see the

damage, and then, with the arrival of a deep, sharp pain she gave a loud cry. She bent double, grabbing at the edge of the bed with tears stabbing her eyes. This shouldn't be happening. Babies chose to come in the middle of the night when it was most inconvenient, but when there was always someone around to help and comfort. A husband, a mother.

Poppy gave a huge sob, remembering in an instant that her mother wouldn't be there to offer any help. And right now she wanted her so much. A second pain made her yelp with fear as much as pain, and she hobbled to the window, feeling tacky and wet, desperately trying to see if Len was anywhere near. The midwife had told her in the cheerful, maddening way she had, that first babies normally took hours to come, so there would be no need to panic, even if her waters broke and the pains began in earnest. There would be still be plenty of time.

'Tell that to the army,' Poppy ground out in an attempt to stay calm.

There was no sign of anybody outside, and the drone of the tractor seemed to be farther away than before. She glanced at the clock. Wasn't she supposed to time these pains? She couldn't even think of that right now. She was more concerned in seeing how long Sam had been gone, and how soon she could expect Florrie back from the village.

It would be ages, she knew, and panic swept through her. Supposing nobody came back in time? Supposing the baby decided to come with a rush? What was she supposed to do? She didn't know what to do. All she knew was that she didn't want to face this alone.

She struggled out of her damp knickers, throwing the offending garments into the washing basket in acute embarrassment. She hobbled back to bed and sat on it, wondering what to do next. Trying to haul the bedcovers off the bed might not be the best thing if she was really in labour – and by now she was in no doubt – but she couldn't just sit here doing nothing.

A hammering on the farmhouse door made her jerk up her head, and she limped across to the window again, feeling about a hundred years old as she did so.

'Who's there?' she shrieked. 'Whoever you are, I need help! Is it you, Len?'

Almost sobbing with relief, she leaned out as best she could, but she couldn't see anyone at first. She knew it couldn't be Sam or Florrie, because neither of them would be knocking on the door. And she knew at once that it wasn't going to be Len either, since he would have Dog yapping all around him.

Someone moved back from the farmhouse to stare up at the window. Someone small and scruffy, who was gaping up at her as if she was an apparition.

'Bloody hell, what's up, Missus? Me mum's only sent me to buy some eggs,' Billy Flint stuttered.

Poppy didn't stop to ask whether God or fate had persuaded Mrs Flint to send him here this afternoon – probably just to get him out from under her feet. The Flints often bought eggs from them and today Billy was heaven-sent.

She shrieked again. 'Billy, see if you can find Len Painter for me. No, better than that. Go down to the village and find Mrs Hobbs and tell her I need her *urgently!*'

She saw him flinch and take a step backwards.

'I ain't bloody going near her. She does the layin' out and me dad says she paints the faces of dead bodies and brushes their hair to make 'em look presentable before they go in their coffins.'

'*Billy!* Do as I say. Mrs Hobbs is going to help me have my baby and it's coming *now*. I saved your life once, and if you want to return the favour, for God's sake go and get the woman this minute!'

And if you say bloody hell once more, I think I shall kill you.

After a few more seconds he turned and ran, and Poppy could only pray that he would do as she asked. Her nerves were jangling, but she was somewhat lulled by the fact that there hadn't been another pain for at least – she glanced at the clock – ten minutes. Perhaps, after all, it had been more of those practice pains and she had been panicking for nothing, she thought hopefully. But the sight of that wet bed and the discomfort in her nether regions made her abandon that thought. This was the real thing, all right, and just for a moment, no more, came a surging excitement that this was the day when the baby was actually going to arrive.

The excitement was quickly smothered by another pain, and she leaned over the bed, pressing her hands down on to it while she gritted her teeth and tried not to cry out. But why shouldn't she cry out? Why shouldn't she scream and yell if she felt like it? There was no one to hear, and Sam always said the animals on the farm had better sense than people did, letting out their feelings in great roars and bellows when they were in pain, rather than bottling it all up.

So she did just as her instincts told her to do, bellowing and yelling and cursing the pains that gripped her in a vice, threatening to split her in two each time they arrived, and making her puff out her breath in exhausted gasps when at last they began to subside.

She lost count of time, but it seemed like

hours before she became aware of other voices coming through the fog of her screeching.

'Let's get rid of these bedclothes and make the girl more comfortable,' she heard Florrie say, and as if through a mist she felt her mother-in-law pulling her away from the bed, and other arms were pushing her gently on to a chair. Strong, efficient, capable arms, and she almost wept with relief as she looked up into the cheerful face of Mrs Hobbs, the midwife cum layer-out of dead bodies.

The irony of the two occupations had often been a cause for mirth among local folk, but Poppy had no such thoughts now as she clung almost pathetically to the woman's arm as Mrs Hobbs ran her hands professionally over Poppy's stomach.

'There was nobody here, and I thought I was going to have my baby all alone,' she gasped. 'I was petrified.'

'Good heavens, there's nothing to be scared of,' the woman soothed. 'Birthing's a perfectly normal thing, and if it weren't, the human race would have fizzled out many moons ago. Women were made to bear babies, and nothing happens very fast, so from the looks of you I'd say you were coming along very nicely, my dear.'

Poppy glared at her. How dare she belittle what she had already gone through? Didn't she know how very much it bloody well

438

hurt? And how about Shirley's experience with Luke? That hadn't gone smoothly, had it? She felt the sobs in her throat and willed them away.

'I want to have the gas and air,' she whimpered.

'And so you shall, just as soon as we get you back into a clean nightgown and into bed again. Mrs Lovering is seeing to all that.'

She was infuriatingly calm, thought Poppy, but that was her training, she supposed. It was better than panicking. She had done enough of that for herself. She remembered Florrie then, and realized she had been working efficiently all this time, and that the bed was now stripped of the soiled bedcover and blankets and that the bottom sheet was clean and dry. She had produced another of her nightgowns and between them, the two women helped Poppy into it. As she emerged from the folds of linen, she met her mother-in-law's eyes. They were surprisingly moist.

'Thank you,' Poppy mouthed.

And then she felt the beginning of another pain, and almost fell on the bed. This time tomorrow, she thought dizzily, seconds before Mrs Hobbs pulled the gas and air machine towards her and pressed the mask over Poppy's mouth and nose, she would be able to leap into it.

She breathed in and out deeply, as Shirley had advised, and felt the blessed floating sensation again as the gas and air relieved her of the worst of the griping pain. Floating ... soaring ... flying high in the sky, like that woman in the song, and conquering the world ... filling her with wonderful, blissful sensations that made her feel that she too could conquer the world.

She began to feel in control of the pains now. Each time they began she grabbed for the mask, and each time they receded, the mask was gently taken away from her and her senses returned to the practicality of what was happening in the bedroom. At some point Florrie had gone to boil water for washing the baby, and to fetch clean towels. At other times Poppy had been conscious that her mother-in-law was pressing a damp cloth to her forehead and urging her to grip her hand as tightly as she liked. The gentleness of her astounded Poppy. She hadn't expected it. She hadn't wanted her here. She wanted her mother. She wanted *Sam*.

'Where's Sam?' she moaned. 'What time is it? He should be here.'

It dawned on her that it was getting dark. Sam should have been back from Penzance hours ago. Nothing had happened to him, had it? She couldn't bear it if it had, when the son that he wanted so much was about to be born.

'Sam's downstairs, Poppy love,' Florrie said. 'This is no place for fathers. He'll be sent for as soon as the child arrives.'

No place for fathers? What nonsense was that? She wasn't so doped by the gas and air that she couldn't think lucidly in between bouts. What better place was there for a father than here with the woman he had loved so well? But trying to make such opinions known would probably scandalize these two old biddies. These *so kind* old biddies, she amended, who were doing all they could to make this time bearable.

She gave a sudden scream, louder than all the others, and scrabbled for the gas and air mask. To her horror, Mrs Hobbs took it away from her.

''Tis time to push, my dear, and you need all your strength and your wits about you now. Do as I say, and your baby will be with you before you know it.'

Is that right, you old bat? She prayed she hadn't screeched it aloud, but she was so fearful now at what was happening, that all she could do was to gaze mutely at Florrie's face and clutch her hand tightly.

'You'll have to be thinking about what to call the baby very soon now, love,' Florrie said encouragingly to keep her mind occupied. 'He'll have a proper name and be a proper little person in no time.'

'He's always been a proper little person,'

Poppy snarled, pushing with all her might. 'And we'll think of his name when the time comes, like we always said we would.'

If she could have crossed her fingers at the thought, considering how tightly her nails were digging into her palms now, she would have done.

'It won't be very long now,' Mrs Hobbs said, still cheerful.

'I want Sam. I want my mother,' Poppy whimpered again.

Sometimes, through the haze of the pain she had imagined she could see her mother, as placid as ever, but giving silent encouragement to this beautiful daughter who knew she must look anything but beautiful by now, her face contorted with pain, and her dark hair lank and stringy with sweat. Her mother had been hovering above her with that other woman, the one in the song.

Poppy frowned, trying to concentrate on something other than the pain that was engulfing her again. She didn't know any other woman who hovered in the air, and she wondered briefly if she was truly going mad. She'd heard that pain could do that to you.

'One last push, Poppy,' Mrs Hobbs was saying excitedly, losing her coolness for once. 'Come on now, we're all longing to see this wonder-babe of yours.'

She gave an enormous shove, and felt as

though she would burst. And then something warm and hot and wet slithered away from her, and seconds later she heard a healthy cry. She craned forward, to see the midwife holding something aloft, something that was moving and alive, and making its first sounds as it emerged into the world.

Florrie was craning closer as well, and for an instant Poppy felt like weeping at the loss of this moment that should be hers alone. But then she saw the almost sweet look that transformed Florrie's face. She remembered how Florrie had lost Evie all those years ago, and she couldn't begrudge her anything.

Florrie looked at her. 'It's a girl, Poppy,' she said huskily, and Poppy knew at once that Sam's mother felt no sense of sadness and loss because there was now another girl in the Lovering family instead of the boy she had craved.

'Let me hold her.'

Poppy held out her arms, still trembling from the effort of giving birth, and the midwife placed the towel-wrapped baby gently in Poppy's embrace. At the same moment they heard Sam pounding up the stairs and storming into the bedroom.

'Is it here?' he rasped, although they all knew he must have heard those lusty first cries.

Poppy looked up from her awed inspection

of the baby's tiny, crumpled face, the dark hair so like her own, and the tiny fingers, already grasping hers by instinct. She reached out a hand to Sam and he came nearer, to kneel beside the bed to take his first look at his child.

'We have a daughter, Sam. A beautiful little girl. Are you disappointed?'

She searched his face anxiously, praying that he wouldn't be. But there was no hint of anything but joy on his rugged features.

'God, no, just as long as you're both all right. How could any man be disappointed, having two beautiful girls to love?'

'Are you going to give her a name, Sam?' his mother urged, too superstitious after her own long-ago tragedy to want to delay it.

'That's for Poppy to choose,' he said steadily. 'After this achievement, she deserves the final say in it.'

Poppy smiled, her finger stroking the soft down of the baby's cheek. As she did so, the baby opened her violet dark eyes, gazing up at Poppy and blinking at the light of this strange new world she had entered.

Poppy drew in her breath. It was all so amazing. So wonderful. Mrs Hobbs had joked about her being a wonder-babe but that was exactly what she was. A wonderful, wonderful babe...

From out of nowhere her head seemed to be filled with the sound of that old song that had been playing on the wireless what seemed like a very long time ago now. She remembered those half-awake dreams as she drifted into sleep, soaring up, up into the sky – just like that flying woman who had achieved something wonderful, and had had a song written about her.

Here in this room, hours later, Poppy had been soaring again with the blissful help of the gas and air, and she realized now that the feelings had been one and the same. And being a true Cornish woman, she had never been one to ignore an omen that was almost mystical, and which had presented itself so beautifully.

'Her name's Amy,' Poppy said softly. 'She's our wonderful, wonderful Amy.'

This Large Print Book, for people
who cannot read normal print,
is published under the auspices of

THE ULVERSCROFT FOUNDATION